RALLY TO THE STARS!

For Lucia, Kate, Milo, Michael, Harriet and the Tiwi people.

You can only be the revolution.
It is in your spirit, or it is nowhere.

Ursula K. LeGuin

Whereof one cannot speak, thereof one must be silent.

Ludwig Wittgenstein

Prologue

Rally

42HX-138 → Earth Orbit

October 21, 2027 → April 29, 2029

There were two beds. One was synthwood and had many blankets with bright whimsical patterns piled on it. The other was reflective steel and covered by a single sheet of artfibe integrated with the powsup at its foot. Both beds were secured to a steel frame fixed in the plain rock floor. There was a small desk behind the beds, a small door in front of the beds, and plaststiff storage containers stacked under the beds. Tubes, wires, and other medfast apparatus cluttered the small room in the middle of the asteroid.

Rally walked through the door and around the beds to the desk. She reached down with her gloved hand and began working diligently through the compads scattered across the work-stained, thought-worn surface. Most were totally dead, or had been smashed, and did nothing for her. Her excitement flared as one appeared to come to life, but it could only display an endless scroll of force/vector calculations, the endlessly recursing solution to some long forgotten trajectory equation connecting points that no longer existed. Nothing on the desk worked for her.

Pivoting fluidly in the low gravity, Rally looked at the bodies for the first time. They wore no masks. No tubes protruded from them. When the end was inevitable, when they were all alone and had only death for company, they chose what dignity they could. She wondered what she would have done, stranded in the debris of her dreams, knowing how unlikely it was that anyone, human or otherwise, would ever witness her end. She hoped she'd try to keep a little piece of grace. She tried to envision herself lying so peacefully as her choices turned to dust.

Their eyes were shut and their faces well-preserved. Their atmosphere died slowly; their bodies were not smashed against the walls or torn apart by sudden decompression. They wore many layers of clothes. Rally could see sweaters, shirts, and something that looked like a bathrobe. How cold did it get before their oxygen ran out or they succumbed to hypothermia? "I wonder if their teeth chattered," Rally asked herself aimlessly, half-smiling to herself inside her helmet. She wondered briefly about the relationship between the amount of atmosphere necessary to breathe and the amount necessary to carry sound.

Rally stared into their faces for a long time. She tried to imagine what they'd felt, lying there, as their dreams crumbled and the oxygen they'd worked all their lives to create hissed slowly out of their failing airlocks. They did not look bitter. But they did not look happy.

Rally turned back to the desk and began to go through the drawers. There were more broken compads, empty containers, a small box of jewelry, and a holophoto of Howard and Delilah standing in front of the Great Pyramid dated September 14, 2017. Rally looked at the picture for a long time. She tried to imagine what Howard and Delilah had been thinking; whether they'd had any inkling what was to come. She pictured them in their hotel room in Giza, laughing together confidently. They'd been happy there, Rally thought, putting the holophoto back.

In the back of the bottom drawer, she found a plastiff box fashioned into the shape of a log and covered with stickers. She recognized the Amsterdam coat of arms but was drawn immediately to the two ends of the log. Somebody had carved *"YILOTI"* in both ends with some primitive tool and Rally knew instantly she'd found what she was looking for. In the language of her childhood, a precursive language isolate spoken by fewer than two thousand people, her father was telling her "forever" in a way nobody else ever could.

She packed the log into her back pouch, skimmed quickly through the meager remaining mementos, and stood up once again to face the bodies. She felt a vague duty to bring them "home," whatever that was.

Rally glanced again at their faces. Looking down between the bunks for the first time, she saw two slender arms poking out from underneath their different blankets and two gloved hands clasped tightly together. Whether they sought warmth, strength, validation, or just human contact, they'd reached out to each other sometime before the end and hung on together through it. Rally knew she wasn't going to pull those hands apart. Whatever "home" meant, she thought, they'd found as much of it here as either of them ever had anywhere else.

Glancing softly at the cold dead faces one final time, Rally walked out of the room and prepared to abandon the asteroid. She strode briskly through the crew halls, finding nothing interesting in the other small rooms. She stopped briefly on both bridges and in both comcenters to make sure there weren't any active running systems. She checked the engineering rooms for gross malfunctions and she started to make her way out the cargo tunnel and back to Earth.

It is not particularly difficult to pull a human female and her space suit weighing 157.069 kilograms out of the rotational gravity well of a 12.031 million ton partially hollow irregularly shaped asteroid rotating at 1.624 revolutions per second. But there's a fair bit of math involved. You don't want to tug on the human too hard, or she might hit her ship and break something, or even bounce off into space. You don't want to tug too softly, or she will try to go into orbit around the asteroid and/or your ship. That happened to Rally once on her first trip to L_1. Her tender was low on power and the *Hab A Good Time* extended a umbicord so it wouldn't have to use energy docking and undocking. They'd underestimated her mass and didn't account for the influence of the tender. As a result, they'd tugged just a little too softly and she'd started floating into orbit around the *Good Time* while they slowly and carefully recalculated and reeled her in. The lesson she learned drifting in space that day was not to hurry. In space, the fewer things you have to do in a hurry, the longer you tend to live.

Rally and her crew were experts at going just slow enough. When she reached the end of the cargo tunnel, she connected her umbicord. "We've been thinking of you," she heard Rico say. "Are you OK? How are they?" "I'm fine," Rally said. "It's not exactly what I expected." "Do you want to talk about it now or are you ready to come back?" "I'm ready to go home," Rally said. "I just don't know what that is." "Wherever it is," Rico replied calmly, "let's get you over here first." Her direct language and practical approach helped Rally stay in the moment, another key survival skill in space.

Rally pushed the button in her suit that transmitted her weight and location to the hatch on the *Farluk* and heard the long beep confirming that her suit's computer, the hatch computer, and the ship's main computer all agreed that 157.069 kilograms needed to travel 176.111 meters. After a short wait, triple beeps signified that the three computers agreed how much force to apply on what vector. Rally subconsciously braced herself as the umbicord recoiled gently and she began moving away from the asteroid's influence—its physical influence.

The lifeline tethered her to the closed crew hatch of the *Farluk* where she waited while her suit, the hatch, and the ship scanned her suit for microbes, viruses, or other unwelcome companions. The computers agreed that her suit had maintained its integrity and that no bugs were trying to ride it into the ship—no known bugs, Rally reminded herself, since computers were notoriously poor in dealing with the unknown. After another triple beep the hatch slid open and Rally moved into the airlock. After more scans and tests, the airlock pressurized and she began the laborious process of removing her suit.

When she took her helmet off, she heard soft music playing over the comsys and smiled. It was one of her favorite songs, a traditional ballad her mother sang, "Yoyi Yimwalini Wangatunga," the dance of the basket and spear, set to a swing beat with horn accompaniment by a multiethnic group of surfer musicians. Rally loved the contrast between the traditional lyrics about the never-ending dance between basket women and spear men and the lively joyful music that made her want to forget everything and dance. It made her happy, knowing that Rico and the rest of her crew cared for her, thought about her, and played her music to ease her return.

After the music ended, she had no excuse to remain in the airlock alone. Thinking about the beaches of Milikapiti with her mother's song echoing in her ears, she opened the door and stepped into the locker room carrying the plastiff log from her father. She still hadn't decided when to open it.

She wasn't surprised nobody was there. Her crew knew when to give each other time and space, and they had things to do. Some crews preferred to spend as much time in deepass sleep as they could, waking only for the mandatory gravity sessions that kept their bodies deteriorating as slowly as possible. Other crews preferred to sleep as little as they had to, spend as much time under gravity as possible, and use the long months of travel to work on their ships and themselves. Her crew was on the latter side of that ledger, and all of them did something besides just keep the *Farluk* going, not that that wasn't itself a lot of work. They took great pride in their ship.

Refreshed, Rally walked out of the locker room and headed for the bridge. As she walked up the transfer, she heard the deep thrum of the engines warming up for the long energy pulse that would send the *Farluk* to where Earth orbit would be 18 months from now. Opening the log would certainly make at least one of those months more interesting.

But before Rally got to the bridge, she ran into Ripley. Ripley and Rico were Rally's closest mates on the

Farluk. On the trip out, Rally and Ripley had been doing battery research, testing different electrochemical variations across hundreds of charge/discharge cycles. Every spacer wants a better battery, and through trial and error they'd created some intriguing combinations. "Wait until you see what's happened!" Ripley told her excitedly, insisting that Rally go to the small corner of the secondary lab where they stored their work as soon as she'd checked in with the bridge.

What happened, Rally soon learned, was a power cell that produced seemingly random test results. Half of the time, its cycle produced almost twice as much charge as it should—more charge than any power cell they'd ever seen. The other half of the time, however, the cycle produced no charge at all. It made no sense: how could the same cell, receiving the same charge, react so differently?

Ripley was fascinated by their discovery and determined to refine it into a version that was more predictable, if not necessarily more useful. She kept doggedly charging and recharging their test batteries and making small, almost undetectable adjustments as they drifted across the solar system. Rally, on the other hand, found it harder and harder to work on their battery project, to perform maintenance support, and even to prepare the crew meals and clean the galley and mess and heads with Rico and Ripley every third day, which had always been her special time with her best friends.

Instead, Rally found herself thinking more and more about her family. She was the child of two children from broken homes, but her parents loved each other deeply and unconditionally. They generously shared that love freely with her, with her mates, and with the people around them. They'd created loving communities around themselves even as their relationships with their own families faded to the edge of non-existence. Rally had never met her mother's parents or her father's mother. As far as she knew, she had no siblings or cousins. The only other family she had was the man who'd sent her on this mission, her grandfather Stanley.

Stanley, Rally's father told her once, saw her as his opportunity to have the obedient son he'd never been. Stanley and his son weren't close, but after Rally was born Stanley visited regularly. His self-avowed purpose was to make sure his only grandchild learned hard truths about the world, not the "poppycock" her father "spouted." Stanley believed in rules and doing what you were told.

And he wasn't entirely wrong, Rally thought to herself one day while she was cleaning a section of hosing in the water cycler. They couldn't survive together out here without routines and responsibilities. Everyone worked every day, and they had to coordinate their efforts. So Rally rededicated herself to her ship and her crew, finding joy once again in the good humor of her mates when she and Ripley and Rico prepared a particularly good meal; the feeling of success when they cleaned and specked a particularly tricky maintsys.

Finally the *Farluk* drifted slowly into a high Earth orbit and Rally could no longer avoid talking to people outside her crew. She decided to begin with the most difficult conversation and comtacked the office of the Senior Climate Commissioner at the North American Unified Central Cooperation Center of the United Peoples and Nations of Earth—aka her Grandfather Stanley.

She waited an appropriate time to be comtacked to somebody so important, magnified ever so slightly by the orbital delay, and finally heard his deep voice as his trim comtar sprang to life. "Hello Rally. Welcome home." "Thank you Grandfather," she replied, wondering briefly to herself what exactly he meant by 'home.' "I'm glad to be here." "What did you find?" Stanley asked in his brusque fashion." "I found them. They're both dead. Nothing worked. No burn engines. Failed life support. Their atmosphere died slowly. Everything was intact." Rally had learned at a young age how to give a proper report to her grandfather.

"Makes sense," Stanley replied. "A crew lifeship drifted near the moon about a year after you left. They sent a ship to intercept it. My sources tell me that everyone aboard

10

was dead, but we don't know very much more than that." "That's too bad," Rally replied. "I'd hoped some of them might have made it." "At least they got off that damn rock before they died," her grandfather replied. "And so did you. What are you doing now?" "I think I'm going to Milikapiti," Rally replied. "I need to dance. I need to sing." "It's a miracle it's still above water," Stanley said softly, "a miracle built on many lives and lifetimes of work." "And many more generations of dreaming," Rally added even more softly. "I'll call you again before I come back up here."

Closing his com, Stanley Burpelson looked slowly up to the sky, as if he could see his only granddaughter orbiting hundreds of miles above him, and sighed softly. "Well," his omnipresent aide de camp Sabull Popper asked insistently, "what did she say? What did she find?" "She said she found dead bodies and no engines," Stanley replied. "But I'm more interested in what she didn't say."

Chapter One

Stanley

Cliffs of Moher, Ireland

June 16, 2021

No matter what happens, Stanley thought, somebody always finds a way to take advantage of it. Here he was on top of a 700 foot cliff bracing against the fierce warm wind that forebode landfall of possibly the most destructive storm ever to strike Ireland. The air was dripping with moisture. It was heavy, clinging, tropical air. It felt very different from the chilly damp air Stanley associated with London fog and Dublin rain. Stanley felt like the air was even more out of place than he was.

But he was the only one standing on the top of the cliff worrying about the weather. There were ten or twenty other people on the visitor's platform. All of them were focusing intently on the real action happening on the waves at the bottom of the cliff. Pointing their binoculars and shouting excitedly to each other, they were mesmerized by the tiny black figures on shiny white surfboards riding the giant waves pushed against the cliffs by the approaching storm. There were even more people in boats out on the water watching the surfers and the holovid drones filming their every move. Somebody much more clever than Stanley had taken advantage of the unprecedented climate storm to stage a surfing contest. Stanley was just hoping the storm might help him save his planet. There was no question, he thought, who was more likely to succeed.

It was "The 2021 Aileen Odyssey" according to a poster he'd seen that morning in Galway. He wondered whether any of the surfers thought about the literary significance of that title, on this date. Did anyone read Joyce, or even Homer, any more? Stanley doubted it. People didn't read much of anything these days. They didn't have the attention span for it any more. It was hard to imagine that, once upon a time, people looked forward to gathering together for six hours a night, three nights in a row, to listen intently to a rhapsodist, a professional reciter, tell them Homer's tales of wily Odysseus, breaker of cities. Stanley tried for a moment to imagine what it would be like to live in a world where everyone could pay attention to the same thing for six straight hours.

Those surfers and their drone cameras, Stanley thought, were so much more attuned to the modern mind than he was. Each ride lasted about twenty seconds. That, Stanley told himself, was about all people today could handle. Each ride was a self-contained story. Tidy, predictable beginnings. Dramatic but comforting middles. Spectacular endings guaranteed, whether the surfer ejected violently across the waves or sailed gracefully into the grasp of the waiting jet-skis to be towed out for a sequel.

Stanley pulled his eyes away from the surfers and stared straight out into the storm. How could he tell its story in twenty seconds? It was too much, too large, too complicated. He looked down at the spectators on the boats and tried to pretend people like that could be persuaded to do the right things if they only heard the right messages. But he knew in his heart that people just weren't like that. They weren't going to save themselves. They needed rules and discipline to save them from themselves.

What they needed, Stanley knew, was to embrace their places in new systems and find new roles in life. But these climate storms were so chaotic they marginalized the very idea of law and order. Climate storms made regularity look old-fashioned and tried people's faith by revealing all the hidden faults in their social structures. Only new social orders could restore their faith, but it was hard to build anything in the face of a storm. It was hard enough to just stand still, Stanley thought, but somehow they had to move forward.

The storm was born almost two weeks ago when a strong low pressure system formed over the Greenland Sea, just south of the Arctic Ocean and almost due north of the cliff where Stanley stood. About the same time, a large ridge of high pressure developed in the Mid-Atlantic northwest of the Portuguese island of Madeira to Stanley's southwest. The low pressure system pushed cold air down the Denmark

Strait over the cold arctic water of the East Greenland Current while the warm air in the high pressure system rode the trade winds north and east over the unseasonably warm waters of the Canary Current and the North Atlantic Drift.

All of that, Stanley thought, had happened hundreds of times before. The cold low pressure system drove south, the warm high pressure ridge drifted north, and when they collided they birthed a North Atlantic extratropical cyclone. A Nor'easter, that's what old New England fishermen used to call them. It didn't happen this late in the season very often, but it wasn't unprecedented.

But this storm, which they were calling Molly— appropriately enough, Stanley thought—was unprecedented. It didn't keep moving west and it didn't make landfall in North America like every Nor'easter before it. The Gulf Stream waters and the June temperatures in the Mid-Atlantic were both unseasonably warm that year. Warm enough for thunderstorm activity to build inside Molly and moisten and warm its lower levels. Warm enough to change Molly's core from cold air to warm air and allow it to start gathering energy as the vapor evaporating from the ocean in the 85 degree heat condensed back into liquid water. Molly morphed into a subtropical cyclone with bands of thunderstorms stretching over 500 kilometers and generating wind gusts up to 250 kph. And now it was following the warm waters of the Canary Current straight towards the

Emerald Isle.

Molly certainly wasn't going to be the worst storm Stanley had seen. He'd worked for APORLACT, the worldwide climate storm response agency founded by the UN, since its inception eighteen months earlier. He'd been through some of the biggest climate storms and he'd learned a few things. He'd learned that single storms, however massive, were never as deadly as double or triple storms striking in quick succession like combination punches. Last September, three storms rolled across Jamaica in a nine day span. The death toll rose exponentially in each storm and by the end there were no multistory buildings left standing on the island. Thankfully, Molly was the only storm facing Ireland.

Stanley also learned that timing and location mattered a lot. When massive tropical super-cyclones hit the Philippines in August it was tragic. Thousands of people died. But it wasn't unexpected. People knew what to do. They'd grown up with the idea. Nobody in Dublin's long history ever grew up with the idea of a subtropical cyclone dropping several feet of rain into the River Liffey and flooding the city on Bloomsday.

Stanley stared into the approaching storm one last time. Maybe after a few more years of this, he thought wearily to himself, nothing will ever shock anyone again. The effects of warmer temperatures and rising seas were so unpredictable and interacted so chaotically that sometimes he felt like nothing would ever be impossible again. Shaking his head, he pulled himself back off the cliff and walked briskly to his car. Whatever happened, he told himself, the only way for them to defeat it—the only way for his planet to survive—was to work together as a single team playing by a single set of rules.

Shaking the water off his coat, Stanley bent his tall athletic frame into the back seat of the town car. "You don't want to take a look?" he asked. "No," the quiet dark-skinned woman replied dismissively. "I've seen quite enough storms already, thank you."

Stanley was trying very hard to get along with this woman, but she could be so disagreeable. They'd gotten off to a bad start years ago. It was before APORLACT, at a geosciences conference in Switzerland of all places. Stanley was sent by the Air Force to sit on a panel discussing urban air pollution simulations. G'ranger Apuatimi came looking for allies in her never-ending fight to save her South Pacific island home. They'd met briefly at a reception. As soon as she found out who Stanley was, she'd made it clear how she felt about the American military and what they'd done in the South Pacific. Stanley held his tongue in her presence, but after she walked away he'd remarked "saved helpless islanders from the Japanese fascists, that's what we did in the South Pacific."

Apparently it got back to her, and apparently she had a good memory. Five years later G'Ranger and Stanley met again. They both presented at an APORLACT organizational planning session in Honolulu last year. As soon as she'd seen him, she handed him a $20 bill "for the war effort." He'd tried to apologize, but she'd had none of it, walking away once again. Since then, as he'd become more and more central to APORLACT's efforts in the Caribbean, he'd watched her become more and more prominent in the South Pacific. Finally, both of them were named to the board of directors earlier this year.

There were more than 30 directors. This was the first time they'd really had to acknowledge each other or work together in that capacity. They'd been sent to Dublin three days ago, when it became clear that Molly was going to make landfall. They were managing and supervising the APORLACT pre-disaster response team. There were five of them on the team-management committee, but G'Ranger and he were the only two directors and the rest took all their cues from them.

Stanley was born into a military family. He became a man in the military. Civilian committee decision-making and politics was difficult for him. If he was going to be honest, Stanley thought ruefully to himself, civilian life in general was hard for him. His dad Wally, a proud navy man, was one of the first sailors killed in Vietnam. His radar tracking plane crashed south of Hue during a test flight in February, 1960. Stanley was not even three years old. He'd never regained any memories of his dad and his mom had never recovered from her loss.

The day after his father's funeral she'd moved him from San Diego to northern Wisconsin iron-mining country. Finally, mercifully, she'd passed away last year at 84. She'd been in various assisted care facilities for 15 years. She'd never re-married. Stanley was her only child. Her brother and sister died long ago. Stanley hadn't seen her for four years before she died. He'd had to supervise her move to a different nursing home. He'd always tried to find time for her, Stanley reassured himself over his nagging guilt, but he knew he'd always put his career above his family and he felt bad about it.

He'd looked forward to joining the Navy his whole life. Growing up playing football and hockey, Stanley learned to be a good teammate. He knew he'd be a good shipmate, like his dad. But to his eternal disappointment, he never got to fight in Vietnam like his dad. The war ended before he was old enough. In the post-war years, he was unable to secure the commission to the Naval Academy he'd always dreamt of. He settled for the Air Force Academy outside Colorado Springs instead.

Reflecting briefly over his 35-year military career, Stanley allowed himself a small smile of satisfaction. He'd done well. He'd made a difference. By any standard he was one of the great meteorologists in Air Force history. In the first Gulf War, his models of dispersion tracks from the destruction of Saddam Hussein's chemical weapon storage facilities proved uncannily accurate. He'd saved lives.

Rising through the ranks to larger leadership challenges and greater responsibilities, Stanley often wondered how much he'd lost outside the military. He'd never married. He'd never had a lasting relationship. He'd known only fleeting, flighty love, never solid, lasting love. He did have one child, a son who'd been taught by his mother to disdain Stanley and everything he stood for. They had a distant relationship at best. Stanley had tried hard to build a closer relationship with his granddaughter, who'd just turned twenty-two, but it wasn't easy. Families, he thought, were so much messier than the military.

Since the Air Force sent him to APORLACT, he'd struggled to work with civilians like G'Ranger. Not, he smiled to himself, that there were many like her! She thought the world would be saved by dreaming a new consciousness. She liked to talk about dancing new dances. Sometimes it was all Stanley could do to keep from laughing out loud at her.

But, Stanley had to admit, she was just as committed as he was to saving the world. Maybe even more committed. He tried hard to respect that about her. "Shall we start back to town then?" he asked her. "To Galway?" she replied. "Do you want to stay on the coast tonight and watch the storm? Should we just go back to Dublin?" They were officially on a fact gathering trip and were scheduled to report back to the committee in Dublin tomorrow afternoon at 1:30.

Stanley wasn't sure what the point of gathering any more facts was. Everyone agreed what was happening. The world was getting hotter and the weather was becoming more unpredictable. But nobody agreed what to do about it. Most people weren't doing anything about it. It was too big for them. They were too bogged down in their narrow little worlds. Too busy trying to keep food on their tables and keep their kids alive. Those were the people Stanley was fighting for. But he needed more of them to fight with him.

Some people had given up. They'd turned their backs on the Earth itself, written it off as a lost cause. Using vast resources and unthinkable stores of energy Earth couldn't spare, they were fleeing to space like rats tearing apart a leaky ship to build rafts. They were trying to build space colonies. Habs, for habitats, that's what they called them. The Chinese and their corporate allies on the moon were selling them blocks of lunar regolith for outrageous amounts. They'd all turned their backs on the Earth and had no compunctions about leaving the little people behind to die with the ecosphere

APORLACT was fighting to save the ecosphere for the little people. But sometimes it seemed like all they ever had were tiny victories and big defeats. Fewer people drowned because they helped move some of them out of a storm's path, but millions were left homeless after a storm took an unexpected turn. People rebuilt a seawall in a harbor faster because they brought materials and engineers, but the rice crop failed due to flooding. They made a difference. They did good. But nothing they did was very inspiring. Nothing they did grabbed people's attention like a holovid of one of those surfers catching a cyclone wave perfectly and riding it gracefully to shore.

It was a question that had lingered in the back of Stanley's mind for a long time. Every so often, it wriggled into the forefront of his mind. It made him think about whatever he was doing at the moment and ask himself whether it could grab people's attention and inspire them to commit themselves to APORLACT's program to ensure the long term survival of humanity on Earth. Standing on the cliff watching the surfers, he thought sadly, didn't even come close. Nothing he could do out here on the Irish Coast could ever come close.

"We might as well go back to Dublin," Stanley replied. "It will be easier if we stay ahead of the storm."

"I'm sure Odysseus himself would agree," G'Ranger replied, smiling at Stanley for the first time that day. "He would,"

Stanley nodded. "If only we had as many gods on our side."
"Maybe we do," G'Ranger allowed. "Maybe we just don't
know how to let ourselves recognize them. Maybe we don't
know how to let them help us." "Maybe," Stanley muttered.
He was too tired to fight or to laugh. He told their driver to
take them back to Dublin. They didn't need to gather any
more facts.

They drove for a while in silence. "Do you think the
gods could save us if we let them?" Stanley asked. "Maybe
the gods are just as powerless as we are." "Maybe they are,"
G'Ranger agreed. "Maybe we've dug a hole so deep even
the gods can't lift us out of it. But at least the gods won't
lose faith or stop fighting or give up on their Earth." That,
Stanley thought, was what they agreed on. Neither of them
would ever stop fighting to save life on Earth.

"Do you have children?" Stanley asked. He knew
G'Ranger was from the South Pacific, but little else about
her. "Nope," she replied in a friendly tone. "Never got
married, never had kids. For half my life I was too busy
trying to conquer the world, and now I'm too busy spending
the rest of my life trying to save it. What about you?" "That
sounds a lot like me," Stanley replied. "Too busy, too
distant, too single-minded." "Yet here we are," G'Ranger
responded, "doing all we can to save everyone else's kids."

"I do have a son," Stanley admitted. "But I'm pretty
sure he'd get a big laugh out of the idea of me saving him.

His mother never thought any more of me or my profession than you did." "And she never married you?" G'Ranger asked, avoiding his remark. "Married me?" Stanley laughed. "We never even went on a proper date!" He couldn't help but smile. It had been a long time since he thought about Jasmine. He could still see her brilliant green eyes and long red hair glowing in the Midwestern moonlight.

"If you don't want to talk about it," G'Ranger started, but Stanley interrupted her. "No, it's fine. It was a different time is all. 1974—you probably weren't even born yet! I was still in high school. I went to a big college football game. She was a student. Our team won, we got caught up in the excitement, and…" "And you have a son together," G'Ranger finished. "Yes," Stanley nodded. "And now a granddaughter."

"The same thing happened after the war," G'Ranger nodded. "People got caught up in the excitement of the moment and slept with the victorious soldiers. Then, months later, when the soldiers were long gone, they had sons and daughters and struggled to care for them alone. The aftereffects rippled down through the generations." "My child and his mother never struggled," Stanley interjected. "I always made sure of that."

"Everyone struggles," G'Ranger countered. "I'm sure you did what you could—everyone knows how upright and honorable you are." Stanley was taken aback for a moment, but looking into her dark eyes he could tell she meant it. "Thank you," Stanley nodded. "It was a struggle—is a struggle—for all of us," he admitted.

"But without struggle," G'Ranger mused, "what meaning does life have? Isn't that part of Odysseus's lesson? What meaning would his life have if he'd just stayed in Ithaca with Penelope drinking wine the whole time?" "That wouldn't be much of a story," Stanley agreed. "But maybe it would have been a better life." "Would it though?" G'Ranger asked thoughtfully. "I guess it depends on what makes life good." She looked at Stanley with a bemused smile. "I don't think the two of us are likely to answer that question tonight!"

No, Stanley thought, they certainly weren't. He let her remark hang in the air as they drove through the warm Irish night. He didn't know what to say. It was the kind of question he hadn't asked himself for a long time. It was too late, he thought, for him to try to answer questions like that. Discussions like that were for young people. His job was just to keep the young people alive long enough to have that opportunity.

He looked back at G'Ranger, who'd opened her compad and settled back into her dark seat for the ride to Dublin. He'd never realized how committed she was. He'd never before been able to look past the parts of her he found ridiculous and see her strength. Stanley respected that strength. And that respect, Stanley knew, was all you needed to work together alongside somebody. You didn't have to like them. You just had to respect them.

Chapter Two

Howard

Port Angeles, Washington, U.S.A.

September 11, 2001

Howard Gall sat by himself at a two-top in the gloomy dining room watching ice melt into his scotch and listening to his world fall apart. It was his third scotch. He'd been sitting by himself for four hours and thirty-five minutes. For twelve hours before that he'd loaded five batches of six hundred twenty-one pounds of chips and seventy-six gallons of white liquor into the number eight digester at the pulp mill. Howard believed in numbers. He believed in himself. He wasn't sure whether he believed in anything or anyone else.

Every so often he heard somebody come into the bar, where the televisions were, and all his P.A. friends and co-workers told each other one more time how shocked they were by what they saw. Even more regularly somebody on television said something stupid and his friends and co-workers howled at them. This was Howard's third summer at the mill. He'd worked with these people, gotten drunk with them, played softball with them, but he'd never felt such contempt for them until today.

Howard wasn't shocked. Howard didn't care what people on TV said. Howard understood what it meant for people to fly airplanes into skyscrapers and murder thousands for no apparent reason. It meant everyone on Earth was held hostage by the most unscrupulous and least reasonable human scum; that there was no way on Earth to make your family safe; that the barbarians would never stay outside the gates.

The ice cubes in Howard's scotch dissolved into chips as he pondered his future on this cowardly old world. His bags were packed and there was a plane ticket on the counter of his apartment so he could fly back to Boston Friday and start his senior year at M.I.T. on Monday. Classes were actually supposed to have started today, but a senior with a 3.9 GPA didn't really worry much about missing the first day of a kinetic topology seminar.

Another howl went up from the bar. "They're sending missile destroyers to New York and D.C." Jake yelled, sticking his head into the dining room. "Maybe there are submarines or something!" Jake was one of the two or three people at the mill who could load chips or stack pallets faster than Howard. That seemed only fair, since he was an all-American wrestler at U.W., not a theoretical math student at M.I.T. But sometimes Howard swore Jake was the stupidest person he'd ever met. And yet the people at the mill considered Jake one of the smart ones. Humanity, Howard thought, did not have high standards.

"Are you working again tonight?" Howard asked his

friend. Jake's face contorted in surprise. "Working? Are you crazy? There's no way that mill will be open tonight." Howard wasn't so sure. If it was his mill it would damn well be open. If somebody was going to ram it with a submarine it wouldn't really matter one way or another in the long run. "Nobody's working tonight. How could anyone work after this?" It was the most brilliant thing Howard ever heard Jake say, even if he didn't know he'd spend the rest of his life trying to answer that question.

"They'll probably shut down some lines at least," Howard allowed. "Let's get another drink." They walked through the pool tables into the smoky bar and looked up at stock footage of destroyers crashing through the sea. It looked to Howard like the destroyers were somewhere in the South Pacific, not the Mid-Atlantic, but his co-workers were cheering them on and he couldn't bring himself to temper their mood. People liked action at a time like this. But as far as Howard could tell, it was all over. Four planes hijacked. Two direct hits. One glancing blow. A mystery of ruin spread across the forests and fields of Central Pennsylvania between Pittsburgh and D.C.

Talia, who'd watched Jake and Howard hustle pool, argue about sports, and pick up local women for the last three summers, worked her way down the bar and poured their drinks. "What do you think Howard?" she asked, "Are those destroyers going to find anything?" Howard smiled.

"Nope. Those ships are going there because the President put the military on high alert, and if the military goes on high alert but doesn't do anything people get upset and start asking questions." "Like how come those fighters they launched from Massachusetts didn't get to New York before that second plane?" Jake chimed in. "I guarantee somebody is going to eat a plateful of crap on that one."

"Maybe" Howard said. "They were probably worried about Boston. Hell, what if they'd flown to New York and then a plane crashed into Fenway Park? If they didn't know about the other plane or where it was going, then maybe flying in circles to conserve fuel while their people on the ground tried to figure it out made sense. But you're right: somebody is going to eat a plate of crap over this, and they probably could have covered their ass by doing something. People will always prefer leaders who act confidently, even if they're wrong, over somebody who waits and waits and waits, even though waiting and doing nothing is often the smartest thing to do. We're just hard-wired that way from millions of years of chasing and being chased across the plains of Africa."

Jake and Howard sipped their drinks in silence as the towers fell over and over and over on the televisions until Howard began to feel its meaning slipping away through sheer repetition. "This is driving me crazy," he told Jake. "You and the rest of America," Jake replied. "How old were we when the Berlin Wall fell, like ten? Do you even remember that? Did you have any idea what that meant? This is the biggest event of our lifetime, the first thing everyone our age will remember forever." Howard nodded. "Of course we're going to remember," he said quietly. "The question is whether we're going to do anything about it."

"What do you mean," Jake asked. "Of course they're going to do something about it. They're going to bomb whoever did this back to the Stone Age." "What if they're already living in the Stone Age?" Howard countered. "What if they like the Stone Age? What if they want to bring us down to their level?" "Nobody likes getting the shit bombed out of them" Jake replied confidently. Howard wasn't so sure about that.

"When people get the shit bombed out of them," he started, "they invariably rally around their leaders, who inevitably use the opportunity to bombard them again with propaganda about how glorious they are. 'I have nothing to offer but blood, sweat, toil, and tears.' The British loved that crap. London got the shit bombed out of it, tens of thousands died, and Churchill became one of the most beloved rulers in English history. 'Nothing in life is so exhilarating as to be shot at without result.' Bombing the shit out of London worked out pretty damn well for him! If these bastards have deep enough bunkers, they might want nothing more than for us to bomb the shit out of their miserable little countries and make them heroes."

"So what are you saying?" Jake asked. "That we shouldn't bomb the shit out of the fuckers who did this?" He waved his arm and drink in the general direction of the TV. An earnest CNN reporter was standing outside a military base in Louisiana behind a graphic headline *President Bush en route to Strategic Air Command.* "We're going to bomb the shit out of them whether we should or shouldn't," Howard replied slowly. "I'm saying this is bigger than that."

"Bigger how?" Jake replied. "Bigger because it shows how fragile and unsafe life is," Howard replied. "No matter how hard those poor bastards in those towers worked, no matter how rich they were, no matter how powerful they were, they couldn't do anything to protect themselves from a bunch of illiterate peasant zealot fucks with box cutters. What's the point of life if you can't protect yourself and your people? What's the point if your destiny isn't under your control? These illiterate peasant religious freaks breed faster than you can kill them, so you can't protect yourself by killing them all. You can't build a wall across China or Scotland any more. There's only one place left to go where the illiterate peasant fucks can't follow you."

"Where's that?" Jake asked. "Up there," Howard said in a low serious tone, pointing to the ceiling. "They're too fucking stupid to get to space. Illiterate peasant religious fucks aren't smart enough to live in space. Unfortunately, we aren't doing any better ourselves at the moment." Jake laughed. "You're kidding," he said. "You want to build a spaceship so you can run away and hide?" "No," Howard replied. "I want to build a lot of spaceships and start over and take the people I care about with me and leave behind all the other fucked up vermin who overpopulate this miserable shithole of a planet."

A buzz went up from the crowd and Jake and Rally turned to the TV like everyone else just in time to see a faraway shot of an airplane landing on a runway in the middle of a desert behind a graphic reading *President Bush lands at Offutt Air Force Base in Nebraska*. "What the hell is he doing in Nebraska?" a wiry old man wearing a Kodiak chew ballcap next to Jake wondered. "It's some kind of command post" a tiny woman next to him replied. "He's going there so they can nuke those terrorist fucks." Everyone drank to that.

"You're serious," Jake asked Howard once the buzz died down. "Your answer to this is building spaceships and leaving the world to the fucking terrorists?" "It's the only answer," Howard replied. "How long have people been trying to civilize the world? Five hundred years? A thousand years? Does it look like the world is getting more fucking civilized to you?" Howard asked, waving his arm at the TV, which was showing the two towers collapsing over and over on split screens. "Does that look like fucking 'progress'?"

Jake considered that for a while and finished his drink. "No," he said, "that doesn't look like progress. But there's a lot of progress they aren't showing; people growing more rice in Vietnam and shit like that." "That's not progress," Howard quietly explained. "That's just a better way of doing the same thing. Progress means new ideas, new ways of living. You know how video games used to have different levels, and you had to use different strategies to beat all the different levels?" "Yeah," Jake replied. "Or there was a different boss at the end of each level and you had to finish everything on that level before you could kill that boss."

"Exactly!" exclaimed Howard. "And you couldn't just use the same moves, or do the same things, to kill each boss or beat each level, you had to change strategies and do different things and find different shit?" "Yeah," Jake agreed. "But what are you getting at?" "Well, what if the moves and strategies we use now aren't the ones that will let us beat this level and move on to level two, to space? What if the entire history of humanity is just the history of level one and we haven't figured out what we need to learn for level two yet?"

"That's a hell of a level!" Jake laughed. "But I see what you're saying. So the strategies that worked in the past aren't going to work in the next level, up there." Jake gazed

34

at the roof. "They're not working now," Howard replied. "You know how in a video game when you missed some important clue and had to waste a bunch of hours wandering around randomly doing a bunch of shit that didn't add up to nothing until you found it?" "Yeah," Jake said. "That happened to me all the time." "Well," Howard continued, "I think that's what's happening now. I think we missed a clue, or something, that would have taught us, or at least some of us, how to move to level two, and now we're just mucking about randomly through outdated level one bullshit like this." Howard pointed again at the TV, which was showing a political map of the Mideast.

"That's some heavy shit," Jake said thoughtfully. "But you might actually for once be on to something. Talia," he called, "this round's on me!" Talia brought them two more glasses of scotch. Jake raised his glass silently to Howard. They drank slowly and watched the reporter in the middle of the Nebraska desert explain what a MIRV was and how many kilotons of nuclear destruction the righteous forces of America could rain down on the miserable terrorist scum who'd brought down the towers. Suddenly their world didn't feel like a very progressive place.

They sat quietly for another ten or fifteen minutes and finished another round of scotch. "So what's the secret?" Jake asked. "What secret?" Howard gave him a puzzled look. "The clue we missed," Jake replied. "The thing that's going to let you beat level one and move on 'up there.'" "I don't know," Howard admitted. "I wish I did. I think it has something to do with realizing that not everyone is equal and not everyone is capable of being rational. For the last 200 years, all the philosophers and politicians have more or less agreed that everyone is fundamentally equal, not that they have any idea what that means, and that everyone is capable of being a 'democratic citizen,' of following the rules, of being rational." "Are you saying they aren't?" Jake replied? "I'm saying that maybe the idea that the whole world has equal rights and is capable of justice is part of what's keeping us back from level two," Howard said. "When people first started exploring the world, they didn't just grab a bunch of random people and go. They were selective. And I think that we're going to have to be pretty damned selective about the first people who start exploring level two."

"Well of course you are," Jake replied. "Shit, look at how many people try to be astronauts—that's got to be one of the most selective professions in the world. You've probably got the math for it, but even if you got in the best shape of your life you might not make it because you're not a pilot." "But astronauts don't really live in space," Howard countered. "They launch up and fall back down. I'm talking about people actually leaving and starting over—like people used to do in Alaska, except in space you have to build your own wilderness." "Can they do that?" Jake asked. "Build spaceships you could live a whole lifetime in?" "I don't know," Howard replied. "But after this, I'm sure as hell going to find out."

"So you're saying that in space everyone will have equal rights and justice?" Jake laughed. "Talk about pie in the sky!" "No!" Howard replied forcefully. "That's not it at all. I'm saying that maybe equal rights and justice are what's keeping us from going to space. I'm saying that as long as we keep trying to pretend that everyone is equal and can be enlightened, we might be stuck here waiting for one of our unenlightened inferiors to fly a planeload of enriched uranium into New York City and cause a real disaster. This?" he waved at the TV. "This many people are killed by crocodiles and hippopotamuses every year. This is nothing but a preview. We can't kill them all, we can't 'civilize' them, and we sure as hell can't protect ourselves from them."

"But how do you keep them off your ships?" Jake asked thoughtfully. "How do you keep people on your ships from having babies who grow up to be religious fanatics?" "I don't know," Howard replied thoughtfully. "That's the big question, isn't it? I just know I'll have a better chance of doing it in a world I made than I ever will here. The idea that the whole Earth would ever become civilized isn't helping because it isn't working. So maybe that happened because people stopped moving forward; stopped exploring;

stopped growing." Jake nodded. "And all they're doing here is making little incremental changes that aren't fundamental enough to finish level one." "Maybe," Howard replied. "The Titanic would have hit that iceberg no matter how healthy the dinner service was."

They thought about that for a minute or two while they watched a vacant runway in the middle of the desert on the TV. "So you're saying that what's keeping us out of space isn't technical, but social? That if people had their heads on straight they could live up there?" "I don't know," Howard replied again. "I don't have a plan and I don't know much about the technical aspects of it. I know that there are two, or maybe more, Lagrange points, named for an eighteenth-century French mathematician, where the gravitational pull of the Sun, Earth, and Moon all more or less balance—I can show you those equations, they're pretty simple—so that objects in those spots can maintain a relatively stable position without expending much energy. I don't know whether any asteroids or smaller chunks of material have collected there. I don't know what the easiest way to move material there is. It's definitely not lifting it from the earth, I know that. Maybe from the moon or from the asteroid belt. I don't know what the technical obstacles are. But what I really don't know is why nobody's trying to do it; why nobody cares about level two."

"Well," Jake opined, "there's not really a huge

demand for spaceship retirement homes and probably nobody's figured out how to make money off of it. Rocks in space can't be worth much, and nobody wants to live there." "You'd be surprised," Howard replied. "Some people think that all the gold and platinum on Earth was deposited by meteors and meteorites. Some people think there might be asteroids out there with as much gold or platinum as on all of Earth." "But then you couldn't sell it or you'd destroy the market," Jake objected. "You could sell part of it," Howard replied. "Enough to pay for a lot of really expensive rocket launches to take things up to your spaceships. But that's not what's important. It would be different if lots of people were trying and failing. That would mean we hadn't finished level one, that we really had missed something. But nobody's even trying. What does that mean?"

"Maybe it means people don't want to live in spaceships in constant danger of springing a leak and blowing up and killing them?" Jake offered. "But three hundred years ago, people did want to live in sailboats with constant danger of springing a leak and drowning," Howard countered. "Look at how many people died on those voyages, yet plenty more kept signing up." "I'm not sure they all had a lot of choices," Jake said. "Weren't a lot of them shanghaied or press-ganged or running from prison or something?" "Maybe," Howard agreed. "But not all of them. Some of them just wanted to keep on going a little bit more, a little bit further than anyone had gone before. Why don't people today want that?" "Cable TV?" Jake laughed. "Maybe people aren't as desperate now, so they don't take chances like they used to." Howard nodded. "Maybe they weren't, but after today they sure might be."

They looked back up at the TV and listened to CNN interview Shimon Peres, the Israeli Foreign Minister, who was explaining how unfortunate it was that Jews in New York City were dying because the American government refused to provide enough support to Israel. "There's a real objective point of view," Howard noted. "Maybe we should go get something to eat?"

Before they could stand up, however, they witnessed something very strange. "We are getting information now that one of the other buildings," CNN reported, "Building Seven, in the World Trade Center complex, is on fire and has either collapsed or is collapsing." "What the hell?" Howard snorted, standing up rapidly. "Either it collapsed or it didn't. What the hell are they saying?" CNN reporter Aaron Brown, in a rare moment of truth that may have been related to the fact that it was his first day on air, then admitted "You, to be honest, can see these pictures a little bit more clearly than I." CNN switched to a view of a building burning below the smoke from the south tower behind a graphic that read *Building 7 at World Trade Ctr. on fire, may collapse.*

"That's weird," Jake said. "Why do they think it's

going to collapse?" "Who knows," Howard replied. "I'm sure there were fire crews in there, but they certainly didn't have time to take structural integrity measurements. Maybe somebody saw some support beams collapse?" "Then wouldn't it already have started collapsing?" Jake replied. "Look, you can see the roofline through the flames: it's perfectly straight." "Yeah," Howard said, "at least it looks like it from here. That fire's been going for a while, right? So they've been in there for some time. I guess we just have to assume they know what they're talking about."

"I'm not working tonight" Jake said, raising his hand to Talia. "If they fire everyone who doesn't show up tonight they won't have enough people left to run two lines. Hell, I'm out of here in a week anyway." "You're lucky you can just drive to Seattle," Howard replied. "I've got a plane ticket to Logan on Friday. What are the odds of that happening?" "Shit," Jake laughed, "that just means that they have to put you up at some crappy motel no-tell in Renton and give you a bunch of vouchers for Denny's. The Warsaw Convention. Who knows, you might like it." "Yeah," Howard chuckled. "It will be a change from school, that's for sure." They ordered another round of scotch and two cheeseburgers and watched the flames and smoke with everyone else until their food was ready.

As they were eating their burgers, the TV switched back to the desert in Nebraska and announced that President

Bush was departing Strategic Air Command for an unknown destination. "That's strange," Howard remarked. "Why would they put him back in the air now? Where could he go that's safer than that strategic command bunker?" "Maybe he's going to New York to make one of those Winston Churchill speeches you were talking about," Jake suggested. "Maybe," Howard agreed, "but he and his people are sure going to look fucking stupid if something happens." "What could happen? Like they said, one of those smaller buildings might collapse, but the two big ones already did, so they could probably deal with that."

Talia brought another round of drinks and they sat in silence for a while watching TV and nibbling on their cold fries. Howard looked at his watch. "Wow, it's 2:20 already" he said. "I've never had an eight hour shift drink before." "Are you sure?" Jake smiled. "I remember that one time last year those guys from the prison kept losing money and buying drinks and you kept buying more drinks and winning more money." "That was different. I had to find out how much they had to lose. This? Everything's already lost and we're just watching the rubble settle." "Yeah," Jake agreed. "I guess everything that's going to happen today probably already has."

Talia brought them their tabs and they paid her. "What a day," Jake said. "We're never going to forget that we were here with each other when this happened." "Nope,"

Howard agreed. "We're all stuck in our memory banks forever." "I'm glad you guys were here," Talia said. "I'm glad you weren't stuck on a plane somewhere or working a pulp line."

Just as they were about to leave, a *Breaking News Alert* flashed on all the televisions and they turned to look up. CNN was reporting that Building Seven of the World Trade Center complex, which had been on fire for most of the day, had collapsed. "Guess they were right about that building," Jake said, not thinking much of it and turning for the door. "Wait," Howard said. "Look at this." Jake turned back to the TV just in time to see a grainy video looking down a city street over a police van into a cloud of dust. As they watched, a large building in the background collapsed and bigger clouds of dust poured down the street towards the camera.

"Did you see that?" Howard asked, staring intently at the TV. "See what?" Jake replied. "That was the building they said was going to collapse. It collapsed. So what?" "So," Howard answered, "See how it collapsed? It didn't fall randomly. It fell neatly into its own footprint. That's impossible. That can't happen if a fire burns out different support beams over the course of an afternoon—that that only happens if something takes out all the support beams at once." "What are you saying?" Jake asked, looking at Howard, who was completely focused on the TV as it replayed the collapse over and over and he estimated the number of support beams, and the weight of the building, and the odds that multiple beams would fail simultaneously, and the dozens of other variables that rushed through his mind even faster than the free-falling building.

"I'm saying that building did not collapse chaotically like it would have if a fire destroyed random support beams over the course of the day. That building collapsed like it was imploded. I don't know what's going on, but I'm saying things might be even worse than I thought; that getting to level two might just have become the most important thing in the world." Howard turned away from the television to look at Jake with wide staring eyes. They were the eyes of somebody who'd just found his life's work.

Chapter Three

G'Sille

Milikapiti, Yermainer (Melville) Island → Darwin, Northern Territories, Australia

March 10 → 11, 1977

G'Sille had never in her whole life seen so many white people. She huddled on the small shelf they called a "bunk," held her little sister Maringka tightly against her, and told herself over and over not to cry; to be strong; to be there for Maringka; to take care of her sister. "I can't stop them," was the last thing her mother ever said to her, barely speaking through her tears. "You must take care of you and Maringka now! *Nimpungi yiloti kapi!*" Good by until we meet forever! G'Sille was almost ten years old. Nothing in her life had prepared her for this.

G'Sille didn't understand these white people. Why did they want to take her and Maringka away from her mother, away from Milikapiti, away from their home and family? Everyone in Milikapiti loved and respected her mother, whose father's fathers were famous leaders and great fishermen, and who was herself a famous singer and an important person at the arts centre where she worked. Her mother never did anything to these white people. Why did they want to make us cry like this? Couldn't they hear Maringka crying? Maringka hadn't stopped crying since the white people took her and G'Sille out of their house and carried them onto their boat. Did these white people have no hearts?

White people had come to Milikapiti before. They liked to fish and play in the waves on surfboards and build fires on the beach so they could drink beer and laugh. They played strange music and sang funny songs but had big smiles and laughed a lot and were friendly. But not *these* white people. G'Sille thought these must be some different kind of white people because they didn't ever smile or laugh as far as she could tell and they weren't friendly at all. They were mean. She hoped they didn't drink beer because she was old enough to know what a mean drunk was.

The white people's boat came roaring into Milikapiti Bay three days ago. Everyone thought it was a big group of fishermen and many ran down to the harbor to see them. G'Sille and Maringka and their mother followed the crowd to join the excitement. To their surprise, the white people who got off the boat first were wearing fancy white uniforms with matching hats. They carried clipboards and briefcases. They weren't going fishing.

Then an old white man with a short grey beard wearing a white suit came off the boat and all the white people looked at him. "I am J. Neville Beatty," he announced to the crowd, "Assistant Commissioner of the Aborigines Welfare Board for the Northern Territories. We have received reports of neglected and destitute children on these islands and I have been sent here personally to investigate those reports and provide appropriate care and remedies for any such children." G'Sille didn't understand what he meant, but her mother tightened her grip on her hand and took her and Maringka straight home. G'Sille saw other mothers hurrying their children home. The old white man kept talking but she couldn't hear what he was saying.

G'Sille had lived in the same small white cottage behind her school's sports oval for as long as she could remember. It was her father's parents' house. After her father died when Maringka was just a tiny baby, not even a year old, his parents moved to Wurrumiyanga to live with her Aunt Mipika and Uncle Peter and her cousins Yreki and Bindi. Uncle Peter was a famous fishing writer who traveled all over the world to catch little fish and write big stories about them. Aunt Mipika taught at the school in Wurrumiyanga. Her grandparents Norm and Carla came and visited her and Maringka often, and at Christmas and for summer vacations their whole family would be together either in Wurrumiyanga or in Milikapiti. G'Sille loved to run around and play games and swim with her cousins. Her grandma Carla told her once that they couldn't stay in Milikapiti for more than a week because looking at the beach where her father drowned was too painful for them, especially Norm.

Grandpa Norm never talked about her father. Other people did sometimes, though, and G'Sille knew that he was a respected and hard-working fisherman and that he drowned at night on South Beach trying to save three children whose raft collapsed. She wasn't sure who the children were or why they were on a raft off South Beach in the dark, but she'd never asked anybody those questions. Her mother did not talk about her father either, at least not with G'Sille. She remembered her father's laugh. She remembered how much he smelled like fish when he came home at night and how tightly he held her after he cleaned up.

When they got home, her mother told Maringka and G'Sille to go clean their room. She went into the kitchen and began washing the spotless walls. "What's wrong Momma?" G'Sille asked. "I don't know baby," her mom replied quietly, walking over to her and glancing down the hall to make sure Maringka couldn't hear. "Remember last year before Christmas ago when that white woman with the clipboard knocked on the door?" G'Sille remembered. "Well, what she was here for was to ask me all these questions about how much money I made, who took care of you and Maringka while I was at work, when the last time you saw a doctor was, what grades you got, and all sorts of things. Now this white man on a big boat is here and I'm scared. Remember what happened to Evna?" G'Sille nodded. Evna used to be her friend, but her parents died and the white people came and took her away. Some people said she lived with a white family in a big house in Perth. Others said she was a prisoner in a uranium mine. But nobody knew. Nobody ever heard from her again after the white people took her away.

"But you're not dead!" G'Sille protested. "I know," her mother smiled, "But your father is, and I'm scared." "Don't be scared Momma," G'Sille remembered saying. "I'm never leaving you!" The very idea had seemed too ridiculous to consider. Now, listening to her little sister crying helplessly on the small bunk inside the white people's dark smelly boat, it was all too real. "I love you Maringka. I will always love you forever and Momma will always love you forever" was all she could mumble but it brought no comfort to either of them.

Assistant Commissioner J. Neville Beatty didn't even come to their house himself. Instead, it was two of the white women with clipboards. G'Sille didn't remember their names, but she'd never forget their faces. They'd marched past her mother and into their house like they owned the place. "As you know," one of them told her mother, "since your husband's death, your children have not had consistent child care on weekends. They don't have regular care when you decide to go to the arts centre instead of staying home with your children." The woman looked coldly down at her clipboard. "For example, our records show that during last

November you admit that you left Maringka alone with only G'Sille to supervise her on at least four different occasions." The woman grunted a *tsk* of disapproval to show her disdain.

"In addition," she continued, "this shows that G'Sille and Maringka were cared for by ten different people at six different locations since then. You identified seven of those people you left your children with as 'cousins,' but our records indicate you have only five cousins." "Two of my cousins are married," her mother explained patiently, "and we call Sufi and Devon 'cousins' because they are like cousins to us." "But they're not really your cousins," the woman replied in a cold disdainful patronizing tone. "And regardless, the real problem here is the stability of your children. It's just not healthy for a child to be passed around to so many different homes with so many different people."

"A child can't develop a sense of self unless he's grounded in a place of his own. Your children need stability and routine, and unfortunately you're just not capable of providing that for them. So, to protect their interests, the commission has ordered that your children be placed, at no cost to you, in the Rella Dixon Home in Darwin. At the Dixon Home they will have the advantages of a stable living situation, a consistent education, and they will be properly prepared to take their places in society. It's in their best interests and will give them advantages you just can't provide out here by yourself."

Our best interests? G'Sille wondered, pulling Maringka even closer. How'd this white woman who'd never met them know what their best interests were? Nothing about the white woman made G'Sille think she had a single generous bone in her body, so the idea that she would go out of her way to help her and her sister did not make much sense. Nothing made much sense at all to her, huddling together with her sister in the dark smelling bunk on the white people's boat. G'Sille just kept stroking Maringka's hair softly and comforting the terrified little girl she loved so much as best she could.

The white women with clipboards kept going in and out until the dark bunks were full of crying children and the dirty boat reeked of urine and fear. If the white people really wanted to give her and Maringka and the other kids advantages, G'Sille thought, they weren't making a very good start of it.

Finally one of the women stopped in front of G'Sille. "And who do we have here?" she asked, trying to pretend like she cared. *If you were trying to help us*, G'Sille thought, *you'd know who we were*. Before G'Sille could say anything to her, the woman reached down and pulled Maringka's dress away from her to read the label the white people put on her when they'd carried her onto their boat. "*Maringka Kerimerini*," the white woman said. "Well, that's a mouthful that won't do much for you. We'll just call you 'Mary

Merini.' That sounds more like a proper name." The white woman crossed out Maringka's name and wrote "Mary Merini" on G'Sille's little sister's tag.

"Now what about you?" the white woman asked G'Sille, reaching down to read out the tag on her blouse. *"G'Sille Kerimerini.* How on earth do you people come up with these names?" "G'Sille was my grandmother's grandmother's name," G'Sille told her. "Do you know your grandmother's grandmother's name?" "Well, wherever you got it, that's not the sort of name that's going to help you in the real world," the woman replied knowingly. "How about 'Sally Rimer'? That's a good Australian sounding name." She carelessly missed the label and left a big black smear on G'Sille's favorite white blouse her mother had put her in to show the white people how beautiful and healthy she was.

"Why do you hate us?" G'Sille burst out. "Why are you doing this to us? Can't you hear Maringka crying?" "Hate you? Oh Sally, you've got it all wrong," the woman replied condescendingly. "We're helping you! I know it seems strange now, but you're going to get to live with white people, to get a modern education, to finally have some stability and order in your lives. You'll be able to go to school for a couple of years and maybe get a real job or meet a nice man and you won't be trapped on that miserable island anymore." "My family's lived on that island for four hundred years," G'Sille replied.

"And they haven't made anything of it or themselves!" the woman growled. "My family's only been in this country for thirty years, but we've built a great ranch and sent four children to college. Now, nobody's going to expect anything like that from people like you, but maybe you'll meet a nice man from a good family and then your children will be practically normal. But nice men don't want wild girls who run around like primitives. They want well-mannered girls who can keep a proper house and cook a proper meal."

The boat shuddered as the engines roared to life. G'Sille felt herself moving away from the dock and into the ocean swells. "Good, we're off!" the woman smiled. "Don't worry Sally," she said enthusiastically, "I know things seem strange now, but you and your sister and the rest of these children will look back someday and think this was the greatest day of your lives! Now, can you try to get Mary to stop crying for me while I get on with these three over here?"

But Maringka had already stopped crying. Now she was looking up into G'Sille's eyes. She was searching for answers and looking for help from her beloved big sister. Looking back into her sister's eyes, G'Sille saw nothing but trust and faith. And G'Sille couldn't do a damn thing for her. It felt even worse than listening to her cry.

They held each other on the shelf for what seemed to

G'Sille like forever. The lifting and bowing of the boat through the waves seemed to calm Maringka, the child, grandchild, and great-great-grandchild of legendary fisherfolk, but G'Sille still didn't have anything to say . The stinky hold got quieter and quieter as the white women with clipboards finished their charting and the children began to fall asleep.

"Hey Silly" a voice whispered from under their bunk. "Is that you?" G'Sille, holding on to the side, leaned over the edge and peered down into the darkness below them. "Who's that?" she asked. "It's me, G'ranger!" she heard the voice say, and she saw that it was indeed G'ranger Apuatimi. "What are you doing here?" G'Sille blurted out without thinking. G'ranger Apuatimi was the daughter of Jean Baptiste Apuatimi, who was a great artist. The Apuatimis were one of the most important and highly respected families in Milikapiti—one of the most important families on the whole island! How could the white people take G'ranger away?

"The white people said my mom couldn't take care of me by herself," G'ranger replied. *By herself?* G'Sille thought. Everyone in Milikapiti respected and looked up to Jean Baptiste Apuatimi and would have done anything she asked. G'ranger, on the other hand, at least in G'sille's opinion, was a spoiled little brat who talked too much, didn't share well, and couldn't be trusted. Once, G'Sille and her friends were pretty sure, G'ranger had let Kim Kantilla's dog Cruiser off her leash and lied about it after Cruiser disappeared. "So where do you think they're taking us," G'Sille replied, still in shock that the white people would take Jean Baptiste Apuatimi's daughter away from her.

"To a home in Darwin," G'ranger replied. "Can you believe it? We're going to get to live in the city! Have you ever been to Darwin?" "No," G'Sille replied sofly. "You're going to love it!" G'ranger exclaimed. "It's all brand new – they rebuilt everything after the Christmas cyclone." Three years ago a tropical cyclone had swung around Melville Island on Christmas Eve and smashed directly into Darwin, destroying much of the city. People in Milikapiti said it was the worst storm in a hundred years.

"I wish the *jaratinga piyanikumuni* had smashed them all to bits!" G'Sille whispered powerfully. "Get to live in the city? Are you crazy? Couldn't you hear Maringka crying?" "But she's just four," G'ranger replied. "She cries all the time." "No she doesn't," G'Sille told her. "Not like this." "OK, it's hard on her," G'ranger admitted. "But I can't wait! Do you know how hard it is to live on a tiny island where everyone idolizes your mother? Where people can't wait to tell your mother something bad about you to get her attention? Where no matter what I do, I'll never be anything more than my mother's daughter?"

G'Sille was taken aback. She'd never thought being

Jean Baptiste Apuatimi's daughter could ever be a bad thing. She'd always thought G'ranger liked being spoiled. G'Sille had even been jealous of her. But maybe G'ranger talked too much and did stupid things because she was trying to get attention for being her own person, not just for being her mother's daughter. "Aren't you going to miss Milikapiti?" she finally asked.

"Maybe someday I will," G'ranger replied confidently. "And if I do, I'll go back and visit, or maybe I'll have a vacation house there and go for the fishing like those white people from Sydney. That's where I'm going to live after Darwin. I'm going to go to college there, and study languages and economics. You can't do that on Milikapiti, can you?" "No," G'Sille replied, "I guess just the language classes at the arts centre." "I'm going to learn French and Spanish and Chinese," G'ranger stated matter-of-factly. "Then I'm going to travel all over the whole world!" G'ranger's voice rose with her determination as she declared this, and one of the white women stuck her head around the dirty corner of the boat and told them to be quiet before they woke the younger children up.

G'ranger smiled up at G'Sille. "You'll see, Silly! This is all going to work out great for us!" G'Sille tried to smile back, but her heart wasn't in it. Her head was spinning. G'ranger Apuatimi was the last person G'Sille would have ever expected to want to leave Milikapiti and go to Darwin. But when G'Sille thought about it, what she said kind of made sense, even if she still didn't trust G'ranger very much. G'Sille knew what it was like for people to only think of her as her dead father's daughter. She didn't like it. And G'ranger's mom was even more famous and important than G'Sille's father! Maybe it made sense for G'ranger to want to go to Darwin and set out on her own. She was almost eleven after all.

But G'Sille still felt like she was going to start crying again every time she thought about her mother. Maringka was sleeping, but she looked like she could wake up and start crying again any minute. Maringka didn't want to go to college in Sydney and learn Spanish and traipse all about the world. She wanted her mom! G'Sille knew deep in her heart that it was not right for the white people to take Maringka away. But she wasn't so sure about G'ranger. And that made it very difficult for her to figure out how she felt about herself.

She didn't want to go to Darwin. She wanted to go back to Milikapiti and run into her mother's arms. But she was just as clever as G'ranger, if not more so, and the idea of traveling to China and Japan and faraway places like that was certainly something she was going to have to think about. She'd always assumed she'd stay on Yermainer for the rest of her life. But now, the first time she'd ever left her islands, she was already traveling to Shanghai and Tokyo in her mind. That was certainly something to think about.

She held Maringka tightly in her arms as the smelly boat bounced up and down through the night and stared into the dark cabin thinking about marrying one of the Milikapiti boys and working in a kitchen for the rest of her life and about going to college and to Sydney and flying on an airplane to Tokyo. If she could fly on an airplane to Tokyo, she could fly back to Milikapiti and see her mother again! But she still didn't trust these white people one bit. G'Ranger's dreams about traveling the world were a far cry from the black smear the careless white woman left on G'Sille's best blouse. She had a hard time connecting those dots. And how could she take care of Maringka if she was flying all over on all sorts of airplanes?

She rocked Maringka up and down with the swells of the ocean and tried to imagine how being torn from her mother and taken to a strange white people's home in Darwin could be anything but evil. She was still trying to wrap her head around all the different futures that she'd had yesterday in Milikapiti, walking on the beach with her mother, and all the new futures she had today when she felt the engines slow and knew the boat was entering Darwin harbor.

Chapter Four

Jake

Lunar Elevator Base Alpha

October 31, 2019

Jake's mouth fell open as he saw the skinny luminescent cables that meant fame and fortune for his tribe snake slowly down the lunar sky like the most valuable lottery tickets in the history of the world. They'd done it! He couldn't believe it. He leaned back and laughed. And on Halloween no less! Quite a trick for the grandson of Irish immigrants who'd supported his father and six uncles by running the toughest cop bar in Philadelphia for thirty years. His father was a beat cop in Philly, then a detective in Columbus, Ohio, and finally retired as a chief in Camas, Washington, the small mill town on the Columbia River where Jake grew up. Now here he was on the moon, only a few hundred miles from Neil Armstrong's footsteps, making history.

"We did it!" he heard Mike shout. "Oh My God, we did it!" "Not yet we haven't," Jake reminded him. "Let's all keep our minds focused and stay in the present right now. I don't see no cartful of angels coming down those cables to pour champagne and run their hands through your hair! Like the man said, it ain't over til it's over, and it ain't never too late to finish like a champion. So let's just stay together on target here and get 'er done, OK?" Jake wasn't sure when or where he'd learned to talk in clichés like a platoon sergeant from a bad old movie, but sometimes it lightened the mood and kept everyone working together.

There were nine of them up here on the moon together. They'd been here for eight long weeks, roughing out the massive base station and installing the huge columns that would tether the cables. Each cable was roughly 45,000 miles long, almost twice the Earth's circumference at the equator. The cables would connect the lunar surface to the space platform the rest of his tribe was building at L_1, a point 25,000 miles above him where the celestial masses of the Earth and the moon more or less balanced each other out. From there, the cables would stretch back towards Earth almost another 20,000 miles to their counterweight platform.

L_1 was important because smaller objects like spaceships and space colonies could maintain more or less stationary orbits there without unsustainable levels of inefficient effort. His tribe was betting everything they'd ever had or ever would have, including their lives, that it would be the most valuable place in the solar system for the next 100 years or so. Watching their cables drop slowly towards the arresting harness below it looked like they just might be right.

Jake wished Howard could see it come to life. "Here's your key to level two," he said to himself, thinking back to that day eighteen years ago that people said changed everything. After today, he thought, that phrase might take on a whole new meaning. As far as Jake knew, however, Howard had still never been off earth. Last year Mike, Nigel, and Jake went to Brisbane, Australia, to negotiate their initial titanium supply. They were watching the sun set over the Story Bridge and drinking Sichuan margaritas at Madame Wu when Jake brought up the idea of asking Howard to join them.

It hadn't gone over well. Mike and Nigel knew how dismissive Howard could be of people who disagreed with him or made small mistakes. "I saw him once at an applied math conference at NYU," Mike said. "At a panel on circuit design. One of the commentators made a passing remark about the output waveform of one passive integrator having similarities to a different input waveform he'd talked about. Howard went apeshit. He jumped out of his seat and stopped the panel while he went to the whiteboard and demonstrated how the waveforms were actually different." "I heard that story!" Nigel confirmed. "I heard the waveforms were totally peripheral to the presentation and he went on about them for seven minutes."

"At least," Mike agreed. "It was so marginal and he was so serious and everyone was so annoyed. What did Polina say the other day when we couldn't figure out whether the bunker floors should be flat or concave—being happy is better than being right? Howard seems like just the opposite, like being right is more important to him than being happy." "That wouldn't even work for us down here right now," Nigel commented. "And I'll bet that up there it's gonna be even more important to make compromises and live with lots of imperfections." They'd finished their drinks and gone back to their hotel. Jake never brought Howard up with his tribesmates again.

He still considered Howard his friend though. Jake hadn't talked to him in five or six years, not since he spent a weekend in Tahiti with Howard and his girlfriend Delilah. They'd taken long ocean swims that demanded all their energy and let them spend their evenings just relaxing. Jake liked Delilah. She'd seemed like a calming influence on Howard. But Howard was still as passionate about space colonization as ever. Jake hadn't followed the news much, but the last time he saw one of Howard's speeches it made Jake feel like the point of space colonization was for the colonists to confirm what a genius Howard was.

If you think you know everything, you can never learn anything. You couldn't think like that on the moon. Jake and the rest of his tribe learned that forever on the very first day they landed. Chiara, who was their smallest tribesmate but had grown up on the Naples waterfront and could outshout and outcurse any two of them, decided she didn't need to test the regolith under the third corner of the supply shelter she and Mike and Polina were erecting because it looked just like the regolith under the first two corners. That was her last mistake. The hollow under the corner caved in and two walls collapsed on her, severing her umbicord. Mike and Polina couldn't get the debris off of her fast enough and she suffocated loudly, spending her last breaths on horrible screams Jake and his tribesmates would never forget.

Knowing in the abstract that living on the moon was risky and people would probably die was a lot different from trying to figure out what to do with Chiara's body. After they buried her under a rock outcropping, they all moved more slowly and became much more enthusiastic about double checking each other and asking endless questions. Survival on the moon was impossible without all of them questioning everyone else's actions all the time. Maybe ego was more necessary for survival on the plains of Africa millions of years ago, but here on the moon humility and a willingness to learn new tricks were proving infinitely more important.

Jake figured that was a big part of "level two thinking," which was his term for the kind of mindset it would take for them to survive up here. Living on the moon didn't come naturally. None of them really knew anything more than what they'd learned in the last seven weeks; they were still making it all up as they went along.

There'd been 25 of them originally. They all had

different reasons for joining together. Mike had been one of their main organizers. He'd worked for NASA for ten years before falling victim to budget cuts and staff reductions as the agency focused more and more on unmanned exploration. Mike's motivation was simple: he just wanted to see people get to space. Nigel joined because he thought space colonies could alleviate global warming and help save Earth's environment. Others signed on because they saw the possibility of getting rich.

Jake wasn't blind to the potential profits, but mainly he just wanted a great adventure as part of a trail-breaking team. He'd spent seven years as a special operations soldier with tours of duty in Iraq and Afghanistan. He'd spent five years working on the highest-producing crab boat in Dutch Harbor. Both experiences convinced him that politics was a waste of time and the only thing that mattered was being surrounded by people he could trust with his life.

They'd formed their tribe on January 30, 2018, and now, not even two years later, they were on the verge of being arguably the most important 23 people in the universe. Two of them had died. Chiara here on the moon and.Grace Comet six months ago in a test of their capsule rotation system that generated gravity for his tribesmates living in space and making the impossibly thin amazingly strong cables that would haul 75,000 pound blocks of regolith up to L_1 and bring supplies back down. Since he was watching it happen, it must be working, but that didn't mean it had become less risky or that the rest of them were more likely to survive.

The two capsules those fourteen tribesmates were living and working in were 25 meters in diameter, orbited L_1 every five minutes, and rotated around each other every four minutes. That combination of cyclical rotation generated just a little less gravity than the surface of Mars. They didn't really know what would happen to their bodies if they spent longer than they should in that kind of microgravity, but they felt pretty confident about staying there for a year.

Their radiation shielding was much, much more experimental: a electromagnetic maze of wave radiation bouncing around the gap between the inner and outer hulls of their two capsules like a twenty-first century slash fire that would, if everything went exactly right, redirect just enough solar radiation back into space and keep them alive long enough to build their cables and retreat down them into their radiation proof bunkers on the Moon. Lives, not just hopes and fortunes, were riding on those slim silver strands of fiber dropping down the lunar sky.

But there were still many hours, if not days, before the cables were ready to loop through the tether. The tether was ready for it. They'd figured out how to arrange an array of solar mirrors and focus a beam of light into a laser powerful enough to melt a huge pile of lunar soil into a sort of building block with a consistency somewhere between concrete and adobe. Mike and his wife Mannie O'Kelly had spend six months on Earth testing formulas for a kind of mortar to hold the blocks together by blending powdered aluminum and regolith. Tests here showed it worked even better than they expected.

Nigel and his wife Hazel Stone had trekked 295 miles back and forth across the moon and retrieved the refining and smelting equipment they'd launched eight months ago. Thanks to them they were able to refine ilmenite, a common lunar mineral, into titanium, iron, and oxygen. Their elevator cables would be anchored to the lunar bedrock by solid titanium beams and secured beneath fifteen columns of 74,275 (lunar) pound stone blocks. According to the engineers, the cables could hold five times as much load as they would ever use. Because the whole point of connecting the moon to L_1—or, more technically, to their platform and anything else in close orbit around L_1—was that once something got from one point to the other, you didn't need to hold it in place any more. Gravity stopped working against you and started becoming your ally again. And if stuff was worth a lot more at one end or the other, or people wanted to get from one end to the other, and you were the ones who controlled the elevator, you stood to become incredibly rich and powerful and famous.

Their goal was to boost thousands of stone blocks

and batches of mortar from the lunar surface to L_1. Their tribesmates up there would release the blocks from the elevator cable and mortar them together in different configurations. Things got a little hazy after that, which Jake figured was fair enough, since building huge inhabitable space colonies out of fused blocks of lunar regolith 70,000 miles above the Earth was almost certainly the craziest, most ambitious engineering project in history. For Jake, that was a big enough adventure in itself.

But some of his tribesmates, like Nigel and Mannie, believed they could build big enough colonies for enough people to leave Earth and move to space to save the planet. They maintained that all the big environmental threats— global warming, water pollution, deforestation, biodiversity loss, etc, etc—ultimately stemmed from overpopulation. Move enough people to orbit, they argued, and you stop environmental degradation at the root by removing the surplus population driving the dangerous pollutants and degradation.

Others, Jake was sure, were closer to Howard's view that the Earth was doomed. Going to space, Howard believed, was necessary for humanity to survive the death of the planet. Jake hadn't heard anyone come out and say that on the moon yet, but he had his suspicions. Most of his tribesmates, Jake was confident, weren't looking much past their ambitious short-term goals. Like him, they had a healthy skepticism of things happening in a predictable, orderly fashion or bringing about any particular result.

Once the blocks were in relatively stable orbits around L_1, there were at least two plans for how to put them together. The simplest design was more or less a giant hollow cigar but the hope was to eventually build something more like a giant hollow donut. There were complicated mathematics involved, but as far as Jake could tell the bottom line was that some people could live and manufacture or grow things in a giant hollow cigar for some time, and a lot of people could live pretty darn comfortably in a giant hollow donut for a long, long time.

Walls of lunar regolith blocks—perhaps supplemented by their electromagnetic slash fires, if those worked and they survived—would in theory block enough radiation for humans to survive indefinitely. The donuts in particular could theoretically be rotated to something close enough to 1 g for humans to not really notice the difference. Cigars could be used for manufacturing and as the world's most expensive construction trailers for building donuts.

Because even though the 75,000 (lunar) pound blocks were impressively massive as Jake looked at them stacked in piles of five across the surface of the moon, it was going to take a whole damn lot of them to build a cigar, let alone a donut, big enough to make it worth the trouble. Their tentative plan for the first small cigar, which would only be about 150 feet long with an interior diameter of a little less than 50 feet at its widest point, called for 1425 blocks.

More imaginative minds than Jake's had drawn up plans for a massive donut with a 450 foot interior diameter, sprawling across almost a mile of space, with solar mirrors to provide light and power and a central hub docking station which would remain weightless. They said they could build that with a mere 130,000 blocks. The dream was that someday people would build donuts that big and bigger as a matter of course; that people would live comfortably in space without thinking twice about it.

Whether that meant that enough of the billions of people whose consumption, byproducts, and waste were destroying the planet would migrate to space to allow the Earth to survive, and perhaps even begin to heal, was an open question. Whether it meant enough people would migrate to space for humanity to survive the death of the ecosphere was an open question. Whether Earth would continue to struggle along while they sold the most expensive luxury vacation resorts in history was another open question. But last year the Kaskawulsh glacier receded far enough to completely drain a river it had fed for hundreds of years. The rate of sea level rise increased by more than a third, putting more than 10 million Bangladeshis in danger of losing their homes in the next five years.. Desertification in Africa was on pace to claim two-thirds of the arable land within the next eight years. They might disagree about a lot, but they all knew the dangers were real.

If their tether worked, they figured they could eventually send about 36 blocks and twelve batches of mortar up it every day; one every half hour, propelled very very slowly by the huge solar panels they were building and the small electric motors that were sitting in their first storage bunker. Before they could put that much weight on the tether, however, they had to send blocks up one at a time to fill out the mass of their space platform and launch their counterweight platform back towards Earth so their blocks didn't pull their platform down out of the lunar sky.

They needed to lift almost 2500 blocks—more than a cigar's worth—of counterweight before they could start lifting building blocks, and they expected that to take about twelve weeks. The second set of blocks they thought they could lift in just six weeks. In theory, they would start working on a cigar right away and finish it in another six weeks. They were optimistically hoping to be able to build a cigar every twelve weeks.

At that point, they were basically counting on people being ambitious enough to start clambering for the opportunity to pour in a bunch of soil and an atmosphere and build themselves a home. Nobody really knew how to do it yet. But they were all pretty sure that once they built a few cigars there'd be no shortage of people wanting to give it a shot and willing to pay for the opportunity.

Which raised a bunch of questions his tribe couldn't really answer. For instance, how were they going to decide who got to move into any given cigar or donut? They'd already made some vague promises about "first refusal rights" to the Chinese government—with extensive conditions and qualifications and legal fine print—in return for help with their initial launches of crew and supplies. They'd made other vague promises about "the benefit of humanity" to the United Nations in return for permit approvals and relative freedom from bureaucratic meddling.

But now they were up here and everyone else was down there. They had supplies for a year, divided between their orbiting capsules and their lunar bunkers. Jake didn't expect anything to go the way anyone thought it would, or for anything to work out neatly according to anyone's plan, but he was confident they could survive here long enough to build at least two cigars.

Would those cigars wind up going to anyone who brought them enough nutripacks, rare metals, and powdered aluminum to live long enough to able to build the next ones? It might come down to that, especially if there weren't that many people interested in betting their lives on their ability to terraform a bunch of lunar soil mortared together like melted Legos three quarters of the way to the moon.

Because for the foreseeable future, there were going

to be things they needed that they couldn't make on the moon. They were going to need a lot of chemicals and supplies. So either they had to sell blocks for money to buy them; or they had to trade for them; or they had to figure out how to get them somewhere else, like the asteroid belt.

But there were a lot of things they could make themselves. Their immediate priorities were sustainable air, power, water, and food. Power wasn't that difficult on the moon. They'd already figured out how to make photoelectric panels out of lunar materials and the limited stock of metals and rare earths they'd brought. They built big panels and the sun never stopped shining. Making glass and glass fiber on the moon was not difficult once they had a reliable power supply. Aluminum was the third most common element in certain areas of the moon and silicon and oxygen were the most common just about everywhere.

They refined ilmenite into titanium, iron, and oxygen. They made mortar and bricks and solar panels out of aluminum, glass, iron, crystals, and titanium-reinforced molten lunar rock. Those were engineering challenges, but semi-reasonable ones.

Air, water and food were much more problematic. In theory, once they had enough power, they could run an electrical current through moonrock and produce hydrogen and oxygen. But it was going to take *a lot* of power. Nobody had ever built ten square mile solar panels on earth before, let alone on the moon where the panels would be vulnerable to meteors, radiation, and other threats they hadn't even imagined yet. The theories were all there, though. They knew how to convert sunlight, which the moon had a more or less endless supply of, to electricity. They knew they could make air and water out of the hydrogen and oxygen they produced. They knew they could grow food with water and carbon dioxide, which their bodies continually produced.

Most importantly, they knew that if they could do all this on the moon, people could do it anywhere. In theory, you could close the ends of a cigar or a donut, pour the right mix of elements and chemicals into it, spin it, and start creating an ecosystem where people could live. Nobody had ever done anything like it. But if they proved it was possible, they would give humanity its ticket to the stars.

Jake figured if they lived long enough they'd build two cigars and trade one of them for the stuff they needed to take a shot at building a donut and creating a viable hydro cycle. If it worked, they'd build another one, and some more cigars, make more deals, then build two more, and so on. With any luck other people would start doing new and different things around them and the whole thing would take off and go viral and save humanity.

Jake didn't really expect things to work out like that. In his mind, this was all a crazy experiment with a really low

73

probability of success. Simply watching the thin glowing cables tumble down the lunar sky was itself such a huge achievement that he felt like they'd already succeeded and whatever happened afterwards wasn't really all that important. The most important thing was they'd done it. It really was just like Howard said all those years ago. They'd cashed in all their chips, all their connections, every resource they had, and they'd committed all of it to each other. Any thing beyond that was gravy.

And yet here he was, watching his gravy float down the lunar sky in front of him. They'd built this amazing thing with no parallel in any recorded human history. Jake had been part of a lot of successful teams before, but this tribe, with these stakes, made him feel better about himself than anything else he'd ever done.

Jake looked around the base and saw Nigel and Mike bouncing around in his direction. "What's up?" he asked softly. "Time for a radiation breather," Mike replied calmly. "The three of us have been out here for more than four hours: time to go lie in a dark cave for a while." They didn't really have any scientific basis for thinking that limiting their exposure to surface radiation to four hours at a time would help them live on the moon any longer. Everything they knew about the effect of radiation on the human body told them clearly and unambiguously that the effects were cumulative; that if your total surface exposure was 24 hours it didn't really matter if you were out there for 24 hours straight, or you spent an hour a day out there for 24 days. Solar radiation didn't care or notice and showed no mercy.

But nobody had ever lived on the moon before either. And they didn't have any reason to think four-hour shift limits could hurt them. For all they knew, it might have some sort of reverse psychosomatic effect: their bodies would resist the radiation better if they convinced themselves that limiting their exposure would make a difference. Maybe their cells would somehow miraculously adapt and start shedding radiation into the cold lunar bedrock as they lay silently in their dark bunkers and thought about what they were doing. Jake thought about his mates from the crab boat and how they'd fare up here. He imagined them pouring water into a cigar and trying to stock it with crabs, or maybe crayfish. *The first orbiting trophy pond*, he smiled to himself.

If nothing else, he thought, taking regular breaks like this gave them time to daydream and it made it less likely that they'd spend too much time working, get tired, do something stupid, and kill somebody. Sometimes, Jake thought, you tried to do something for one reason and it wound up helping you in a completely different way you never could have predicted and probably wouldn't understand. Jake figured that was probably what would happen with their cables.

Chapter Five

Jasmine

Oberlin, Ohio, U.S.A.

May 5, 1994

"Today I found my friends. We had breakfast at
IHOP." Jasmine had no idea what her only child was about
to say. "Then we took naps. Now we're here, and it's just
my luck, I'm supposed to speak to you today about
'Learning and Labor,' which some of you might know is the
motto of Oberlin College." Jasmine didn't know that. She'd
never been to Oberlin before. She'd never been to a college
graduation before. She'd dropped out of college her junior
year because she was sick of people staring at her pregnant
belly. Now her baby boy was graduating from college, and
they'd asked him to make a speech. That was different.
Usually people just wanted Grok to shut up.

"Don't ask me to lie: before they told me in no
uncertain terms that I'd be speaking today about 'Learning
and Labor,' I never even knew Oberlin had a motto, much
less what it was. Any minute, somebody's going to tell me
we have a winning football team too!" Jasmine thought he
might look up at her when he said this, but he was looking
over towards his classmates with a smile on his face.
Probably he didn't think about that football game in Madison
all those years ago as much as she did, even though he never

would have been born if that team hadn't won that game. It almost made her smile, thinking about how capricious life was. One team happens to catch a ball that happens to bounce one way and not another and twenty years later her little boy—that young man—stands at that podium and speaks to this huge crowd of wealthy and important people.

"So, if you're anything like me, you've probably never really thought much about that motto before." No, she'd never thought about it at all. And she wasn't sure any of the other students were anything like Grok. If they were, she sure felt sorry for their parents. But she'd done a hell of a lot of labor to give him the opportunity to stand up there and talk about his learning. Jasmine looked around the grandstands at the other parents. They didn't look like her. She was wearing a beautiful green and brown dashiki from Mali over her best pair of jeans with a comfortable pair of nylon walking shoes. They were wearing suits and cotton sundresses and polished leather shoes with heels. They looked successful and popular and content. They all looked the same, like they were all friends already. They were smiling cheerful insincere smiles. Jasmine wasn't very good at faking. She wondered if it made her look even more unhappy and unsuccessful than she felt.

"Probably all of you together haven't ever spent as much time thinking about 'Learning and Labor' as I have the past few weeks. I've thought about it so much it makes me sick. Today, for better or worse, I'm going to share those thoughts with you. It may or may not be what they expected." Though he tried to keep his tone pleasant, Jasmine could hear the adrenalin, anger, and hostility filtering up through Grok's voice. He had been the happiest little baby, she remembered. When he was two or three he would run and laugh and play and fall down and smile all day long. Then her father died, and she had to start working day jobs, and her mother started having her problems, and everything went to hell and took little laughing smiling Grok away with it.

"My first reaction is that it was total nineteenth-century bullshit. Just a cheap advertising ploy by bourgeois academics with manicured fingers and silk gowns to give themselves some illusion of solidarity with the working class. 'Learning and Labor,' us and them, even though we weren't them, and none of them would ever be one of us." Jasmine hoped Grok wasn't about to give a Marxist lecture. When he was eleven, he insisted on going to school barefoot so he could better identify with the 'wretched of the earth,' as he called them. That lasted about two weeks. Wisconsin winters made cowards of many. She was able to persuade him to wear a pair of fur lined mukluks a member of the local Ho Chunk tribe might have worn in the winter, giving him some sort of authentic local connection. All the Ho Chunks she knew wore Sorel boots in the winter, but she kept that to herself.

"But then I started thinking that wasn't fair. It's not fair to us and it isn't fair to John Frederic Oberlin, the man for whom our school is named." Life isn't fair, Jasmine thought. It wasn't fair that she had to raise Grok herself while his father ran off and watched clouds in the Air Force. "John Oberlin was a pastor who lived in eastern France from 1740 to 1826. What he was mostly known for, what I think this school honors him for, was attempting to better both the material condition and the spiritual life of his parishioners. I'm not sure, in fact, whether he felt there was any meaningful line to be drawn between the two. One of the things he is most remembered for is building roads and bridges to connect the villagers he served. I've never heard of a pastor who built roads and bridges."

Jasmine saw Grok start to relax as he eased into his speech. He'd never been afraid of crowds, she thought. He'd never cared very much what other people thought. The only person whose opinions he'd ever really feared was Stanley. Their connection had been so tenuous that Grok must have been terrified his father would disappear completely. "John Oberlin was also a teacher who built and opened several schools in his parish. He relied on his housekeeper, a poor woman named Louisa Scheppler with no formal education or experience, to help him write his curriculums. I don't know a lot of pastors who would treat their housekeepers as equals and work collaboratively with them on school curriculums."

Did Grok actually know any pastors, Jasmine wondered? She tried to remember if she and her son had ever gone to church together, but nothing came to mind. She'd been raised a Lutheran, but had never really adopted that faith as her own, and once she'd gotten to Madison she didn't think she'd ever gone to a Lutheran church again, except maybe for a wedding or a funeral every now and again. She did yoga and from time to time practiced meditation on her own, but she hadn't been part of any organized religion for a long time.

She didn't really know about her son though, which made her feel sad. She'd never tried to exercise much control over Grok. Whether that was because she believed in freedom or because she was scared of losing him to his father—who for his part tried to exercise as much control as he could in his limited time with Grok—she couldn't really say. Stanley couldn't be here, Grok told her yesterday at lunch, because he was overseas somewhere. Exactly where was apparently top secret. Control and secrets were two of Stanley's favorite things.

When she'd found out she was pregnant with Grok, Jasmine remembered, it had taken almost a week to make Stanley talk to her. When she finally got him on the phone, his main concern was making sure their child didn't stand in the way of his college. He didn't tell her he'd joined the Air Force until Grok was almost three years old. When Grok was seven, Stanley spent a year in Antarctica without telling them. But whenever he did show up, Stanley always had a plan. When Grok was ten, Stanley took him on a seven day trip to five baseball games in three different cities. Grok was never interested in sports, but he pretended to be a fan so he wouldn't upset Stanley's plan. Not many ten year-olds were capable of that, Jasmine thought.

"In addition to practicing medicine, founding a library, and introducing improved agricultural techniques, one of the other things John Oberlin did for his parishioners was founding a savings and loan bank. His bank was more like what we'd call today a credit union. His goal was to give the villagers tools, financial tools, to improve their lives, not to get rich." That's what all the kids wanted to do today, Jasmine thought, get rich. It's like all the things she and her friends believed in and marched for and wrote poems about in the 60s had totally inverted themselves in their children. She'd done a sculpture about it once called "Melting Beauty" and a yuppie from Chicago bought it for $12,500. Now Jasmine had $57.86 in her savings account and was unlikely to qualify for any loans from anyone.

"So after I learned a little bit about who John Oberlin was, I started thinking again about 'Learning and Labor.' And it seemed clear to me that one of the meanings, what some might call the 'intentional meaning,' of our motto is that an admirable life, a worthy way of life, involves both 'Learning and Labor,' and perhaps even building some kind of bridge between them. John Oberlin labored mightily so that his learning about religion, agriculture, medicine, masonry, education, and economics would benefit the villagers he served. The men who founded this college admired him so much that they named our school after him, and not in an ironic way. I think our motto was meant to honor these admirable qualities of our school's namesake." Jasmine figured there was probably more than that to the story of John Oberlin. What about that housekeeper, Louisa, for example? Jasmine figured she was probably not unattractive and there was a good chance John Oberlin had been sharing more than curriculums with her.

That's just how men were; how people were. She'd learned that the hard way when Grok was just a baby and she was just starting her sculpture career. She naively accepted a more established male sculptor's offer to use his kiln. The first time she'd gone to fire something, he'd been waiting for her with a bottle of wine. It wasn't his first. He started touching her and when she resisted he got angry, like it was all her fault. She'd been lucky to get away. She'd tried to educate her son, but for now he still basked in the idyllic innocence of the young.

"I think the motto has three main lessons about

'Learning' for us. First, 'Learning' isn't something that happens in isolation; in an 'ivory tower.'" Strange, Jasmine thought. Her son was one of the most isolated people she'd ever known. "It means that learning is synergistic. That scholarship among people with different temperaments, talents, and convictions is more productive than scholarship by people who all think and believe the same things." Jasmine didn't think Grok had ever had a best friend, let along a group of friends with diverse backgrounds and wide-ranging points of view. The last time she could remember a friend of his coming over to play was when Grok was seven or eight. After that, he'd been a loner who spent all his free time reading.

"It means that diversity really does have an inherent value. For scholars, for communities, and in every workplace." But people didn't want diversity, Jasmine thought. She remembered her last day job. She'd worked at a medical office after her dad died. The doctors were all the same. They all looked the same and they all thought the same. They all talked the same, for God's sake. They all had wives they despised. They all fooled around and every one of them tried to sleep with her. They all played fast and loose with the rules and their money, partying and padding their bills. Was Grok saying one older female Hindu doctor who didn't drink or take drugs would have saved them all from themselves? That would at the least have made it all more interesting, she had to admit. But the doctors would have laughed at the very idea. One reason diversity didn't work, at least in Jasmine's experience, was that the people who needed it the most were the ones least likely to seek it out and the ones most likely to resent it.

"One corollary of that is that knowledge is inherently social; that the nature of ideas is to be shared. That doesn't mean people can't have new ideas. It means that people have more new ideas and better new ideas when they're part of a learning community." Jasmine felt like she was part of a forgetting community. She and the rest of her old friends had a brief vision of what life could be like during the 60's and they'd spent the last twenty years trying hard to forget it, or just blot it out.

"The second lesson is that learning is holistic. That people who study lots of different things know and discover more than people who study just one thing. That came as a surprise to me. It seems like all of us have spent, or at least should have spent, the last four years studying just one thing. Standing here watching people get their diplomas today, it seems to me like somebody who really understands C++ or Windows, because they spent the last four years studying code, should have a lot brighter future than somebody who dabbled in a bunch of subjects."

Jasmine wasn't sure what exactly Grok studied at Oberlin. He'd told her at lunch yesterday that he was graduating with a "self-designed" major that "incorporated" philosophy, history, music performance, and rhetoric. Jasmine figured the college was probably sick of listening to Grok and happy for him to move along. He'd been on scholarship, so they weren't making any money off of him. Stanley had offered to pay Grok's way to Princeton, Harvard, or anywhere else. His test scores would have gotten him accepted just about anyplace. But Grok had insisted on taking a scholarship, much to Stanley's annoyance. Jasmine was delighted to see her son growing up and moving out of his father's shadow.

"But that's not what John Oberlin did. He didn't try to become the nineteenth century's leading expert on bridges for rural roads in eastern France. He only learned just as much about bridges as he needed to build them. Sometimes what's best for one person isn't necessarily best for her community or her world. Sometimes somebody who studies a lot of things a little gets a better education than somebody who studies a little thing a lot." Most of Grok's classmates looked bored, or hung over. Jasmine wasn't sure they believed in anything at all. When she was young, she believed in the inevitable victory of peace and love. Now it was difficult for her to imagine peace and love surviving their latest defeats.

"I think John Oberlin would say that a coder with more exposure to other topics is going to be a better citizen that a coder without that exposure and is going to contribute more to her community over time. I think John Oberlin would say that coders who don't just write code are going to write better code and make more breakthroughs than coders who do nothing but write code. Specialization does not promote innovation. There is no innovation without diversity.

"John Oberlin's third lesson about learning is that it is spiritual. Oberlin wasn't trying to make his villagers better chemists and masons so they would be more intelligent. He was trying to make them better people. I don't think Oberlin would think much of learning that didn't make the world a better place. He was very much a man of God; he was born before the 'death of God' so famously described by Friedrich Nietzsche, who was born about twenty years after Oberlin died and was Oberlin's opposite in just about every way possible." People who were so arrogant they thought they could make other people better, Jasmine mused, weren't always fun to be around. She'd met a love-drug-crazed hippie guru like that the summer after she finished high school. She spent two weeks on his so-called commune before she saw through the curtain of his charisma. Mostly he'd wanted a lot of sex, expecting her and the other women to massage his ego and feed his vanity. That, according to him, was the way for them to become better people.

"Nietzsche was unfriendly, unpopular, and passionately opposed to the 'herd mentality' of the ordinary villagers Oberlin championed. Oberlin was friendly, popular, and passionate about elevating the lot of his herd of villagers. His learning was not dry, academic, or destructive, like Nietzsche's, but instead was practical, social, and constructive. Learning without spiritual improvement is empty." That was the great thing about being young, Jasmine thought. Young people could believe their spirits would just keep improving their whole lives. She'd believed that once. Then she'd raised a child alone and run her solo sculpture studio for fifteen years. Mostly she worked in concrete and Portland cement, making large abstract outdoor pieces. She tried to make art that was dramatic and infuse it with a positive spirit. But it was hard for her to say she had higher spirits than when she started. She'd infused too much of her energy into her work.

"If learning should be synergistic, holistic, and spiritual," Grok continued, "what about labor?" What about labor, Jasmine thought? Grok's first job was at the library in Stevens Point. He was supposed to shelve books, but would inevitably start reading them instead, until somebody found him nestled in the stacks when the library was about to close. The librarians liked him and thought he was clever, so they never fired him, but he quit anyway so he could go to some concert in Chicago. Stanley gave him money for that.

Stanley always had money. Jasmine never wanted any of it, but it gave her another reason to be terrified of losing Grok. She'd been so proud of him for taking this scholarship and not letting Stanley pay for his education. Looking at Grok, she felt very proud he was so comfortable standing on his own two feet.

"I have to tell you," Grok said, "it was hard for me to think about what labor meant in John Oberlin's world, in the 1810s, because so much of our vocabulary about labor starts with Marx. But Oberlin labored in a pre-Marxist world, with no clear consciousness of class, let alone class consciousness, so I'm going to try not to impose any class structures on him. But I'm going to try not to idealize his pre-industrial world either.

"Oberlin's first lesson about labor is that it is good. Working, building things, improving conditions, exercising stewardship over the earth, all these are good things. But they're not good if they're not shared. I don't think John Oberlin thought the accumulation of wealth was a sign of divine favor. I think he thought good work was service to others; service to the blessed community he was trying to create in rural France. Service for others was part of his divine world. He served God by enriching his community. He built bridges for his village, not temples to himself." It was hard to serve a community when you didn't feel like part of one, Jasmine thought.

She felt like Grok was skipping over a bunch of things that seemed like big problems to her. She'd felt like part of a community when she was young: a beautiful community with a vision of a world of love and peace. Once she got pregnant though, everything was different, and she'd felt it right away. Then after she left Madison she never really felt like she fit in anywhere ever again. That's why she spent so much time working in her studio by herself.

"His second lesson about labor is that it is shared. Without romanticizing Oberlin's villages into some sort of Eighteenth Century Mondragon Collective, his spiritual willingness to treat his villagers on equal terms seems to have led to collaborative workplaces: to banks, road building crews, and schools that were neither feudal, where the peasants could manage their production any way they liked as long as they had the king's share ready on time, nor industrial, with owners extracting surplus value by managing the worker's production as finely as possible. His workshops were something else. Something where the peasants felt his love and acknowledged his leadership but all of them were still in it together." Jasmine thought that was ridiculous. How could Grok know what love peasants in France 150 years ago felt or didn't feel? Of course they told their pastor what they thought he wanted to hear. That's what people do.

"Now let me be the first to admit that's a totally

idealized version of history. I don't know what actually happened. I don't know if anyone knows what actually happened. For all I know Oberlin was a tyrant and a jerk. But I think that's the story the men who founded this school wanted to believe. Sometimes myths are more important than reality." Grok had never really been hungry, Jasmine knew, never spent the night outside cold and wet, never wondered whether he would survive the morrow. Stanley had made sure of that. But sitting here listening to him talk Jasmine wondered if he was too soft. Life was going to shit on him soon enough, she thought to herself, as it did everybody, and she hoped her son was strong enough to survive it.

"What else should I say? Probably I should stop there. It's a nice myth, a good story. Most of you are still awake." Stopping was hard, Jasmine thought. She thought it was probably the hardest thing about making art, knowing when it was done. God, how many pieces had she ruined by not knowing when to stop? Just one more batch of concrete, one last layer on the base, she'd tell herself, and all of a sudden 40 or 50 pounds of concrete were crumbling over her feet. "But I'm not going to stop. I'm not going to just talk about the eighteenth century. I'm going to talk about our reality, or at least our myths. I'm going to talk about some of the ways that I think this school named after John Oberlin doesn't live up to my own personal myth of John Oberlin that I spent the last two weeks thinking about, or maybe making up.

"I'm going to try to skip over the easy targets: the disconnect between the campus and the city around it; the almost complete lack of physical labor by students; the focus on individual studies over group projects. Instead I want to use the myth I've created to talk about some bigger issues." Once again, Jasmine had no idea what her son was about to say. He had bounced around so many schools of thought. He'd tried to teach her about Marxism, existentialism, libertarianism and a bunch of other things she didn't even know what to call, much less understand. It made it difficult to be his mother sometimes when he called home filled with excitement over his latest intellectual journey and spent several hours passionately enlightening her. At least he always wanted to share his learning with his mother, Jasmine thought, smiling and thinking about how much she loved her son.

"The first thing I want to talk about is what appears to be an ever-growing disconnect between physics and religion. But putting it that way probably doesn't make it sound like much of a problem. Physics is objective and cumulative; religion is subjective and sudden. If you think about physics more generally though—as the physical sciences—and about religion most generally—as the art of spiritual improvement—maybe it will be less obvious that those should be kept segregated. At least it isn't obvious to me, and it sure wasn't obvious to John Oberlin. He saw himself in the tradition of Descartes, Hume, Kant, Hobbes, Newton, Spinoza and the other thinkers of the Enlightenment who tried to fit everything together. It's fair to say none of them ever really succeeded—and in a way I'm glad because the world would be much more tedious and less magical if we knew everything—but they tried. By trying, they made huge advances in religion and in science that still shape the parameters of our thoughts 200 years later. John Oberlin would not think that was a mere coincidence."

Jasmine wondered what it was like for Grok to be twenty years old and confident he would someday figure out the universe in a way nobody else ever had. She couldn't imagine having that kind of confidence. That was the Stanley in him. Neither of them ever doubted themselves for an instant. But their confidence also drove them apart once Grok stopped being the ten year-old who travelled around the country watching baseball games he wasn't interested in and turned into a young man every bit as self-assured as Stanley.

"But if you look at what people are doing today, which as students we pretty much have to, you will see more and more specialization and fewer and fewer grand unified theories. Sure, every now again somebody will write a 'popular' article about 'Quantum Buddhism' or some such, but the very nature of those essays belies any pretense of serious work. I think John Oberlin would remind us that neither the universe itself nor humanity's place in it is any more complicated today than it was in 1795 – or 450 BC for that matter—and that if you can't explain something to your mother then there's a good chance you don't really understand it." Grok did finally look up at his mother then. He smiled at her and paused briefly. She smiled back, thinking of all those late night phone calls about Derrida and Kierkegaard and Pythagoras. She'd understood every word even when she had no idea what he was talking about.

"One manifestation of that disconnect between religion and physics is that religion still works in the language of things, even though physics now tells us that our universe at its most fundamental level is composed of events, of fuzzy energy interactions across time. We don't notice this as much as we should, because our philosophers are themselves specialists, with few or no institutional incentives to try to construct grand conceptual schemes incorporating ethics, ontology, epistemology, aesthetics, etc, etc." Jasmine thought 'grand conceptual schemes' sounded a lot like code for telling other people what to do. That's something Stanley would have, she thought, a grand conceptual scheme. And he'd believe in it so much that the idea that anyone else could have reservations or questions about it—or suggest improvements, Heaven forbid—would drive him into a rage.

"If our philosophers were constructing grand conceptual schemes, of course, none of them would ever succeed, not any more than Hobbes, Locke, or Kant ever did. But just because you don't succeed doesn't mean it wasn't important to try.

"One more special message to go," Grok continued with a smile. "The last thing I want to talk about today is the structural division of the Oberlin community into 'students' and 'faculty.'" They hadn't actually given him his degree yet, had they? Jasmine smiled. There's no way her son could talk himself out of graduating in the last part of his speech, but part of her—a part she hadn't felt so in touch with for a long time—really hoped he would. "Because I don't think John Oberlin's banks, his bridge-building companies, or especially his churches were ever structured like that. I don't think John Oberlin believed certain people were more godly than others. I don't think John Oberlin believed anyone had nothing to learn from anyone else. I think John Oberlin believed everyone was better at something than anyone else was. I think John Oberlin believed everyone had something to teach to, and something to learn from, everyone else."

Jasmine tried to think what she could learn from some of the uglier people she'd struggled with over her life. He was right, she realized. They all taught her something. Maybe not something good, or anything very important, but there was always something. There were always lessons. The yuppie who bought her statute taught her how two people could see the same statute so differently. The hippie sex-guru taught her to look past charisma. The drunken doctors taught her that people with status and riches weren't always admirable.

"I think John Oberlin would challenge us to approach every encounter with every human with an open mind. To appreciate every meeting as a chance to learn something. Segregating our community into 'faculty' who teach 'students' can hinder that mindset. Although I've learned a lot from my professors in formal 'educational' settings, I think I may have learned even more over the last four years from you, my fellow students, in informal discussions. So that is the final thought I have to share after pondering our motto for two weeks: keep an open mind in every encounter with every human because they all have something to teach you."

Jasmine stood with the rest of the crowd and applauded her son. The ceremony wrapped up and she made her way down off the platform and onto the cool grass of Tappan Square. She was smiling now. Her smile was absolutely authentic and grew even bigger when she caught sight of Grok. He was explaining something earnestly to two professors and didn't see her walk up behind him. She stood for a moment, beaming with pride, until one of the professors noticed her and looked away. Grok turned to her. "Hi Mom!" he said with a grin. Jasmine suddenly swelled with tears and couldn't speak as she wrapped her arms around her only child and held him tight with love and appreciation.

Chapter Six

Ripley

Stoner's Bridge Mining Post

November 20, 2022

Ripley careened across the 50-foot bridge at the middle of the mining post in less than half a second. That had been one of the most difficult adjustments for her to make—the speeds at which experienced people could cover ground up here. There was a bit of a trick to finding the most efficient gait: it wasn't quite a sprint but rather something of a cross between skipping and ice skating. Running was dangerous because it was so easy to go out of control. Jumping was inefficient and ungainly. But once Ripley learned how, her long legs and strong heart made her one of the fastest people on the moon. Right now, she was using every bit of her speed to get away from Stoner's Bridge as fast as she could.

According to her friend Preemo, whose security teams regularly traveled long distances around the post, the key to maintaining control was for the moment of inertia when your boot actually contacted the regolith to be as long as possible at any given speed. It was risky enough that people generally limited themselves to two or three skipsteps at a time, enough to move 50 or 60 feet in a couple of seconds, especially inside the post. She was taking a chance going so fast but she knew it was her best risk.

Glancing at the dark buildings as they flashed by, she didn't see many signs of occupancy. There were around 450 or 500 people here now, but they had room for more than a thousand. She'd been in some of these buildings before, back when this part of the post was still working. For her first twelve months on the moon she'd run loaders stacking habricks for the elevator. Some of these buildings had been where she helped the mainteam keep the loaders running. One time she'd helped move a pallet of spare loader parts from the elevator into a dark building flashing by on her left. That was one of the last times anyone had ever sent any really useful parts down the elevator. Everybody had been so excited and felt such a connection with the people up there at the other end of the tether, like they were all working together.

Now mainteam buildings looked like nobody had been in them for years. Ripley remembered learning in physics class that if you went really really fast you'd experience time more slowly than an observer "at rest" relative to the rest of the universe. From what she'd seen on the moon, however, the opposite was true: moving so fast made people live even faster. Nobody had been here for even three years but they'd done so many amazing things in that short time. They'd bound together so tightly. And they'd changed so much—for better and for worse.

She passed another building where newmooner orientation used to be, back when people still arrived fairly regularly. That's where she'd met Rico almost two years ago. Her loader team and Rico's telemetry team both needed bodies. They'd found some exceptionally capable people. So capable, in fact, that she was running as fast as she could across the moon so she and Rico could get away from them before it was too late.

She made a sharp turn away from the center of the post at the deserted building where California Pete and some of his friends had tried to start their Southside Cafeteria. She'd been to at least three of their funerals since she met her last newmooner. Life, death, and politics moved fast on the moon and people took their food pretty seriously. Now she had to move even faster or she might be stuck on this post for the rest of her life.

She slowed her pace by taking a stride a bit higher so she could look around at bit. She could see a dim light in one of the storage canisters, thank God! Who'd have thought she'd ever have to sneak around and hide. Hide from her enemies? Had it really come to that? On the moon? How incredible and amazing, how sad and disappointing people were that after just three short years here, on this most alien of worlds, they already felt at home enough to start persecuting and discriminating and ostracizing and maybe even killing one another.

It's not like death was hard to find on the moon. Somebody died every month or so. Last week five people on a mortar crew died when a rover axle snapped in two. A wheel flew off and crushed their umbilical mainline. They'd done everything exactly by the book. The axle was forged with a slight flaw but barely passed inspection. It was one week away from the end of its service life. The odds of it hitting their mainline were thousands to one. But they were all still dead. That's why she was so astonished to think political disagreements could lead to cold-blooded killing. Maybe murder was actually easier where life itself was so precarious.

In the beginning, when the firstmooners came up and built their tether harness at Touchdown, forty-seven miles northwest of Stoner's Bridge, they had crew chiefs, in an informal kind of way, and they all gave each other extra respect in their areas of expertise, but they didn't really have any political structures. Nobody was planning to live on the moon then: they wanted to start mining habricks to build cigars and donuts around L_1. They wanted to build themselves nice tidy little worlds in space, not try and tame something as unruly as the moon. Thinking they weren't staying must have made their mission a lot easier.

In fact, as far as Ripley knew, the firstmooners never really talked much about politics at all. They called themselves a tribe, but she figured that was probably more for morale and PR than anything else. None of them worried about what any of it meant. They just came up here on borrowed money and empty promises and fast-talking doublespeak and equipment they didn't pay for. They just started lifting habricks into space and they probably never even thought once about what a world of shit was going to come of it. Most people worked like that.

But once people saw those habricks floating up that tether, they got really jealous really fast. Suddenly everybody wanted to see their own habricks floating up their own tethers. Including organizations like the Chinese government, Amazon, and FC Barcelona, with enough money, power, and resources to crash the firstmooners' party. The lunar race of 2020 left the crazy tribes of adventurers with vague ideas about lifting habricks to make space habitats shaped like cigars and donuts behind. It replaced them with the world's most powerful governments and corporations, armed with spreadsheets, procedure manuals, and very specific and detailed business plans. They'd sent their best organizational people so maybe it shouldn't be surprising to see those people starting their own organization and executing a hostile takeover.

That's how Ripley got here. She'd been a low-level manager at Amazon, steadying and increasing the constant delivery flow of bread and pastry products from factories to distribution centers to homes across Northern California and

101

Southwestern Oregon. The call went out for mining loader operators and she applied, on a whim as much as anything. All the physical and psychological tests they put her through must have turned out OK though, because after a two week training course in Sri Lanka they sent her to L_1 from Amazon's launch facility on Diego Garcia, the Indian Ocean island Jeff Bezos bought from America after the first great climate storms in 2019. Four months after she applied she was on the moon. She'd read once that astronauts used to train for years before they first left Earth. Either Amazon thought it knew a lot more about space travel than the military or it didn't value life as highly. Probably both, she thought.

Life on the moon had started out great for Ripley. She displayed an intuitive knack with her loader that made her a favorite of all her shiftmates and she managed to get along with everyone in her dom. She met her best friend Rico, who ran away from a bad marriage in Grenada when she was 15 and worked her way up the FC Barcelona corporate ladder to the moon. She had a brief romance with a Cafeteria cook, which if nothing else meant she ate well. She worked hard, kept her nose clean, and accumulated stock credits and bacsal at an impressive pace.

As she slowed down and circled the lit storage canister to make sure she hadn't been followed, she remembered calculating once that if she loaded habricks for five years, took a year off, then did another four years, she would have more money than she could ever spend by the time she was 40. Now, walking towards the door, she laughed at herself for thinking her job, or anything else on the moon, could last for ten whole years.

There was a note on the lock door to "Keep Your Gear On." Ripley could see that the lunalock inside was wide open. Apparently they wouldn't be staying here long, or they were prepared to evacuate at a moment's notice. Would it really come to that? As far as she knew, the only dead people so far had been killed in spontaneous fights between equally hot-tempered combatants. That was a lot different from killing people in cold blood, wasn't it? Either way, she thought, the best plan was to get out of here ASAP and not give any of the particularly zealous moonfirsters a chance to draw that line in blood across their throats.

She opened the door and saw Rico sitting on a bench with Sudomo and a woman she didn't recognize in a Chinese spacesuit with its distinctive red stars and white boots. Ripley smiled and was glad Sudomo was there. He used to run the Cafeteria at Ripley's dom. He'd effectively been in charge of feeding a third of the people on the moon and was used to pressure situations. Sudomo knew a few things about stress and crisis management and was a good person to have with them in this pinch.

The Cafeteria had been a "cooperative" project

between Amazon and F.C Barcelona. In theory, that meant that both companies contributed labor and money and all their employees got fed in one big cafeteria instead of two small ones, taking advantage of economies of scale. In practice it'd been a lot more complicated than that, which is why Sudomo was sitting in a dimly lit storage unit wearing a spacesuit and hoping to get off the moon alive.

As a rule, plans and deals and rules and systems made on Earth weren't working out so well for the people actually on the moon. Sudomo had been here almost from the beginning, and from what he'd told Ripley, it all went pretty well at first, when everyone was still trying to get everything built and all their operating systems working. As long as they'd had a common goal, a specific mission, they'd all worked together to survive. Sudomo's Cafeteria had been a warm, friendly place back then—a place where everyone knew your name and people met as individuals with little or no thought for different institutional loyalties. As much as anyone could ever relax up here, that was the place for it: a place for Ripley to eat soup and steal glances at her lover.

But soon enough all the buildings were built, all the mining systems were up and running, and the endless stream of habricks started rolling down the lunarail to Touchdown and up the tether to L_1. You'd have thought people would have relaxed and been happier then. You'd have thought they'd have enjoyed the Cafeteria even more. But looking back on it, everyone agreed that just the opposite happened and that's when the divisions between the Amas and the Barcas really began to arise.

After about four months, people stopped coming to the Cafeteria at all and started cooking for themselves in storage containers, using emergency supplies and stores spirited from the Cafeteria by people who used to work there. Not long after, a joint committee of Amas and Barcas presented Sudomo with a duly enacted memorandum of understanding and reorganization sent from Earth. They proceeded to take everything of value from the Cafeteria. Then they spent ten hours dividing it up to the last grain of rice, like two spoiled sisters splitting their shoe closet. Finally, inevitably, the moonfirster movement emerged in reaction to that silly and strange conflict—a pox on both your houses, Ripley thought, which was sensible as far as it went because they really did need unity to survive.

But now the moonfirsters were taking over, and it was becoming clear they were going to insist that everyone do everything their way forever. That, Ripley had a problem with. Not so much with any specific rule or way of doing things, but with the general concept of staying on the moon and living under somebody else's rules for the rest of her life. If she'd wanted military discipline, Ripley thought, she'd have joined the army, not Amazon.

Ripley didn't recognize the woman in the Chinese

spacesuit. That wasn't surprising. The Chinese crews generally kept to themselves. Under the general three way division of labor imagined in executive boardrooms on Earth three years ago, Chinese crews manufactured the habricks, Amazon was responsible for delivering them to L_1, and Barca crews handled infrastructure and maintenance, logistics, marketing, admin, and human relations. Like everything else, it hadn't worked out quite like that. You couldn't deliver the habricks to L_1 without quality controls, which meant Amas inside Chinese mining and fabrication plants. You couldn't calculate booster output without real time information on the delivery sleds, which meant Barcas on the Amazon supply line.

Ripley had to admit, the way everything had gotten so mixed up and become so different than what the men in suits had envisioned, the moonfirsters really did have a good point. All of them on the moon absolutely did have more in common with each other than with anyone on Earth. They really did need to be one lunar team, not extensions of different Earth teams. But that didn't mean she wanted to spend the rest of her life here. There was a whole galaxy out there and she had big dreams.

"I'm so glad you're here," Rico said, standing up to touch faceplates with Ripley. "We have a lot to talk about and some important decisions to make in a short time." "We sure do," Ripley replied. "How much time do you think we have?"

"We don't really know," Sudomo answered. "That's why my friend Maringka is here." He made a short but very formal bow towards the Chinese spacesuit. "Maringka, I am honored to introduce you to our friend and fellow conspirator, Ripley." He bowed again to Ripley. "Ripley, I am honored to introduce my friend and, it seems, potential accomplice to our conspiracy, Maringka. Maringka and I became friends in Tokyo a long long time ago. She was the chief information security officer for the Chinese embassy and I was a humble purveyor of satay and rendang in Jiyugaoka Meguro.

"As you may have noticed, Maringka is not herself of Chinese descent—I will leave it to her what parts of her story she will share with you, or not—and she became a frequent, if not daily, patron of my humble establishment. One thing led to another, we became friends, and she began bringing other diplomatic types to my café. She was in no small measure responsible for the financial success I enjoyed at that time. The very financial success, in fact, that ultimately led me here, searching as moderately well off middle-aged men will for one final great adventure. But that is neither here nor there. We are not here to listen to my troubles except as they relate to our current situation.

"Maringka, I cannot say that my friendship with Ripley has lasted for so many years, but I know her to be a person of integrity and can vouch for her confidence and trust. She will not tell anyone you were here unless you tell her to." "Of course not," Ripley answered, bowing much less formally to the woman in the spacesuit, who appeared to be around Sudomo's age. "Sudomo has been a great friend and help to me, and any service I could perform for his friend would be an honor." Ripley often found herself speaking more formally around Sudomo. Some people had that effect. It wasn't so much that he was old, just dignified. Ripley tried to remember if she'd ever heard anyone curse in his presence and couldn't. That was pretty unusual for a chef.

"Thank you Ripley," Maringka replied in an unfamiliar accent with a slight bow. "I am honored to meet you and glad you have had the good fortune to enjoy Sudomo's friendship." She turned and bowed more formally to Sudomo. "I am here because Sudomo is my friend, and although he was graceful enough not to mention it, because I am in his debt. I would honor that debt by doing whatever I could to help him and his friends regardless of the cost. As it happens, however, I believe it is also in my interest and the interest of my country to help you." Ripley was glad to hear that Sudomo's friend was going to help them, but had no idea how it could be in her interest or in China's interest to do so.

"I am 49 years old," Maringka continued, "which I

believe makes me the second oldest person on the moon. I have been a Chinese citizen for 38 of those years, having been adopted from an Australian orphanage by Chinese diplomats when I was eleven. I have been a member of the Chinese Communist party for 33 of those years, having joined the party when I was sixteen. I have been an officer of the Chinese People's Liberation Army for 30 of those years, having enlisted at nineteen. I am currently responsible for the safety, health, loyalty, performance, and behavior of every Chinese person on the moon." Ripley and Rico both involuntarily let out a quick breath at that. Sudomo's old customer was the most powerful person on the moon! Why in the world would she come here to help them escape?

"As you know, many, if not all, of those people are now moonfirsters. For better or worse, their loyalty now lies with their lunar comrades, not the three billion Chinese people on Earth who made it possible for them to come here." Ripley looked at Sudomo, who was nodding his head. She had no idea that so many Chinese were ready to break ties with their country and stay here for the rest of their lives. "I think that because I was born into one culture and taken from it by another before I was adopted into a third and became 'Chinese,'" Maringka continued, "I may perhaps have a better understanding than many Chinese military commanders would about why so many of 'my people' have chosen to follow this path. They see how many people die here and cannot help but wonder whether following my orders relayed from Earth gives them their best chance of surviving. Our leaders on Earth are always behind the curve; always out of date. More fundamentally, though, they are not here fighting with us. It is hard to be in solidarity with those who do not fight your battles alongside you."

She paused for a minute and Sudomo interjected softly "And from those I've talked to, there isn't much of a plan to rotate them back to Earth." "That's right," Maringka nodded. "In its wisdom, the Politburo Standing Committee has decided that because it costs so much to transport crew from China to L_1 to here, those of us up here are now deployed 'indefinitely.' In all honesty, it is likely that they assumed people would die off fast enough that so long as they kept sending replacements nobody would be here long enough to start complaining about wanting to go home. But, as you know, people's attitudes when we were building the mining post were much different than they are now."

Rico and Ripley nodded in agreement at that. They'd seen for themselves how their very successes had created the squabbles and disagreements that were leading to this first lunar revolution. "Regardless of how and why it happened," Maringka said with a short chopping motion of her left hand, as if to signify the uselessness of speculating about such things, "several Chinese teams and many Chinese individuals have been involved in this 'moonfirster' movement from its very beginning, if not before. Five days ago, a committee of them told me about a 'Declaration of Sovereignty and Solidarity' that they'd written in conjunction with their Barca and Ama counterparts. Stripped of its philosophical underpinnings, it basically calls for the establishment of a unitary lunar military government with full control over everyone and everything on the moon."

"Military!" Ripley exclaimed. "What do you mean? I thought the military wasn't allowed on the moon? How can they do that?" "They claim to reject all terrestrial authority," Maringka replied, "but I will say their Declaration borrows heavily from the very Chinese Communist Party practices and ideologies that the moonfirsters claim to reject. It is a very detailed plan for a military coup. Touchdown and the two mining posts will each be governed by a military committee. Every crew on the moon will have a chief appointed by that committee and subject to its control and discipline. Every crew will be subject to the control and discipline of its chief. Every crew will have another member anonymously appointed by that committee to report on its chief. I think it's safe to assume that their Declaration spells out in detail what every chief and every crew is responsible for and what privileges they have in return."

"And none of them," Sudomo added softly, "will have the privilege of leaving the moon." "That's right,"

Maringka nodded. "As I said, the Chinese government does not currently plan on paying for anyone to return from the moon to Earth. Obviously, when they find out that none of the Chinese up here are working loyally for them any more—and that their rebellion has spread to the employees of the government's Barca and Ama allies—it is not likely to make them more generous in that regard. And frankly, even if the Politburo sent a special luxury rocket to bring us back, I suspect that many would be hesitant to return: the people who run my country are not known for their short memories or their forgiving hearts."

"But what about the Barcas and the Amas?" Ripley wondered aloud. "They could go back home if they didn't do this. That's what Rico and I have never understood—why would they turn their backs on Earth? I've tried to talk about it with Preemo and some of his crew a few times, and Rico has too, but you know how it is if they get suspicious of you." She looked at Sudomo, who was nodding. "My understanding," he began, "is that they have done the math and calculated the difference between how much people are paying for habricks at L_1 and how much Amazon and F.C. Barca are paying them to live and die up here making those habricks." "But they knew that when they came up here," Ripley protested. "Nothing has changed!"

"Everything has changed!" Maringka blurted. "People are paying hundreds of times more for habricks than they were a year ago." Sudomo nodded. "I have friends at L_1," he added, "who tell me that in the last four or five months several capsules full of would be habsters showed up at L_1 and just sat there, unable to procure habricks, until they ran out of supplies and died. People used to want to build habs, but now they are desperate—literally dying—to build habs." "But why?" Ripley puzzled. "Why did living in habs suddenly become so much more attractive to people?"

"It didn't," Maringka replied. "Living on Earth suddenly became much less attractive. The projected rate of ocean warming increased, which means sea levels are rising faster than people thought: water expands when it is heated. Warmer seawater means larger low-pressure systems and more violent storms: climate storms are becoming a regular occurrence in the Mediterranean, not just the Caribbean and Southeastern Asia. Coastal cities all over the world are threatened. Some people are already being displaced. So a lot of people seem to think a nice dry hab would be a much better option." "And every hab," Sudomo added, "is built with habricks. The people who make those habricks now have a monopoly on tickets to escape a worldwide disaster. They can and will get people to give them whatever they want."

"But so what?" Rico asked. "So what if they get all the money in the world? They'll still be stuck up here." "You think you'll be able to buy habricks with money?"

Sudomo asked with a hint of a smile on his face. "Not a chance. That's still happening today, and the people who are still getting those habricks might be the luckiest in history. Once the moonfirsters are in charge, it's going to take a lot more than money. If you want a hab, you're going to have to figure out a way to lift a bunch of stuff to L_1 that we—*they*— can't make up here. Heavy metals, rare earth elements, plant genetics, new inventions, things like that. Maybe drugs, maybe children, maybe human organs. Who knows how low people will sink. The refugees will do whatever they have to do—and pay whatever they have to. That's why the moonfirsters figure they'll get whatever and whomever they need to build terradomes, to make water, to dig caverns, and to do whatever else they've decided is necessary for people to live up here indefinitely."

"If you stay," Maringka smiled, "you'll be one of the chosen people! You too can plunder the corpses of the dying coastal populations." "But I don't want to live here," Ripley scowled. "I wanted to work up here for a few years and move on." "Me too," Maringka assured her, "which is why I'm here helping Sudomo rather than sending a security crew to chase you down. It is not right for 500 people to hold the rest of the world hostage!"

"Then come with us!" Ripley exclaimed. "If you're Sudomo's friend, he will find a place for you at L_1 in somebody's hab!" She looked at Sudomo for reassurance.

"Unfortunately it's not that simple," Maringka replied calmly. "It is one thing for the three of you to disappear—no offense—but if I leave, the moonfirsters will think I am part of some plot against them, not that I want to disappear and run a little café with Sudomo under a different name in a quiet corner of somebody else's hab." "What will you do though?" Rico asked. "I will do what I have always done," Maringka said. "I will survive. I will learn. And I will work for a better future for myself, my friends, and the friends of my friends."

"So what can we do?" Ripley asked, puzzled as to how she and Rico could possibly help this woman who seemed to know everything. "You can tell the truth!" Maringka exclaimed. "You can tell the truth about what happened up here. About how impossible it was for Earth-bound organizations to manage people on the moon. Because, you know, the moonfirsters are not entirely wrong. Living on the moon, which is what we all started doing once we started actually rolling habricks up that tether, is fundamentally different from living on Earth. The idea that lunar colonists would be good little soldiers spending a tour of duty up here in service of Earth-bound goals and objectives just isn't ever going to work. You've all been here long enough to know how hard living here is, not just individually, but collectively: how your lives are constantly in your teammates' hands. You can't survive up here without fanatic levels of loyalty to each other. You have to be willing to die for each other two or three times a day. But that kind of loyalty doesn't leave any room for loyalty to 'China' or 'Amazon' or anyone else who's not up here risking their lives right there alongside you. You can't serve the Earth and the moon."

"But then why aren't you joining them?" Rico exclaimed. "I mean, if you think they're right?" "Because their solution is wrong," Maringka replied. "They are right about the problem: working for people on Earth is wrong and won't work. But military rule is not the answer. I don't know what the answer is, but that's not it." "I still don't see how we can help," Ripley stammered. "If we leave and you're here, what could we possibly do?" "Like I said," Maringka replied, "you can tell the truth. About what happened, the good and the bad. And you can learn. Sudomo says there are other friends of his at L_1, in some of the habs that have deployed. Learn from them. Help the habsters figure out what we could not do here: help them figure out the right way to live together up here! Help them figure out how not to destroy the habs like they destroyed the Earth."

Ripley looked at Rico, who was nodding in agreement. They both looked at Sudomo. "Some of my friends up there," he told them all, "have been asking themselves these same questions about how best to survive away from Earth. They have organized an assembly of all the habsters." "You must tell them what is happening here," Maringka repeated. "I will make sure you get there—that at least is still within my power." Rico looked back at Ripley. Ripley nodded back at her. "We will tell them what happened," Ripley assured Maringka, "and we will try to learn from them." They all bowed to each other again very formally. Maringka left to organize their escape route while Ripley and her friends sat silently in the empty storage container and thought about what to tell the habsters.

Chapter Seven

G'Ranger

Basel, Switzerland

November 23, 2015

G'Ranger looked down into her cup of tea and thought about the ocean. She'd been to the Café Zum Roten Engel hundreds of times since she started university. It was a small café in the Schweizerdeutch fashion. Fanatically clean. Generous cups of tea for students to sip and ponder big ideas. Salads simple enough for student budgets but elegant enough for visiting dignitaries. Staff who were attentive, but not familiar. The kind of place where just about anyone would feel at home. Despite it all, G'Ranger didn't feel very comfortable as she sat looking into her tea and watching the rainy Monday lunch crowd filter in and out.

She'd broken up with her university boyfriend Pieter here. In 1993, the day before they'd graduated. They'd been sitting at that long table at the front window where four young Japanese tourists were sitting, giggling and sipping coffee. He'd wanted her to marry him and go back with him to Klaipeda, Lithuania, where his family had started a group of businesses catering to the fledgling Baltic Sea cruise ship industry. She'd loved him very much, but the thought of living in a dark, cold, patriarchical land where she didn't speak any of the languages was just too much. And besides, who was going to pay to cruise on that cold, stormy sea? She smiled. Last year, Klaipeda had been visited by more cruise ships than Riga, in Latvia, for the first time ever. Pieter's family owned expensive homes in London and Paris and she'd heard people talking about his future in politics. He'd married a tall blonde woman from a Finnish merchant shipping family and they had three beautiful children. Sometimes people surprised you.

Pieter wasn't the only rich and powerful man who'd courted G'Ranger, though perhaps she'd cared for him more than most. Her family hadn't mattered to any of her suitors and she'd never gone to Milikapiti, or even Darwin, with any of them. Only a few had ever met her mother, Jean Baptiste. She'd never married or had a child of her own.

She'd never really settled down. After university, she'd gone back to Darwin and worked for a company called Pegasus Networks, trying to get in on the ground floor of the Australian internet. Like its namesake, however, the company never made it to the top of the mountain and went belly-up after a few years. It almost took her down with it. She'd been sick of Darwin anyway, which seemed small and provincial to her after her university years here in Basel. She used her last few thousand dollars of savings to lease an apartment in Singapore, which had one of the strongest Asian internet presences in the mid-1990's, and reinvent her career.

That worked out great. She loved Singapore and still owned a small apartment there. She thought Switzerland and Singapore had a lot in common, for good and bad. They were both islands of prosperity with airs of superiority but neither of them felt inaccessible. You couldn't change them, but you could make yourself part of them. But she'd never really been at home in either place. She'd never really been at home anywhere but Milikapiti, where she still felt like a stranger.

G'Ranger made her fortune in Singapore though, working as a systems developer, analyst and security engineer for Singapore Airlines. She'd worked ferociously there for fifteen years and accumulated some serious stock options. Then, in 2010, her mother got sick. G'Ranger left the airline and returned to Milikapiti to provide hospice care for her.

By then she'd done enough and been away from Milikapiti for long enough to fall in love with it, with her people, all over again. True voyage is return, she believed, as long as you know you can never really go home again. She'd made herself into a new kind of person, a cosmopolitan Tiwi Islander. She'd never felt overshadowed by her mother's life and artistic accomplishments in Milikapiti again because she was so proud of her own life and the things she'd done. Jean Baptiste was still the strongest person G'Ranger had ever met. Probably the most deeply rooted as well. Even when she could barely speak, she spoke with the only real authority there is—the authority of her truth. But G'Ranger had found enough of her own truth not to feel intimidated by her mother's authentic voice. She was strong enough herself to share some of her journeys, to take her mother places she'd never been. She belonged there in Milikapiti with her mother. It felt good. Maybe that's why it was so unfamiliar.

Her people and her island had certainly changed since she'd been taken to Darwin. They had broadband now! There were others like her who'd left the islands, made their way through the wider world, and found their path back to Yermainer. They brought with them not only new ideas but a new familiarity. Like their ancestors, they were exceptionally well grounded, but in different ways. G'Ranger's great grandparents had seen the white world as a curious novelty. Her grandparents had learned, at a great cost, to take its threat seriously. Her parents fought to preserve their culture against it. Her generation learned how to live in both worlds—at least the ones who hadn't been crushed between them. G'Ranger wondered if any of them, or any of their children, would ever learn enough to save any of their worlds.

G'Ranger knew that change could be good or bad but was always different. In the last sixteen months of her mother's life G'Ranger had many wonderful, enlightening, fanciful, provocative conversations with Jean Baptiste: the matriarchal artist who grew up without electricity or running water and the independent engineer who took for granted having the accumulated knowledge of the world at her fingertips. Her mother wanted to learn everything right up to the very end. She never lost hope: not for herself; not for her people; and not for her planet—though G'Ranger wasn't sure you could talk about them like that, as separate things, in the western fashion, if you really wanted to understand her mother.

One of the things G'ranger and Jean Baptiste Apuatimi spent a lot of time talking about was the future of their world. Milikapiti and Yermainer, which had been home to their family for so long, were, like every other island in the South Pacific, becoming increasingly vulnerable to the ever-rising seas. The city itself was at sea level, and the highest point on their island was only a hundred meters or so higher than Bukit Timah, the 166-meter peak of Singapore Island. Unlike her adopted homeland, however, G'Ranger's native home possessed little wealth, few resources, and almost no influence to combat or adapt to the impending changes. They didn't have a tram, or tourists, or much of anything except their songs, dances, paintings, and stories. Their accumulated cultural wisdom was all they had and she was terrified it wouldn't be enough to save them.

Jean Baptiste's last paintings were almost exclusively variations on the theme of rising waters. G'Ranger had one in the kitchen of her apartment in Singapore that showed generations of Apuatimi dancers and singers beneath giant waves under the ruins of Milikapiti. Painted with bold wide brush strokes in multiple hues of blue green, it was simultaneously scary and inspiring—the dancers floating to the rhythm of the sea and the singers' song soundless under the waves. Many times G'Ranger listened to her mother tell her how her people, her family, had been part of the ocean for so long that it could never really destroy them; that they would always be able to join the ocean's song; that they would always be part of the great ocean dance. But G'Ranger was not just her mother's daughter; she was more than educated and informed enough to know the scientific reality—even if, during her mother's last days, she felt more and more that it was her native culture, not her accumulated knowledge, she needed to hear in her heart.

After her mother passed G'Ranger felt ever more strongly called by the song of the rising ocean, as she came to think of it. Finally, at 45, she re-invented herself and became a self-funded amateur climate change activist. She got herself to Warsaw in 2013 and met several representatives of the Alliance of Small Island States, which had no Tiwi Islander representatives. She quickly became an unofficial part of the South Pacific group. She got to know several Palau Islanders who had barely survived the Haiyan Super-Typhoon earlier that year. The results of the Warsaw talks were particularly disappointing for their group, and for all the small South Pacific Islanders, who remained the most vulnerable on the planet. G'Ranger felt the song of the rising ocean growing even stronger in her heart every day, but she still had no idea what it was telling her to do.

This latest conference, the 2015 Swiss Geoscience Meeting, hadn't been any better. She loved Switzerland, and they took climate change very seriously here, even if they were surrounded by mountains that would at least hold off the sea until the final bitter end. Walking around Basel she'd been proud of how many solar panels, windmills, vertical gardens, and electric cars she'd seen. But these small steps weren't slowing the oceans fast enough to save Milikapiti. And nobody at the conference wanted to talk about that. Nobody wanted to talk about anything but small steps. She understood why. Small steps were themselves barely feasible politically, if at all, so that's what people could get grants to do and what they could find jobs to study. Nobody was going to pay for anyone to work on something with no chance of ever being considered, let along implemented.

The corollary was that small steps were treated like huge victories. It was the only way for people to feel any sense of accomplishment. After all, it's hard to carry on bravely in the face of defeat forever. Saturday night she'd had dinner with Onifire, a Brazilian social scientist G'Ranger had known for ten years. Onifire had come to Switzerland from Kenya, which had the fastest growing and most successful solar installation rate in the world. People were proud of that. But the Kenyans were about to start shipping crude oil out of Mumbasa as well. Onifire had spoken emotionally about how hard it was for her to reconcile the two developments.

G'Ranger and Onifire had been part of an international economic systems development team in Nepal in 2005. Rival royalist and Maoist factions there called a brief truce and reached out together to the UN, the World Bank, the INF, and the rest of the "world community" for "normalization," whatever that was. Ming Fai, the IT Director for the Singapore government, reached out to G'Ranger, who'd just supervised a complete reboot of the terminal, tower, and traffic software in conjunction with major hardware upgrades and the installation of a military runway at Changi. The World Bank wanted to do more or less the same things at Tribhuvan International and Tenzing-Hillary, Nepal's two largest airports, so G'Ranger and her team wound up rewiring a sizable chuck of the Kathmandu Valley and connecting it to eastern Nepal and the tourist zone around Mt. Everest.

Onifire wound up in Nepal by mistake. She'd been doing PhD work in anthropology in Rio when she'd taken a summer job as a research assistant for an economic development project in Bolivia. Three days before she was supposed to go back to Rio for school, two members of the economics development team that was to represent Brazil in Nepal died in a plane crash in Santiago. Her team got the call instead, and gained the dubious honor of being the only people in living memory to actually fly "down" to Tenzing Hillary, which at "only" 2,845 meters was more than 1000 meters lower than their departure strip outside of La Paz. Having made that unrivaled and highly dangerous trek between two of the world's most sacred and inspiring mountainscapes, Onifire spent the next six months teaching elderly Nepalese women and their bored granddaughters how to brew coffee and tea to sell to the wealthy western climbers who were supposed to be their economic future.

It wasn't the kind of thing G'Ranger would have picked an anthropology grad student to do. G'Ranger met her when Onifire brought Dia Thapa Magar, an elderly Nepalese woman with the most joyful smile G'Ranger had ever seen, to Tenzing Hillary airport. Through some combination of bribes, family connections, blackmail, salesmanship and unmitigated chutzpah, Dia had gained the exclusive right to serve food and drink at the airport, and she'd come in person to make sure G'Ranger's computer installations would include wifi for her customers, preferably at no charge to her. "What exactly are you teaching her?"

G'Ranger had asked Onifire later that day, after spending some time with Dia. "I don't know," she'd laughed, "but we have a great time together and she says nice things about me to the suits with clipboards."

Dia got her internet. She insisted on giving G'Ranger and Onifire lifetime employee discounts (6%) to show her appreciation. G'Ranger smiled, thinking that at least if worst came to worst she'd have her choice of high mountains to retreat to. But as far as she knew, neither of them had ever returned to Nepal. Onifire finished her Ph.D. by writing a provocative thesis on "21st Century Reverse Cargo Cultures," which is what she called the westerners who, seeking out "authentic spiritual lessons," "primitive religious connections," and other indigenous inspirations to fill the gaps in their own lives and cultures, sought out totem artifacts to display as tokens of their enlightenment. Dia had been one of the stars of her book, along with a woman from Bali named Ni Ida Ayu Ngurah who ran something called the Yoga Barn Guesthouse.

Basically Onifire found that people from so called "less developed" cultures had a much more highly conceptualized understanding of their interrelationships with their western clientele and their respective ideologies and cultures and a lot more malleable attitude towards their own cultures than anyone had ever realized. It was actually the westerners who had trouble seeing both worlds, and who were almost universally incapable of synthesizing them, which is why the affirmations they sought were never really reflected in their "real" worlds. The so-called 'primitives,' on the other hand, were much more self-reflexive, more culturally literate, and so adapted, integrated, combined, and evolved new world views much more readily.

Her book catapulted Onifire to a small degree of academic fame, modest fortune, job security, and a lifetime of invitations to conferences with people who liked to be described with phrases like 'thinking outside the box,' 'paradigm shifting,' and 'interdisciplinary approach.' She lived in London now and taught at the School of Oriental and African Studies. G'Ranger had been to four or five dinner parties at her townhouse in St. Pancreas over the years, and she'd always met the most interesting people. People who weren't afraid to dream big or fail big but were terrified not to try. That's the kind of people G'Ranger was interested in now. She was sad she wasn't meeting many of them at climate change conferences.

Yesterday she'd spent ninety minutes talking about creating more secure routing redundancies for bank data from the South Pacific Islands. Which was important, but she was never going to find a game changer by helping people cope better with losing. Not that she wouldn't do all she could to help with their networks, but it wasn't the kind of thing that would make you stand up and shout. That's what she was looking for. Something to fall in love with. Something to sing about.

So when Onifire asked her to stay in Basel for a couple of days after the conference and meet with some people, she'd agreed right away. Now she looked up from her tea past the laughing young Japanese tourists and saw Onifire walking across the Andreasplatz with two American men who didn't look like they could recognize a big idea if it walked up and smacked them in the face. One of them was an almost painfully large black man. He must have been over two meters tall, and surely he weighed more than G'Ranger and Onifire together. His back was slumped. He was breathing heavily. He looked like a balloon slowly deflating.

The other one was white and wore a hat with huge earflaps that had long strings hanging down almost to his waist. He looked tired. He was very skinny. Underneath his earflaps and down jacket, G'Ranger could see that he was wearing a white dress shirt and a narrow black tie and that neither of them was particularly expensive, or fashionable. The large man wasn't wearing a tie or a hat. His green sweater was decorated with rows of oak trees. But he was smiling. The skinny man looked like he hadn't smiled in a long time.

They crossed the platz and G'Ranger waved as Onifire pulled the door open and ushered the two Americans past the Japanese tourists, who weren't laughing any more.

"Guten Tag" G'Ranger smiled, standing up as they shuffled over to her table. "G'Ranger my friend! Good afternoon to you," Onifire replied enthusiastically. "It is good to be here! We were delayed at the University this morning and I am glad to see you."

"I am Howard," the skinny tired man said, shaking his hat off of his head and extending his hand directly at her in the American fashion. "Onifire tells me you are a skilled software developer and a capable hardware installer—a rare and valuable combination—and that you might contribute to my project." He stared at her intently. G'Ranger glanced at Onifire, whose mouth turned up in a small smile as she moved forward to embrace her. "G'Ranger, meet Howard Gall," she said formally. "Howard has had a long weekend. Few delegates share his passion or his convictions."

"Howard has the convictions of ten men!" the large man said. G'Ranger couldn't tell whether or not he was being sarcastic as he sat down at her table and let out a large sigh. "What does it mean to be a person of conviction these days?" Howard asked. He seemed to be speaking to himself. "It means nothing, and it means everything, just like it always has!" the large man replied. "G'Ranger, my name is Wells, Mark Wells, and I apologize for sitting down like this but the Swiss altitude is hard on me. You might find that somewhat ironic, given the nature of our project."

He looked up at her with a friendly gaze and she

could only glance sideways at Onifire again. "Oh … no," G'Ranger started. "Please make yourself comfortable! The tea here is very good." Onifire took her by the hand and laughed. "I'm sorry G'Ranger!" she said, looking at the skinny man as his eyes narrowed. "I didn't think I could do justice to the breath and scope of Howard's vision, and so I perhaps have not shared as much with you as they might think." "What!" Howard exclaimed, "I thought she was interested. Do you think we can just waste our time like this?" "She's interested in meeting you, Howard," Onifire replied. "And we're here now, and your plane doesn't leave until tonight, so can we please just share a cup of tea and some of our stories with each other?"

"Very well," Howard said curtly. "My story is that I will not rule out the chance to preserve a nucleus of human specimens." He stared at G'Ranger even more intently. "It's a quote from a movie about nuclear annihilation," Wells interrupted. "Howard likes to shock people." "I don't enjoy it," Howard retorted. "But somebody has to tell it like it is." "And how it is, is?" G'Ranger asked, glancing at Onifire yet again. Why did she think G'Ranger would be interested in this? "How it is, is over," Howard replied in the calmest tone she'd ever heard. "You've been to the conferences; you've read the papers; you've talked to the people who know. It's simple: humanity isn't smart enough, or good enough, or whatever enough, to stop exploiting the

environment before … you die, she dies, everyone dies."
She looked at Wells. "Another movie quote," he admitted,
shrugging his shoulders. "He does that. It's from a different
movie about power, evil, and big breasts.

"But what he's saying," Wells continued, "however
inartfully, is that climate annihilation, not nuclear holocaust,
is the supreme evil our generation must face. He thinks
humanity will not defeat that evil." "Defeat it!" Howard
interjected, "they can't even see it!" "Whether through
inertia or greed," Wells continued, "but regardless, Howard
is trying to rescue some people from the end of humanity."

"Are you talking about mine shafts?" G'Ranger
asked, having figured out one of the movies Howard was
talking about. "No," Howard replied, his mouth turning ever
so slightly upward in a vague hint of a smile. It was the
closest G'Ranger ever saw him come. "Unlike nuclear
winter, the planet cannot recover from the damage humanity
will inflict before its end in just a few hundred or a few
thousand years. People cannot crawl back into the ground
and devolve into moles!"

"What then," G'Ranger asked? "The oceans? Is that
why you thought I'd be interested?" "Yes and no," Wells
replied. "Wells is interested in the oceans," Howard said
dismissively. "He likes luxury." "Everyone likes luxury,"
Wells laughed. "That's why they call it luxury. But
sometimes it's hard to tell what's a luxury and what's a

132

necessity." He smiled at G'Ranger. "What are you interested in?" she asked Howard, staring intensely back at him for the first time.

"I'm interested in moving forward," Howard replied, settling slowly back down into his chair. "Whatever humanity does or doesn't do—whether the whole world suddenly started living like the most ecofriendly hippies in history and stayed that way forever—this planet is going to become inhospitable for one reason or another sooner or later. Best-case scenario, it's the death of the sun in about a billion years. Worst-case scenario, a big asteroid smashes into the moon next year, creating a cloud of dust particles that moves into earth orbit and cuts off the light of the sun. Either way: 'you die, she dies, everyone dies.' I don't want that to happen. I just recognize that it's happening now." He looked up passionately at G'Ranger once more. She'd never met anyone who took the fate of humanity so personally yet with such indifference. "I want to take us—some of us—up there" he finished, pointing up towards the ceiling.

"Up there?" She followed his finger. "You're building ... spaceships?" She glanced at Onifire for the last time, wondering just what her friend thought of her to arrange this conversation. Spaceships weren't going to save Milikapiti. "Not spaceships" Howard said, ignoring her glance like he'd seen it many times before. "Spaceships

133

come back. I'm building homes. I'm building worlds."

"So you're not trying to save the world at all!" G'Ranger exclaimed. "You just don't want to die with the rest of us." "None of us want anyone to die" Onifire said calmly. "There's more to the project." "Not really," Howard said. "The world's dying. We don't know exactly when or how or why it's going to die. It doesn't matter. Either some people get off of it before then or nobody does. It could hardly be any simpler."

"Howard's been telling people that for ten years," Wells added. "But, for whatever reason, they haven't exactly flocked to him to be saved. Three years ago, however, whether in a moment of weakness or clarity, Howard agreed to add a second element to the project." "Let me guess," G'Ranger said. "You want to build submarines as well as spaceships?" At least she couldn't complain that these Americans didn't dream big. But they dreamed of saving themselves and letting the world die like they weren't really part of it. It didn't sound like a very beautiful dream to G'Ranger.

"I told you, we're not building spaceships!" Howard exclaimed loudly. "Yes, you are," Onifire said, reaching out and touching his arm, "they're just spaceships that will travel forever. And yes," she continued, turning to G'Ranger, "we want to build permanent undersea habitats as well as permanent orbital habitats. I told you she was smart," she said, staring across the table at the two Americans.

"I will just clarify," Wells added, "that, as ambitious as those aspects of our project are, they are not, perhaps, our most audacious dream. Though Howard disagrees, some of us are convinced that we will never be able to truly break free of Earth's gravity well unless we take our oceans with us: that the seas of Earth do not have to perish when—or if—this world dies. As you probably know, our bodies are essentially water with a few floating minerals. As you may or may not know, water is perhaps the most effective radiation shielding in the world. For those reasons, among others, some of us feel that the undersea habitats are not just a worthy goal unto themselves, but they will also stimulate the development of essential elements of our orbital habitats. It is that aspect of our project we're here to talk about. We—or at least some of us—seek not only to 'preserve a nucleus of humanity,' as Howard puts it, but to preserve some part of the ocean as well, thinking, or perhaps feeling in our hearts, that the two are connected. That's what Onifire thought you might find interesting. That's why we're here."

"That part is foolishness," Howard scoffed. "You cannot lift seawater to orbit. Too expensive, too much pollution. It's insane! At best, we might be able to recreate something close enough to seawater to fool some simple algaes." "That's why it's a dream, not a plan," Wells responded patiently. "Who knows what will come of it all, if anything." He shrugged. "Who knows what will come of any of this? One does not stop fighting just because victory is elusive. But for now," he continued with a dismissive wave of his hand, leaning towards G'Ranger, "all of Howard's years of work, everything we've done, is headed for a big test." He glanced at Howard, who gave him the slightest of nods. "We're about to build our first undersea habitat and we want you to help us design and install our IT. We want you to play computer god in our brave new world."

"You're building a submarine!" G'Ranger said incredulously, managing to keep herself from laughing. These mismatched Americans looked like they'd struggle to buy tickets on the Darwin ferry, let along build something nobody else ever had. "Yes," replied Wells, "but you really shouldn't call it a submarine. It's a habitat, or 'hab' for short." "And where are you going to do this?" G'Ranger asked, still convinced that they couldn't be serious. "We've built a 500,000 square foot manufacturing facility at Kota Kinabalu port in Malaysia. Our corporate base will be a little south of there, in Brunei. We will assemble materials there from around the world. We've designed a hab that will be about a quarter mile in diameter. There will be four main levels and some sub-levels for maintenance and infrastructure. Our initial budget is two billion American dollars. I don't know where the IT budget currently stands, but I assure you it will not be less than generous."

G'Ranger saw her shocked look mirrored on Onifire's face. "It's true," her friend assured her. "I've talked to the accountants. The money is there." "From who? Are you all working for the Chinese military? For Apple?" "For me," Howard replied softly but firmly. "I spent the best years of my life accumulating this money so that I could do this. I assure you that at least for the undersea hab the budget is enough and the technology is available. The water does have one significant advantage," he acknowledged with a nod to Wells, "it is much cheaper and easier to sink things than to boost them. So I start here, and I learn the lessons that help me get up there." He pointed at the ceiling again.

"What lessons?"G'Ranger asked. She was beginning to take these people seriously. "I thought all the tech was already on the shelf?" "We think it is," Wells answered, "although I'm sure there will be disappointments, problems, and innovations." "Then what lessons do you need?" she asked. "We need to learn how to live in habs," Howard replied. "Humans have never lived in worlds they made themselves. It will take an almost complete re-education. Every instinct will have to be retrained. All our social, moral, and political instincts developed for life on Earth, life in an open environment. Unfortunately, those instincts we evolved so well turned us—some of us—into greedy selfish savages. We reward standing out, not fitting in. By doing so, we've destroyed our environment, which for tens of thousands of years we incorrectly thought was infinitely unbounded. Now, having destroyed that womb, we must learn how to imprint social, moral, and political instincts that will give people the discipline to live together in an environment that is extremely bounded, exceptionally finite, and exceedingly vulnerable to minor mishaps. The great irony is that only by mastering that discipline, by learning how to live selflessly, predictably and with great sacrifice in a closed environment, can humanity take the great leap forward to life among the stars, which from our perspective are themselves actually infinitely unbounded and limitless, in a universe that might itself be infinite."

Chapter Eight

Sabull

Manhattan Special Administrative District

December 25, 2024

Sabull Popper took the elevator to the fourth floor. It was dark and quiet. He walked out of the elevator and stood in the hallway motionlessly, listening to the background machinery hum around him. Somewhere behind the staff room door a single diode intermittently blinked red. Sabull didn't see or hear any signs of life. It was 6:35 on Christmas morning—a good time for secrets. Maybe some boys and girls still believed in good secrets, like Santa Claus, but Sabull, born into a nominally Hindu and devoutly irreligious family, never believed in Santa Claus. Sabull knew every secret had its dark side, and those were the sides he liked. That was the currency he trafficked in. Sabull didn't believe in much, but he coveted a lot.

"Popper, is that you?" Teng Blao's voice blared out of the speaker overhead as the young Chinese man's comtar appeared suddenly in the comport, clear and bright in the dark, silent building. "Merry *focking* Christmas, arsehole" Teng laughed with a curt smile and a demented East London accent. Teng's comtar wore a garish traditional open-fronted coat and a lavish Fu Manchu style mustache that made his smile even more demonic than it already was. His rich eyelashes were nearly an inch long and framed his big black eyes perfectly.

"*Cao ni zuzong shiba dai,*" Sabull replied in an even more annoying accent. He imagined Teng looking at his own comtar with its horn rim glasses and Lincoln beard and wondered how the vile Mandarin insult sounded on the other side of the world. "Fuck your ancestors too," Teng laughed. "Fuck you, fuck me, and *shen jing bing* us all, most likely." "*Shen jing bing* us all," Sabull repeated. "That is exactly the problem. That's exactly why I'm here to talk to you. The whole world is going insane."

"The world's always been insane," Teng replied. "We just have to be mad enough to stay one step in front of it until we die covered in wealth and glory." "Oh, that's all," Sabull sneered. "And it's the fucking Chinese on the moon who are the most insane of all! What the hell is going on up there? Where's the wealth and glory in that?" "Ah, yes," Teng nodded. "That is a problem."

"A problem?" Sabull raised one eye. "That's a pretty optimistic way of looking at people who are blackmailing the whole fucking planet, wouldn't you say?" He stared intently at Teng's comtar, wishing more than ever that he could actually look the man in his eyes and that he knew what his real deal with the moonfirsters was.

Teng's demonic smile slowly expanded into a giant jack-o-lantern grin. "But I only say problem to appease your

140

sensitive white devil ears Popper! For me I see great opportunity! Six years ago I was nobody! I couldn't afford a plastic booth in the back corner of the third floor of the Hong Kong Trade Expo Center to try to sell satcom and viscope futures to mid-level bureaucrats at second-rate trade conferences. Now look at me!" Teng's comtar rotated slowly through 360 degrees. "I have my own tailor!" Teng's grin faded as his face filled the comport and he looked closely at Sabull. "The mooners are your problem, Popper, not ours. They're not blackmailing us! For us, they're just another opportunity."

Until they are your problem, Sabull thought. And if that happens—when that happens—you'll never see it coming, if you're telling me the truth. But if you're lying, if you already see it coming, why aren't you scared? Sabull didn't think Teng was a good enough liar to hide real fear. "Opportunity?" he asked. "Not much of an opportunity for you, if the moonfirsters have anything to say about it." "All opportunities have problems," Teng replied. "When the first great climate storms created millions of refugees, there was an opportunity to coordinate and implement relief efforts. But there were lots of problems to overcome in order to realize that opportunity. The mooners are no different."

"Except that the refugees had nothing, didn't work together, and were generating income for you. The moonfirsters have habricks, the most valuable commodity in

141

the world, they work together much better than you ever will, and they are plundering the planet like no emperor in history." "Like I said, there are problems," Teng agreed. "But they are the kinds of problems great merchants have. Nothing great is easy! We are the first great galactic traders!" Teng laughed. "The greatest middlemen in history! The mooners will not treat directly with you, and you will not deal directly with corporate disaster profiteers, so here we are! We are what you need and who the mooners want— and if we can only dip our beaks a little, I will be showered in seven lifetimes worth of riches and glory."

"And then you can die," Sabull smiled. "Everyone dies, Popper," Teng retorted. "The only questions are how you live and what you leave behind you." "And this is how you live?" Sabull snorted. "Pretending to provide for poor people by acting as a go-between for people who never acknowledge your existence and will be only too happy to see you dead?" "Different strokes for different folks, isn't that what your American bosses say?" Teng replied. "But remember, I'm British!" Sabull retorted proudly.

Although England had finally been permanently absorbed into Europe even before all the world's countries were themselves absorbed into the UNP, Sabull still considered himself a loyal British subject. Born in Pakistan to a family with British ancestry, he'd been sent as a ten-year-old to live with relatives in Chichester and developed a passionate patriotism for all things English.

"British, American, Chinese, Eskimo … who cares? Your problem, Popper, is that you can't see the future happening above you. You've never even been to orbit, have you Popper? You think that what matters are the little people scurrying around down here desperately trying to rearrange the deck chairs to forestall the inevitable for another ten or fifteen years. They're all going to die Popper! All of them!"

Not all of them, Popper smiled softly to himself, trying to suppress his nagging doubts. He'd long ago come to terms with massive climate change casualties. Almost a half-million died after the first great climate storms in 2019. Just one small Philippine city, Pagadian, lost sixty-thousand people that day—almost a third of its population—when thirty-five foot storm surges swept Panguil Bay across the island, turning the Zamboanga Penninsula into Zamboanga Island. More than five million had died since. Cities in the Ganges Delta like Barisal, where more than three-hundred thousand people once lived, were ghost towns. But there were very few models where the entire species perished.

Even in Barisal, Popper knew, a few thousand determined people stayed and fought to survive as the city fell further and further below sea level and became more and more isolated. It was almost inevitable that a few remnants of humanity would survive any natural disaster. The moonfirsters knew that as well as he did. It was almost as inevitable that Popper would find a way to be one of those survivors, or so he felt. Looking at Teng's comtar's ridiculous mustache, he was almost sure Teng felt the same.

Sabull had been no more than a skinny Paki teenager with a faltering grasp of English when he entered the Chichester High School for Boys, yet he'd been able to secure a place at Downing College (he'd never admitted to anyone that he'd actually been pooled by King's). There he began a long life of maneuvering his way into old boys' clubs by any means necessary. Sabull didn't know just how many people were going to die in the end, but he'd always been good at identifying leaders—the survivors—and making himself useful to them somehow. But he didn't have any way to make himself useful to the moonfirsters, and now he was hearing rumors of a plan to make Earth inhabitable. If anyone could tell him if they really thought they could do that, maybe it was this crazy young man from Hong Kong who'd somehow connived and blustered his way to the top of a charitable climate relief organization in Southeast Asia that subsequently became one of the moonfirster's main intermediaries.

"But the people up there," Teng continued, his comtar gesturing rapidly upwards with both hands, "some of them are going to make it, Popper! There are over 1500 of them on the moon now, and they haven't boosted anything from Earth for more than two years! Two years, Popper!" "They don't need to boost anything," Popper snarled. "The habsters fight for a spot in line to give them anything they want!" "Isn't that how business works Popper? Build a better mousetrap and the world will beat a path to your door … even if your door is a million miles high. But now they're mostly taking luxuries—things they could live without. Things they don't even need. Things they can't even use! Last month they traded 68 habricks for the world's largest collection of Elvis memorabilia. Elvis has left the fucking planet Popper! 'Blue moon, without a love of my own'—come on and sing with me, Popper! "

"Our planet is dying and they're plundering the corpse" Popper retorted angrily. "If the habsters would just stay here and work together with us …" "Work together *for* you?" Teng laughed. "For what? To push the rock a little further back up the hill? I understand," he continued, his comtar's arms chopping down suddenly in the comport, "that we are not here today to resolve that debate. And although I would never presume to give you diplomatic advice, I suggest that in regard to our immediate situation today it does not really matter whether Earth is dying, whether people will survive its death, whether habsters are hastening or halting its death, their death, my death, or your death; however intellectually fascinating those questions might be."

"Point taken," Popper nodded sarcastically. "But I

enjoy our discussions so much." He didn't want Teng to know how serious he was, Sabull thought. Teng thought the world was dying slowly, and he was fine with that. So was Sabull. Pretty much everyone had come to terms with that. What scared Sabull was the thought of the world dying quickly, before he had time to make proper plans; to find a way to profit from it. That's what the moonfirsters were threatening and he needed to find out if Teng, the self-fancied galactic tradesman, knew anything about it. "Some other morning then," Teng replied with a sloppy, disrespectful bow. "Now what are we going to do about the mooners?"

"To start with," Popper began, "you need to cut them off the omninet!" The Amazon team that built the expanded L_1 platform at the top of the firstmooners' tether had installed netsats in those facilities as a matter of course. Their equipment could provide broadnet connectivity to Touchdown and the entire inhabited surface of the moon surrounding it. There was equipment at Touchdown, Sabull knew, to connect the underground areas there as well.

Which meant that, before the moonfirsters declared their independence and told the Chinese government and its corporate partners to pound sand, an uneducated Chinese laborer who spent most of her time on the moon operating industrial molding equipment could spend what few off hours she had netting people on Earth and enjoying the same access to the omninet as a full professor at CalTech in California on Earth. That was pretty amazing.

But it all changed when the workers became moonfirsters and took over, imposing military discipline. Apparently, prime omninet access and promises of future riches paid back on Earth hadn't been enough to keep the workers happy in their lunar caves once they'd realized what people were paying for their habricks. Sabull wondered whether fear and the never-ending supply of exotic drugs, rare art, ornate gemstones, and the other luxuries would-be habsters were launching to L_1 now were working any better.

After the coup, Amazon and the Chinese government had cut omninet access to the moon entirely. But without bases and facilities to make habricks, they weren't making any money from the L_1 platform and their interest waned. Two years ago, after the habster convention, the habsters were able to buy out the corporations and the Chinese and take control of the platform and the counterweight. As a result, to a certain extent, they took control of omninet access to the moon.

So the moonfirsters had the habricks to make new habs, and the habsters had the netsats that would allow the moonfirsters to access the omninet once again, and the hablicants desperate to escape Earth had whatever the moonfirsters demanded they buy, beg, borrow, or steal. Connectivity was a major subject in the first halting negotiations between the habsters and the moonfirsters. It was somewhat awkward. The moonfirsters didn't really want just anyone on the surface with a simple receiver to have omninet access, but their leaders were rightly paranoid and so wanted all the information they could get.

Back on Earth, the leaders would have preferred not to let anyone off-planet on the omninet. But the public was fascinated with the habsters—they all dreamed of being one—and demanded to be able to net them. Also, Sabull and his superiors wanted any dissidents on the lunar surface with simple receivers to come to their senses and rejoin the human community. The habsters wanted more habs built, which required people from Earth and habricks from the moon, so they did their best to please everyone, despite their philosophical distaste for the regimented lunar military regime and the wage labor capitalist Earthers. Most of the frustrations Sabull had over the inefficiencies created by the three different systems were tempered by the realization that those inefficiencies, these different systems, were the lifeblood of people like him who knew how to leverage others' differences for fun and profit.

Teng's so-called charity, by virtue of mediating negotiations between the moonfirsters and the hablicants as a supposedly impartial party just trying to save climate refugees, was therefore more or less in position to decide what kind of omninet access the moonfirsters got. Teng, like

148

Sabull, found his niche leveraging differences. In Sabull's opinion, he'd been erring on the wrong side. Omninet connectivity gave the moonfirsters far too much information, and they gave back almost nothing in return. The moonfirsters were far too clever and much too disciplined, he thought, while the good UNP citizens were disarmingly open about their world and its flaws.

Teng's comtar released a great guffaw. "Cut them off? You're crazy! How can I do that, Popper? Be reasonable! The habsters all use the omninet, everyone on Earth who can afford it uses the omninet, and you want me to persuade the mooners to give it up? Our share of the habricks is not so large Popper—they'd just sell them to other groups, or to hablicants directly!" "They couldn't sell them to hablicants directly if you cut off their connectivity though," Sabull pointed out. "OK, maybe that's not something you can do immediately," he continued, "but there's more habsters now, and so less netsat bandwidth available at the platform. If nothing else, you can slow down their connection a little." One of the first moonfirster threats Sabull had considered was some sort of omninet attack, but he didn't see how that could threaten all, or even most, life on Earth.

"You think if we don't give them bandwidth through the platform that's going to slow them down for a second?" Teng asked. "What's harder to get, Popper, a portable satcom or Elvis Presley's fucking gold-plated diamond-encrusted toilet seat? You think I can cut them off? That's the whole fucking problem Popper—they have the habricks everyone wants. Nobody can cut them off from anything!"

Yes, yes they can, Sabull thought. I can. I can cut them off from everything. You just can't think big enough to see how I'm doing it. You just don't know what's happening in the asteroid belt. But do you know what's happening on the moon?

"We need better sources," Sabull said, changing the subject. "I thought you had a relationship with that fat Indonesian on the *Hab a Nice Day*?" Popper asked. "He knows all the important moonfirsters. Can't he get you information?" "He's on the *Nice Day,* not the moon," Teng replied. "And he's a cook! Hardly a man placed to trade important secrets, even if I trusted him, which I don't. His best friends are mooners." But he'd left them behind, Sabull thought, and he started over in a hab with a bunch of strangers. There must be something about the moonfirsters he didn't like. But what was there about the moonfirsters that Teng wouldn't like? He needed some kind of leverage over this brash youngster.

Popper knew that Teng was not much older than 30. He'd told Popper once that he'd been born on a Star Ferry en route from Kowloon—nobody knew exactly where—and the prissy white English lawyers his family hired had still been

150

arguing about his legal status on June 31, 1997, the day before written laws no longer mattered much and their lawyers took the last planes out of British Hong Kong. The Teng family, like most of the old Chinese families, survived the change without incident, taking advantage of the English departure to secure two fine new storefronts in Happy Valley.

Teng Blao was the black sheep of his family. He'd left Hong Kong Polytechnic after his sophomore year for Chang Mai, where he was involved in an illegal data mining operation before he turned 21. Popper knew he'd lived in Taipei, Vienna, and Brunei since then, bouncing around different enterprises of varying legitimacy. At some point he'd gone completely legit, taking over a struggling vidpro outfit in India that he'd been able to merge with a bankrupt satcom carrier in Jakarta right before the first great climate storms struck in 2019. Everything his companies owned had been destroyed, but somehow he'd blundered into a seat on the board of a Malaysian conglomerate disguised as an Islamic charity that became one of the largest APORLACT climate relief contractors, managing contracts for billions of dollars across SE Asia and East Africa. Under the new United Peoples and Nations structure, Teng's so-called charity became one of the primary intermediaries for selling habricks in those regions on behalf of the moonfirsters.

"So we don't have any sources, we can't keep them

off our omninet, and people are lined up to give them anything they want," Sabull summarized. "And you're fine with all of that, so long as you get your pound of flesh." "We really do help refugees, you know Popper," Teng replied, a hurt tone in his voice. "We've resettled more than ten million people into communities where they produce less pollution and have higher standards of living. We're making a difference."

"Sure," Sabull sneered, "you're practically the second coming of Mother Theresa. But there's just one problem, isn't there? You've already admitted you think they're all going to die!" "Like I said, Popper, everyone dies," Teng retorted. "There's no shame in extending their lives a little longer. They'd not begrudge me my fair share of wealth and glory for that!"

"They would if they knew you were helping the moonfirsters!" "Why is that? I do not think you and your masters understand these refugees very well, Popper. Have you ever been to a refugee center? I have. I've talked to these people in their own languages. Have you? No, of course not, you're a bloody Brit." Like many people, Popper had more than one comtar. Unlike most, his had different skin tones, ranging from the chalky white skin of a Newcastle accountant to the dark brown pigment of a Sri Lankan dock worker. That one helped Popper appear authentic. But in his first comtack with Teng, before he knew much about him, Popper had used his whitest comtar, the one he used to portray authority to people he'd never actually meet. Popper realized now that might have been a mistake.

"Bloody Hell!" he exclaimed in the purest English outrage he could muster. "You can't tell me these poor bastards want to help the moonfirsters destroy us!" "We were destroying ourselves long before the moonfirsters stole the tether from the Chinese and their corporations," Teng replied. "The refugees don't think the mooners are trying to destroy us! They admire them, think they're heroes. The problem with you, Popper," Teng continued, "is that you've spent your whole life trying to understand rich people. You don't understand poor people at all. You think a poor person gets upset when the mooners want a pound of uranium for 1,000 habricks? Not in the least. Only rich people get upset about high prices. Poor people are impressed by them."

This clearly wasn't getting him anywhere, Sabull thought. Teng didn't have any context, couldn't appreciate the scope of the mooners' threats. "Maybe your poor refugees are impressed by the moonfirsters' outrageous demands," Popper admitted, "but that doesn't mean they'll be impressed by threats and blackmail." "They don't see threats and blackmail," Teng repeated. "That's what I'm telling you. The high prices make them respect the mooners, not hate them."

"That's the problem," Sabull countered. "That's what I'm telling you. The prices aren't the only threat any more. Up to now, the moonfirsters have only threatened us with not sending any more habricks up the tether. In the last few months though, we've heard whispers that they have other, more offensive cards up their sleeves. We've heard talk of them threatening to destroy Earth!"

"A thousand mooners are going to destroy Earth?" Teng laughed. "Popper, you can't seriously believe that. What are they going to do, throw habricks at you? They'd burn up on re-entry. They can't touch you." "Maybe not," Sabull admitted. "I don't know if they can, but it worries me to think they might *think* they can." "That's why you're worried about their omninet," Teng said. "You think they're going to hack something important?" "I don't know what they might do," Sabull replied. "If I knew, I'd be trying to stop them instead of wasting my time here trying to find out what you know. You know nothing!"

"Nothing," Teng agreed, looking straight into Sabull's horn-rimmed eyes. "Most of the people I know are pretty convinced the Earth is already destroying itself and all the mooners have to do is sit and wait patiently for a hundred years or so." "Maybe you're making a difference," Sabull replied. "Maybe you and the habsters, boosting everything precious in this world to the moon, have moved enough people to space to reach a tipping point where humanity will survive on Earth for another few thousand years or more."

"Maybe," Teng allowed. "But you and I both know the science says otherwise. Maybe they're just threatening you, bluffing." "The threat is always greater than the execution," Sabull replied. "Even you should know that. Especially an execution that only works once. I don't think they want to destroy the Earth. Why would they change anything right now, with the whole world lining up to hand its treasures over for their habricks? It's protection, Teng. It's their insurance policy against the rest of us. And don't try to pretend you don't understand why they want an insurance policy."

"They want an insurance policy against assholes like you Popper!" Teng's comtar's eyes started turning red. "They know people like you will never leave them alone!" "Leave them alone?" Popper snarled. "How can we leave them alone unless we're sure they will leave us alone? And they're not going to leave us alone until your fucking habsters have delivered everything they can get their hands on to them. Think about it, Teng," Popper urged, "if you're a habster, and you've handed over your last dollar and everything else you can get your hands on to the mooners for some habricks and a few hundred kilos of fucking regolith, aren't you going to do what the moonfirsters tell you? If you're in trouble out there, the moonfirsters are the only ones who can save you! The habsters all rely on them; they all owe them!"

"And you wish they owed and relied on you instead, Popper," Teng retorted. "You don't know the habsters! They don't give a crap about you or the mooners! They think you're all remnants of the horrible, inefficient past. They think you're already dead, you just haven't realized it yet. They're pioneers, Popper. You wouldn't know a pioneer if one crapped in your hat. They just want to build their habs and find their own paths. They don't want to talk to you or the mooners, let alone rely on either of you."

"Everybody's gotta serve somebody," Popper retorted. "Right now they're serving the moon. But the times they are changing."

Chapter Nine

Mark

Bandar Seri Begawan, Brunei

January 20, 2019

Its motto was: *Serving all the food you crave under one roof.* But nobody came to the Delifrance Café on the ground floor of the Badi'ah Hotel for the food. Or for the service, which appeared to be designed to make sure nobody disturbed the Filipino waiters and bus staff while they chain smoked cheap unfiltered Champion cigarettes and played endless games of 16-tile mahjong for even cheaper stakes. People went to the Delifrance because they were in a hurry, because they were desperate, or because they didn't want to be seen. Mark Wells was there because he didn't know what else to do. When he didn't know what else to do, Wells ate.

He sat by himself at the smallest corner table with three plates of dim sum (Chicken Pau, Beef Ball, and Prawn Dumpling), two pieces of French toast, and an order of fish and chips covered in curried tartar sauce. None of it looked very good. Wells really liked the idea of eating much more than he actually liked to eat. Getting something to eat gave him a purpose when he had none. Actually eating reminded him how fat he was and took his purpose away from him.

He pushed a soggy slice of French toast up onto the side of his bowl and wished he'd taken a taxi down to the

Burger King across from the Royal Regalia Museum on the other side of the Sungai Kedayan water village instead. Every time he drove by there he thought of the little paper crowns he used to wear at Burger King when he was a kid and wondered if they ever gave them out here. He wondered if anyone had ever worn a paper Burger King crown into the Buildings Royal Regalia museum across the street. One of Wells' strengths was not pretending to be more than who he was.

One of his weaknesses was interpersonal conflict. Wells was an only child. His parents were killed on his eighth birthday, December 21, 1988, when their flight from Frankfurt to Detroit exploded over the dark skies of Lockerbie, Scotland. His dad, Frank Wells, taught art history in Ann Arbor. He went to Frankfurt that winter to consult with city officials about displaying publicly a series of famous murals by Jorg Ratgeb, a 15th and 16th Century German master. His mother Alyce Wells went with him because she'd never been to Europe—she'd never even been out of Michigan except for a few excursions across the river to Windsor and a single class trip to Chicago.

They'd left their seven-year-old son with Frank's graduate assistant, Sophie, a disenchanted and unsuccessful artist from Des Moines who wore black lipstick and liked to talk about other people's problems. She'd been Mark's regular babysitter for three years and Frank's student for five. After Frank's death, she wound up dropping out of school and moving to New York to resurrect her art career. Mark never heard of her again. But she'd been one of his favorite babysitters. She was so obsessed with herself that she never left room for anyone else, and he could just float through her storms. It was the beginning of his long history on the sidelines of his own life.

Sophie wound up taking care of Mark for two weeks while Frank's parents, Alyce's sister, the State of Michigan, and the federal government tried to figure out who was going to take him on and how they were going to pay for it. Mark never knew exactly what sort of relationship his dad and Sophie had, but she took Frank's death pretty hard, and she wasn't exactly full of light to start with. It was not the merriest of Christmases or the happiest of New Years in the little blue house on Brooklyn Avenue that year.

Sophie mostly ignored Mark and kept her crying to herself. But sometimes she worked herself up into a frenzy and started screaming at him, demanding answers to questions he wasn't old enough to even understand. He learned that trying to answer only made her more upset. He learned that sometimes people just scream at you for no reason, and it doesn't have anything to do with you. He'd reminded himself of that a lot over the past couple of weeks. He reminded himself daily that if screaming back could make any difference, then they wouldn't be the kind of people who just screamed at you for no reason.

Finally, Frank's parents, Ted and Alice, showed up in their 1976 Buick Skylark to take Mark back to their ranch house in Traverse City. Mark had never been to Traverse City. He soon learned it was very different from Ann Arbor. All the kids there had already known each other forever. People didn't come and go from Traverse City like they did in Ann Arbor. He never stopped being an outsider, even nine years later when he graduated as the valedictorian of his class of 915 students—one of the largest in the state.

Unfortunately for Mark, 1997 was also the last year the Traverse City Central High Trojans were the only football game in town: the new Traverse City West Senior High Titans were supposed to take the field that fall, and all anyone cared about was what was going to happen to "their" football team, even though most of "them" weren't going to be there any more anyway. Most agreed that the Trojans would no longer be a state powerhouse with nearly half of their team going over to the Titans.

Three weeks before Mark's parents plunged to their death over Scotland and six weeks before he moved to Traverse City to live with his grandparents, the Trojans had claimed their last Michigan Class A football championship, squeezing past Novi at home in the semi-finals and handily besting Redford-Detroit Catholic Central in the championship game at the Pontiac Silverdome. Mark hadn't

160

been part of that victory and wasn't part of the communal despair over the split into Trojans and Titans. But sometimes he felt like he'd brought their whole football team down with him—really their whole community—and he didn't know whether to feel guilt or schadenfreude.

His grandparents weren't football fans either. Ted's small accounting office, where Alice answered the phones, kept the records in perfect order, and put a small bunch of white flowers on Ted's desk every Monday hadn't changed much in the past 30 years. Mark tried once to convince his grandfather that digital computers were the future of accounting, but to no avail. Ted wasn't stupid, but he wasn't ambitious either. He'd made himself exactly the sort of home he wanted. He read the *Record-Eagle* every morning and watched Lawrence Welk every Thursday night. In retrospect, taking on his half-black 18-year-old grandson must have been pretty tough on Ted. He never screamed at Mark, but he was never passionate about anything Mark did either.

Mark wound up at the University of Maine on a mathematics scholarship, meaning he was somewhat talented but not nearly prodigal enough for an Ivy League scholarship, much less MIT or Caltech. That never bothered him. He was happy enough just to avoid East Lansing and leave Michigan behind forever. When he was a sophomore, he applied for the Semester by the Sea program at the

Darling Marine Center in Walpole, mostly because he'd fallen in love with Moni from New Jersey. That hadn't gone far. She left him for a local boy with a boat two days after they got there.

Mark's love affair with the sea, on the other hand, brought him all the way around the world to the shores of the South China Sea. He never forgot the first time he realized how much more alive the ocean was than the arms of Grand Traverse Bay or the shallow and polluted waters of Boardman Lake. He never regretted his journey here, but sometimes he wondered whether it would turn out any better than Walpole had.

Wells had known Howard Gall for more than ten years and didn't understand him any better than he did the ocean. Wells thought he'd understood Howard enough to move forward with him on the hab project, knowing how hard it would be. He wasn't sure whether or not Howard was right about escaping the end of the world, but he was pretty sure hab life was going to be an important part of the future. Maybe ten or twenty other people in the world were gifted with Howard's burning mathematical insight. But maybe there weren't any more than that who were as dogmatic and single-minded either. Because after eighteen months of constant battles between Howard and anyone who didn't want to do things exactly the way Howard wanted, Mark was starting to have second thoughts. Maybe sometimes, Mark thought, when answers come so easily and seem so natural it's more difficult to navigate through life's grey areas. At least the ones that aren't mathematical. Probability and uncertainty are very different things.

Right from the start Wells had seen first hand just how comfortable Howard was with probability and mathematical grey areas. He met Howard in Macau during one of Howard's fortune-building projects involving high stakes blackjack card counting. Mark had just finished his post-dissertation fellowship at the University of Hong Kong and was giving a lecture at the Macau Science Center. Howard and thirty of his trained blackjack minions were there to plunder $100 million from fifteen different casinos in a disciplined nine-week rotation carefully designed to make sure the casinos never knew they'd been there.

They'd met at a roulette table when Wells made an offhand remark about the relationship between the period of the wheel's rotation and the period of the ball's rotation. Howard had given him a long discomforting stare and later, as Wells was leaving, Howard appeared next to him in the casino driveway and asked "Are you gaming that table?" in his trademark direct fashion. Mark's blank stare answered the question, but Howard kept talking to him anyway, and they wound up eating crab congee soup and talking about the world late into the morning. Wells wasn't sure he'd ever met anyone in a casino late at night who wasn't a character of some kind, and Howard certainly qualified. But Howard, unlike most, never asked Mark for anything. That, along with his obvious intellect, piqued Wells' interest.

Three years later, Howard called out of the blue and started asking Wells questions about algae. One thing led to another, and before Mark knew it, Howard had convinced him to join his project and start designing space aquariums. Howard wanted to freeze-dry algae, send it to orbit, and revitalize it using water extracted from lunar soil or captured asteroids. The algae would remove carbon dioxide from the atmosphere, produce oxygen and hydrogen to make pure water, and even provide a source of food. It was a beautiful dream and Mark fell in love with it right away. Mark was fascinated by the hab vision in a completely non-ideological way. He figured that whatever reasons people thought they had for building little worlds in the sky probably wouldn't make much difference in the end. Just the building was enough for him, and he soon realized Howard had the cash to make it happen.

Mark didn't know exactly what else Howard had done to accumulate his billions. He knew that he'd spent a short time working for a Wall Street investment bank right after he graduated from M.I.T. in 2002, and that he'd been involved in developing some of the first algorithmic trading strategies. Wells suspected that Howard had been one of the few people on the right side of the collateralized debt bubble before the financial crisis in 2007. He was an early investor in Uber and Airbnb and cashed out at the right time. Now he was prepared to spend all his money on his vision of space colonization, which was both the blessing and the curse of it. A blessing to have Howard's seemingly unlimited resources behind them, but a curse for their project to be limited by the expanse of one man's vision, however talented that man might be.

Wells stared down into his bowl of curried tartar sauce and cold French toast for a moment or two until he was startled by an upbeat voice behind him. "Where be your gibes now? Your gambols? Your songs? Your flashes of merriment that were wont to set the tables on a roar? Not one now?" He looked up to see Howard's wife Delilah. "Unquiet meals make ill digestions," he replied. "I hate the idle pleasures of these days," she countered, pulling one of the small red chairs up to his table and sitting down. "I am determined to prove a villain."

Delilah and her mother had both been members of the acting company at the Oregon Shakespeare Festival in Ashland for years and she knew most of the plays by heart. Mark had a high school English teacher who made him read most of the plays and the kind of memory that didn't forget much. He also had a knack for spouting improvised doggerel and a lifelong habit of attending as many amateur and low-budget Shakespeare performances as he could.

When Howard had introduced him to Delilah, he'd made a crack about her daylight shaming Howard's lamp and, without hesitation, she'd responded "What man art thou, stumbling over my night?" They'd been good friends ever since.

"What villainy today?" Mark asked her, pushing another bit of cold mushy French toast around his bowl. "None but our own," Delilah replied, the smile fading from her face. "Our villainy in sinking those poor people to the bottom of the ocean and pretending we know what they're going to do down there." Mark looked up at her. "They're going to do what Howard wants them to do," he said slowly. "Just like the rest of us." Delilah laughed. "I thought we were better friends than that!" Mark sat up in his chair. He wasn't sure how honest about his doubts he could be with Howard's wife.

"I'm starting to wonder if we're all making a big mistake," Delilah continued. "What do you mean?" Mark asked. "What mistake?" "Oh, we've made mistakes aplenty. We could sit in this charming little café and vet new mistakes well past the coming dawn. But our big mistakes are the ones that could kill people." "We're not going to kill anyone," Mark replied. "Our latest risk assessment shows a very low probability of catastrophic failure." "Yes," Delilah agreed, "I'm sure your calculations are exceptionally accurate. You're still in charge of risk assessment, aren't you?" "Yes," Mark admitted, not quite sure where she was going or how serious she was.

"And what are the factors in those equations? You've quantified the chance of systems failure, right?" "Of course," Wells replied. "In every hab system, and every subsystem, and every system interconnect, and attempting to account for external contingencies, which we hope to reduce significantly with our fleet of support vessels." "Exactly," Delilah said, leaning towards him, "you've calculated the risks associated with every hab system and every hab connection and every external contingency you could think of. But what about internal contingencies?"

"What do you mean?" Mark asked, still not understanding. "There are no internal contingencies. The master schedule sets everything out. Everything's going to run on Howard's plan, which includes contingency plans for everything that could happen down there." "You don't really believe that, do you?" Wells looked at her as if for the first time. "If you believed that, you wouldn't be sitting over there in that dismal corner of this godforsaken diner pushing that crappy food around your bowl." "I guess we kind of have to believe it," he muttered. "That's the way Howard wants it."

"Oh, that's absolutely the way Howard wants it," she agreed. "Trust me, nobody knows more about the way Howard wants things than I do. But nobody but me knows how often things don't go his way either. He's a genius, Mark, not a magician. I shouldn't have to tell you that. You've been there. You've seen what happens when somebody sees a different way of doing things. Remember when Onifire left? Did anyone ever tell you that story?"

"No," Mark admitted. "I wondered about her."

"She did her job," Delilah said. "She's an anthropologist. She studies how people live together. She told Howard people weren't going to be predictable and certainly weren't going to doggishly follow his nine-month plan or automatically execute his contingencies every time something went wrong. She told Howard that if he leaves 1225 people down there for nine months, at least one of them is going have some kind of mental crisis serious enough to pose a danger to the entire project. She told Howard that controlling the habinauts' lives from the surface would make the project either 'tragic or meaningless or both,' and she said she was hoping for meaningless so that it would just waste his money and not kill anyone."

"What did Howard say?" Mark asked. He was surprised he hadn't heard. "It was in a social constructs committee meeting" Delilah replied. "Howard totally dismissed her. He said they weren't going to pick anybody who'd have a serious mental crisis. He told her that the whole point of him building this was so he could leave those kinds of people behind." Mark looked down into his bowl.

"Howard does like to see people in black and white." He jerked up suddenly. "Not literally! I didn't mean to say ..."

"I know exactly what you meant," Delilah interrupted, reaching out to touch him on the arm. "I never told you this, Mark, and it really shouldn't matter, but Howard told me about you for two years before I met you. In all that time he never mentioned you were black." "My mom was black," Wells replied. "My dad was white. Did you assume I was white?" "I don't know. I guess I never really thought about it, which probably means yes." "And I guess I never really thought about what color you were," Mark said, "which probably means I assumed you were white too." "So both of us, white and half-black, assumed the person we didn't really think about was white," Delilah said, looking straight into his eyes. "What that means is we come from a place with a pretty fucked up racial history."

"That we do," Mark agreed. "But I'm not sure Howard thinks about that. He sees 'good' people and 'bad' people. He thinks that if he fills his hab with 'good' people nothing 'bad' will happen. He thinks his habinauts will have so much on their plates they won't have time to think about what color their skin is or where their ancestors came from." "And what do you think?" Delilah prompted. "Do you think nothing 'bad' will happen because all the habinauts are 'good'?" "I hope so," Mark replied. "But I'm not sure what you're saying. I think that being white or black—or half of each—is part of who we are, that it shapes us and the world around us like some kind of aura, or gravitational field. I think that if you don't see that, you're not 'color-blind:' you're 'reality-blind,' because that's a part of us, part of our reality. So are you saying Howard can't pick 'good' people without knowing if they're white or black?"

"If race is part of who somebody is," Delilah said, "which I think is what you just said, then doesn't not knowing anybody's race mean Howard's making his picks of them based on incomplete information?" "But it's not relevant information," Wells insisted. "Who cares what color they are or who they like to sleep with or what they think about God or whether they shave their body hair or a zillion other things about them? All that matters is whether they're more likely than the other hablicants to increase the overall probability of the mission's success."

"And what is that success?" Delilah asked insistently. "Completing the nine-month mission without disaster and landing healthy habinauts in front of a million cameras on Jerudong Beach," Mark replied, nodding in the direction of the ocean. "And you don't think those cameras will judge us differently if 1225 white folks march triumphantly up the surf?" "That's not going to happen," Mark replied. "We're getting thousands of hablicants from around the world every week."

"But since you're on the risk assessment team, not

the habinaut selection team, you're not really in a position to be sure? Has anybody asked you about it?" "I'm pretty sure you're the only one who's asked me what I thought about racial identity since we got here," Mark agreed. "People don't like to talk about it. I don't like to talk about it. Does it matter?" "Does it matter that the selection team isn't looking at the racial or ethnic identity of the candidates?" Delilah replied. "I think you're exactly right. I think Howard sees 'good' people and 'bad' people, and since he's trying to be a good progressive twenty-first century forward-thinking person of consciousness he doesn't think skin color, religion, gender, or sexual preference have any relevance to whether or not somebody's a 'good' person."

"And you think it does?" Wells asked. "No, of course not!" Delilah snapped. "Don't be silly! That's not the question. The question is simple: does how many people of different skin colors or religions or sexualities you throw in there together have any relevance to their ability to spend nine months living together in a bubble on the bottom of the ocean? Think about it Mark—even if they all pass all the personality tests with flying colors and are all highly motivated to succeed and are all totally committed to every detail of and every contingency in Howard's nine-month plan, doesn't it seem like it could make a difference if there were 800 straight black male Muslims, 400 lesbian white female atheists, and 25 gay white male Jews down there?"

"That's statistically impossible," Wells assured her."
"Of course," Delilah agreed. "But it would be something
you'd want to know about, right?" "I guess, but isn't the only
alternative some sort of quota system for all these different
kinds of people? I thought by judging each candidate solely
on his or her ability to contribute to maximizing the
probability of mission success, we were avoiding all of that.
No quotas, no discrimination, only each candidate's merits.
'Only the best need apply.'"

"We are certainly doing our best to convince
ourselves and the world of that," Delilah allowed. "But if a
big difference like that would matter, then there's no way we
can honestly say that little differences—differences that are
statistically inevitable—can't possibly matter. We can't just
pick 1225 'good' people to live together one at a time,
Onifire told us, because human success is determined in
groups, not by individuals."

"But the only way to pick our group is to pick the
best individuals," Mark protested. "What are you saying, that
we should have had people apply in groups of 1225?"
"Actually," Delilah replied, "that's exactly what Onifire
suggested. But then she said even that wouldn't really solve
the problem." "Solve it?" Mark snorted, "it would make it
much worse! I can assure you that our 1225 individuals will
be way more racially, sexually, and religiously diverse than
any group of 1225 that would have applied."

"You're absolutely right. And again, that's exactly what Onifire said. She said that the fundamental problem doesn't really have anything to do with skin color or diversity or any of that. She says that the fundamental problem is that living in a hab, living in a relatively closed environment, is fundamentally different from living on Earth, living in a relatively open environment." "Of course it is," Mark admitted. "That's why we're doing this, so we can learn how to do that! That's the whole point!"

"I thought so for a long time too," Delilah replied sadly. "I really wish I still thought so. But that's not what we're doing. We're not sending the habinauts into a closed environment." "Of course we are! What do you mean?" "Whose orders are they following?" she asked him softly. "Howard's of course. It's Howard's project!" "And will Howard be living in the hab with them?"

Mark was stunned. He'd asked himself many times whether or not Howard would, in the end, decide to join his experiment. In the end, he'd always convinced himself Howard would wait for the first space hab. The mission plan called for Howard to remain aboard the chief support vessel.

"Is he going to?" Mark asked. "I thought he might." Delilah looked up at him. "Not as far as I know," she replied, staring at him. "I've asked myself that as well. But I think he'll stay on the surface and run his experiment." "I think so too," Mark replied. "But so what? What does that change?"

"It changes the point of what we're doing," Delilah said. "We're not trying to find out whether people can live in a hab. We're trying to see whether people can take orders in an enclosed space for an extended time. Well, spoiler alert— they can! Nuclear submarine crews have done that for years! And that's all our habinauts are—a glorified submarine crew."

"But there's never been a submarine crew this large," Mark objected. "The scale of the hab is totally different." "I didn't say the whole thing was pointless. I'm sure lots of technical insights will be gained." "But?" "But if habs are going to 'save a nucleus of humanity,'" Delilah said with air quotes, "then the habinauts have to live in them forever, by themselves. Not live in them for nine months, following somebody else's orders, on somebody else's schedule." "And that's why this is a first step," Mark replied. "We can't just start giving people one way tickets without figuring out how to do it first!"

"But that's what Onifire said, Mark—that we're not figuring out how to do it. What she said is that the only people who will ever really figure out how to live in a closed environment are people who grow up in a closed environment and have the instincts for it. She said not a single hablicant can possibly have the instincts for living in a closed environment because for the last two million years every human instinct has developed in an open environment."

"But if that's true," Wells said, "then humanity can never live in habs, because there will never be a first generation with any of those instincts." "Maybe that's true, but that's not what Onifire thought. She thought that the only way to create habinauts was to grow them and that only people who grew up with instincts learned in a closed environment, even if they developed those instincts in an environment that wasn't in fact closed, would ever truly be able to live in habs."

"And what do you think?" Mark asked, still uneasy about discussing the project's flaws with Howard's wife in his hotel lobby over the remains of cheap whitefish. "I think she's 100% right," Delilah replied. She looked straight into his eyes. "I think Howard is 100% on the wrong track. And that's why I'm on my way to the airport right now. I'm leaving Howard, leaving the project, and flying to Mexico City to meet Onifire and learn more about this *Escuela Neuvos Talentos* that Grok Martin built on the Pacific coast of Nicaragua fifteen years ago. I hope you'll think long and hard before you help Howard continue any further."

Delilah pushed her red plastic chair back to walk around the table and give Wells a long farewell hug. He assured her he would think long and hard and watched her walk out of the lobby. Wells knew, and he was pretty sure Delilah knew, that he wasn't the kind of person who could change lanes instantly and make a dramatic exit like her. Even if Howard's submersible hab project was flawed and imperfect, he reassured himself, it would spur progress towards the ultimate goal. Maybe it wasn't the smartest way to spend Howard's money or the most efficient road forward, Wells thought, but it certainly couldn't hurt anything.

Interlude

Rally

El Ostional, Nicaragua, Earth

March 30, 2010

Two pieces of tomorrow were deep in Rally's mind keeping her awake late into tonight. She'd never had this much trouble falling asleep. She'd never had so much to think about. Tomorrow she'd leave the Escuela with her father Grok and her mother G'Sille in the old white Jeep the adults used to bring people and supplies from town. They'd travel halfway around the world on trains and planes and boats all the way to her mother's childhood home on Yermainer, or Melville Island, off the north coast of Australia. They wouldn't get to *Mili ka piti*, as her mother had taught her to say the name of her hometown, until the day after the day after tomorrow.

She hadn't left El Ostional, or seen any openers, for four years, ever since the Escuela started when she was just a tiny little girl who loved animals more than anything. She'd turned eleven six weeks earlier, on Valentine's Day. Her mother always told her she was born on Valentine's Day because she was so full of love. Lying quietly on her back listening to the deep honking bullfrogs and whistling crickets, she thought about how much she loved her mother and her father and her mates and about her mixed feelings about tomorrow's trip to Milikapiti.

Her mother and father were two of the most important people at the Escuela, but they always made time for her, their only child. On her eighth birthday, just a year after the Escuela opened, they'd spent three days together hiking from Playa El Ostional to Playa La Flor as a family. Her mother had stopped them every time she saw a new plant and helped Rally collect a leaf from it. Rally saved all the leaves in a special notebook. When they got back her mother helped her identify all the plants on the opennet and they talked about how all the various species fit together in the different ecosystems they'd walked through.

Grok wasn't that interested in the plants they collected, but near Playa Anima he'd found what he thought were fragments of pottery fired by Nahoa people, who'd lived here for thousands of years and were now slowly disappearing. He told her stories about how the Nahoa lived next to the river and wove plants together to make fish nets and told each other funny stories about the brave jaguar cub and the clever monkeys who liked to play tricks.

Grok loved telling stories. Sometimes, when Rally was grouping with her mates, it embarrassed her because a lot of them didn't think he was very funny. But other times, like when he told her about the Nahoa, she loved him even more. That made her feel the kind of funny she was feeling now about this trip around the world. She loved her mates.

She loved her parents. But she didn't love everyone the same.

Nothing mattered more than her mates—that's what she'd been taught her whole life. They were here at the Escuela learning how to live in a closed environment, which was much harder than living in an open one. Openers could take advantage of other people or waste resources and just keep moving on to new territory. Closers couldn't do that. Closers would only ever be as strong as their weakest link because they were so mutually vulnerable. She and her mates had to be as strong and capable as they could be because any one of them could bring disaster on them all. She'd never let her mates down and they'd never let her down. She knew that. She knew that her future, her safety, rested in their hands, not hers. But they still weren't her family. They still didn't matter to her as much as her mom and dad.

It was even more complicated, at least in her mind, because not all of her mates had parents. Like her friend Yestrey, who always wanted to help Rally clean the animals' cages. Yestrey was an orphan from London who didn't even remember anything about her parents. She came to the Escuela with Case Henry and his sister Susan and their parents, who did remember Yestrey's parents. Yestrey didn't have anyone but her mates and their families, but their families weren't her family.

Case Henry's parents died when Rally was just nine and Yestrey and Case Henry were only six or seven and Susan was just two or three. They'd been installing a water wheel in the Rio El Ostional when a log floated downstream and trapped them beneath it. None of the children were strong enough to pull the log off and they drowned before any other adults appeared. They were buried next to the river by the waterfall up the hill from the Escuela.

Rally and her mates all made sure to spend extra time with Case Henry and Susan after that, and to make sure they knew that they were all there for them, that they all loved them, but Rally wondered whether any number of mates could ever really make up for having your mother and father die a tragic death like that before your eyes. Rally wondered if it was even fair for her to be mates with Yestrey and Case Henry and Susan when she had a mother and father and they didn't. She wondered what Susan thought when she saw Rally and her mother loving and hugging each other.

Last night, when Rally asked G'Sille why they were going to Milikapiti by themselves, without any of her mates, she knew there'd been some traces of guilt in her voice. She didn't want to have anything more than anyone else. Her mother's reply hadn't made much sense to Rally. She'd talked about how Rally was the oldest one of her mates, how she'd been at the Escuela longer than any of the others, and how she was reaching an age where it was time to see the world of openers and learn how different and unique she and her mates were. Rally was really confused about that, but she could tell how proud of her G'Sille was, and she didn't want to sound ungrateful or ask too many questions.

Rally knew that for thousands of years people thought the Earth was endless and infinite. They believed there would always be more islands, more forests, and more resources waiting for them down the road. This premise, Rally knew, led openers to develop unsustainable belief systems that prioritized taking, harvesting, and consuming over sharing, growing, and preserving. The pretense of endless resources helped openers justify atrocious practices: burning irreplaceable petroleum to fuel cars; poisoning coral reefs with cyanide to catch fish; dumping industrial waste directly into oceans; and the rest of their unsustainable economy. They were learning a new way of life at the Escuela. They were learning how to be sustainable and live together in a closed environment anywhere, even in space.

But it was hard for her to understand how being special and unique and teaching the openers went along with lifting her mates up and making everyone strong to keep everyone safe. It seemed like you couldn't have it both ways and had to pick one or another. Either you were special and unique or you all had to stick together and be the same. How could both be true? If she was special and unique, how could any of her mates know how to make her strong enough to keep them all safe? If her mates were special and unique, why would they want to make her stronger? How could a group of snowflakes find enough common ground to save the planet, or to live together in space, or even here at the Escuela? How could they all be miracles and still live together like closers? She'd asked her dad that, and he'd looked at her in silence for a long time.

When he finally spoke, he told her one of his stories. "Once upon a time," he started, "there was a troop of baboons, who lived on a nice savannah in Central Africa. There were mommy baboons and daddy baboons and baby baboons, and they all lived there together. One day, one of the mommy baboons and two of her baby daughters went down to the river to look for fish. But when they got to the river, they didn't see any fish. Can you guess what they saw?" "A tiger?" Rally guessed. "Nope," her dad smiled. "Not unless one escaped from a zoo. Tigers don't live in Africa. Did you know that?" "I forgot," she answered. "A lion?" "That's a better guess," Grok grinned. "But think about how many fish a big lion would have to eat to fill itself up." "A mess of them, huh," she agreed. "A big mess," he smiled. "Nope, it wasn't any kind of cat. It was a little baby bonobo, which is a kind of chimpanzee, with her head just barely sticking up out of the water. Do you know the difference between chimpanzees and baboons?"

"They're both primates," Rally remembered from

biology group, "but a baboon is a monkey, so it has a tail, and a chimpanzee is an ape, so it doesn't?" "That's right," Grok said proudly. "You sure do remember things well! Anyway, yes, the little baby bonobo peeking her head out of the shallow part of the river had no tail at all. And she wasn't catching any fish either. She was just sitting there with her head sticking out of the water looking at some rocks on the shore." "Why weren't any other bonobos there in the water with her?" Rally asked, feeling a little sad for the baby in the river all alone. "That's a good question and it's the probably the same question the mother baboon was asking herself, in her own way. Mother chimpanzees usually stay within about twenty feet of their babies for three or four years after they're born, so the mother baboon knew that the mother bonobo was probably not too far away."

"Were the baboons scared of the baby's mother?" Rally asked. She didn't remember ever grouping about whether monkeys and apes would try to kill each other and she wasn't sure whether baboons were bigger or smaller than chimpanzees. "I don't know," Grok replied, "because I don't know how a baboon thinks. But I know what happened. What happened is that the mother baboon grunted a few times to let the little bonobo know she was there and alert the mother chimp if she was nearby. The little bonobo turned its head to look at the baboons but didn't stand up out of the water or try to run away. And the mother baboon didn't hear anything that sounded like a mother bonobo, just the water flowing down the river around the chimpanzee."

"Why didn't the little bonobo try to run away?" Rally asked. "Wasn't she scared? Didn't she want her mommy?" "She did," Grok agreed. "She was really scared and really wanted her mommy. But when the mother baboon crawled down to the river and sniffed the little baby bonobo, she found out why it didn't run away. She saw that the baby's leg was stuck under a rock on the bottom of the river, and her arms weren't long enough to reach it without pulling her head under the water."

"So what did the baboon do?" Rally asked curiously, scared that the story would not have a happy ending. "She reached down and pulled the rock off of the little baby's leg," her dad assured her. "And then the baby bonobo crawled out of the river and ran up the other bank and dove into the trees calling for her mother. And then the mother baboon grunted at her daughters to come down to the river and they splashed each other and smiled and laughed and caught three little fish that they ate and four more little fish that they took back to their tree to share with the other baboons."

Grok stopped talking and sat looking at his daughter silently for a long time. "That's it?" Rally asked him. "That's all that happened? That's the whole story? That's not funny!" "It's not funny at all," Grok agreed. "And it's not very captivating. Not much happened. It's very ordinary. But sometimes ordinary things are the most important."

"But what's important about the little baby stuck in the river?" Rally asked.

"What's important," Grok told her, "is that bonobos and baboons, apes and monkeys, have more than 90% of the same genetic makeup as people. So they're a lot like us. And they're a lot like each other. But they're not the same as us. And they're not the same as each other." "But then why did the momma baboon help the baby chimp out of the river?" Rally asked. "Because despite the momma baboon having a tail, and the baby chimp having none," Grok explained, "they still had more in common than their differences. That doesn't mean that things always happen like this. If that had been a daddy baboon, or if the momma bonobo had been a little closer, or maybe if she'd been a little hungrier, then maybe the momma monkey would have tried to kill and eat the baby ape. But this time she didn't."

"So what made her decide to help the baby?" Rally wondered. "I don't know," Grok replied. "Like I said, I don't know how baboons think. I don't even know how I think! But what you said is really important. The mother baboon decided. For whatever reason, she decided to help that baby. That's what monkeys and apes and dolphins and people do— they decide. They make choices." "That's what makes them different," Rally agreed. "But why do they make the choices they make?"

"That's a great question. But I don't think it's one we'll ever be able to answer. Because dolphins probably make choices for different reasons than apes, and people probably make choices for different reasons than dogs. Dolphins make a wider range of choices than dogs and people make a wider range of choices than dolphins. There are species of algae that, at most, make one or two really small, almost meaningless choices their whole lives, and nobody really understands them. Some people think that you can never understand enough about the reasons for a choice without interfering with the choice itself; that your attempt to understand a decision can only succeed if it winds up affecting the decision and so preventing you from understanding what would have happened if you hadn't gotten involved in the first place."

"But what does that have to do with us going to Milikapiti?" Rally groaned. Sometimes she wished her dad would just give her an easy answer. "For one," Grok replied, "it says that we're going to Milikapiti because your mom and I decided we were." Rally just kept looking at him. "Monkeys and apes are different," he replied brusquely. "But they have more in common than their differences. Openers and closers are different. But they have more in common than their differences. You and your mates are different. But you have more in common than your differences. Your mother and I are different. But we have more in common than our differences. We promised ourselves—and we promised you—when we agreed to start this school, this experiment, that we would never teach you to look down at anyone who was different. The momma baboon didn't look down on the baby chimp because she was different. She reached across their differences to help, to lift her up. That's exactly what we're trying to learn to do at the Escuela, to reach across differences and help lift each other up. And if you never learn anything about openers, you're never going to be able to do that."

Rally sighed and turned over onto her stomach as she heard a troop of howler monkeys join the nighttime jungle choir. She wondered what kind of animals lived in Milikapiti and tried to imagine herself falling asleep to the sounds of kangaroos and koala bears. Finally she fell asleep and dreamt about dozens of momma bullfrogs working together to pull a frightened baby kangaroo out of a burning bush.

Chapter Ten

Teng

Phnom Phen, Cambodia

August 29, 2019

Teng was just beginning to understand how bad
things were when the power finally came back on. The killer
typhoon that hit them reportedly made landfall 500
kilometers away, on the other side of Vietnam near Mui Ne,
just over four days ago. It got to Phnom Phen shortly
thereafter and the heavy rains and wind pounded them
relentlessly for almost 24 full hours. For a whole day he'd
been unable to see the street below his window. He'd seen
motorcycle tires blown three stories high. He'd watched
houses peel apart layer by layer like cakes with too much
butter. Now it was barely even drizzling, the trees in the
hotel driveway were hardly shaking, and the TV was
warming up. He'd survived somehow.

But the winds here had 'only' been a little more than
220 km/hr. There had 'only' been a little less than half a
liter of rain. 'Only' one river had flooded. There were 'only'
15,000 or 20,000 people whose homes had been destroyed
and were 'camping' in and around the Olympic Stadium.
Nobody knew how many were dead, 'only' that they'd
apparently fared much better than Ho Chi Minh City,
Manila, Manado, Davao City, and countless other people

across Southeast Asia. Nobody really knew anything, just bits and pieces picked up here and there from people who'd ventured out of the hotel or had visitors.

Climate storms, people were calling them. Teng vaguely remembered seeing reports about them on TV and the internet last week. One formed west of Australia in the South Indian Ocean and headed northeast towards Northern Australia and Southern Indonesia. The other formed north of Guam and moved southwest to the Philippines. Teng remembered the newspeople saying the storms would never meet, since no tropical storm could ever cross the equator, and treating them more as curiosities than threats. Well, they'd been much more than curiosities, even if Teng had no idea at the moment how or why or what the full extent of the disaster would turn out to be.

He'd been able to speak briefly with his cousin Jocelyn at his parents' house in Hong Kong that morning. It was the first time he'd had any cell service since the typhoon hit. Even in Hong Kong, 2000 kilometers away, there'd been flooding, power outages, panic, looting, and violence. Jocelyn told him their family was safe, as far as they knew, but Teng could hear the fear in her voice. She probably heard the fear in his as well. He was scared as hell. Surviving a storm like this was so totally impersonal, so completely out of his or anyone's control. If you were in the wrong place at the wrong time you just died. And it was starting to look like most of Southeast Asia had been in the wrong place this time.

Teng hadn't left the fifth floor of the InterContinental Phnom Phen since the power went out in the middle of the night four days and fifteen hours ago. He'd only ventured out of his suite a few times to talk to some of the others stranded there. A few had ventured out of the hotel but not for long. Five days ago Teng would have said he'd have been one of the first ones going out to explore but faced with the explosive winds and driving rain he'd huddled inside his suite with no desire to expose himself to the storm or its aftermath. If sitting out the storm in his hotel suite was such a humbling experience for him, Teng kept wondering, what was it like for the people who were actually stuck out there in it?

He'd limited himself to turning his cell phone on once a day, carefully taking the battery out after each unsuccessful attempt, but he was still dangerously low on power. The first thing he did when he heard the power go on was plug his battery in. His phone powered up but still didn't show any incoming calls or any messages. That was the scariest thing of all. If nobody had called him from Jakarta or Haldia, did that mean they were all dead? His phone refused to connect to the internet at all even when he had cell service, which he didn't understand. Satellites didn't get flooded.

190

The InterContinental staff had, for the most part, remained at their posts throughout the deluge. Some of them had gone out just long enough to bring their families back to the hotel. Built in 1999 on relatively high ground between the airport and downtown, it promised to stand long after the poorly constructed homes in the surrounding neighborhoods blew to the ground. As soon as the power went out, they fell to the refrigerators and freezers and wasted no time passing out boxes of fruit and cheese and seemingly endless plates of eggs and steak and other perishables.

Teng's first two days inside the hotel eating huge meals and snacking continuously on fresh fruit while being cut off completely from his phone, the internet, and TV news were a surreal experience for him. Like most people his age, Teng had grown up taking for granted that he could access the history and ideas of his world any time he wanted. He'd assumed he could find out what was happening anywhere in the world in real time and text his friends and colleagues at will.

He hadn't liked being stuck here alone very much at all. Luckily, the hotel water was still working and he was able to drink as much as he liked and take cold showers. Every time he poured himself a glass of water he told himself how blessed he was and offered a short prayer for all the people without water. But mostly he felt helpless. He felt blessed and helpless at the same time, which bothered him in ways he couldn't put in words. He spent a fair amount of daylight time looking out his windows and trying to figure out what was happening to the city around him.

The InterContinental was one of the tallest buildings on Mao Tse Tsung Boulevard. From his fifth floor room about halfway up the north face of the building, he could see at least a kilometer down the street towards the center of town and the Mekong. What scared him the most was how few people he saw out there. Last week, the street had been full of scooters and bikes and taxis and people all day and every night. On the third day after the storm he'd looked down right before sunset and hadn't seen a single person.

Yesterday his concierge, Bong, told him that all the fresh and perishable food in the hotel had been eaten or distributed. Bong had assured him that the hotel still had hundreds of pounds of rice and plenty of propane to fire the stoves, so there was no danger of starving. But instead of just cooking meals whenever they liked and passing trays up the stairwells and around the halls, they were going to start serving in the lobby. Now that the power was back, Teng wondered if they'd still do that. He had a feeling maybe this wasn't going to end quickly. If he was going to be here for a while, he appreciated how lucky he was to have hot meals served to him.

Now his TV came on, but it wasn't finding any channels. He clicked around the dial a couple of times with no luck and finally turned it off. He didn't understand how the global channels like CNN, RT, and CCTV could be down because of the storm. Maybe it was a problem with the local infrastructure. He stuck his head out the door to see if he could hear anyone else's TV, but there was only silence.

Teng walked slowly back across his suite to his bed and lay down. With power, he told himself, came hot showers and AC and, eventually, TV and internet. There was no point in worrying about Jakarta or about any of his people. Either they'd made it back to Haldia ahead of the storm or they'd survived like him or they'd been destroyed by the storms. He prayed for them all, to any gods who might listen, but he was smart enough not to count on his prayers changing anything but himself.

What he could count on was that, however bad these storms were, there were still going to be training videos. There were still going to be people who wanted to come home at the end of their day and watch movies. He still had a chance. He was in Phnom Phen because it was more or less halfway between Haldia, the Indian port city downriver from Calcutta where the nearly bankrupt vidpro company he'd bought last year, BollyMadras Films, had its dingy warehouse full of outdated equipment, and Jakarta, where a struggling satellite communications startup called DataBank kept what was left of its equipment and other capital assets in four dingy storage units 50 kilometers west of Jakarta airport outside a dirty industrial suburb called Cikande. He hoped to merge the two failing companies and use their equipment to produce and distribute secure programming. He dreamt of growing it into an actual film company and producing real videos for markets across Southeast Asia.

He'd brought Salman and Sanjay, his only two remaining Indian production employees, here to meet with the DataBank principals. He thought the meetings had gone pretty well. The DataBank people were all tech, all the time. They knew perfectly well they weren't going to come back from the dead on their own. They didn't have the mindset for it. Like most techies, their vision was buried so far inside the cell molecules they didn't even care about the forest. They ridiculed the forest, thought it was beneath them. Teng wasn't sure they thought he had enough capital or connections to somehow build a real programming distribution company out of the hodge-podge of outdated equipment in Haldia and Cikande, but he didn't think anyone with more capital or more connections was going to be flying them to Cambodia any time soon either. He suspected they'd happily take the easy way out he'd offered them.

But they'd left for Jakarta the day before the typhoon hit without making a final commitment, and he had no way of knowing whether they'd made it back, much less whether they were going to take his deal. Traveling west away from the storms, Salman and Sanjay had left for Haldia that same night. Teng assumed their flight to Calcutta hadn't had any problems, but who knew what happened after they got home? Teng lay back on his bed and tried to visualize dutiful Apple and Nike employees intently watching BollyMadras training videos in factories across Southeast Asia via DataBank satcoms, but he kept seeing walls of water washing over the vidscreens instead.

After a while, his cell phone rang and he sprang upright. It was the most wonderful noise he'd ever heard. He dove across the bed and grabbed it but saw only "Unavailable." He answered anyway, something he rarely did. "Teng here."

"Mr. Teng," a male Asian voice replied in Australian-sounding English, "my name is Yadi Song, and I am the manager of the Daftar Banten warehouse here in Cikande, Indonesia. I understand you are yourself in India?" "Yes I mean, no, Mr. Song," Teng replied uncertainly, "I am right now in Cambodia, Phnom Phen, although my production company is yes, itself, it is located in India. In Haldia." "Very good," the voice continued, "and how are things there in Phnom Phen?" "I don't really know," Teng admitted. "I have been stuck in my hotel room without power for four days. Not good. Flooding, some looting. How are things there in Cikande?" "Things here in Cikande are very bad," Song continued.

Teng's heart sank. Mercy of all gods, he thought to

himself, how could anything be big enough to wreck havoc from Hong Kong to Java? They must be 3000 kilometers apart. He tried for a second to calculate how many people lived inside the area that extended from Hong Kong to Jakarta, and his mind recoiled. They were talking about hundreds of millions of people on both sides of the equator. Teng remembered again what the newspeople said about typhoons not crossing the equator and wondered if he was misremembering or if that was no longer true.

"I am very sorry to hear that," he told Song. "What do you know?" "I know that a good part of Jakarta is underwater," Song replied, "and that millions of people have lost their homes and are fleeing the city for higher ground. I know that our power goes out sporadically, that our water system is damaged, and that the looting and violence have already begun." "I am very sorry," he told Song again, his voice shaking. "Why are you calling me?"

"I am contacting all our customers," Song continued, "because Daftar Banten is taking preparations to try to assist as best we can in the continuing crisis. My records show that you are the managing partner of DataBank, and that your company has four units of electrical equipment here in our warehouse." "It does," Teng replied, confused. "I mean, DataBank has four units, but I am not the managing partner. I run a vidpro company in India called BollyMadras. I met with three DataBank partners last week and proposed a merger, but nothing is final." How did his name get in this man's files? Was this some sort of trick to hold him liable for their equipment? Teng's mind began spinning.

"I see," Song replied. "One second ... Ah, yes, it seems that this all happened very recently. The DataBank warehouse registration was revised through our website just over 72 hours ago. Not long before we lost power here, in fact. This of course did not come up on my list of managing partners and agents to call. My apologies. The registration states that DataBank is now a wholly owned subsidiary of something called BollyMadras. It lists your name and shows an address on Balughata Road, Haldia, India 721602. Is that your company?" "Yes, that's it," Tong replied slowly, trying to process how the merger could have closed during the storm without his knowledge.

"Well, Mr. Teng," Song continued, "it appears that your merger succeeded. Congratulations!" "Thank you," Teng replied, although he felt like he could hear sarcasm in Song's voice. "Assuming you're right, why are you calling? What's wrong with their ... with our equipment?" "Nothing's wrong with it," Song assured him, "at least as far as I know. This doesn't really have anything to do with the equipment itself so much as the four units the equipment is currently occupying. We are going to need those units. For people." "Oh, of course," Teng agreed. "Of course. God, yes. Why would you even call people? Don't tell me you are keeping people out in the storm!"

"No," Song replied. "We are not keeping anyone out in the storm. The storms have passed. It is the aftermath we must now face. We're going to do what we can to keep people healthy and alive until things get 'back to normal,' whatever that means." "Good! And good luck! But I still don't understand why you're calling me." "You are not a lawyer, are you Mr. Teng? No, neither am I. But apparently my boss's boss has talked with several of them about this. Simply put, if we vacate those units without your consent, which as you say we will certainly do if we need to, you may have certain legal rights when things are 'back to normal,' and you may bring some sort of claim or action. If, on the other hand, you consent to this vacation now, you will not bring any claim or action, and my boss's boss will have one less thing to worry him at night."

How typical, Teng thought. Maybe an eighth of the planet was at risk of dying in the streets and slums of Southeast Asia after storms the like of which the world had never seen, and this guy's bosses were putting the screws to him about Teng suing them two years down the road over a bunch of mismatched and outdated satellite gear he'd never even seen. "I see," he told Song. "And what's in it for me if I make it easier for your boss's boss to sleep at night by giving away every capital asset DataBank owns?"

"Another merger, of a sort," Song replied. "Daftar

Banten, the warehousing company, is, even as we chat here so pleasantly, in the process of transferring ownership of this facility, and a number of its similar facilities on Java, to an entity known as Rumah Pelarian, effective immediately. We are offering you and your parent company, and the other owners of warehouse unit leases, membership in Rumah Pelarian in return for your consent to vacate your units immediately, with no guarantee of safety or return for any of your property."

"Membership? You mean stock? How much? At what valuation?" Teng had never dreamed of having any part of a refugee shelter company in Jakarta, but he prided himself on his flexibility and open mind. "Not stock," Song continued in the fashion of somebody who'd given the same explanation many times already that day. "Membership. Rumah Pelarian is neither a corporation nor a charity. It is neither a partnership nor a non-profit, although it shares many characteristics with such entities. Rumah Pelarian was created yesterday, after the scope of this disaster began becoming clear, under a relatively obscure provision in Indonesian law that enables the formation of what are called *zakat waqfs*. Are you familiar with sharia law, Mr. Teng?" "No, not really," Teng replied, trying to follow Song's story.

"Your religion is your concern, of course," Song continued. "But '*zakat*,' the giving of alms to the poor and needy, is one of the five pillars of Islam. Every Muslim with

199

a certain amount of wealth, which is called *nisab*, is required by sharia law to share something, the *zakat*, with those who do not have *nisab*. *Waqfs*, again under Islamic sharia law, are a kind of inalienable religious endowment, somewhat akin to a charitable trust and also like a church in some ways. So, *zakat waqfs*, which are legally recognized under Indonesian law, albeit rarely used here to date, can roughly be described as inalienable charitable trusts for the benefit of the poor and needy. A membership in Rumah Pelarian, our *zakat waqf*, means that you and your company ... BollyMadras ... would join our collective efforts to help the poor and needy—to take care of the refugees that are even now flooding towards our warehouses."

"But I'm not a Muslim," Teng blurted out. "And I don't think Salman or Sanjay or any other BollyMadras employees are—I don't even know!" "There is no legal requirement that members of a *zakat waqf* practice the faith," Song replied. "And though on a personal level I may hope that you do submit to faith in Allah, surely that is more likely to happen if I work with you to do good than if I just put your electronic equipment out in the rain and wait to see if you sue me?" "I see," Teng replied, not seeing how membership in this Islamic trust could benefit him any more than a worthless lawsuit over outdated electronics that were discarded to give succor to people fleeing one of history's great disasters.

"As a member of your ... trust," Teng began, "would we be obliged in the future to give—to share—more than our four storage units?" "A good question," Song answered. "Your mind opens quickly to this new idea despite the horrors around you. But, as you know, the future is the future, and we do not know who will be blessed with prosperity, with *nisab*, in that future and who will not. If there are many members, engaged in many pursuits, some of those pursuits will find favor with the world and others will not. Those who are fortunate will share with other members who are less so. If the membership as a whole is more fortunate than not, the *zakat waqf* itself will extend those blessings to others who have even less."

"Share how much?" Teng asked. "How much is this *nisab*, and how much will the members give—or get?" "Traditionally," Song explained, "the *nisab* is the equivalent of 200 silver dirhams or 20 gold dinars. In Indonesia, several different organizations have been minting and using dirhams and dinars for several years to promote alternatives to interest based banking and inflation based currencies. Dinars weigh about 4.4 grams and dirhams about 3.1 grams."

Teng was silent for a moment. He was trying to wrap his head around this new Indonesian religious entity and at the same time calculate the real value, if any, of the DataBank electronics stored in Song's warehouse. The DataBank accountants had dutifully recorded the cost and calculated the depreciation of their assets, but he'd pitched his merger on the basis that DataBank's intangibles, its (admittedly limited) ability to do actual satcomm work, were its real value. After sitting alone in his hotel the last few days watching pieces of people's houses careen randomly down Mao Tse Tsung Boulevard it was hard for him to put any value on anything intangible.

Song's trust sounded to him like some sort of Islamic *keiretsu*, the Japanese term for a family of companies with interlocking stockholders and boards of directors, with a charitable component of some kind. In Hong Kong, they really were family businesses and they called them *chao dai*, historical dynasties. But their charity was definitely kept strictly inside the family. Maybe, Teng thought, glancing out the window at the broken buildings below, a disaster of this scale could bring a wider spectrum of people together.

"Why now?" he finally asked Song directly? "Why is this, this … *zakat waqf* the right tool for this moment?"

"Another good question!" Song answered happily. "I really do hope that we are fated to meet someday, Mr. Teng. Why now? On the one hand, there are those who would argue that it is never the wrong time to create a *zakat waqf*. If times are good, they say, then it is crucial that those who have less still have enough to keep them happy; enough to keep them from upsetting the apple cart, as the saying goes. If times are bad, on the other hand, then they say that it is important that those who have nothing do not lose hope because one of them could be the one who turns things around for everybody."

"So it's an insurance policy either way," Teng said more or less to himself. "Yes, in a way. And like any insurance policy," Song continued, "it's only as valuable as its surety is reliable." "So why are your members so reliable?" Teng asked. He'd pretty much concluded that just about anything he could get from Song was, in the end, going to be better than suing the warehouse in an Indonesian court for jettisoning DataBank's used equipment in a moment of global tragedy. But he wanted to hear more about why Song thought it was the right move now, not even a day after the storms finally dissipated.

Teng looked out the window again at two houses a few blocks over in the direction of the Olympic Market. One had lost its roof completely and he could see a crumbled interior wall and a swath of debris. The other was relatively unscathed with just a couple of broken windows and a few missing pieces of siding. Would those people work together to fix their houses, he wondered, or would the fortunate family just look out for itself? *They say disasters bring out the best in people*, Teng told himself, hoping it was true.

"I know nothing more about most of our members than I do about DataBank or your company, BollyMadras, that I just now learned about," Song replied. "As I said, we are extending this offer of membership to all our tenants in all the warehouses here on Java that will be used to house refugees for the duration of this crisis. I cannot vouch for the reliability of any of our members aside perhaps from our company, Daftar Banten. To a certain extent, it is a lottery, a numbers game. Daftar Banten owns several warehouses, each has many tenants, and each has some small chance of great success." "Then why do this?" Teng replied. "Why not just empty everyone's units and take your chances down the road."

"Because," Song replied calmly, "although I cannot vouch for the reliability of our members, I can report that my boss's bosses are of the opinion that the form of our enterprise—the *zakat waqf*—will itself offer invaluable structural advantages, and that simply reforming Daftar Banten itself into a *zakat waqf* would not be enough to give us the full benefit of those advantages." "What do you mean?" Teng asked. "What can a *zakat waqf* do that a different kind of corporation cannot? Why can't Daften Banten do all this itself?"

"At the moment," Song admitted, "it perhaps makes very little difference and Daften Banten could itself perhaps do all that can be done right now. But the thought is that this great catastrophe is likely to lead to certain changes, which will make certain opportunities available to our *zakat waqf* that would not otherwise be available to Daftar Banten alone." "Like what?" "The feeling among my superiors,"

Song reported, "is that the social and political consequences of these climate storms will be both widespread and far-reaching. Are you seeing the pictures there in Phnom Phen?"

"No," Teng told him. "Our power just came back, but the TV is not picking up any channels."

"That may be deliberate," Song told him. "Some believe that communications are being blocked to keep the full scale of the disaster from becoming known. I disagree, but in the end it will not matter: the pictures show a swath of devastation almost 4,000 kilometers wide." "I talked to my cousin in Hong Kong," Teng said. "It's pretty bad there." "It's pretty bad everywhere in Southeast Asia," Song agreed. "And the thought is that because this was such a great disaster, the response to it will not be the normal country by country rebuilding. My superiors expect the UN and other global political entities to take a larger, more visible, more active role in the aftermath of this disaster, these disasters, whatever we wind up calling it. They believe that a *zakat waqf* will be favored by those entities because of its religious and charitable characteristics, and that they can position Rumah Pelarian's members to provide a wide variety of goods and services to the relief and reclamation projects, which, *Insh Allah*, will benefit both the members and the wider community."

"Favored why? Why would religious charities have any advantages?" Teng knew that all bureaucracies had blind spots, but he didn't see anything to make an inalienable religious trust special in the global relief world. If anything, wouldn't they want to avoid religious entanglement, or at least deemphasize it? "At the moment," Song replied calmly, "they wouldn't have any advantages. But, as they say, you can't make big money unless you zig when everyone else zags and it turns out you were right.

"The feeling is that there will be much public and institutional sentiment towards making sure that what people call the 'disaster capitalism complex' does not profit from this tragedy. The hunch is that those sentiments will lead to a future where 'not for profit religious charities,' like Rumah Pelarian, will be favored over purely corporate entities like Daftar Banten. It's a gamble. But it's also a kind of insurance policy, a trade of some of BollyMadras' potential for a share of other members' potential. Most of all, it's a way of doing right by all these poor bastards staggering out of Jakarta with little hope and nothing more than what they could grab as their lives collapsed around them."

"When you put it that way," Teng smiled, "there's hardly a choice, is there. OK, as managing director of BollyMadras, parent company of DataBank, I agree to vacate our lease on your four storage units and authorize you to take any reasonable actions with respect to our equipment and to become a member of your Indonesian trust—what did you call it, Rumor Pelirien?" "Rumah Pelarian," Song replied.

"Welcome. Congratulations! I hope we meet again in circumstances that are better for all because of our conversation today." The phone went quiet.

Teng stared silently out the window at the street. People were starting to mill about, and he could see them bowing and hugging each other, sharing their obvious joy and relief at having survived. They were smiling and laughing, gesturing ebulliently at one another. Teng looked up and down the boulevard. It was covered by a layer of broken glass and surrounded by debris in every color of the rainbow. But people kept running through the wreckage into the street and finding moments of joy with each other amidst the rubble.

Chapter Eleven

Paul

Denver, Colorado, U.S.A.

April 19, 2012

It's not like it had never happened to him before. Ehrlich had been giving speeches, lectures, and talks around the world for almost 50 years now. Maybe, he thought to himself, he'd seen more than his fair share of zealous, single-minded, long-winded amateurs because of some of the things he'd said and written. That was probably fair enough. Once, in 1994, on a pleasant May afternoon in Fairbanks, Alaska of all places, he gave a general talk and Q&A at the Institute of Arctic Biology that was interrupted no less than seven times by a well-meaning older gentleman with a long white beard hell-bent on convincing him that a small blue and gold butterfly his team had trapped outside the Costa Rican town of San Vito the year before and identified as a female *Memphis niedhoeferi*, generally seen only in Mexico, was actually a female *Memphis acidalia*, generally seen only in Colombia.

In that man's mind, molded by the long interior winters, great stakes—maybe the fate of the planet—rested on whether one butterfly was flying further south across the mountains towards the equator or another was flying the opposite direction across the water away from the equator.

No fanatic like a butterfly fanatic Ehrlich reminded himself. Every time he published something lepidopteran, his voicemail, inbox, and mailbox inevitably filled up with deep, heartfelt complaints about how wrong he was and how much his stupidity pained his readers. But one thing was for sure: 18 years later and three thousand miles to the southeast, the fate of the planet was definitely at stake. Not just here, but everywhere.

So maybe it was good for everyone that these two were at least as passionate about space colonization as that wizened old curmudgeon had been about butterflies. Biodiversity was important in every population, even one as unique as that strange group of non-academics who felt themselves called to share their views of the world at academic conferences, promoting their causes and quests among people who'd been carefully inoculated against chasing dreams. And from what he'd heard thus far in Denver, maybe things had gotten so bad that dreaming about something as unrealistic as space colonies was all anyone had left to hold on to.

He'd walked downtown past the capitol towards the zoo with Clive Hamilton and Corey Bradshaw last night for vegan comfort food and they'd scared the crap out of him. Even if the whole world started acting like responsible adults tomorrow, their work showed it was still going to hell. The time for action was long past. Four degrees Celsius average

209

global warming was now the irreversible baseline. Coastal inundation, bigger cyclones, water scarcity, and decimated biodiversity were the inevitable future consequences of unsustainable growth. The loss of biodiversity in coral reefs alone was tragic enough to silence him as he sat and shoved his food about aimlessly, staring at a picture of General Woundwort facing down the farm watchdog. It seemed an apt metaphor for the coming climate battles—greedy rabbits being torn to bits by rabid dogs.

As he listened to Corey and Clive banter amicably about whether Jakarta or Rotterdam was best suited to survive massive unprecedented inundation in any recognizable form and speculate about what crops would be most efficient in the warmer troposphere of the anthropocene, Ehrlich reflected back to the days when he'd always been the most pessimistic person in any room. He hadn't always been right, but the world had moved a long way in his direction. He felt some responsibility for that. Now, standing in front of 75 sociologists who'd come to hear him talk about sustainability at a conference with an oxymoronic 'real utopias' theme, he didn't feel any responsibility at all for the two amateurs screaming past each other. But, he thought to himself, he felt it was important that they were here screaming, whether or not anyone but him was listening. Dispassionate people weren't generally first adapters. Maybe the world had finally moved past him and these two were just confirmation. Or maybe all those years of feeling like the crazy one in the room just made him enjoy listening to people who seemed even crazier.

The two men were about 30 and 40. Both appeared to be in pretty good shape. The younger man was very skinny and had hard, hard brown eyes. His brown hair was clipped short. He wore a tan tweed sport coat, an old yellow tie, and grey trousers with a white shirt. Ehrlich would have bet just about any amount that he'd worn that exact same outfit to more than ten other conferences, talks, or seminars. Looking around curiously at his professional colleagues, Ehrlich wondered how many of them would admit the same. There were a few, sprinkled through the audience, with shiny shoes and sharp creases in newer suits, but the vast majority didn't dress much better.

"You will never know that believing the world is dying is not itself a self-fulfilling prophecy!" the older of the two declared. "You are part of the world! Maybe you are part of what is killing it!" "Yet nobody thinks I have the power to save it," the younger man replied. "If I were the one killing the world, I would save it by jumping off a bridge!" A quick murmur went through the audience at that. Ehrlich had to agree with the crowd: from the look of the man, suicide might be a real concern. Over the years he'd heard about several unaffiliated amateur zealots who'd taken their own lives. The suicide rate among academics with institutional affiliations, on the other hand, was exceptionally low, especially for tenured professors. Perhaps, Ehrlich mused, that was a particularly morbid consequence of how much more committed the crazy zealots were to whatever quests they followed than his peers were.

Most of the "real" sociologists in his audience were infinitely more committed to advancing their careers, sending their kids to good colleges, and having enough to retire comfortably than they were to any intellectual, spiritual, or moral ideal. Prospering in their worlds was far more important than changing them. These two, on the other hand, looked like they'd never have kids in college, careers, or enough to retire at all. Every word they said, though, made it clear how truly they believed in the changes they wanted to make. But at least one of them believed in something that wasn't a real utopia at all. Probably both of them did. Truth, Ehrlich knew as well as anyone, was slippery and in short supply.

The younger man's worn brown loafers, Ehrlich noticed, were unpolished and uncared for, but were actually a very expensive brand. Probably a gift, Ehrlich thought. Even those in the audience that shared the young man's casual style, however, didn't share his intensely serious visage. They'd learned to not take themselves so seriously; to find little moments of humor in each other; to not make every conference a matter of life and death. Ehrlich could tell the younger man took himself deadly seriously and doubted he'd laughed very much in a long time. Ehrlich would have wagered a lot of money that he was single and had no children.

The older man wore generic blue jeans and a plain black long sleeved shirt. His long black hair was braided neatly into a ponytail and, together with his dark features and eyes, gave him something of a tribal look. He was very handsome. His dirty athletic shoes looked like they'd been handed down from previous generations, and Ehrlich was willing to wager they had little or no tread and would leak in the smallest puddle. He'd probably never worn that exact outfit before and might never wear it again. It was obviously not something he thought or cared about. He was still young enough to believe that this academic audience would judge him on the truth of his words alone, that his appearance, like his (lack of) credentials, was irrelevant to the truth value of what he said. At the same time, he was old enough not to care what other people thought. It was not a sartorial combination.

Ehrlich looked around again and saw a few people in similarly casual dress, most of them older, with pleasant, bemused looks on their faces, entertained by this interruption without taking it very seriously. The prospect of imminent chaos at a sociology lecture was, for most of them, much more interesting than the dire warnings about the imminent consequences of unsustainability he'd been giving before the disruption. They'd made their peace with their lives long ago and no longer had any interest in wrapping their latest research up in bows and fighting to change the world. They'd found their own private utopias with their families, and Ehrlich suspected the same was true of the man with the ponytail—that he had a wife and kids somewhere who gave his life a balance his interlocutor might never find. Yet he was clearly just as passionate about saving his world.

"You can't negotiate with the Earth!" the man with the ponytail said. "That's what Dr. Ehrlich is telling us. He's telling us the only way to maintain anything like the kind of civilization we have now is to increase our resource base dramatically. We can do that! We can create resources in space and decrease Earth's population at the same time! We're living off of Earth's capital, and that's not sustainable—that's what he's established. That's a fact; his research proves it. But he's not considering adding new capital to that equation. Sustainability is possible through a combination of creating new capital resources and moving resource consumption off Earth. That's what space colonization can do! It can create resources in a way that reduces the terrestrial population!"

"Reduces the population?" the younger man with the crew cut scoffed. "Are you incapable of basic math? What if you moved twenty-thousand people into orbit in the next

214

two years? That's so far past the most optimistic projections that really it's not even worth discussing—but let's say you inspire people to some kind of superhuman effort. How many more people than that will be born in those two years? You're lighting a match on the surface of the sun and pretending to bring light to Mars. And you're using a ton of energy to do it!"

He stopped and looked up at Ehrlich. "Energy use is the single best measure of how fast we're destroying the planet, isn't that what you said? Energy-intensive efforts to move a few thousand people into space will inevitably push the rest of humanity further and further down the path of destruction. That doesn't mean it's not the right thing to do. It doesn't mean everyone has to die. But it means we have to be realistic. Either we're all going to die here together or some of us are going to get away. Those are the only two choices. You can't seriously believe that it's better to all die here together—that if there aren't enough lifeboats for everyone, we shouldn't build lifeboats for anyone?" He stared longingly at Ehrlich like Noah looking up at God asking for permission to build the ark.

"But the Earth's not going to die in the next two years!" the man in the black shirt shouted back. "We've got some unknown amount of time before we all die. One and a half Earths—that's what he said we need for seven billion people." Ehrlich nodded instinctively, then caught himself, not wanting to be pulled in to their conversation any more than he already was. "We can build another half-an-Earth's worth of resources up there in 50 to 100 years. Knowing that we're up there building those resources will give people here an incentive to adopt the sustainable principles Dr. Ehrlich is trying to teach us about!" He looked down at his notes. "Population rescaling, social equity, shock buffering, natural capital planning—that's what he's saying we need. You really think that people are going to accept those solutions after you tell them that they're all going to die? And, by the way, you're going to accelerate their demise by using their limited and declining energy and resources to save your happy few? You're insane! The only way they're going to accept his solutions is if there's a big pile of gold for them at the end of the tunnel." He raised his arms dramatically and pointed to the ceiling with both hands. "Out there in the asteroid belt, there's the biggest pile of gold that anyone's ever seen. In 250 years, we could build another two or three Earths worth of resources!"

He had a point there, Ehrlich thought, nodding in agreement once again. It was something he'd struggled with for a long time as he'd tried to warn the world what was coming. Real changes probably required giving people a reason for hope. Telling people that the science showed they were on a path to doom generally wasn't enough to make a critical mass of them change their behavior in any meaningful way. Some of them just didn't care. Some figured if they were going to hell, they might as well get on with it and burn out as brightly as they could along the way. Sometimes, he thought, whole generations were like that.

His generation, the so-called flower children of the sixties, was like that. They gave up on love and peace, at least on any systemic scale, decided greed was good, and took to meaningless consumption with a rare intensity. No matter what you thought of the books Ehrlich and his compadres had written, the songs his idols had sung, the poems they'd written, he was pretty sure his generation had, on the whole, pushed the Earth further into decline. They hadn't even slowed the process, much less found a new path steered by love instead of greed. They long ago stopped becoming their revolution and started being part of the problem.

Neither of these men was old enough to be a baby boomer like him, Ehrlich thought. He figured the older of the two had been born in the early 70s and come of age in the early 90s. The fall of the Berlin Wall, the end of the Cold War—those were the moments that shaped his early adult life. A sense of possibility, a new vision of hope. He'd seen them, at least briefly. Ehrlich wasn't sure whether that brief moment of optimism had lasted all the way to 9/11, but it certainly didn't survive much longer. Great fear makes all possibilities seem hopeless. The man with the ponytail hadn't quite embraced the great fear completely, Ehrlich thought, he still believed survival was possible for the many, not just the few. He still believed in hope.

The younger man with the crew cut, on the other hand, would have been just 18 or 20 on that fateful day shortly after the turn of the last century. It was natural, Ehrlich thought, for him to be so ready to accept the climate death of 99% or more of the human race. He would have grown up with no hope at all, just fear. No wonder he dreamt only of saving himself and a few select others; he'd written off the majority of humanity years ago. He felt no shame at leaving his dead behind. He'd never been taught hope so he never believed in hope.

"He says there will be another 2.5 billion people in 40 years," the grim young man replied, pointing at Ehrlich again. "40 years after that, what, another four billion? 150 years after that? Many fewer, because civilization will certainly collapse long before your 250 year plan fails it miserably. And nobody is going to stop us from leaving. Most people aren't as thoughtful as you," the crew cut man smiled grimly. "Most people don't even know that he says their future is doomed," he jerked his finger at Ehrlich again, "and most of those who know don't give a crap. Half of the people won't ever learn of their pending doom, half of the rest won't believe the information is true, and half of the rest will still be happy to take our money. They'll all think we're

218

crazy."

"And you'll have no compunctions about taking advantage of them!" the man in the black shirt countered. "You'll treat them like they're already dead! You'll waste their resources and degrade their environment to save yourselves." "You'll do the same thing!" the reply came from the man in the crew cut as he picked up his briefcase and started moving towards the door, eyes locked on his opponent. "You'll do the exact same thing. You'll just pretend that you're doing it to save them."

Ehrlich looked up at the door and saw a group of concerned staff members in maroon shirts and black pants moving nervously into the crowd clutching their walkie-talkies and brandishing clipboards. "Wait," he said before he realized he'd started talking again. "Our guests raise some interesting points." He looked down at the two of them, looked at his lecture notes, and looked back at them for an uncomfortable moment. His whole career he'd felt sympathetic towards passionate non-academics like these two. He'd often wondered what would happen if they got a chance to fully speak their piece. Now he was almost 80 years old. He didn't care much about decorum and he was curious how they'd handle their moment in the spotlight.

"Before I resume my talk—which I do intend to finish in the allotted time," he assured the rest of the audience, which continued to perk up as things went even further off track—"I'd like each of you to give us a brief summary, an elevator pitch if you will, of your theories about the relationship between sustainability—which, after all, is what we're supposed to be here talking about—and space colonies." He caught the eye of the pony-tailed man in the black shirt, who, Ehrlich suspected, had a more complicated ideology than the other man. "Since our friend on my right," Ehrlich gestured towards the man with the scuffed expensive loafers, "was about to have the last word, why don't we give him that and ask you to go first?"

"Some say last words are for fools who haven't said enough," the handsome, darker-skinned man replied without missing a beat. "But to answer your question, the relationship between sustainability and space colonies is a new way of thinking. For many thousands of years, humans have proceeded under the false assumption that the worlds consists of 'things' that 'move' through time. That is incorrect. Neither that chalkboard nor I is a thing and neither of us moves through time. We are actually 'events,' unfolding interactions of energy and time."

Ehrlich thought he could actually see the little flurry of interest that had risen from the disruption vanish from the audience. Nothing was guaranteed to alienate social scientists so much as a claim that some 'new physics' made some such ideology or the other absolutely true.

"That outdated idea that people, trees, rocks,

minerals, whales, etc, etc, are all things moving through time, was a very powerful idea. It describes more than 99% of the human experience quite well. As a result, what we call 'Western civilization' fooled itself into thinking that the world had an infinite supply of new things, that there would always be more things just a little further out there, and so concluded that having more things was better than having fewer things. As Professor Ehrlich has taught and showed us for years, however, having more and more things turns out not to be such a good way of living. It turns out to be unsustainable and world destroying.

"Interestingly, though, if the universe keeps expanding forever, that ideology might actually be tenable, despite being strictly inaccurate. More urgently, however, whether or not that ideology is tenable in a relatively short-term sense depends on whether or not people achieve large scale space colonization and master living in space. If we colonize the solar system, our resources will once again be unlimited in any practical sense because the 'one and a half Earths' the Professor says seven billion people need is but a minute micro-percentage of what is available in the heliosphere. Even near-Earth space contains many more resources than even 40 billion people could use.

"So, if we learn to live in space, we can potentially continue to live like having more things is unambiguously superior to having fewer things for a long long time. I believe, however—and some may find this ironic—that people who think and live that way, people like us, will never be able to master living in space. Because although the solar system itself may be practically endless, the space colonies people must learn to inhabit in order to colonize it will themselves be just the opposite. They will be bounded, closed, finite, like no previous habitat in all of human history. Only by mastering life in a closed system, in a space colony, can humanity move from a spaceship that was once, for all practical purposes, an open environment—Spaceship Earth—to another spaceship that is now, for all practical purposes, an open environment—Spaceship Solar System."

Ehrlich smiled at that, although looking around the room he could see that he was one of the few who'd followed the point. Even the near solar system, he realized, from the asteroid belt to Venus, contained hundreds, maybe even thousands, of Earths worth of resources. If all that capital became open for development, humanity could once again worship greed and accumulation, at least for as long as it took to colonize and process all of it, which would be a long, long time. And by then, they'd undoubtedly have opened up the great gas giants, Jupiter and Saturn, and their moons, great storehouses of treasure, creating additional resources to plunder. They'd move on and on and on, conquering and destroying the natural world on an ever-increasing scale across the universe.

But, the dark skinned man seemed to be saying, people couldn't survive together in artificial hollowed out space colonies if they thought like that. That was the irony of it, he said. Ehrlich saw his point: you could only get at the abundance of space by learning to live without abundance. Ehrlich wasn't quite ready to buy in, but it had a certain ring of truth to it nonetheless. But weren't the technical challenges the only real hard parts? Soldiers and sailors lived in submarines, he thought. They lived there for a long time. What was the difference? Why would living in space colonies be any different from serving aboard submarines?

"My small contribution towards such mastery and such colonies," the ponytailed man continued, "has been to rework certain philosophical arguments which were based on incorrect premises: that people are 'individual' 'things' who have 'rights' and 'duties.' I have reformulated those arguments by substituting the correct premises: people are events who make choices." Ehrlich looked around and saw that the earnest young man in the black shirt had now lost his audience completely. He could almost smell their disdain. He'd just told them that, in addition to a new physics, he'd also rewritten the history of philosophy. It was so outrageous it made Ehrlich smile again. That was more than he could have hoped for. Nobody with any kind of academic career could ever do anything like this and survive. But maybe none of them would survive unless somebody did it, Ehrlich thought. He'd been explaining it slowly and methodically for years and arguably hadn't gotten any further than this passionate young man with big dreams.

"My 'elevator pitch,' then, is pretty simple," the ponytailed man continued. "To live in a closed environment, our political and social rules and norms need to be derived from a restatement of the categorical imperative in physically accurate terms: don't make choices for other people. By acting always to increase the choices available to others, people will have the best chance of surviving and prospering in a closed environment like a space colony. Or to put it in another way: to survive and prosper in a closed environment like a space colony, people will have to become completely sustainable, to minimize entropy in ways we can't even imagine." He looked up at Ehrlich with a completely serene visage. "By learning how to live sustainably, people will open the resources of the heavens, which are for all practical purposes limitless." Ehrlich looked back at him and felt a strange pride in his earnest eloquence. Ehrlich certainly wasn't ready to sign off on his new physics or his new philosophy, but his ideas were interesting. Additional resources would solve a lot of problems.

"He's right about one thing," the younger man responded quickly. "We have to open the resources of the heavens. Because the resources of the Earth are doomed. You heard him—he's never going to move a million people to orbit before another four million are born to replace them! The Earth, my friends, is doomed. That's my elevator pitch. It's doomed and we have to admit it and start dealing with it. Best case scenario, this planet manages to hang on for a few million years until the Sun becomes a red giant and swallows it. Worst case scenario, an asteroid hits the Moon in a few months. Most likely, humans continue to plunder and reproduce like mad and you've got another 50 or 100 years. Either way, the Earth, like all of us, is mortal, and its best years are far behind us." He looked directly at Ehrlich, then at the man in the black shirt, then he swept his vision around the crowd, looking directly into as many eyes as he could. "None of you can save this planet any more than you can live forever. But you can save yourselves.

"Some of you might think a few million years sounds pretty good," he continued, "but you're kidding yourself if you think humanity is going to last even a small fraction of that time. Look at the consequences Dr. Ehrlich has been telling people about for what, 30 years? Ocean warming, mass extinction, biomonism—they're all real. And what have people done about them? Nothing!" He looked up at Ehrlich with his hard steady eyes. "Not only are you not going to save the planet, most of humanity is going to die without ever hearing your name or learning that you foretold

225

their doom, much less implementing your so-called remedies.

"But that's not even the worst thing! Not only do people ignore their impending doom and refuse to make even small compromises, but what do they do with the time they have left?" He turned and swept the crowd with his eyes again. "They kill each other. They plant explosives in markets and drop bombs on each other from robotic planes. They're fighting a gang war on the Titanic after the Captain's sounded the iceberg alarm!"

He looked up at Ehrlich once again. "My elevator pitch, as you put it, is that space colonies offer a subset of people a sustainable alternative to the impending death of the Earth. Good people," he continued in a confident voice, "can work together to leave the bad people down here and start over up there. For too long, we've pretended, and maybe even convinced ourselves, that all people can be good; that nobody is born bad. But if you look around, that's just not true. Some people are incorrigibly evil, and there's nothing to be done about it but leave them behind. Some people are incapable of the discipline that true sustainability requires and there's nothing to be done about it but leave them behind. Unfortunately, that will be as true in space as here on Earth. That will be true as long as people are people."

Ehrlich could see people around the room nodding.

226

He was a little surprised. Innate human evil, after all, was somewhat antithetical to the entire sociological project. But he could see the attraction of what the young man offered. A new start, a chosen few—these were dreams that had always resonated. It was a clean, simple message, and it was easy for people to get their heads around it.

"So I don't pretend that life in space will be glamorous, or fun," he continued. "And I don't pretend that it will be some kind of new age playground where everybody gets to make their own choices. Space will be strict, rigorous, and disciplined. Only a small number will be suited for it—people who can conform to society without ever asking society to conform to them. Undisciplined non-conformists won't last long in space. Sustainability in space means routine, discipline, and predictability. Life on Earth is unsustainable because too many people forget their place and demand to receive more than they give. Life in space offers the rest of us a chance for sustainable survival in the security of people who know their place and are content to get less than they give."

"Thank you both," Ehrlich nodded as a half-hearted round of polite applause drifted across the room, "for sharing your ideas on sustainability, space colonization and possible futures. The invitation to this conference said that the idea of real utopias embraces the tension between dreams and practice and I think you have given us an excellent

227

demonstration of that tension." He could see the audience settling back into their comfortable seats. "Resuming our previous discussion on designing to promote social equity," Ehrlich fell back into the familiar rhythms of his lecture. In the back of his mind, though, he knew the world needed to hear more unfamiliar ideas that made people uncomfortable.

Chapter Twelve

Onifire

Regents Park, London

April 20, 2022

The best thing about Regents Park, Onifire thought to herself for the hundredth time, was the never-ending variety of people. It wasn't as touristy as Hyde Park or as self-consciously British as Hampstead. It was mostly just plain. Neat grass surrounded by clean sidewalks. It didn't tell you what to do or who to be. Maybe that's why it attracted so many interesting people to come and do so many different things. Today she'd seen some American kids playing baseball next to the cricket pitch, stopped a young couple from Pakistan or India to pet their darling old English bulldog 'Marley,' and watched a busload of elderly Japanese women stroll slowly through the gardens. She'd only been here about twenty minutes.

And it was such a pleasant walk from her home in St. Pancreas. The joy of walking through and by so many gardens and beautiful landscapes on her way to the park never failed to lift her spirits. Today she'd heard a cheerful flock of cuckoos in Gordon Square chirping as she passed by, sharing their joy at the coming summer. She'd stopped to listen to them for a good five minutes.

Maybe on her way home, she thought, she'd walk

around the other side of University Hospital and go through
the University to Russell Square. One of her closest
colleagues, Kat Morgan, had her office there, across from the
Cabmen's shelter and next to the Brunei Gallery. She and
Kat had been working together on a biodiversity project in
the Loru Rainforest on Espiritu Santo in the Vanuatu Islands
for the last three years, ever since she'd left Howard Gall's
doomed submersible project behind in Brunei. A shudder
went through her at the thought of those poor souls she'd
helped send down to the bottom of the ocean. Trapped
helplessly on the safety of the ocean floor as their control
teams capsized and collapsed in the climate storms above
them, they'd plummeted into anarchy and madness. Two
years later, she still felt guilty Howard hadn't taken her
warnings. She wasn't sure whether or not Grok Martin and
his people in Nicaragua had either, but she'd find out soon
enough.

She hadn't talked to Howard since she'd stormed out
of his social constructs committee meeting and found her
way back to London and the relative stability and safety of
academia. Her friend G'Ranger, who'd gone back to
Singapore before the climate storms destroyed the project
and was now working with some sort of vidpro foundation in
New Greater Jakarta, told her that none of the IT people
who'd survived that disaster were still working with Howard.

Even Mark Wells, who'd been so loyal to Howard

and his vision, was gone, working with aquatic mammal preservation groups in Hawaii. She'd had lunch with him last December when she was there for a biodiversity conference. Howard himself, Wells had told her, was still plunging ahead, as determined as ever that in the end he would be the one to save a select few; as confident as ever that he'd turn out to be the hero. Not even losing his wife, Delilah, to the work Grok and G'Sille Martin were doing had diminished Howard's belief in himself. She'd seen Howard being interviewed on holovid from Russia just a few weeks ago, in a friend's apartment, but her pain was still too fresh for her to listen to his voice, and she'd excused herself to the restroom until the program changed.

Her biodiversity project on Espiritu Santo started in 2016, three years before the first great climate storms. Ten years before that, the French National Museum of Natural History had led an unprecedented effort of more than 150 researchers from 25 different countries to comprehensively document the terrestrial and marine flora and fauna of the island. Fifteen years later, they still didn't have a comprehensive list and they knew they never would. They simply couldn't count fast enough to be sure none of the species they counted went extinct before they finished counting. The climate storms, which swept through the Vanuatu Islands two or three times a year now, didn't help.

She and Kat were there as cultural liaisons. Their

role was to facilitate the project's interactions with the locals. Few people knew that the Vanuatu Islands were the home of one of the world's largest concentration of different languages per capita. There were only about 300,000 people in all of Vanuatu but they spoke more than 110 different mother tongues—an average of fewer than 3,000 people per language.

And people here certainly weren't isolated in remote mountain valleys. They almost all lived in villages on the shore. On Espiritu Santo itself, as she recalled, there were only about four semi-isolated inland villages, and she was pretty sure none of them had more than 200 people at the very most. On the coast, on the other hand, there was a village at least every twenty kilometers or so, some of them with 1000 people, or more. In New Guinea, people spoke so many different languages because they'd lived in isolation for so long. On Espiritu Santo it was because they'd lived at the crossroads of the South Pacific for so many generations.

She remembered that on their first day in Port Olry, she and Kat had been so eager to count how many different languages they could hear in a day. They'd come across fifteen, in a town of about 4,000 people. The two of them could only speak three of those—some cultural liaisons they'd been! Luckily, most of the people the biodiversity project had contact with were trying to sell them something or trying to chat up her or Kat. For a place where so many different people had come together over so many hundreds and thousands of years, it was still very much a man's world on Espiritu Santo. Linguistic diversity alone didn't necessarily promote cultural adaptation, they'd decided, any more than biodiversity inevitably led to interspecies cooperation.

Once it became clear that the original goal of compiling a comprehensive list of species living on or around Espiritu Santo was unreachable, the project's mission evolved into an attempt to track the loss of biodiversity as closely as possible. Once they realized they couldn't catalog all the flora or fauna, they were determined to be a lot better at chronicling its demise. And there'd been a lot of extinction and biodiversity loss to report in the last three years.

The first great climate storms in 2019 hadn't touched Espiritu Santo. They'd swept up from the Indian Ocean and down from the North Pacific and bounced off each other and around the equator in Indonesia, the Philippines, Malaysia, and other places that were—from their perspective—comfortably far away, safely on the other side of Australia. That didn't last.

Just a bit more than a year later, in September of 2020, the water in the North Tasman Sea between Brisbane and Norfolk Island reached historic high temperatures of more than 28° Celsius. For perhaps the first time in history, an early fall tropical cyclone, Anne, developed almost 30° south of the equator and, driving towards even warmer water, moved northeast through Vanuatu, Fiji, Tonga, Samoa, and the rest of the South Pacific. The physical devastation was widespread, but it was nothing compared to the spiritual effect on the islanders.

For thousands of years, the peoples of the South Pacific faced great storms coming from the warmer tropical waters closer to the equator in their north. Those storms generally struck in February and March, after the southern summer had warmed the subtropical waters. Pam, in March 2015, and Winston, in February 2016, had killed more people and caused far more physical damage than Anne, but the psychological effects Onifire and Kat saw and documented were on a completely different scale. The islanders had seen the tides rise a few degrees. They'd read about ocean warming and climate change. But nothing had prepared them for a ferocious September storm forming off Brisbane and wrecking destruction on the islands to the north and east. It was literally their world turned upside down.

Since then, life in the South Pacific had changed, with a sense of urgency unlike anything anyone on the islands had seen for generations. People were reaching out politically, working together locally, and standing up for each other in front of the world as best they could. Their voices had been heard, at least to some extent, and they'd been able to make at least one big change in the world. The UN agency for climate storm prevention and recovery, APORLACT, had drastically expanded last fall beyond its original mission, which was limited to the area of Southeastern Asia directly affected by the first two storms.

Now, after Anne, APORLACT had jurisdiction over recovery and prevention efforts in pretty much every nation that was within 35° of the equator and felt threatened by ocean warming and climate storms. More than two-thirds of the world's inhabited islands were in those latitudes, and as people started to see more climate storms and watch APORLACT spend more money, more and more of them started feeling threatened. It was a lot of territory and a lot of people. It gave APORLACT great power in a lot of places for an undefined period of time—a big change from a single recovery effort in Southeast Asia. Here in London it had the world government conspiracy folks up in arms, making speeches and prophesying doom.

One of APORLACT's governing principles, by UN resolution, was to avoid supporting disaster capitalism—to keep people from profiting from environmental tragedy. To implement that goal, the agency adopted a rule that not-for-profit organizations that were not officially associated with any single government had extensive preferential status when it came to contracts, grants, personnel, and just about every other activity associated with its climate storm damage recovery and prevention efforts. Conveniently, the Espiritu Santo Biodiversity Project was a joint venture between France and Luxembourg and became one of the first organizations to qualify as a preferred APORLACT vendor in November, 2019.

Some of their people had been on the ground on Espiritu Santo for the better part of a decade at that point, and the locals mostly trusted them enough to want to cooperate, especially when they began to see APORLACT spend money. Their project became the natural link between APORLACT and the islanders. They transformed quickly from compiling lists of species into a much more active role and implemented a wide variety of measures to save species, minimize the overall biodiversity loss, and empower islanders to resist future storms and increasing temperatures. They hadn't had a major spring storm this year, at least not yet, and they'd learned how to build barrier walls that provided protected space for mollusks, sea cucumbers, starfish, and other intertidal species—small victories, but substantial ones in the eyes of the islanders fighting for their lives.

Onifire's role as cultural liaison had evolved just as rapidly into some amalgam of human resources director and project coordinator. Sorting through files of resumes, she drafted people into teams for different recovery and prevention projects. She spent most of her time in London now, traveling to Espiritu Santo only two or three times a year, as she was also responsible for teams across Fiji and Samoa. Somehow it was often easier to stay in contact with them all from her office here halfway around the globe.

As she left the gardens and moved north up the Broad Walk towards the zoo, she wondered what was happening on Espiritu Santo today. The rainy season was about to end, and the new threat of early fall storms was at least four months away, so it was as good an opportunity for action as they'd have this year. More and more, though, the projects and people at her desk were focused on building new bureaucracies.

Sometimes she feared that the project, with APORLACT's blessing, was more deeply entrenched in disaster capitalism than any single corporation ever could have been, even if it was officially a non-profit. They were still profiting. They had an artificially small number of competitors and had been first to market by a wide margin. It was unreasonable to expect anyone else to compete with them, at least in the South Pacific, and they continued to pile up projects, money, and contacts.

Onifire wasn't sure how she felt about that, or about the project's recent focus on the 'emerging market' in her home country of Brazil. The accepted wisdom was that there weren't very many tropical storms in the South Atlantic because the intertropical convergence zone—what sailors

237

called the 'doldrums'—typically moved further north during the Northern summer than it moved south during the Southern summer; because the Atlantic was so much narrower at the equator than the Pacific; and because the water of the South Atlantic was generally colder than the water of the South Pacific. The oceans continued to warm, however, and it was certainly possible for a tropical storm to hit Brazil—Hurricane Catalina had destroyed thousands of homes in 2004.

But people in her native country, Onifire knew only too well, hadn't faced great storms for thousands of years. Hurricanes weren't part of her culture and so were even more dangerous to Brazilians than late winter storms like Anne were to the South Pacific Islanders. The preparations Brazil needed were mostly physical, not spiritual—her people were as mentally strong as any and had realized the dangers of climate change as early as anyone. Many of the higher-ups felt this meant a great growth opportunity for APORLACT and, by extension, for the biodiversity project. There were about 300 million people in Brazil and more than 80% of them lived within 200 km of the Atlantic coast between the equator and the Tropic of Capricorn. If the South Atlantic started producing climate storms on a regular basis, she knew, they'd need all the help they could get. That would be good for her project but catastrophic for her country, which left her feeling depressed and confused.

She walked past the Ready Money Fountain and saw a small crowd had gathered around a group of performers— clowns, jugglers, and tumblers—who were marching loosely around the green to the sounds of circus music. She turned off the path and walked across the lawn to look for Grok and G'Sille, knowing they'd be unable to resist the seemingly spontaneous performance that was actually a daily show— she'd seen it several times.

And, indeed, there they were in the back row, laughing and applauding. From the first time she'd met them, Onifire had been struck by what a perfect pair Grok and G'Sille were, at least physically. Not that either of them was exceptionally beautiful, though they were certainly both attractive. They just fit together really, really well. Grok was a medium size white man with slightly dark features. Onifire figured he had some Mediterranean ancestors, maybe from Spain or Italy. He wore his hair in a long braided ponytail and dressed very casually. G'Sille was much darker skinned and had much darker hair that was cut much shorter in a classic contemporary style. She dressed better and her clothes fit her much better than her husband's did. As soon as they looked at each other you could tell they didn't care. As soon as you looked at them you knew they were together.

Four jugglers stepped forward and began tossing brightly colored clubs back and forth. She caught G'Sille's eye and moved politely through the spectators towards them.

"Hello!" Onifire smiled as she found a place next to G'Sille. "As soon as I saw this, I knew you two would be watching!" G'Sille laughed. "And why shouldn't we take a moment?" she replied, sweeping her arm across the scene. "They're very good! And it is wonderful to see you!" "Thank you," Onifire smiled back. "It's good to be here with both of you! This is one of my favorite parks and these are some of my favorite performers. I thought your daughter was coming? I bet she'd have enjoyed this."

"She'd have enjoyed seeing you!" G'Sille replied with a slightly less joyful smile, "but she felt like she had to stay back in El Ostional. If this thing with Grok and the habs works out, she really wants to be one of the first, one of the first ones—we're actually calling them missionaries, which probably isn't the most sensitive phrase to use." "One of the first on a hab?" Onifire blurted. "But she's still just a child … a teenager! How do you expect her …" "She's 23," G'Sille replied. "She's a very mature young woman."

"She's a dreamer, like her mother," Grok said, turning to join the conversation. "There's no guarantee any of the hab people are even going to ask to listen to me, let alone turn to us, to our daughter, for guidance. Nevertheless, Rally is convinced she will be living in space next year! And so she's back in El Ostional doing her 'astro-training,' running up and down the beach to gain strength and trying to read everything that's ever been written about small scale water purification, waste processing, and solar power." He smiled at his wife. "If I didn't know anything about the power of your family's dreams I'd laugh out loud at her."

"Sssh," G'Sille hushed him quickly. "Don't make fun. You know dreams can't be put in words."

Dreams can't be put in words, Onifire thought to herself. They sure can't. Maybe that's one reason why it's so hard for us to share our dreams together. "I'm sure Rally will be an exceptional … astro-missionary?" she told the couple, "or whatever else she decides to become. There's no doubting that! But," she nodded at Grok, "like you said, that's a long way from now! What about you two? Do you think the habs are going to reach out to you? Do you think they want to learn what you have to teach?"

"I don't know," Grok replied. "I really don't. As you know, the firstmooner tribe didn't really have a plan— or, some would say, they had many contradictory plans, especially about what to do if they did actually manage to build habs. They called them 'cigars!' Like trying to build the first human space colonies wasn't grand enough! People forget that it was only about eighteen months ago that they finished their counterweight and the L_1 platform and the first few blocks for actual habs started moving slowly up their tether!"

"I did forget that," Onifire agreed. "It seems like so much has happened since then! The Chinese trying to claim

L_1, Jeff Bazos buying that island, Diego Garcia, and building the world's biggest spaceport, the firstmooner tribe making their deals with the UN and the Chinese and then with Amazon and the Barcas ... it's all been so crazy! For some reason I always thought that if people went to space, it would all be so planned out and orderly, even though everything I've ever learned about anthropology would have told me it would be exactly the opposite, like this: chaotic, messy, and unplanned. I'm just surprised so few people have died."

"Only a few," Grok agreed. "And, as far as I know, all of them have died by mistake. Died because a beam collapsed, or a test went wrong, or two chemicals accidentally mixed together. So far, I don't think anyone's intentionally killed anyone else up there. But I fear that time is rapidly approaching." "You could say the same thing about the climate storms down here," Onifire interjected. "People have died, but it's all been natural causes so far. There's no reason to think that will last, that nobody will ever be desperate or incompetent enough to resort to violence as their homes are swallowed by the rising waters."

"I told Grok just last week," G'Sille exclaimed, "that we're living at a time of crossroads. Either people learn to go forward in peace and tribal love, or they'll descend back into war and tribal fear. Isn't that what you told us in Seattle?"

Seattle was where Onifire had met Grok and G'Sille

at a conference after walking out of Howard Gall's project. She'd told them what she'd told him: people were inherently unpredictable and hard-wired for both violence and peace, for competition and cooperation, but above all they were wired for learning. People could learn to be just about anything, Onifire reflected, but they were almost never content just being who they were.

Howard never appreciated that. People were never going to be content living in his submarine under his orders forever because it left them nothing positive to learn, no room to grow. If the only things left to learn were secrecy, destruction, and rebellion, that's what people would learn. That was human nature. That's what she'd told Grok and G'Sille in Seattle. She told them that if they told their students they were building perfect worlds the students would learn how to destroy them because learning—doing, changing, becoming—is more fundamentally human than any possible way of life, no matter how idyllic it might seem at first.

"I told you that people couldn't live in habs without growth, learning, and change, and that pretending things are perfect will just make them discover imperfections," Onifire said. "But do you really think people are going to start killing each other in space?" "People are people," Grok replied. "That's one of the things I've learned from you! We can try to bring out the best in people, try to put people

243

in systems that promote their success, but we can't turn them into robots." He laughed. "What's the challenge in building a spaceship full of robots? Everyone and their brothers are already doing that!" "But the robot ships will help the habs, right?" Onifire asked. She knew that different robotic projects were underway, but it was hard to know how they were related to any of the hab projects.

"Who knows," Grok replied. "All the robot projects have one thing in common: they're designed to make money for people here on Earth. If they can do that by helping people on habs, then I assume they'll do that. If not? If their masters back home don't see a profit in stopping, a robot ship might sail right by a dying hab without batting an eyelash." "They're interested in minerals, not people," G'Sille agreed. "Mostly trying to find a shortcut to the asteroids; trying to bring back a huge nugget of gold and platinum." "I wouldn't count on the mooners either," Grok added. "Once the people up there realize how much their bosses are making on every block they send up to L_1, they're going to start asking some hard questions. They're going to start playing for themselves, just like everyone else."

"Not everyone!" Onifire said. "Have you been following the successes of APORLACT and our biodiversity project? We're playing for the three billion people who live less than 35° from the equator now. The UN is really coming through with funding, supplies, equipment ... we're really starting to do some good things for people!" "You haven't seen anything yet," Grok replied, shaking his head. "Grok," G'Sille started, but he continued. "We spent a week with my father last month. He's now the American Deputy Under-Secretary to the UN Climate Change Council. He says the UN is really close to establishing a governing council for Southeastern Asia and the West Indies, the two areas hit hardest by the climate storms. A governing council, he says, which will replace the existing nations: Cuba, Haiti, Malaysia, Indonesia … just gone, wiped out with a stroke of their pen!"

Onifire gasped. She'd heard the anti-world government types railing on against this, but nothing so concrete. "All of the nations?" She asked, trying to remember all the countries in those areas where the storms had been most active. "All of them," Grok confirmed. "And, by the way, you didn't hear that from me!" "Grok and his father are not close," G'Sille added, "but they do trust each other, and he did ask us not to talk about it. And Stanley does love Rally very much. She's his only granddaughter!" "Of course," Onifire assured them, thinking nobody would believe her anyway. "But what about APORLACT? What about our project? How is this going to change the relief and recovery efforts?"

"Good question," Grok said with a smile. "Nobody really knows, because there's never been a world government before. Maybe it will be like Ancient Rome, or Ming China—those are probably two of the closest historical parallels." "But you think it's a bad idea?" Onifire asked. "You don't think it will help relief efforts?" "Oh, it will almost certainly help relief efforts," Grok admitted, "especially, I imagine, in places like Haiti, where the local government has been a failure for a long time. It will make the relief efforts more streamlined, more efficient, more regular."

"But you aren't welcoming this change?" Onifire asked. "What worries you?" "I do worry," Grok admitted. "I worry about loyalty, about pride, about the future. I know it looks like a unitary government structure has all sorts of technical and logistic advantages. But I'm not convinced people will buy into it. It's too big, too abstract, for most people to be able to put their pride and faith in it. It's too big to be organic, too big for everyone to feel like part of it. The idea of the human race as one big tribe with universal love and harmony sounds great. That's where this is headed. Bureaucracies generally don't get smaller. But, like you said, it doesn't leave any room for growth, for healthy changes."

"But if the hab people do invite you and your astro-missionaries up there," Onifire asked quizzically, "isn't that what you're going to tell them? Aren't you going to say they need to be one big tribe and send your students up there to show them how?" "I don't think so," Grok replied. "Maybe that's how it should have started, maybe that would have been the best way to do it, but things are moving way too fast for that now. There are enough blocks for a new hab going up that tether every seven or eight weeks now. If they invite me and the students up there, I think what I'm going to tell them is that they need to have a big tribe of tribes, that not every hab needs to work the same, and that people need to have a chance to experience different habs, different strategies, different ways of living in space." "How are they going to coordinate that?" Onifire wondered. "Probably not in any way we can control or predict," Grok replied. "That's the beauty, and the frustration, of being human!"

Chapter Thirteen

Delilah

Climate Support and Recovery Base Patrick,

Brevard Sub-subadministrative District

September 13, 2024

"So you're Howard Gall's ex-wife, and you're working for the Martins on their mission to support the habsters?" The tall, clean-cut man in a plain UNP uniform without rank or identification walked quickly into the small conference room without greeting or introduction, pulled the other flimsy white plastic chair up to the cheap white plastic table where they'd sat Delilah an hour ago, and cut straight to the chase. "Actually, I like to think we're all working together for bread in Athenian stalls," Delilah replied sarcastically, confident this UNP man in front of her had little understanding of Robin Goodfellow.

She'd had a tough 48 hours. The people from the UNP found her early yesterday morning at the CSG spaceport in Kourou, on the other side of the Caribbean. She and her mates from the Escuela were there working with groups of hablicants who encamped outside the fence and attempted to negotiate for habricks and lift capacity to chase their survival, their dreams, or both. She'd been up the whole night before with a group of Maoris who'd been there for six weeks. They had plenty of lift capacity booked—

three passenger flights and seven cargo flights—but they wanted to build a huge hab with more than 3000 habricks. That was virtually three entire months of lunar production, and the moonfirsters were demanding a veritable treasure trove of heavy metals and rare earth elements far beyond the islanders' abilities to procure.

She'd spent the night urging them to revise their plans, assuring them they would find a way. She had a harder time convincing herself. Since the moonfirsters broke away from their corporate sponsors early last year, the price of habricks had increased by several thousand percent. To make it worse, the moonfirsters wouldn't take cash or gold any more, just rare and valuable items that could be tethered down from L_1 to the lunar surface. They published a list every week or so, and Earth prices of any new items instantly skyrocketed. The moonfirsters could make bear shit the most valuable thing in the world tomorrow if they wanted to.

The UNP had pulled some strings with her people down there. That was clear enough. Grok and G'Sille both comtacked her yesterday to ask her to come to Florida and take this meeting with the representative from the UNP Climate Committee, APORLACT. She'd agreed, but she might not have if she'd known that it involved a late night rocket plane to Cape Canaveral, a high speed transcar ride to the base, no sleep, bad food, and a lot of waiting around in a sterile room with uncomfortable plastic furniture.

Typical UNP, Delilah thought. Everything's on their schedule, and they make me move as fast as possible, even though they're going to wind up asking me for something. Something fairly important judging by how much effort they've put into it. They should be kissing my ass. She thought of Claudius and Gertrude welcoming Rosencrantz and Guildenstern and immediately beseeching them to spy on their friend Hamlet. That didn't turn out well for anyone, she reminded herself.

"Swaggering together like hempen home-spuns you say?" Stanley replied in an awful Irish accent. He looked Delilah straight in the eye and gave her an insincere smile. But his eyes didn't smile. His cold eyes reminded Delilah of Howard and she wondered if this UNP man shared her ex's obsessive nature. "Interesting you say that," he continued. That's exactly why I've brought you here. I want—I need— my son and your ex-husband to work together on the most important mission in history. I'm Stanley Burpelson, Rally's grandfather."

"Grok's father!" Delilah thought. Grok never mentioned that. She'd never heard Grok say much about his father at all, only passing references with vague hints of power and influence. She remembered once Grok told a story about having lunch in a hotel in Tokyo and the meal ending when two groups of solemn bureaucrats interrupted, one group to take Stanley back to the embassy and another to take Grok to the airport. Delilah thought Grok had said he was eight years old and hadn't seen his father again until he was ten. She tried to remember anything else Grok said but came up blank. How strange, she thought, for Grok's father to have Howard's eyes.

"Why didn't Grok tell me I was coming here to meet you?" Delilah asked. "He didn't know," Stanley replied. "I haven't talked to my son since he began working with the habsters two years ago." "Why not?" she blurted. "It's complicated," Stanley admitted in a less confident tone, looking down. "I did not—do not—have a good relationship with his mother. I must admit, I have never been the best father, for a wide variety of reasons. But that's neither here nor there: my son managed to become a fine adult in any event. Two years ago, when I last saw Rally and her parents in British Columbia, I was the American representative on the APORLACT central committee. It was an important position but not necessarily a powerful one. Elected officials were still calling most of the shots then, even in the severe climate storm areas. Then, of course, as you know," Stanley continued, "the American government, along with many others, was formally incorporated into the UNP's new administrative structure of nations and peoples, just about six months ago now."

Of course Delilah knew. Everyone in the world

251

knew. She'd been back in Ashland the day it happened, visiting her parents. People there were still going apeshit. A group of the most upset had taken up arms and occupied two visitors centers and the gift shop at Crater Lake National Park, north of Klamath Falls. The Ashland public radio station, which had long branded itself Jefferson Public Radio, became Jefferson Resistance Radio and turned into the epicenter of the political movement against incorporation in that rural region.

Other occupations and opposition groups responded across the country. Different towns, counties, and the State of Idaho had declared independence, or secession, or revolution, or something. So far, the UNP hadn't raised a hand against any of them, content to let them make speeches and build barricades in remote areas while it moved to assimilate the federal bureaucracy and quietly take control of key economic centers across the country, where production and distribution of consumer goods had been largely unaffected. Delilah had mixed feelings about it. She approved of efficiency but at Kourou she'd seen how regimental and uncaring the UNP could be to unsuccessful hablicants.

"And how's that working out?" Delilah replied sarcastically, wondering what his point was. Stanley smiled. "That's been pretty complicated. I'm sure you know that." "But how's it working out for you?" "For me? For me, it has been a trying and difficult, but not unrewarding, time. As a member of the APORLACT council, I now have significant responsibilities with regard to climate recovery and relief programs across North America. Those responsibilities come with corresponding powers, which I am attempting to use for good. We all are."

Stanley paused and smiled at her again. "When, or if, the history of our age is written, undoubtedly there will be some who will cast APORLACT as villains. Villains of necessity, perhaps, but villains nonetheless. So be it. On this day, and for my part, I can only assure you we are trying to do the right thing, however elusive that might be." "Elusive indeed," Delilah agreed, still not sure where Stanley was going, what he wanted her to do, or why he thought she or anyone else could ever convince Howard and Grok to work together. She never would have seen that coming. She couldn't think of two less likely partners. "Indeed," Stanley continued. "If we didn't think it needed to be done, we wouldn't be doing it. And once the council gained those responsibilities and that power, it put me in a position where meeting with my son, with the so-called 'spiritual father of the habsters,' was … difficult."

The UNP, Delilah suddenly realized, didn't know what to do about the habsters. They hadn't decided whether Grok was right and the habsters would help save the planet or whether Howard was right and the habsters were destroying the planet even faster, or whether they were both wrong. Delilah looked closely at Grok's father, wondering what he thought, but she couldn't read those inscrutable eyes that reminded her so much of Howard. In any case, for two years there'd been an ever-increasing number of habsters boosting more and more resources up to L_1 as the swarms of hablicants trying desperately to come up with anything the moonfirsters wanted continued to grow. It was going to be hard for UNP to maintain any kind of detached neutrality much longer.

Delilah thought about some of the hablicants she'd met at CSG and how they'd had such very different things to say about the UNP. She'd thought it came from them. She'd assumed that the UNP lived up to its image and treated everyone with the same cold neutral regularity. But that was a myth, she realized. Some of them believed in the habsters, and some of them hated them, and somehow they were trying to build a world government together? What could go wrong? Idiots full of sound and fury, she thought. Somehow they had to learn to be more than that.

"Well," she continued slowly, looking back up at him and smiling, "How lucky you are that it will be so much easier for you to collaborate with Howard! He's just in North Korea, working with your enemies! No problem there." "Indeed," Stanley smiled, "if any of this was easy I wouldn't need your help and I wouldn't have had to take you

254

away from your Maori hablicant friends at CSG and bring you here to have this conversation you are obviously enjoying so thoroughly. It's fair to say, in fact, that I wouldn't have done that unless I felt I absolutely had to."

He had a point there, Delilah admitted. Grok didn't talk about his father much, but everyone at the Escuela knew who he was and knew how committed he was—knew he was a lot like his only son in that regard.

"If you can't meet with Howard or Grok," Delilah continued, "why not find somebody else to do whatever it is you want them to do? Having been with Howard for more than four years and on Grok's team for close to five, I can assure you that both of them are replaceable. Eminently replaceable, in fact. Really you're almost certainly better off without either of them. And having both of them involved on the same project is, if you don't mind my saying so, insane. It's so insane that it would be funny if I hadn't been awake for the last 48 hours and I wasn't sitting in this miserably uncomfortable chair." Delilah leaned back as much as she could without worrying about breaking the plastic and crossed her arms over her chest, wondering how long it would take him to hear her say no.

"Did you know they met in 2012?" Stanley replied calmly, as if he'd expected her incredulous denial. "They've known each other longer than you've known Howard." "No, I didn't know that," Delilah replied. "Apparently neither of

255

them felt it important enough to mention to me. And so despite what, a decade of opportunity, they're not working together, have never worked together, and, in case you haven't noticed, rarely have anything even remotely good to say about one other? Now, I admit, that's something I may have contributed to. In fact, I'm probably the last person who'd ever convince them to do anything together." She looked at him curiously. "What is you want them to do anyway?"

Stanley sat up even straighter and looked her square in the eyes for a long moment. Every time she looked into his eyes it reminded Delilah of Howard and his brilliance and his passion. "I want them to do what they've both always dreamt of doing," he said softly. "I want them to go further than anyone has ever gone before. I want them to take a ship to the asteroid belt and bring back an asteroid so we can start building habs without having to boost everything good in the world into space and hand it over to the moonfirsters!" "An asteroid!" Delilah exclaimed. "How could they do that? Why would they do that?" "My hope," Stanley continued, "is that they will be able to do it because they have been dreaming of doing it their whole lives.

"You know the two of them as well as anyone" he continued. Delilah had long ago come to terms with that part of her history, but always on the assumption that Grok and Howard would never work together. "You know," Stanley said "that what they both really want is to stand on the bridge of their own ship like Captain Kirk and 'boldly go where no one has gone before.' Tell me they don't!" Stanley was leaning forward aggressively in his chair now. Delilah leaned forward too, resting her arms on her knees while she thought about it. She wasn't going to let Stanley intimidate her into anything, but was he right?

Howard, she thought, absolutely. Howard wanted to be a great leader. Captain Kirk? Not even close. Howard wanted to be Moses and lead his people to the Promised Land. She wasn't sure about Grok though. Grok was more cerebral, more abstract, but at the same time more grounded, less self-absorbed. For Grok, she thought, reaching the destination was more important than being the one to get there first.

"I know it sounds crazy," Stanley continued. He stood up and put his hands on the back of his white plastic chair. "Think about those Maoris, your friends down at CSG. Now think about hundreds, maybe thousands, of hablicants like them. Some of them have already bought flight time and are trying desperately to find whatever the moonfirsters want before somebody else does. Some of them are building ships or spaceports. Some of them get to L_1 but never get any habricks and just wait there, helplessly, until their systems fail and they die. Others are just starting out. But whatever they're doing, more of them are doing it every day. More and more people are working harder and harder to go to space, and they're willing to ship everything precious in the world to the moon in the process! Does that seem like a sustainable plan to you?"

"But it's working," Delilah protested. "People are up there building habs! Some of them might make it work. Maybe enough of them will make it work to make a difference down here. Just because things get shipped to the moon doesn't mean they'll never get shipped back." Stanley smiled. "I see why you are working on my son's project and not with Howard. I wish I could be so optimistic. As we discussed, however, my role with APORLACT compels me, for better or worse, not to believe only in dreams." "Only?" Delilah asked. "Does that mean that you do believe in one of their dreams?"

"I believe in everyone's dreams," Stanley replied, "but I also have to plan for everyone's future. Everyone except the moonfirsters, that is. They've made it clear that they don't want us on their team any more, so I don't have to worry about them. I have to worry about everyone else, about the other 99.9999% of humanity. I'm planning for a future where twelve million tons of rock and heavy metals moves slowly out of the asteroid belt, eases past Mars, and slides into Earth orbit, just a little bit closer than their platform at L_1. It's easier to launch from Earth to a twelve million ton rock because it has some gravity to catch you.

It's easier to build habs from rocks than from habricks. It's actually twice as fast: you build habs with material you remove from the asteroid, and at the same time you're making more habs out of the rock itself. You have heavier elements, natural radiation shielding, the list of advantages goes on and on ...."

"Thomas Edison had the same list of advantages for DC power over AC," Delilah replied. "But Westinghouse got to market first. So did the mooners." "They did," Stanley agreed. "They've sold and delivered more than ten thousand habricks in just over two years. There's no doubt that what they've built, what they're doing, is one of the great accomplishments in human history. But do the math! That rock sitting out there waiting for us is twelve million tons. That's the equivalent of 320,000 habricks! Just how long is it going to take for 320,000 habricks to crawl ever so slowly up their cute little tether?"

Delilah could see his point. The math was on Stanley's side. If it took the mooners two years to lift just 10,000 habricks, it would take a lifetime for them to lift 300,000. Howard would see that instantly, she thought. He'd be enthralled by the possibility of accelerating the process. "We don't have enough lifetimes to wait for them," Stanley continued. "Whether those people up there are going to save us, or survive us, or something else entirely, we just don't have time to do it a few thousand habricks for a few tiny habs at a time." His passion was contagious. Delilah started trying to imagine what it would be like for a habster watching Stanley's asteroid drift into orbit and realizing the neighborhood just changed forever real fast.

"But won't the mooners build more tethers or make bigger habricks?" she wondered. That's what Grok would ask, she thought, how other people would respond. "Maybe they will," Stanley nodded. "But once we've moved that twelve million ton asteroid, we'll set our sites on two eighteen million ton asteroids, from two different parts of the belt. That's over a million habricks! There's just no way for them to keep up with that pace. We think we can build a ship that can go to the belt, build engines, and bring back that twelve million ton rock in about three years and four months. If we launch the next two ships in the third year, when the first ship is about halfway back, they'll bring us 36 million more tons in years seven and eight. It's over at that point— do the math! We've got a million habricks. They keep plodding away at 1100 or 1200 a month, they'll have fewer than 100,000. We'll outnumber them almost ten to one even if they somehow double their production!"

"Then what happens to the mooners," Delilah asked, "when your asteroids make heavy elements commonplace at L_1 and bring twenty times as many habs for the Maori hablicants and the rest of them? How do they survive?" "That's not my problem," Stanley replied. "That stopped being my problem when they declared their independence. I'm UNP, remember? Peoples and nations 'united'? They're not united; I'm not concerned. But honestly I have a feeling they'll be fine."

"Because they'll have everything they need?" Delilah asked. "Because they'll have learned to really live on the moon by then? If they can live on the moon, why couldn't they live on Mars?" She looked up at him. "How many habricks is Mars … 700 quintillion or so? Maybe the math works out for them in the end?" "Maybe it does," Stanley agreed, surprising her slightly. "I didn't say the moonfirsters were my enemies. They're not on my team, but they're not my enemies either. Let's hope space is at least big enough for that!" That didn't sound like Howard, Delilah thought. Maybe Stanley did have some of Grok's compassion in him.

"Even after all they've done," she prodded, "you still hope they make it work?" "They're still people," Stanley nodded. "Of course I do. Make no mistake; I'm not against people living in space! But because of my position, my job, my task, is to try my best to make sure that living in space helps my team as much as possible. My team is APORLACT. My team is the United Peoples and Nations of Earth. I don't know whether my son is right, whether we can move enough people up there fast enough to tip the balance down here, but if we can move more people up there without making things here worse, I'm all for it."

He looked at her intently. "Maybe I'm humble enough, or old enough, to admit I don't know what's going to come of it and accept a lesser role, doing what I can. And what I can do is put those two on the most advanced spaceship ever built, give them parts and blueprints for making the biggest engines in history, and send them off into the cold black yonder to this rock and hope for the best." Delilah liked humility and was starting to realize why Stanley was one of APORLACT's leaders. He was making her feel like he wanted to make everything better.

Howard and Grok, she knew, were going to be drawn to Stanley's plan like hungry dogs to leftover meatballs. But she still wasn't sure he'd thought it through. "How do they work together," she started before he cut her off abruptly. "They don't," he interrupted. "Well, they travel in the same ship, to the same asteroid, with the same mission, but not together. We send two crews. One crew follows Howard. Howard gives the orders, they do things his way. The other crew works with my son. They do things however the habsters do them. They all make choices for each other, or whatever it is that they do. One crew is in charge of launch and acceleration, the other deceleration and rendezvous."

"But what happens if and when they get there?" Delilah asked, trying in vain to imagine either Howard or Grok standing calmly to the side while their ship ran the other's way. "It's a big asteroid," Stanley continued. "We send three sets of engine parts—we would have sent two anyway, for redundancy—two sets of blueprints, two stores of supplies, two of everything plus an extra set of mission critical parts. Each crew starts with the same stuff. Each crew sets up on a different pole of the rock—the rock we've picked out is basically spherical and so the engines could be located at either pole. Then whichever crew's engines are operational first gets to be in charge on the trip home."

And gets to have their theories about living in space validated in front of the whole world if that asteroid eases ever so slowly past Mars and into orbit, Delilah realized, looking at Stanley a little closer. He'd put his finger on exactly the right button.

She was amazed at how simple yet far-reaching his plan was. He was giving them what they'd always dreamt of—the chance to be the one who showed people how to live in space. She wasn't sure whether his scheme was crazy or brilliant, but she knew she wouldn't have much trouble convincing Howard or Grok to take him up on it. Not when he'd raised the stakes that high. After all she'd been through, Delilah thought, building Howard's submersible hab and bringing Grok's students from the Escuela to L_1, if Stanley's plan worked this was the thing she'd be remembered for. The scale of it was so much larger than anything else, she felt compelled to contribute.

"Why me?" she asked, resigned to her task. "There

must be others." "There are," Stanley replied, "but they both know how reluctant you would be to do this. When you ask them, both Howard and my son will realize you overcame your reluctance. That will give them comfort and encouragement." "Howard and Grok you mean?" she asked, realizing that she had yet to hear him call his son by his name. "You know who I mean," he snarled, standing up. "You won't use his name?" she asked. "Seriously? I mean, a son by any other name ..." "He was my son!" Stanley replied angrily. "He should have my name, not this name that shames me!" Delilah saw him take four deep, measured breaths. "I was not involved in the selection of my son's name," he continued in a calmer tone, "and it is not the name I would have chosen for him. So I choose not to use it. What of it?" "Nothing, I guess," Delilah replied, embarrassed at having opened such a deep wound. "Nothing so long as you still believe in him" "I believe in him," Stanley assured her calmly. "I believe in him as much as I believe in anybody."

Assuring Stanley she would tell Howard and Grok about his plan, Delilah stood up and started back to Kourou. It made her a little uneasy watching Stanley get so emotional about his son's name after discussing the fate of millions so dispassionately. All of them, she realized, were driven by more emotions than they'd care to admit, weaving a web of mingled yarn that might yet prove strong enough to save their world.

Chapter Fourteen

Sudomo

The *Habudo Maru*

October 30, 2026

"Specialization is for insects!" It was an unofficial motto of the habster community. Somebody had inscribed it with beautiful calligraphic flourishes on a wall panel in the bodily waste recycler Sudomo used most of the time. Ever since he'd lived in Tokyo around the turn of the century Sudomo had been infatuated by the Japanese fascination with bodily waste. He'd grown up in a village outside Malang where footrests for squatting more comfortably over an open hole were signs of prosperity. Now he lived in space and relieved himself in what was undoubtedly one of the most expensive washlets in history—'toilet' didn't come close to capturing its grandeur.

This washlet, Sudomo mused, was the product of nothing but years, decades, maybe centuries of specialization. Yet here it was, in the bowels of one of the greatest human constructions in history. Here he was, in a famous space colony, enjoying a restroom experience more luxurious than 90% of people back on Java could even imagine, courtesy of people who as a matter of principle rejected specialization. It seemed contradictory somehow, Sudomo thought, but it wasn't like they were building any more of them and they'd gladly help anyone who wanted to copy or improve on it.

Sudomo was one of the oldest mates on the *Habudo Maru* at the moment. The *Maru—the circle—*that's what they called their home. He spent more time thinking about philosophical issues than his mates, and he'd been part of the wage labor economy much longer than most of them. He'd certainly been a lot more specialized—he'd been a cook, and eventually a chef, mastering a single style of cooking, dry *rendang*, a stylistic family of dishes developed in his native Indonesia as a way to preserve meat in the tropical climate. He'd been an apprentice to Master Chef Yamien Nyong Choi at the Mie Belitung restaurant in Tanjung Pandan, on the west side of Belitung Island, where he'd moved at seventeen, chasing a young girl named Wulandari around the beach for most of the summer. Eventually, Wulandari had gone home to Medan, in North Sumatra, and enrolled at UNIMED to study nursing.

He'd lost track of her shortly thereafter, but Sudomo and Master Choi never lost touch until, at the age of 92, Master Choi was one of two hundred people killed in the Fu De Ci temple collapse in Kelapa Kampit during the first great climate storms in 2019. When they'd peeled the rubble off three days later, rescuers found two infant survivors sheltered under Master Choi's dying body. His death hit Sudomo much harder than losing his own father, but it

266

inspired him to do more for others and set him on his journey to the moon and from there to the *Maru*.

Master Choi taught him much more than the art of *rendang*. He'd learned about leadership, about loyalty, about people, and about profit, that much debated word. Habsters didn't believe in profit, at least officially, but every one of them knew which habs were doing well and which ones were struggling and might be in danger of being out-rotated at the next biannual habster reconvention, where they all had an opportunity to convince others to adopt new hab parameters and take possession of a hab that could not muster the same quorum of support. But our choices are never really infinite, Sudomo knew, and sometimes pretending they are just blinds us. The first two reconventions had been formal, uneventful affairs, without any habs actually out-rotated or any revolutionary new parameters proposed. So far, Sudomo thought, the habsters were being fairly conservative, sticking with what worked and avoiding big risks.

Master Choi never wanted to take big risks either. Security was all he'd really sought. He'd cautioned Sudomo against seeking great profits many times, warning that the costs were too high and the risks too great; that greed led inevitably to disloyalty, dissent, and distrust. A solid business and a reasonably well-appointed life, Master Choi taught him, were things you could pass on to your children. Vast riches, on the other hand, only corrupted youth. "Hire

267

ambitious children from poor families, treat them fairly, work harder than you expect them to work"—that was Master Choi's employment philosophy in a nutshell.

Sudomo wasn't sure how that applied to the habster economy of choice. It was hard to be greedy where there was little to accumulate without it spoiling. Ambition was a little harder to define, but you couldn't deny that people preferred to have more choices most of the time. Supposedly that wasn't greed, because choices weren't mutually exclusive like capital, but Sudomo wondered sometimes if that difference really made any difference. People worked just as hard to make a variety of great foodstuffs here, he thought, as they did in downtown Tokyo where the rewards were infinitely more tangible.

Some had warned that there would be no innovation in an economy without capital, Sudomo remembered, but the habsters had put that one to rest. Even if they all died tomorrow, necessity, not greed, would always be the mother of invention. Their very existence was so precarious that they had no choice but to continuously keep coming up with better recyclers, better ways to store food, better batteries … the list never stopped growing. People weren't going to stop innovating in space, Sudomo thought. The question was whether a time would come when they stopped sharing their innovations so freely. He'd seen on the moon how quickly things changed once the blocks started flowing steadily up the tether and people started sharing fewer ideas less often.

Free sharing of ideas among different habs with different people living under different rules in different conditions was the best possible recipe for survival and comfort in space. That was the hypothesis they'd all signed off on at the first habster convention. So far, it seemed to be working, even though people definitely still had egos. When John Racker on the *Habalone* came up with his first primitive seawater recycler last year he hadn't keep it secret. He shared the plans freely across all the habs, just ten or eleven of them back then, and every one of them tried to make his idea work in their own way, experimenting with different processes on the dried samples that traveled around the different habs.

It was actually somebody here on the *Maru*, Sudomo remembered, who'd found the perfect combination of heat and pressure to reconstitute seawater that, if not authentic, was close enough to fool 90% of marine species into staying alive. Just about every hab used seawater now, and the mooners would be shipping blocks to them for years to come in exchange for sharing that process. With reconstituted seawater and dehydrated fish eggs, you could raise a lot of protein on just algae and hard work. Maybe you could live in space without sushi, Sudomo thought, but most people would choose not to.

And things hadn't worked out so bad for John Racker

either. Respect had always brought rewards money never could. Racker would be welcomed, recruited even, on any hab, and any habster would be excited to group with him in any circumstances. Racker had more choices open to him than he did before he had that idea. Maybe that sort of thing wasn't as substantial as a pile of gold bars, but it was a lot less fragile, and the only one who could ever diminish it was Racker himself. Sudomo had known his share of riches and had experienced perhaps an equal measure of respect and admiration. To his mind, the latter was more precious by far.

Sudomo's wristcom beeped and he realized he'd been relaxing—daydreaming really—in the washlet for much longer than he realized. Sudomo's com station rotation began five minutes ago, and Haru, who'd been sitting there listening to the emptiness of space for the last ten hours, was wondering where he was. He felt bad, as he should—he'd stolen those five minutes from Haru and could never give them back. They could only survive out here together by building each other's choices—their economy depended on him feeling bad. Rarely is any external punishment half as harsh as that which a moral person issues themselves. "Sorry," he answered, twisting his wrist in the air to disable his comtar, as was customary under the circumstances. "I'm on my way."

Walking down the narrow supply corridor to access the com station on the very bottom pole of the roughly spherically-shaped Maru, where their antennae had maximum reach with minimum interference, Sudomo thought to himself that, most of the time, the economy of choice worked fairly well—at least as well, he figured—as the capital economy did in situations like this. Most of the time most people didn't steal from each other, and if somebody was five minutes late most people forgave and forgot and moved on with their lives. The advantage their economy had, Sudomo reflected, was how it handled advantages, not disadvantages. Disadvantages, like using bodily force to take something from somebody else, were refreshingly unambiguous and easy to condemn, even in a wage labor society.

Arranging their society so advantages worked for the benefit of all, not just ensuring disadvantages wouldn't benefit anyone; that was the hard part of it. The habsters had committed themselves to Grok Martin's hypothesis that an economy of choice could simultaneously maximize the position of their least well off and give them their best shot at surviving in space colonies. They certainly weren't perfect, Sudomo thought, but they were making a pretty good run.

The *Maru* was his second hab, and without exception his mates seemed happy and successful, at least to him. In theory, anyone could become a habster, even if in practice it was limited to those who could lift supplies and wheedle habricks out of the mooners. That wasn't their fault though—they couldn't help it if the mooners and Earthers didn't play by their rules. But once somebody made it up here, she could most likely join him and Haru in the *Maru* within a few rotations, maybe eighteen months or two years. Some people liked change, while others took longer to find their places. The semi-annual rotation kept them together, helped people move on from difficult situations, and reminded them that the habster project as a whole was more than any one hab.

Any improvement they made in the *Maru* would, in principle, be available to every habster, just like Racker's seawater. No one was ever left behind. But nothing happened instantaneously, Sudomo thought, that was the catch. Early adaptors would always have a temporal advantage, a flashing moment in time where their innovation was the hot new thing and they danced a little closer to the pulse of the universe than everyone else. And so innovation, which they needed so badly, was still highly prized and rewarded, and every hab devoted significant time and effort to research and development.

Some habs, he'd heard, had cut back or even discontinued com station rotations. They set an alert—a ringtone basically—and went about their business until somebody called them. Others, like the *Maru*, continued to listen around the clock to what went on around them.

272

Sudomo could see the logic in both approaches. Sitting and listening to empty space was boring, and there wasn't much else you could accomplish if you were actively trying to find com signals in the darkness. On the other hand, you never knew what you might hear—or what you might not hear, which was probably more to the point. There were undoubtedly deeper concerns about isolation, and the grass always seeming greener somewhere else, but that was the basic issue: waste time or risk missing something really important. Sudomo firmly advocated for spending the time. Innovation, he'd learned, always started with information, and every com rotation brought some small chance of gathering priceless new information.

"Haru, I am so sorry!" Sudomo apologized as he opened the com station hatch and gave a polite bow to his friend. Haru stood up smiling and returned his bow properly. "I was starting to worry about you," Haru started with a feigned look, letting Sudomo know he'd been forgiven. "I know," Sudomo replied, "somebody of my age, who exercises so little ... I could drop dead any second!" Haru was an enthusiastic martial arts practitioner and long distance runner who frequently reminded Sudomo that statistically the extra five kilograms he carried around his mid-section put him at greater risk "at his age."

"It is no matter," Haru assured him. "I actually enjoy the com rotation! It is good mental exercise for me calculating the relative positions of the other habs and executing the most efficient frequency sweeps." He extended his arms out as if to encircle the moon and all the habs floating around them. "I'd probably be useless if somebody actually comtacked us," he continued, "but I do enjoy the search." "I enjoy it too," Sudomo admitted. "I thought I was the only one! But I'll let you in on my secret—I spend almost as much time listening to the other planets and the stars beyond as I do the other habs! If they call, I'll hear them, sure, but what I really dream of is hearing someone who's not talking to me, somebody else who's just out here passing by for reasons of their own, human or alien."

Haru's eyes flickered as he processed this idea of aimlessly casting about for anonymous signals from undiscovered aliens drifting randomly through empty space. Then, smiling, he reached out and held Sudomo's left bicep with his right hand. "It is good that you dream!" he told Sudomo in a very serious tone. "I have heard it said that we have so many chores we do not have time to dream. But here you are, chasing bigger dreams through this very chore some consider so tedious. That makes me very happy! I am glad you are here, glad you are my friend and my mate."

Sudomo bowed again. "Now I will leave you to your dreams—and to your chores. I am going to have a workout, maybe a bowl of that miso soup from yesterday, if any is left, and a nice sleep! I believe we are slotted to group together in biotics tomorrow, so I will see you soon. I hope you have interesting stories of aliens just passing by to share with me." Grinning, Haru bowed again and pulled himself out of the com station through the hatch.

Sudomo cleared his mind and started sweeping through his comcheck routine. Their antennae were not sensitive enough to receive any internal transmissions from other habs but when you pointed their biggest dish directly at another hab it did register electromagnetic activity. You couldn't eavesdrop, but you could tell how active the hab was, like listening to a beehive to see how loudly it buzzed. It wasn't something that was officially recorded, but Sudomo had friends on other habs he liked to keep track of. He kept a small notebook to record his observations and speculate about what the different patterns of high and low activity might mean. He liked to daydream about his friends on other habs discovering alien life, perfecting superconductors, mastering cold fusion, or something equally miraculous.

Sudomo's ten hour com rotation went fast. He started by checking on as many of the other sixteen habs as he could. Today *Habulous*, which was generally the furthest away from the *Maru* and travelled in the opposite direction around L_1, kept disappearing behind other habs. That effect became more and more frequent as the number of habs continued to slowly increase. Sudomo was no mathematician, not by any means, but he'd figured once that the odds of two habs colliding would become statistically significant once more than 42 habs were all maintaining different slow rotations around L_1. He knew that other, more mathematically inclined, habsters maintained that more than 100 habs could take up station here without colliding. He hoped they were right and he was wrong.

After he checked in on the other habs and jotted down his observations, Sudomo liked to take a quick listen to the Moon. It was far enough away that their equipment could not really distinguish the mooners' electromagnetic activity from the background radiation of space. But, unlike their habs, not all the mooners lived in one place, and they communicated with each other directly by comtar, not just through the omninet like the habsters. Officially, there weren't any mooners on the omninet any more, but Sudomo had his suspicions about that. He knew how paranoid the mooners were and how much they'd covet that trove of information.

Today Sudomo did not hear any activity on the moon, which was unusual. He wished the com station had telescopes or even a viewport so he could look down at the moon and see for himself what they were up to. The habsters and the mooners had a complicated relationship. Everything the habsters believed in, the mooner military regime rejected. The mooners got everything they wanted from the habsters of tomorrow and never really had to deal with the habsters of today. Once you'd paid their outrageous demands and taken possession of your habricks, you really didn't have anything tangible to offer the mooners anymore. All you had was inventions, creativity, intellectual property. Racker's seawater recycler. The *Maru*'s washlet. Things the mooners didn't know they needed but might still want.

But it was strictly a one way street. The habsters had no idea what innovations and inventions the mooners had made. There were 361 people on the *Maru*, which was one of the largest habs. There were only a little more than 3500 habsters in all and the two new habs under construction would only add room for a few hundred more. None of them had any idea how many mooners there were now. Their population was growing, Sudomo knew that. He'd heard them talking about new construction at Churchill Warren, which wasn't on any map of the moon he'd ever seen. You didn't build new cities without bodies to fill them. The mooners were building new cities and every day anything they wanted from Earth floated down their tether. Talented and successful people like that, Sudomo thought, undoubtedly had come up with some new tricks of their own.

The habsters had millions back on Earth clamoring to join them, but only the mooners could send them habricks to build habs to live in. It was, Sudomo thought, just the sort of illogical outcome that typified humanity. The mooners had plenty of space to fill, but refused to bring outsiders into their tightly regimented society. The habsters had plenty of room for more people in their economy of choice, but no space for them. Earth had billions of extra people, but more of their land kept disappearing under the waves every year. Yet instead of working together, the mooners stubbornly rejected everyone who couldn't trade for habricks, which the Earthers tolerated because the habsters offered hope to its teeming billions. At least he hoped they did. Sudomo hadn't been back to Earth for more than six years and had long since lost any desire to return, but he still felt sympathy, and a little pity, for the people down there drowning themselves in the capital economy as their world fell apart.

Sudomo passed the antennae south through the Sea of Nectar and across the lunar South Pole when he realized that a comtack was beeping steadily on his panel. He sat up in shock and his arms reflexively pulled the antennae north, ending the alert. He sat back, shaken. There was nothing at the South Pole. After a second, he found the courage to push the antennae south again, to the pole. The alert started beeping steadily again.

"How can it be?" Sudomo asked himself frantically, feeling his excitement. There wasn't anyone out there! The mooners didn't live at the South Pole! It made no sense! He pulled the antennae back to the Sea of Nectar and pushed it back to the pole. The alert stopped and started beeping again. "This is real!" Sudomo thought. His dreams of discovering alien life took over for a moment and visions from every comtext and comvid about alien contact he'd ever seen flashed through his mind.

What to do? They had procedures for how to respond to comtacks from other habs, or the mooners. But none of them were comtacking from the South Pole. They'd never grouped about how to talk to aliens! He'd just now mentioned it to Haru for the first time. "Should I call for help?" Sudomo asked himself, thinking furiously. Shouldn't somebody else be here? What if this really was the big moment, humanity's first contact with other spacefarers? He reached to the omninet terminal and opened a message pad but the words wouldn't come. "They'll think I'm crazy," he thought. "I'll have to show them something." Sudomo stopped himself, calmed his breathing, and listened silently to the alert until it beeped 100 times.

Finally, finding the calm within himself, he pushed the comtack button to see what the aliens had to say. The comtar flickered and came to life for the first time in months, revealing a white trapezoidal shaped boxy structure like an expanded toaster oven with two long narrow super-structures suspended underneath it. "This is an automatic distress beacon," the comtar intoned in a flat, artificial tone. "This ship requires aid and assistance. Mayday! Mayday! Mayday!" The comtar was silent for a second and then began again. "This is an automatic distress beacon. This ship requires aid and assistance. Mayday! Mayday! Mayday! This is an automatic distress beacon. This ship requires aid and assistance. Mayday! Mayday! Mayday!"

Sudomo stared wordlessly at the comtar and listened to it repeat its toneless distress call for a long time. It sure didn't sound like aliens—even if they were pretending to be human they'd have come up with something more dramatic than that. But who? Whose ships were out there past the moon? What were they doing? The mooners? Somebody else? Sudomo's mind feverishly composed different scenarios while the comtar continued to repeat itself.

Before he could wrap his mind around it, another much stronger comtack started beeping. He looked at the anterminal and saw that it was definitely coming from the moon, from the main com station at Touchdown. But they weren't comtacking him, or any of the habs, he realized. They were comtacking the boxy white ship! He was only receiving their comtack because he was pointing his antennae directly at the ship, at the South Pole, where nobody else would be listening. "Were the mooners building ships like this now?" Sudomo wondered to himself. That would be amazingly fast progress.

Sudomo twisted the dial to see what the mooners were saying to the ship. To his shock, a second comtar shimmered into life revealing the distinctive South Pacific

Islander features of his old friend Maringka!

"Acknowledging Mayday" she said calmly and evenly in her unique accent. "Acknowledging Mayday. Please report status so we can provide aid and assistance. Please report status." He hadn't seen Maringka for four long years, and now, looking at what he assumed was a recent comtar, he saw that they'd been hard years for his friend. Her hair, which had never been exceptionally rich or full, was visibly thinning, and her cheeklines were unhealthily pronounced. Whatever life on the moon was like, Sudomo thought, eternal youth was not one of its rewards.

The white box comtar stopped momentarily. After a long moment of silence, he heard it start again. "Status report begin: computer systems, operational; electrical systems, operational; battery systems, operational, charge level 86%, sub-optimal; habitat systems, operational, atmosphere quality, 93%, sub-optimal; engine systems, operational, fuel level, 2%, critical. End status report." Sudomo sat stunned for a moment as the ship resumed its cries of mayday and Maringka remained silent, her comtar staring silently at the white box.

"Acknowledging status report." Sudomo finally heard Maringka say in a toneless voice. He couldn't tell whether or not she was surprised or determine whether or not the white box belonged to the mooners. "Status report acknowledged. Please report mission parameters so we can provide aid and assistance. Please report mission parameters for aid and assistance." The mayday cries stopped once again and the white box ship was silent for a moment. Maringka certainly seemed to know how to talk to it, Sudomo thought to himself. Maybe it was one of theirs—maybe they were progressing that much faster than the habsters.

"Mission parameters begin: mission objective, evacuate to Earth orbit, not completed; mission duration, one year, ninety-four days, four hours, thirty-two minutes and six seconds, in progress; mission crew, information restricted; mission resources, information restricted; mission communications, information restricted. End mission parameters." And once again Sudomo listened to the white box ship beeping mayday and watched his friend's stoic face as she contemplated what they'd heard.

She didn't talk to it that well, Sudomo thought. It wasn't telling her everything. It wasn't their ship. But one year and ninety-four days! How far would that be for this ship? Was it coming from Mars? Sudomo felt like that wasn't long enough to travel to Mars, but he just didn't know. It was all happening so fast. He saw Maringka's comtar look away from the white box ship comtar to her right, as if somebody else was talking to her. Then her face turned slowly back to her left past the ship until Sudomo could have sworn she was looking right at him. At that moment, another comtack lit up on his board and started beeping so loudly it drowned out the mayday calls.

Pulling his eyes away from Maringka's comtar, Sudomo quickly looked down at the board and saw that the new comtack was directed squarely to the *Maru* from Touchdown. They'd caught him eavesdropping! There was no point in denying it, so he shut off the white box ship comtar and pushed the button that would send his comtar back to the mooners. He'd never been so nervous to talk to an old friend and had no idea what to say.

"*Ni jintian chi mifan lao pengyu*" Sudomo stammered nervously, trying to remember the traditional Chinese greeting Maringka had taught him late one night in Tokyo long ago. *Have you eaten rice, old friend?* If nothing else, it was probably the last thing she expected to hear from the largely-Japanese *Maru*! Her comtar stiffened, then her eyes flickered wide for just a moment before she regained control. But he knew her well enough to see she'd recognized his voice. He had to remember that she wasn't alone, that their conversation was probably on display for the entire mooner high command. He didn't want to get his friend in trouble.

"*Maru*, you're not coming through clearly," she replied coldly. "Do you copy?" "*Maru* copies," he replied, trying to match her detached tone. "Do you copy Touchdown?" "Touchdown copies," she replied disdainfully. "Much better, *Maru*," Maringka continued, twisting her head and showing him the vaguest hint of a smile to register her appreciation at his understanding. "We were getting gibberish there at first! Now what are you doing listening to our private conversations with our ship!" Her voice was angry but her eyes were soft, and he knew she was trying to find a way to communicate with him without saying anything.

"Private conversation!" he blustered. "Why should you have a private conversation with our ship? I was monitoring its beacon while we prepared to render aid and then you interfered." "Your ship, *Maru*?" Maringka replied in a biting tone, rolling her eyes at him. "Please." So much for the big lie theory, Sudomo thought to himself. "Ours by right of first discovery," he protested. "We heard the beacon first! And it's not your ship," he continued in a more reasonable tone, "or it wouldn't have restricted your information."

"It's not ours," Maringka admitted, "yet." She stared at him even more intently. "*Maru* you can do nothing! Our recovery mission is even now preparing to launch, and we will rendezvous with that ship in … less than five hours. There's nothing you can do that quickly!" That was true enough, Sudomo admitted to himself. It would probably take a couple of hours to bring everyone on the *Maru* up to speed on the events of the last five minutes, much less start grouping on how to respond. For better or worse, snapdash military precision in response to faraway events was not a strength of their economy of choice.

"So why did you comtack us?" Sudomo wondered aloud. If she was telling the truth, and he was pretty sure she was, their mission would probably have the white box ship back on the moon before the next com rotation ended. "To bargain," she replied calmly. "The only reason we ever comtack you! You keep quiet about that ship, and we'll credit you 40 habricks. You tell anyone about that ship, we'll shut down the tether—no more habricks!" Her look told him how serious she was. "You know you can only get habricks from us!" She wasn't just acting tough for her audience: she really wanted his attention. But why would she threaten to shut down the tether over this white box ship? And why did she say that about habricks?

He thought frantically for a few moments, trying to figure out where this white box ship came from and why it was so important to Maringka. What was she trying to tell him? Shut down the tether. Habricks you can only get from us. Then, suddenly, it came to him all at once! Asteroids! That ship came from the asteroid belt! His friends Ripley and Rico, the two young women who'd escaped from the moon with him four years ago ... were they on that ship?

Sudomo tried to look composed while he desperately tried to do the math. It was just two years ago, right after the tenth hab, the *Hab a Dream*, launched when Ripley and Rico joined the crew of that ship. The *Farluk,* that was the name of it. Their mission was secret, but before they left Ripley confided in him. They were going to the asteroid belt. The trip out, he remembered Ripley saying, would take them just over a year. This white box ship was critical on fuel because it just came back from the asteroid belt! But Ripley couldn't be on it, could she? She hadn't been gone long enough, he thought. Or had she? Was it possible with the right orbital mechanics? Was L_1 getting closer to or further from the asteroid belt? Did it depend on which asteroid? He just didn't know. It always came down to information, Sudomo reflected, and there was never enough of it.

Either way, Sudomo thought, the habsters didn't send any ships to the asteroids. The mooners didn't send it, or it would have told them everything. Somebody on Earth must have sent this ship. Either they sent it with Ripley and Rico, or they'd sent a different Earth ship. Why? What did it mean for Earthers to send ships to the asteroids? Why did Maringka want so badly to keep it secret? He hadn't found aliens at the South Pole, Sudomo thought, but he felt like whatever was going on here might be almost as important.

He looked more steadily into Maringka's eyes and tried to nod ever so slightly, relaxing his face ever so subtly to show his friend he was trying to understand, trying to help her. He remembered the night she helped him escape from the moon, how she'd taken a shine to Ripley. She told

Sudomo she saw a lot of herself in the young Ama. Why would an Earther ship go to the asteroid belt? What was there?

Rocks, Sudomo realized suddenly. A whole lot of rocks. And if you had a lot of rocks, you didn't need habricks. Like any puzzle, it seemed obvious once he'd solved it and a wave of understanding swept through him. That ship threatened the mooners' monopoly, that's why it was so important to Maringka. If people found out, they wouldn't be desperate for habricks any more. Before he had time to wrestle with the ramifications of that realization, Sudomo's instincts kicked in and he did what he'd always done—he stuck up for his friend "Touchdown," he assured her, "I see no record of any ship. Our equipment may have malfunctioned for a moment there." "Understood, *Maru*" Maringka replied. "I hope we all fix our problems soon." "Copy that Touchdown, *Maru* out."

Sudomo quickly disconnected all comtacks and flopped back into his chair with a loud gasp. So what if he didn't tell anyone about the ship, he thought. That wouldn't make one whit of difference. If Earthers started harvesting asteroids the habster population would explode dramatically and the mooners truly would be on their own. The fragile balance between the three factions of humanity would shift drastically. The Earthers could move whole nations off planet without transferring any energy or resources to the

287

mooners. The few thousand habsters who'd given all they had to the mooners for habricks and mortar would be joined by tens of thousands of new colonists in maintenance-free hollowed out asteroids backed by Earther resources.

Sudomo had watched rich newcomers move into his neighborhood before, during the Tokyo housing boom in 2013. His Japanese friends and neighbors had scoffed at the idea that the influx of wealthy Chinese investors would affect them to any degree. And it hadn't had much effect on their day-to-day lives, just like hundreds of new asteroid habs orbiting L_1 wouldn't really affect the *Maru*'s daily routine. But the Japanese never forgot about the Chinese and, over time, found it harder and harder to feel superior to them. Sudomo feared the same thing happening to the habsters, watching as their pride in their economy of choice slowly eroded and they returned to Earther ways. And that was nothing compared to the total isolation the mooners would potentially face. *Poor Maringka*, Sudomo thought as he brought the antennae back online to finish his com rotation.

Chapter Fifteen

Rico

El Ostional, Distrito Administrativo de San Juan del Sur

Rivas → *The Farluk*

December 7-9, 2025

Rico never tired of looking out to sea. The sea was always the same mystery posing different questions in her mind. When she was five years old her parents had taken her to the coast for the first time, to the *Balcon de Europa* in Nerja. She'd gone instantly, her mother swore, to the statute of King Alfonzo at the end of the promontory. There she'd sat silently for a long time, looking out to sea under the King's right arm. Finally, according to family lore, she'd turned back around and exclaimed emphatically to her parents, "The sea is not ready for me yet!"

Thirty years later, at the Escuela this morning, another little girl of five or six with blonde hair and blue eyes whom Rico had never met walked up to her in the comedory, planted her hands firmly on her hips, and announced in a loud voice, "The stars are not ready for me yet." Rico was stunned. Silent. Finally, she gathered herself enough to reassure the child that the stars would always wait for her. Shaken, she walked away from the Escuela down the beach alone to ask the ocean what it all meant. She felt fraudulent and useless, like thirty years later she was still stuck at the same starting line as the little girl. She was scared the stars weren't ready for any of them. As usual, the ocean's steady rhythm served only to multiply her unanswered questions. She'd never seen this Pacific Ocean before, but all she heard from it was the same old familiar mystery.

She'd never been to the Escuela or Central America before. She'd never gone anywhere on Earth outside Spain, save for her brief stay on the island of Diego Garcia during her Barca training, before she went to the moon. She hadn't spoken to her parents, her ex-husband, or any of her family or friends in Spain for more than three years. Rico felt like she'd left the planet so completely that there probably weren't ten people left on Earth who'd recognize her in a train station queue.

Rico married before she turned sixteen to a man of 27 whose family was quite important in Granada. She'd been dealing with male attention, unwanted or not, long before that. But here in Central America, her soft Spanish olive skin, glossy black hair, big brown eyes, and petite stature weren't helping her, even if she did speak the language. She felt it everywhere, all the time, an all-encompassing cloud of scrutiny and desire that pressed in on her constantly and overwhelmed her with attention that had nothing to do with who she was.

In space, everyone knew everyone, at least by

reputation. Everyone treated her with respect there because they all knew something about her. Maybe they knew she'd operated cutting edge industrial machinery on the moon. Or maybe they knew she'd been an important part of two of the most famous and well-respected habs in the short history of space colonization. A select few knew she'd been chosen to crew on the most advanced spaceship in history. It would be hard for her to float across the L_1 platform without five or ten people recognizing her and stopping her to talk about a shared memory, a common friend, or their future plans. But the people here had no idea about any of that, no idea who she was, and there were so many of them everywhere all the time! People here were strangers to each other yet men felt free to disrespect her because of how she looked with no interest in learning anything more about her.

She was proud she'd been able to maintain her dignity as well as she had. Taking her sandals off and walking barefoot through the choppy green surf, Rico thought that the looks and remarks and smiles and stares and even the cheesy pickup lines and the obscene remarks were, in an odd way, merit badges for the society they were building in space. Sometimes, Rico felt, you didn't realize how good things were at home until you traveled. It wasn't acceptable to act like that in space, for whatever reason. That was surely a sign they'd advanced from the starting line, wasn't it?

But if it was bad here for her, she thought, what about that precious little girl? "The stars are not ready for me yet...." What an amazing thing to say to a complete stranger in broad daylight. She wondered how long the little girl had been here at the *School for New Talents*. She couldn't have been more than six; the Escuela had been here for almost twenty years. It started with just five or six children and a few parents committed to a curriculum based on Grok Martin's ideology of choice. Now there must be 100 kids here, and more than 50 adults. How large could it grow, Rico wondered, before it turned into something completely different?

Turning around, Rico looked back across Salinas Bay. Rico had been born two months after the Berlin Wall fell. She'd grown up in Granada, which was proud to have been the last independent Islamic state in Iberia. She came of age in the early 2000s along with the Euro, the European Parliament, Eurovision, and the rest of the Eurohype. She'd always thought she had a healthy disrespect for borders. Then she'd moved to Catalonia and started working for F.C. Barca. It had challenged her and forced her to reexamine her ideas about groups and boundaries and identity for the first time.

That took her as far as the moon before it all went to shit. She and Ripley had barely escaped. What would they have done, Rico wondered for the thousandth time, if they'd

292

been trapped up there? Would they have found a way to fit in and be happy and adjust and find joy and live out their lives in peace? What had happened to the people who were still up there? For the past three years none of her mooner friends had made any effort to reach out to her, or any habsters she knew.

Some people said the mooners still had some omninet access. If they did, though, they weren't using it to comtack anyone. She and Ripley had talked about reaching out to them many times. Every time, they finally decided the risk of getting their friends in trouble was too great. They just didn't know what would happen, what had happened, to their friends, how the mooner government would react to personal contacts. But she and Ripley somehow got off the moon and avoided that isolation by the thinnest of margins. They'd made it to L_1 and then to the *Hab a Good Time* just a few short days after the habster convention. Maybe she and Ripley would be remembered in some dusty history footnote as the first two habster refugees, Rico imagined.

They'd certainly made their presence felt. The habster convention had lasted more than three weeks. They'd brought Grok and his so-called astro-missionaries from the Escuela for the express purpose of building on Grok's work and choosing a blueprint for their new habster society. They'd talked about initial crews, crew rotations, medical emergencies, new habsters, allocating habricks, famine, disease, unplanned ships from Earth, inventions, chemical storage, inventories, communication networks, different social structures, and hundreds of other things. But nobody ever thought to group about what to do if two hungry and scared young women stowed away in a mortar pod and came up the tether from the moon.

The *Good Time* hadn't really had room, or vitsups, for either of them, but they'd both been welcomed with open arms and they'd all made it work together. Luckily, she thought, most of the habsters believed in doing the right thing more than they believed in their convention, even after all the work they'd put into it. Rules, as the habsters liked to say, were tools for helping people make better choices, not irons shackling them to bad ones.

People down here on Earth didn't do that. They wouldn't have welcomed her and Ripley at all, except maybe as mistresses, or *putas*. She'd been a habster so long she'd forgotten just how strong the taboos against solidarity and mutual aid were down here. She'd become a closer, incorporating the need for mutually chosen solidarity deep within her. She hadn't realized how strong the habster ideology was until she'd traveled here and been surrounded by people who behaved so differently.

Leaving the CSG spaceport in Kourou on her way to the Escuela, she'd seen another little girl standing on the other side of a fence. That little girl wasn't blonde and the stars weren't going to wait for her. She had brown hair and black eyes, like Rico, and her distended belly showed her hunger. Instinctively, Rico threw her water bottle over the fence to her, only realizing what a mistake that was when six or seven bystanders launched themselves towards the bottle and started fighting desperately. Rico made herself walk away without looking back at the hungry little girl, convinced that all she could have done was make things even worse. Even if she'd survived, Rico knew that girl was still thirsty, still miserable, and the stars still weren't waiting for her. It made her feel certain she and the rest of the habsters hadn't moved anything forward very far.

It was just a question of numbers, the habsters liked to assure and reassure themselves. When the right number of people shared the proper amount of resources, without many shortages or luxuries, without the ability to add to their resource pool in any significant way—like (surprise!) on a hab—people generally got along pretty well. If there were too many people who wanted too much, like here on Earth, or not enough people and too many resources, like on the Moon, things usually didn't work out so well. The imbalances incentivized individually motivated action over collective efforts. But she was sure they told different stories about themselves on the Moon and especially here on Earth. People were really, really good at telling themselves how great they were, Rico thought, dragging her toes through the cool sand. But she couldn't deny how much happier people were on the habs, where they had almost nothing, where they had to work as hard as they could all the time and still died regularly, than they were here, where the ocean and the sunshine and a thousand other luxuries were free for the taking.

Walking back up the entrance to the Escuela, she realized how susceptible the people around her, like people everywhere, were to believing their own myths. The people at the Escuela believed unquestioningly that, by reformulating ethical imperatives in terms of choices, Grok Martin had pushed their little village to the top of the human pyramid for the conceivable future. 'Openers,' they called the rest of the people on Earth, and when she heard them say it Rico heard in the back of her mind "Spics," "Injuns," "Wogs," and all the other nasty names people called one another ever since the Greeks coined the term 'barbarian' to mock the 'bar bar' vocalizations of their enemies. It made her feel sad and a little sick, like she'd eaten some bad cheese.

There wasn't that sort of condescension on the habs, not that she'd seen. On the habs, they didn't take anything for granted. It was too easy to die that way. On the habs, they were too busy trying to stay alive to think about the unenlightened billions on Earth. When they did, it was mostly with pity, thinking they'd be dying soon, or with hope, thinking they'd make room for more of them in space. She'd never seen or heard the kind of contempt they felt down here in space. Striding through the central courtyard, she was looking forward to leaving even more than she'd looked forward to coming here. As far as she was concerned, the past was a pretty depressing place for a vacation. She was part of the future of space now and if they weren't perfect they were certainly doing better than this. She'd learned where she belonged, who her mates were, and she was ready to go home to them again.

Waking up the next morning, she gathered her personals and joined some others in the entry courtyard to wait for the truck to take them to La Cruz, where they'd catch a bus to the Liberia airport and fly to the spaceport in Kourou. Three others were coming to the *Farluk* with her. She'd met two of them briefly the day before. Sam and Shawn were fourteen and fifteen years old, kids who'd been at the Escuela for three and four years, and they'd never been to space before. They would be the youngest mates on the *Farluk*, training for greater roles in future endeavors. They were good kids, somewhat in awe of her experience, a little shy, and a little too determined to make a good impression.

Rico had never actually met her third mate personally before, but she knew a lot about her. They had a history. She was an older white woman with long braided hair that looked like it had once been golden brown but was now growing duller and browner, with faint traces of grey. Jody Digger was her name. She had been a habster as long as just about anyone. She'd helped build the *Hab and Hold* with a group of her friends from Chicago, and they'd kept themselves alive and growing for close to a full year before the convention. They'd been more individualistic and libertarian than most. Some of them had stridently resisted coming to the habster convention at all, let alone joining up. Jody had resisted as vociferously as anyone.

Even as she stood and looked blankly at Rico with barely concealed hostility, it was apparent she'd never forgotten or forgiven Rico. "Jody, it's a pleasure to finally meet you," Rico started, nodding her head respectfully and reaching out her hand with her fingers together in the habster fashion. "Is it?" the woman replied. "I'm sure I don't know why." Jody's hands remained at her side and she continued to stand straight up. Her face was tight and she stared impassively into the distance, making it clear she had no intention of talking to Rico any more than necessary.

Shawn and Sam, the eager young kids who they were accompanying to the *Farluk,* stirred nervously in their seats. Rico almost laughed. Those two had been relentlessly taught that everyone in space was passionately supportive of everyone else. They'd internalized Grok's rhetoric of choice and mutual solidarity for years, and now here they were seeing this display of open hostility on the very morning they started their first journey to space. Well, Rico thought, it's probably best they learn right away that you don't have to like somebody to love them.

"That's fair enough Jody," Rico replied, settling on one of the brown wicker chairs to wait for the truck. It was actually pretty easy to understand, Rico thought, why Jody and some of her *Hab and Hold* mates had been so fiercely opposed to the habsters taking her and Ripley in. There was nothing in the convention about taking in strays. They'd argued that letting them join the *Good Time* would inevitably make them habsters, which it had. That, Jody passionately maintained, was a betrayal of everything they'd agreed to, and by extension everything they'd not agreed to. Jody and her mates had survived hard and dangerous months bargaining for habricks, getting to orbit, building their hab, and making it work well enough for most of them to stay alive because they wanted to be on their own, not because they wanted to help others.

People on the habs thought more about Earth back then. There had been, and to some extent still was, a huge divide. Some people, like Jody, didn't really care whether or not everyone on Earth was dying. They just wanted to build themselves as strong a home as possible and survive as long as they could, relying on nobody but themselves. Other people thought they could build enough habs and move enough people to space to keep humanity alive on Earth.

They cared passionately about those people. They wanted to save that thirsty little girl on the other side of the fence by building enough space colonies that were strong enough and large enough for humanity to go on forever, both on and off its home planet.

That debate had never really been resolved. At the same time, it wasn't really something habsters talked about very much any more—at least not the people Rico knew. Living in space was so inherently dangerous that they had too much to talk about just keeping themselves alive, for one thing. No hab had ever been completely destroyed, but people regularly and routinely died on all of them. Rico was as good at living in space as just about anyone. She was that good because she never took anything for granted.

And as far as anyone knew, the mooners weren't building any new tethers or increasing the supply of habricks, which dropped off the tether at the same slow rate, year after year. That was one thing habsters did spend a lot of time talking about, endlessly debating what, if anything, was happening at L_2, the mirror image of L_1 on the far side of the moon. In theory, a tether could be built there more or less as easily; the counterweighting process would actually be somewhat different, but the principles were the same. By definition, though, you couldn't see L_2 from L_1 because the Moon was in the way. So they had no real way of knowing what, if anything, was happening on the far side of the moon—and no way of finding out, short of building a ship and going to look. They didn't have time or vitsups for that, so they argued endlessly instead.

The white truck finally pulled into the courtyard and the four travelers silently loaded their personals in the back. Without discussion, they all climbed on and sat down in the bed of the truck with their stuff. Shawn and Sam whispered together a few times, but Jody and Rico were content to stare silently through their sunglasses at the warm May sky as the truck traveled down the coast and across the peninsula towards the airport.

After their flight landed, looking out the dirty windows of the CSG spaceport shuttle bus, Rico saw muddy rivers of sewage surrounded by ramshackle shacks and favelas, half collapsed shelters of cardboard and cheap plywood held together with duct tape, bailing wire, and mud by dirty, discouraged people—the polar opposite of the fancy surfboard cases and tanned, smiling vacationers she'd seen at the Liberia airport last night. Some of the inhabitants were idly watching the bus go by; others ignored it and went about their morning routines, such as they were. It made her sad. She wanted to believe that she and her habster mates were on the side of the people in the favelas, not the well-to-do surfers on vacation. But up close they all looked like two sides of the same coin and she felt no more of a connection to the grim dirty people in the favelas than she had with the tan smiling surfers at the airport. She felt sorry for them all, trapped in outdated class structures and forced into archaic materialist conflicts.

After a few minutes, the makeshift cardboard shelters gave way to shoddily built tenements. Instead of washing themselves openly in polluted waters, the inhabitants gathered around doorways to smoke cigarettes and drink from cans wrapped in paper bags. Some of them watched the shuttle too, but with more visible hostility. At least it was a connection, of a sort, but it made Rico even sadder and she kept wondering whose side the habsters were really on.

The shuttle continued past the Anse Golf Club and moved steadily west towards the CSG through the warrens of corporate sub-divisions that had sprung up in the last decade. Finally, Rico looked through the dusty windshield and saw the old white Ariane launcher marking the main entrance to the spaceport. They were still about 750 meters away, but the shuttle bus was completely stopped and Rico could see other buses, cars, trucks, and all sorts of supply vehicles going nowhere as a sea of people swarmed around the main gate.

Rico saw Sam and Shawn glance at each other and look questioningly at Jody and her, as if asking for guidance. She didn't know what was happening at the gate, but she was pretty sure it wasn't anything good. She felt like anything could happen any moment down here with people so divided

302

and disunited and constantly tearing each other down. It made her long even more for the reasoned comfort of space, where even she and Jody would set their differences aside and work together. She said nothing but sighed and stretched her arms and settled even deeper into her seat with her eyes closed, trying not to make the kids any more scared than they already were.

That worked for a little more than half an hour. Rico kept her eyes shut and kept reminding herself that there was no reason for them to hurry; their ship to L_1 wasn't scheduled to launch for hours. She was sure Shawn and Sam wanted to hurry. She was just as sure that Jody was keeping as calm as she was, if not calmer.

Finally, half an hour later, Rico heard the front door of the bus open. She looked up to hear their driver entreating two white European passengers not to get off the bus. "We will go through in time," he assured them. "Please, sit and relax. You do not need to go out there."

The two Europeans looked at each other. They were a couple, Rico thought. Probably they were about 28 and had been married for two or three years. He was a tall blonde man with short hair and blue eyes, wearing a suit that fit him well. She was beautiful, wearing a large straw sun hat and a fashionable version of a peasant smock in bright tropical colors. They looked comfortable and happy. Rico thought about the people she'd watched from the bus and understood their hostility a little better. The smiling young European woman took her husband by the arm as he confidently told the driver "You wait here. We are going ahead now. Thank you."

The two Europeans got off the bus and Rico's view was obscured. The driver shut the door firmly and she thought she heard him mutter *"via con Dios"* under his breath. Curious, she stood up on her seat and tried to see what the Europeans were doing. Before she could see them, she heard a loud whooshing sound, like a giant gust of wind, and suddenly black smoke began rushing violently up from the floorboards and filling the bus with the stench of sulphur.

Her first thought, as people's screams surrounded her and she saw people starting to fight for the exits, was for Sam and Shawn, and then Jody. She had to get them out! Taking a deep breath, Rico ducked down into the smoke and pushed through people until she found the two kids huddling together in their seats. Gasping, she pulled them up and got them to all stand on their seat together so they could take another deep breath from the rapidly disappearing cooler air near the roof. They heard windows shattering, but the smoke kept rushing in. Images of the well-dressed Europeans flashed through Rico's mind as she struggled to process the unthinkable idea that somebody, probably those two, had blown up their bus. They were able to breathe twice before even the roof turned black and Rico knew they had to get out right away. Out of this bus and off of this planet full of people capable of such horror.

Holding each teenager by one hand, Rico pulled them up and over the seats in front of them, knowing the aisle would be hopelessly crowded and unsure about going out a broken window. She heard the other passengers screaming at each other as they blocked themselves in the middle of the bus. When she felt the driver's seat, she let go of one young hand and reached out in front of her. As she'd suspected, the driver was gone and she could feel air rushing out his open window. She hoisted the first frightened young body through the window with a great shove, hoping to cleanly clear the windowsill.

Somehow, through the commotion, she heard the child hit the ground outside and smiled as she reached back for the second youngster. *You crazy Earthers aren't going to take us out this easy*, she told herself as she started feeling the complex waves of emotion that sweep over people in the moment they realize they're not about to die. She threw the next teenager head first. She didn't hear a thud, but it didn't matter. She didn't know where Jody was, but there was nothing more she could do. Her lungs were clamoring for air and it took everything she had to pull herself into the driver's seat and roll forwards out the window, trying to aim her body to the right so that she didn't land on anyone. Her last thought as she dove out of the smoke was she hoped Jody would make it.

She woke up lying on her back with a tube in her nose in a sterile white room with four caged overhead lights. Moving slowly, she felt up and down her body carefully. She had a mediv in her left arm, but she couldn't feel any bandages or casts. Her right arm made its way slowly to her head and she realized it was wrapped tightly. "You're OK!" she heard as Shawn and Sam came into her view. "I'm OK," she replied cautiously, still taking inventory of herself and not finding any pain or obvious damage.

"Our launch was postponed," Shawn told her earnestly. "For two hours," Sam added. They looked at each other. "They said it's up to us if we want to go," Shawn said. "Do you?" Rico asked in a gravelly voice. "Here, drink some water," Sam replied, handing her a cup. "We need to tell the doctor you woke up." Sam darted out of the room through a white curtain hanging over the doorway. Rico sipped her water, looked at Shawn's dirty and torn clothes, and tried to start piecing together what had happened.

Before she could collect her thoughts, the curtain moved aside and an elderly Latino man with thick glasses entered. "Ah, you have decided to rejoin us!" he smiled. "I am Doctor Juan Carlos Alvarez," he continued, with a slight bow. "You hit your head on a rock diving out of that bus," he informed her, looking down at his clipboard, "and have

306

suffered a slight concussion." He took a tongue depressor out of his pocket and held it in front of her. "Please follow this." Her eyes tracked the stick. Dr. Alvarez continued his exam, and after verifying that she had a slight headache, did not feel nauseous, was not sensitive to light or noise and felt no numbness or tingling, he pulled the covers off her cot and extended his hand to help her to her feet.

Hesitating only slightly, Rico took his hand, swung her legs to the floor, and stood up quickly and steadily. "Excellent!" Dr. Alvarez noted, letting go of her hand so Rico could stand on her own. As she took her first confident steps, the curtain parted again and two women wearing coveralls came in, followed closely by Sam. One of them glanced at her compad and told Shawn "We need to know right now if you and Sam are going on this flight?"

"What about Rico?" Shawn asked, looking at Dr. Alvarez. "Can she come with us?" Dr. Alvarez looked at the women in coveralls and back at Rico, who looked at Shawn and back at Dr. Alvarez. "Can I?" She asked him. He smiled. "Who am I to tell one of you folks what to do?" he asked. "I'm not sure I could keep you off that launcher against your will unless you had some kind of communicable disease." Rico smiled with him. "OK, should I go? Is it dangerous?"

"It is more dangerous than it would be if you had not hit your head," Dr. Alvarez nodded. "But not that much more dangerous." "It's certainly no more dangerous than staying here!" Rico exclaimed. "What happened? Has anyone caught the people who tried to blow us up?" Dr. Alvarez looked cautiously at the women in coveralls. "The security office is conducting an investigation," one of them replied. "It was probably one of the local criminal gangs that steal resources from the habsters," the other added. "But I saw them," Rico objected. "I'm sure of it! They were well-dressed Europeans like the surfers in Liberia, not like locals at all. And how would blowing up a bus help them steal anything?"

"As I said," the first woman replied, "an investigation is under way." "Perhaps you should stay and tell them what you saw?" the second woman added. That, Rico felt immediately, was not a good idea. The last thing she wanted was to get involved in an investigation to determine who tried to blow up their bus and for what reason. She didn't know much about politics or war, but she felt strongly that none of the Earthers would win anything so long as they needed investigations to figure out who was blowing up buses and ask why.

"So there's no way to know if—when—another attack is coming," she said to nobody in particular. She looked back at Dr. Alvarez. "Doesn't that increased risk," she asked him, "make flying now seem more reasonable?" He looked at the women in coveralls and nodded. "I can

clear her to fly if she wants." Shawn and Sam looked at
Rico. Clearly they did not want to go to the *Farluk* without
her. She reached up and felt her head. It wasn't too bad. She
jumped up and down cautiously. It felt OK. She looked
around the room. "Let's do it," she said quietly. She was
ready to get off this planet and was pretty sure she was never
coming back.

"Right then," one of the women in coveralls said,
making a notation on her compad. "You've got thirty-six
minutes." "No problem," Rico smiled, looking at Shawn and
Sam to reassure them. "Can you take these two to prep and
suit up?" she asked the woman with the compad. "I'll catch
up. I've done it before." The women in coveralls glanced at
each other. The one with the compad shrugged, and,
gesturing to Shawn and Sam, led them out through the
curtain.

Rico started pulling herself together before Dr.
Alvarez could even take the mediv out of her arm. "There
will be other ships, you know," he told her softly as he
bandaged her arm. "Thanks Doctor," she replied, "but I'm
ready to go home." "Well," the kindly doctor said, pulling
the curtain aside, *"via con Dios."* He went out and Rico
stood in shock for just a moment. That's what their bus
driver said to the white Europeans. Was Alvarez connected
to him somehow? It was so hard with these Earthers, she
thought, to know when they were in league and when they

were fighting and with whom. She and Jody might not like each other very much, but at least they were open about it and tried not to make more of it than they had to. "No time to think about it now," she told herself as she shook off her shock, piled together the few personals she saw, took a deep breath, and walked through the curtain.

She recognized the hallway from her trip down and quickly found Sam and Shawn in the locker room at the other end. As soon as she walked in, attendants set upon her and started prepping her for their flight. They inspected her scalp to be sure her wound was fully closed and wound another layer of bandages around her head. "No problem," one of them told her. "We've seen people come through looking way worse!" 'And why do you think anyone'd tell you if they'd died,' Rico thought to herself briefly. Not today, she told herself quickly, and not down here. She was going home.

Rico tried to remember what it had been like on Diego Garcia, the only other time she'd left Earth, but she didn't remember much. When the throbbing roar and gigantic hand of gravity came at liftoff, it was almost anticlimactic. She could see Sam and Shawn touching heads in front of her to share their thoughts and she hoped they'd recovered enough from the explosion to be excited about the trip. Maybe the contempt she'd seen at the Escuela made it easier for them to process unknown people trying to blow up their bus for undisclosed reasons. She couldn't turn her head and didn't see anyone who looked like Jody, but Rico hoped she'd been able to catch this flight too.

As far as she could tell, the boost and recovery phases of their flight were uneventful, and after about twenty minutes she felt the maneuvering boosters fire as the shuttle began the complicated process of docking with the L_1 platform. It felt good to be in space again, she thought. It felt better to leave Earth. She felt like she could finally relax and be herself again without anyone propositioning her or trying to blow her up. She was almost looking forward to the next time somebody came up and in the direct habster fashion shared their disapproval of something she'd done. The launcher docked successfully on the first try and with a minimum of delay she was able to bounce onto the platform.

She looked around expectantly, but didn't recognize anyone. Shrugging, she herded Sam and Shawn over to the tender that would take them to the *Farluk*. She still didn't see Jody. When they got to the tender, she saw that it was already loaded and waiting for them, so they strapped in quickly and undocked.

On the slow trip to the *Farluk*, Rico saw Sam and Shawn looking at her furtively now and again, but they did not make comtack, so she just smiled back at them and let it go. Finally, almost 50 hours after they'd woken up in the Escuela guesthouse on the southwestern Nicaraguan coast,

Rico felt the tender dock and sighed with deep relief. At last she was home!

After they helped unload the tender, Rico and Shawn and Sam went into the locker room to unsuit. Rico had worried that, after breathing fresh ocean air for a few days, the air would seem bland or metallic, but it smelled great to her. Smiling, she looked over at Shawn and Sam, who seemed to be unsuiting a lot more efficiently than they'd suited. Just being in space, Rico thought, helped them learn. "Do you know what launcher Jody was going to come on?" she asked them.

The shock on their faces was immediate. "You didn't know?" Sam exclaimed. "Jody's dead!" Shawn stuttered. "She died at the bus" Sam continued. "She saved us!" Shawn shouted. "She saved you!" Sam interjected. "From the criminals," Shawn agreed. "They were going to shoot us!" Sam stammered. "She stopped them!" Shawn cried. "They shot her!" Sam concluded. Rico stared at the youngsters in shock, trying to process what they were telling her, trying to process that somebody wanted to shoot them, trying to process what it meant that Jody Digger, who'd argued against saving her and Ripley, had laid down her life for her, trying not to cry at how proud of that she was.

Chapter Sixteen

Jong-un

Sohae Satellite Launching Station, Cholsan,

North Pyongan Province, North Korea

October 14, 2023

"I'm telling you, Marshal, that ship can't carry enough space marines with enough supplies for them to be able to assemble that spacedock in orbit before they die." That's not necessarily a problem, Jong-un thought, irritated at the prospect of enduring another lecture from this skinny, annoying American. We've got plenty of people. "And, Marshal, I'm telling you that you can't just send people up there in that ship to die," Howard continued in his nasal self-assured tone. "If they're smart enough to be at all useful once they're up there, they're smart enough to figure out it's a one-way trip. I know you have many space marines who say they're willing to die for you, but do you really want to bet millions of dollars they mean it? Are you going to bet all this that they'll spend their dying days building your station and not trying to figure out some way to survive? I've seen you gamble, Marshal. You make smart bets, not risky ones. Am I wrong?"

Part of the reason this American was so annoying, Jong-un thought, was how quickly he picked up on cues from the people around him. Calling him by his military rank, Marshal, for example. It seemed like he'd done that practically from the moment he stepped off the plane in Pyongyang this summer.

"The main problem, Marshal," the persistent American continued, "as I've told you time and again, is that your designers are in love with themselves! They want to build such beautiful ships. They want their beautiful ships to be self-contained! And they want to send people and their supplies in the same ships. They think it's more elegant. They think it's safer that way. But it's just not. The safe bet, Marshal, is to send the supplies and equipment first, in simpler, cheaper rockets. Then, once the material is safely in place, raise the stakes and send in the space marines—in simpler, cheaper ships. Remember, it does not matter how slowly you go if you don't stop!" The American smiled proudly and looked Jong-un in his eyes, waiting for his approval.

There he went again, Jung-un thought. Another Confucianism. Another smarmy gambling reference. If only he'd managed to work in basketball, booze, and broads, he'd have checked off the entire Western guide to kissing my fat North Korean ass in a single sentence. It amused Jong-un to have people think he was easily distracted and susceptible to flattery. He tried to carry himself in a simple manner and talk in a way that minimized his education, which had been excellent. He liked it when people underestimated him. "A

314

friend should always underestimate your virtues and an enemy overestimate your faults," he repeated to himself. It was a quote from the famous American gangster movie, but Jong-un was certain Confucius would have understood and appreciated the sentiment.

But was this annoying American who worked so hard to kiss his ass a friend or an enemy? What if he was smart enough to see through Jong-un's affected manner? Those were the real questions, weren't they? Jong-un had tried to talk about politics with him on many occasions, but Howard had adroitly brushed him aside each time. "It doesn't really matter who gets to space when," he'd said once, "but if nobody does, we're all going to die." Jong-un figured he had at least as much power over death as anyone else on the planet. He had total control over the North Korean nuclear arsenal. He had dozens of followers who would kill anyone he told them to. He could deal death with the best of them. But not even he had Howard's certainty, his total conviction, his complete devotion to a single vision.

When Jong-un first invited Howard Gall to North Korea he thought he'd get a defeated, downcast man who might be able to make some small practical or technical contributions to the North Korean space program at little or no cost. He thought it would be entertaining for him and his people to see this once rich and powerful American working at trifles for peanuts in the margins of North Korea.

Howard's fifteen minutes of worldwide fame after the first great climate storms in 2019 had been historically brutal. Even Jong-un, who'd been the butt of bad jokes since before he was born, felt bad at the way Gall was treated. Four hundred of Howard's habinauts died on the floor of the South China Sea, probably the safest place in the world to be in a typhoon, or drowned trying unnecessarily to get to the surface, after Howard's surface-based command, control, and communications systems were destroyed by the storms.

If Gall had been down there with his people, Jong-un thought, if he'd built his great submersible experiment to be truly self-enclosed, they'd all have ridden out the storms effortlessly. Their technology didn't fail; their people did. Howard failed because he didn't want to be stuck on the bottom of the ocean and he didn't trust anyone but himself to control his experiment. With better planning they'd all have risen from the sea bottom amid the devastation healthier, fatter, and better rested than anyone else in Southeast Asia. Gall's hab would have been reckoned one of the great wonders of the world, not ridiculed and scorned as the rich man's plaything that drowned 400 innocent people.

Then, later that year, when those crazy young people went up out of the blue and built their lunar tether, Howard would have been the most natural person in the world for them to reach out to. Howard, not Jeff Bezos, Lionel Messi, and the Chinese government, would have had the inside track to build a lunar mining station and send the first habricks up their tether into history. Instead, Howard dropped under the world's radar as best he could while history went on without him. He spent the last part of 2019 in Brunei, winding down his operations there and, with most of his personal fortune tied up in various legal squabbles, trying unsuccessfully to convince the Sultan to partner with him to buy the island of Diego Garcia from the Americans and build a spaceport there.

He'd already caught Jong-un's eye by then, and with the resources of a small country at his personal disposal, it was easy for him to keep track of the American. After he'd worn out his welcome in Brunei, he'd gone to Kazakhstan for several months at the end of 2020. Unable to further his dreams there, and with most of what money he had left still tied in legal knots, he'd left with the New Year and made his way across the border to the Chinese spaceport at Jinquan. That's where Jong-un had reached out to him for the first time, through his contacts in the Chinese government.

But Howard ignored his first entreaties. His advisers thought maybe Howard was too proud or too embarrassed to work with them, but Jong-un realized the issue was more basic than that. It had nothing to do with pride or politics. Howard still wanted to be in charge, to be the boss, the man, and he knew that wasn't ever going to happen in Pyongyang. Or was it? Jong-un thought with a sly smile, trying to

317

remember the last time he'd said no to Howard.

After that Howard had wandered back and forth across Central Asia from Jinquan to Baikonur to Vostochny for another year and a half. He was trying desperately to find a home, to find a place to build the spaceships he still dreamt of. Jong-un let him wander. He kept track of him patiently and followed the various lawsuits that slowly and inevitably separated Howard from the rest of his money. When Jong-un thought Howard had fallen just far enough, he made him a second offer. That one didn't go through any Chinese emissaries—he'd gone himself. In great secrecy, with disguises and decoys, Jong-un traveled to Baikonur and showed Howard the drawings of the *Byeol Bich*, the spaceship he wanted to build in orbit and send to Mars.

Jong-un remembered assuming the idea of working on the first spaceship to Mars would inspire Howard. He couldn't have been more mistaken. The skinny American dressed in rags laughed openly in his face. "Mars? Mars? You fool!" They were the first four words Jong-un ever heard from Howard. It was not the treatment he was used to. But he kept listening.

In some ways, Jong-un was actually disappointed Howard had become so much more sycophantic since then. That was the price he paid for having an entire country subject to his every whim, Jong-un figured. Everything in nature is as it should be, and so there is beauty in every part

318

of it, even if we can't always see it. Howard's survival, like the survival of everyone else in North Korea, depended on Jong-un's attitude towards him. It probably wasn't fair to expect Howard to laugh in his face all the time. But he still treasured the memory.

And the crazy thing was, Howard's convictions, his certainty, had carried the day. They'd spent two hours talking about the future of space exploration at Baikonur, Jong-un remembered, and by the time they'd parted that evening Howard had convinced him that the asteroid belt, not Mars, should be the *Byeol Bich*'s first destination. "It's just a question of efficiency," he'd explained, working through equations at breathtaking speed using seat of the pants estimations for the size of the asteroids he wanted to visit, their elemental composition, their distance from Earth in three years, the chemical composition of the Martian soil, and a hundred other variables Jong-un quickly lost track of. Later, after he returned to Pyongyang, Jong-un had his best engineers and data collectors look up as many correct numbers as they could and check Gall's calculations. A dozen men worked on it for more than a week. In the end, they told him, their numbers were within about three and a half percent of what Gall had done by himself in an hour, without any reference materials, by the seat of his pants.

It would be a shame, Jong-un thought, to kill somebody with that kind of genius. But the American was so annoying, and his plan had so many problems, and he quoted Confucius so much, and he was such a humorless little suck-up! It truly was a test of Jong-un's patience, another trait he tried to hide. Going to Mars had great propaganda value for him and his country. It was a monumental trip that would have assured him and North Korea places in history. And yet Howard, still challenging him even as he kissed his ass more and more, was openly contemptuous of that objective.

"All the people down here are going to die," he told Jong-un over and over. "Only the ones who learn to live in orbit will ever write any history that matters. 'Happiness is the journey itself, not an arrival.' 'If you shoot for the stars and hit the moon, it's OK.'" Jong-un had to spend a week getting drunk at his Wonsan beach resort to recover from that conversation. But in the end Howard convinced him and got his way.

Living in space, in manufactured worlds, was the really big goal. History would belong to whoever mastered that skill set first. Howard was right. Planets were just distractions, or material stores—really nothing but glorified fueling stops. The most accessible, most lucrative, richest material, the really low hanging fruit, though, was the asteroids. Millions of tons of trace elements, heavy metals, and who knows what else, just floating out there waiting for somebody to come get it. Whoever was first to bring a big

320

asteroid back to orbit would vault past the mooners and the habsters into history by the sheer weight of their acquisition.

Howard flew back to North Korea with Jong-un that summer day and, since his arrival, he'd lectured everyone he met incessantly about how they were doing everything all wrong and their only hope in life was to immediately start doing things the right way—Howard's way. Every time Jong-un had occasion to share a meal with Howard, he half expected the man to start lecturing the cooks about their *kim chi*. "Better a diamond with a flaw than a pebble without," Jong-un thought, laughing silently at the thought of the skinny American lecturing one of his fat Korean cooks about their *kim chi*.

In just a few months though, Howard, with his unquenchable self-confidence and unique purity of vision, had somehow made himself indispensible to the North Korean space program. A big part of it was that he just solved math and engineering problems faster than anyone else. Where a normal engineer would have questions and want to explore different variations, Howard saw only the clearest path to the answer. He'd already helped solve major problems with propulsion, power, command, and data handling. Because he was a foreigner—a rare sight in North Korea, let alone at Sohae—he was actually able to move in and out of different groups in ways that Jong-un's Korean subjects, with their more detailed histories and social interrelationships, could not.

"I have never seen you go slowly," Jong-un replied after a moment of thought. "As far as I know, you have never gone slowly. You raced to become rich so you could race to the bottom of the South China Sea so you could race to orbit. Yet now you urge caution!" Jong-un waved his hand at the *Seungliui Balam* resting on the launch tower in front of them. "We will go to space with this ship! With the ship we have! You helped Jae-Wook design those engines. Min-Kyu could not have done these control systems without you. How can you tell me now that they're worthless?" Jong-un felt as close to killing the American as he'd ever been. Flawed diamond or not, Jong-un couldn't allow anyone to question his authority for long.

"But Marshal…" Howard began to reply. "Do not call me that!" Jong-un thundered. "Do not address me! Address our ship! Tell it to her, to the *Seunghui Balam*! The ship you worked on! Tell her why she cannot take our glorious marines to space!" Jong-un felt his anger rising and forced himself to breathe deeply and not let Howard's annoying American arrogance limit his usefulness. "You can take the leader's glories to space," Howard told the ship, slowly and deliberately, his gaze not wavering from Jong-un's eyes. "You will take the glorious leader's space marines to orbit to build the *Byeol Bich*, the *Light of Stars*, the highest achievement of any human civilization ever!"

322

Howard held Jong-un's eyes one beat too long. "But not yet you won't," Howard finally said, looking at the *Seunghui Balam* as if for the first time.

"Not yet?" Jong-un questioned curtly, feeling his patience running out. "Not yet," Howard nodded in agreement. "She is a fine ship! The equal, perhaps the superior, of anything the Chinese, the Americans, or anyone else has ever built! Perhaps you mistake me, Marshal," Howard added quickly, "but I do not criticize this ship!" "Then you criticize me?" Jong-un asked with a sharp edge of steel in his voice. "'To see what is right and not do it is want of courage,'" Howard replied. "How can I criticize what has not yet been done? I only say what I see is right, never anything against you."

Yes and no, Jong-un thought to himself. True, the American didn't actually say anything negative. And there was no doubt it took courage to tell him things he didn't want to hear. He was more than smart enough to know that, and to know the value of people who had such courage and spoke truth to him. But the American saw things in such simple terms. He had no sense for the politics of it all. In his eyes everything was simple. The Earth was dying. If something helped humanity survive its death, Howard was all for it. If it didn't, he had no time for it. Jong-un sighed, thinking of his father. He would have liked this American, he thought. They both were able to see purity in this most impure world.

"So what you are saying is I must leave this ship, our best, the most advanced thing North Korea's ever built, sitting on that launch pad while I build others?" Jong-un started slowly. "Do you have any idea of the cost? Do you have any idea what the Chinese, the South Koreans, and the rest of them will say if we do not launch our finest ship immediately?" Jong-un saw Howard's eyes flicker at that. The American, focused only on getting to space by any means necessary, hadn't considered any wider, more strategic concerns.

"Who cares what they say?" Howard replied. "'The superior man understands what is right; the inferior man knows what will sell.' Will your people know what the Chinese and South Koreans say? Will they care? No! Will history know what they say?" The American paused, and Jong-un could see him taking calming breaths and forcing himself to speak slowly.

"Do not think, Marshal, that I am ungrateful for the opportunities you have given me here, or that I wish your country anything but the greatest success. And I know that I am not always an easy person to get along with, that I do not always 'behave towards everyone as if receiving a great guest.'" That was the understatement of the century, Jong-un thought to himself.

"But being here with you and your people, working

on these projects," the American continued, "has helped me, and so I say this with as much humility as possible: launching the *Seunghui Balam* today will move your space program backwards, not forwards." The American strode quickly over to a table and picked up a compad. Swiping through pages rapidly, he continued lecturing. "Your engineers are telling you that this ship can lift 25,000 kilos of cargo to orbit at about 500 km, a little higher than the International Space Station and the Hubble Space Telescope but still well on the safe side of the first Van Allen belt, moving at a speed of just over nine kilometers per second. That's based on everything going perfectly, but even if she only gets to 420 km at eight klicks a second, which I think is more reasonable, it will be a smashing success." He stopped and looked at Jong-un again. "I mean that, you know. She really is a tremendous ship!"

Howard continued, looking back at the compad. "You're going to send eight space marines up there to build your spacedock, so that's just about 975 kilos of mass, including their personal gear and spacesuits, etc, etc. Your engineers have about 4500 kilos of hydrogen and 7500 kilos of oxygen onboard, along with another 500 kilos of fuel cells, electrical equipment, wiring, transformers, power tools and the like. They claim that will make enough air and water to keep your eight space marines alive for 21 days, while providing enough power for them to assemble two square

325

kilometers of solar panels and one square spacedock measuring exactly 31 meters on each side."

Howard paused, and Jong-un reminded himself not to be swept along by the American's eloquent flow of numbers, to keep his perspective and maintain his authority. "I think their assumption about that oxygen and those fuel cells keeping those eight marines alive for that long is unreasonably optimistic, and I suspect there might be an unspoken assumption that one or more of them will die before the end of their mission, but it doesn't really matter. They have 150 kilos of food, 20 kilos of medical supplies and emergency gear, and 100 kilo reserves of water and oxygen. Finally, since it's not officially a suicide mission, they have a re-entry capsule that weighs 4,800 kilos, with a heat shield that has literally no margin of error.

"That," Howard swiped at the compad again, "leaves 6,355 kilos worth of solar panel and spacedock supplies and materials, along with the body of the ship itself, which is cleverly built in such a way that most of it can be deconstructed and reconstituted into the body of the space dock." "Which is plenty!" Jong-un declared. "I reviewed the blueprints and inventories myself. They will have exactly what they need to build our spacedock and return to Earth covered in glory!"

"Exactly." Howard said, looking at Jong-un like he'd just won the argument. Jong-un looked back at him curiously, not seeing his point, but Howard did not speak. "Exactly," the American said again. Jong-un waited, but could not stand the thought of hearing Howard repeat himself again. "Yes, exactly. You have a problem with that!"

"Marshal," Howard replied, "this is not about me, or you, or any of us who have worked so hard to build this beautiful ship. This is about making sure your spacedock gets built." Howard put down the compad. "When I built my hab in Malaysia, do you know how many parts were listed on my master inventory list?" Jong-un remained silent. Howard hadn't talked much about his hab and Jong-un had consciously avoided the topic, keeping Howard focused on North Korea's future in space, but he was as curious as anyone to hear behind-the-scenes stories. "147,969," Howard continued. "Do you know how many wound up being used? 150,861. That's just under 2% extra parts, which is actually pretty good for a project of that size. That means that for every 50 parts, one of them got lost, or broke, or somebody dropped it and couldn't find it, or whatever. Shit happened. Entropy happened."

Howard picked the compad back up. "Look at this, Marshal." He showed Jong-un a spreadsheet. "Your engineers are claiming those eight space marines can build those solar panels and that spacedock out of 975 parts, not counting the five parts of the ship herself." Jong-un took the compad and saw that the different components and sub-assemblies and so forth did, in fact, add up to 975 listed units. Some of them were 'parts' like 'CPU assembly,' which obviously contained many more parts, but it was still, he thought, a pretty amazingly small number from which to assemble humanity's first spaceport.

"But now look here, Marshal," Howard continued as he took the compad back and flipped to a different page. "How many parts have they loaded on your fine ship over there?" Jong-un took the compad knowing Howard already knew the answer. "975," he recited dutifully, "with a combined weight of 6.356 kilograms." "You see Marshal," Howard exclaimed. "They have no extra parts and are still one kilo overweight! As soon as one of those space marines accidently knocks a single joist, or even a single nut, off into space, they won't have the parts they need to build the spacedock!"

It was a problem Jong-un had seen before. His father and grandfather had demanded perfection from their citizens. When imperfections had inevitably crept into their world, they'd pretended it didn't exist and written it out of their histories and their propaganda. But, Jong-un admitted to himself, you couldn't do that in space. You couldn't announce that your glorious space marines had constructed the first ever orbital spacedock and were making final preparations to build the *Byeol Bich* when any peasant with a primitive telescope or even a decent pair of binoculars could look up at night through the dark skies of North Korea and see for himself that there wasn't anything there.

But his engineers weren't worried about that. It was too far in the future. They were just trying to survive today. They'd all learned at a young age that the best way to do that was to convince themselves that the future, like the past, would be perfect. Perfect, at any cost. "My people plan for success, not failure," Jong-un told the American.

"Your people fear failure," Howard replied. "If they plan for success and things go wrong, the engineers can blame the space marines for losing a piece of wire or letting a bolt slip through their gloves and off into space. As long as they have somebody else to blame, they feel like they're succeeding." Jong-un nodded in recognition, admitting that Howard had identified the root of the problem. His people feared individual failure more than they fought for national success.

Before he could think of anything to say, Jong-un heard cries ring out, followed by gunfire from the western edge of the hollowed out launch pit. Howard and Jong-un instinctively backed away from the edge of the observation balcony and crouched down, looking at each other quizzically as they heard more screams and more gunfire. "Seventy years," Jong-un told himself. Seventy years of total power, secret police everywhere, comprehensive state

329

education, yet every year or so somebody went crazy and threw their lives away like this. Few lived long enough to work together or cause any serious trouble, but even a lone fanatic had that one chance to punch above their weight.

After a moment of silence, both cautiously raised their heads and looked out over the edge of the balcony. More gunshots rang out as they saw a young man in a red tracksuit jump down into the launch pit and start running towards the launch platform and the *Seunghui Balam*. "Stop him!" Jong-un screamed as Howard looked around in confusion.

Special operations soldiers had already taken up positions on the edge of the launch pit and were firing at will. Jong-un saw that the young man was hit in his left arm, and twice in his back, but none of the wounds were critical and his momentum kept him moving slowly towards the launch platform. His red clothing symbolized a unified Korea, which Jong-un knew meant opposition to his 'polarizing' space program.

Jong-un suddenly realized the young man was wearing a red backpack and he knew the danger of that. He grabbed Howard and pulled him down to the balcony floor on top of him seconds before the explosion. "NO!" he heard Howard screaming as the echoes of the blast reverberated around and through them for what seemed like an eternity. Jong-un felt Howard trying to pull away as his instinct to flee kicked in, but he felt much safer with the American covering him and held Howard there until he heard silence.

Released, Howard sprang to his feet. "Oh my God," the American exclaimed as the smells of the explosion and the dead bodies started to reach him and he looked down at the body parts strewn across the platform, "they're all dead." Jong-un started to get up, but before he could move four of his supreme guards were on the balcony, surrounding him and making nervous noises. He could see two of them looking at Howard suspiciously. "He is fine," Jong-un snapped. "What happened?"

"There were four of them," General Yun replied, walking out onto the balcony. "They were able to incapacitate a group of special operations soldiers on the western perimeter with some kind of nerve gas and gain access to the station through their vacant post. They assassinated two pit guards with silenced weapons. The other three held off the rest of our guards just long enough." Jong-un didn't have to ask whether the other three were dead, or whether they'd worn the same red tracksuits. Their treason made him even more determined to colonize space and occupy South Korea.

Jong-un got up and moved to stand next to Howard. His supreme guard would be on edge and he didn't want them to kill the American. At least not yet. He turned and looked at the launcher. The *Seunghui Balam* was lying

331

across the platform with a hole in her side. She wasn't flying today, or any time soon. But she hadn't blown up, he wasn't dead, and all the terrorists had been killed.

Jong-un put his arm around Howard and smiled. "'Men do not stumble over mountains, but over molehills,' eh?" "Marshal," the American stammered, "this is no molehill! Look at her!" "Yes, look at her," Jong-un smiled. "Look at her safely there on the ground, where she cannot fly for many weeks." Howard looked at him, still confused. "Many weeks," Jong-un continued, "for us to build your simpler, cheaper supply rockets and launch them into the *Seunghui Balam*'s orbit, so that our spacedock will still get built no matter how many pieces of wire our space marines drop!" It doesn't matter how slow you are, he reminded himself, as long as you keep moving forward.

Chapter Seventeen

Maringka

Touchdown

February 2, 2025

Walking out of the conference room, Maringka wanted to strangle somebody very slowly. Things should have been so simple, she thought, starting down the dark tunnel towards her quarters. Keep building habricks and sending them up the tether until they had everything they needed to build a sustainable life up here. Maybe it wasn't as grandiose as "crush your enemies and see them driven before you," but it was a lot more civilized and so much easier on the children. But that wasn't the course they'd chosen. They didn't even have enough power to light all their hallways all the time and they were working on their master plan to conquer the solar system.

It had only been two years, she reminded herself, since she and the rest of the mooners broke free from the corporate overlords on Earth and started trading habricks to hablicants directly instead of dutifully posting them on Amazon like good little employees. And they'd done some pretty impressive things in that time. They'd dug in deep, excavating enough tunnels and rooms under Touchdown, Stoner's Bridge, and Stayer's Tower for more than two thousand people to live underground, free of their space suits and safe from radiation. North of Touchdown, they'd built a chamber big enough for fruit trees, bees, and running water, a place where you could see actual sunlight through plastiff skylights with your bare eyes and feel living grass beneath your bare feet. They'd raised chickens on the moon—the lunar gravity meant larger eggs—and they'd seen the first lunar births. Their population grew every month and so far their gravity training regime was allowing dozens of children to develop normally. They'd done so much, Maringka thought as she walked into her quarters and shut the curtain behind her, and now they seemed determined to throw it all away over a trifle. She lay down on her artfibe bed cover and felt it start to heat up in response. What had happened? How had it come to this?

When the mooners declared independence their primary motivations were pride and opportunity. They'd done the math and figured out the difference between what hablicants were paying for habricks and their corporate wages. It was a huge gap and it wounded their pride. Their Earther bosses didn't understand what it took to live on the moon and never gave them the respect they deserved, further injuring their pride. Once they controlled the habricks everyone on Earth wanted, their opportunities were unlimited. All they had to do was make sure they had reliable middlemen to spread word of what they were willing to trade for and to collect their spoils from the masses trying to escape Earth's death spiral of climate storms. Keep the habricks going up the tether and they could have anything on Earth they wanted delivered back down to them. Maybe things came too easy? Maringka laughed softly, thinking what a ridiculous thing that was to say about living on the moon. But that didn't mean it wasn't true.

Maringka landed on the moon in early 2021. She was sent by the Chinese military to oversee the production and construction of habricks at Stayer's Tower and Stoner's Bridge. She tried to remember whether she'd ever really even considered herself Chinese. For a long time she'd tried not to think about it. The Chinese diplomats who adopted her, Wang Yi and Qian Wei, were kind, loving parents. They'd given her more than any orphan could ever have asked for. But they were also important Party members with powerful connections throughout the Chinese foreign ministry and in the central bank. As much as she'd tried, she couldn't have the former without the latter.

So when they'd brought her home with them from Australia in 1985, when she was just twelve, she'd been given many advantages and opportunities because of her parents. Maringka quickly learned that in China those perks came with serious duties and expectations attached.

At that time, the Chinese army offered some of the best opportunities for women in a society still struggling with Mao's realization that "women hold up half the sky."

So when she finished school, along with many other talented and privileged women she knew, she joined the PLA. In some ways, the fact that she was "just" an orphan girl from Australia helped her march quickly up the ranks. She didn't have any extended family or extensive regional ties to threaten anyone and people tended to underestimate her. That was a mistake few made twice. "When the wind blows, some build walls and others build windmills," Maringka thought. She built windmills.

So they'd put her in charge up here, where everyone was an orphan of one kind or another. They'd started with shelter, food and water, radiation shielding, and materials to build their great banks of solar panels. Simple, straightforward stuff. She'd kept them on schedule and working hard together. Morale was high. They finished the habitats and moved on to build the habrick assembly plants and their vast transport systems. Everyone on the moon and back on Earth agreed she'd done a great job and that they'd achieved great success.

But once it got easier for them to survive, Maringka thought, it got harder and harder for them to work together. Part of it was just plain stupidity on the part of the bosses on Earth, like when they stopped rotating anyone home. Another piece of it was how fast demand for habricks became supercritical and they learned they could trade them for anything on Earth they wanted.

But part of it was more fundamental. While they worked together to build shelters and solar panels, when everyone's survival depended on everyone else all the time, it seemed like they'd never really fought with one another about anything. There wasn't time and they didn't have any energy to spare. Grave danger and imminent death were impressive agents of unity. Plenty of people died. They got crushed by habricks falling off loaders. They suffocated quickly when airlocks failed. They suffocated slowly when walls collapsed on their umbilicals. They were electrocuted when solar panels were installed incorrectly. But the tasks at hand had been so obvious they had no choice but to work together. Only after they'd cleared their first hurdles did they have time to stop and look up and ask questions and start bickering about their futures.

She'd tried to warn her superiors back in China and their corporate partners, but they hadn't listened. They kept telling her to stay the course, to maintain discipline. They were so used to being obeyed they'd forgotten that without fear or love there is little obedience and less loyalty. Once the mooners realized they had nothing to fear from and no reason to love their so-called superiors on Earth they stopped obeying. They became disloyal. Finally, they rebelled.

Maringka remembered her last comtack with Marshall Xu at the Jiuquan center. He'd lectured her for letting her people forget they were Chinese and demanded she threaten them with punishments to their families on Earth. Maringka wasn't that kind of leader and it wouldn't have worked anyway. She led from the front, by getting out there and getting dirty with her people, and she knew they'd already come to terms with never seeing their families again. You couldn't gather twenty Chinese mooners without one of them telling a story about Maringka risking her life for somebody. Once, during a petrochemical spill at Stayer's Tower, she'd single-handedly pushed two workers to safety with her left leg planted in a pool of hydrofluoric acid that burned through her protective suit and got about 90% of the way through her survival suit before they got her to the medfast. She'd been about fifteen seconds from, at best, losing her leg above the knee. Nothing builds loyalty like risking your lives together.

And so people respected her. They were loyal enough to her that, when they decided to proclaim their independence, they were honest with her. They came to her and openly shared their plan, trusting her not to betray them. And she found, to her initial surprise, that she was more loyal to them, to the people who'd built the lunar bases with her, the people who'd gone out and risked their lives next to her, than she was to China or the Chinese government. Her adopted parents were long dead, she had no children, and other than her long-held desire to revisit her birthplace in Milikapiti, she had no reason to ever go back to Earth again, which was good because she honestly didn't know whether or not they'd ever let her go back.

And so she'd gone along to get along. She'd agreed to the military principles and disciplined regimes set forth in their Declaration of Sovereignty and Solidarity. She stood down and accepted a position as an honorary senior adviser to their central command and coordination council, the 4C. She kept her head down and worked hard cleaning locker rooms and kitchens. She watched as they broke the population down into crews, assigned chiefs to direct and discipline every crew, and chose consuls—spies really—to watch and report on every chief and every crew. She saw them spread endless amounts of propaganda, assuring everyone that they were humanity's chosen few, living the best possible life in the best possible world for the best possible reasons. She tried to stay out of the spotlight and give the best, most honest advice she could to anyone who asked her for it. The most important goal for any politician, she'd realized, was to convince as many people as possible that just about everything was just about perfect and the politicians were hard at work on the rest. People wouldn't try to change perfection or steer away from it. One of the byproducts of their rebellion was that the politicians in charge were so young. Young, courageous, and growing ever more fanatical about their cause. They were convinced they knew the right way to do everything.

That, she thought, was the fundamental mooner premise. They believed in right answers and were confident they had them. She called it "the mooner way," although she'd never shared that with anyone. What was the mooner way to mop the kitchen floor? You used exactly one liter of grey water, half a liter of clear water, and 100 mL of strong soap. You poured the grey water into a red five-liter bucket first, then the soap, then the clear water. You put the mop in and stirred five times counterclockwise while you rotated the mop clockwise two turns. You started as close to the biggest stove as you could, rubbing a clean spot on the floor near the center of the stove bottom. Then you pulled your clean spot back until it filled the room, using two handed strokes and rinsing and straining your mop (by pulling it up through the strainer with your right hand while holding the strainer handle down with your left) every fourteen strokes. Maringka mopped two or three kitchens every day, and sometimes she lost herself in the ritual and came away glowing with energy and lifelight.

What was the right way to develop leg and thigh muscles on chickens raised in lunar gravity? The mooner way was to make all your chickens—layers, breeders, and feeders—spend the same amount of time—30 minutes a day—on the same centrifuge at the same setting—1.15 g, or 115% of Earth normal. Maybe that wasn't perfect, but it worked. Your chickens didn't die and you ate meat. As time

340

went on, though, Maringka watched it become less and less acceptable to question "the mooner way" or to experiment with different ways of raising chickens.

At first, Maringka thought, the Declaration and 4C and the mooner chiefs were up front about the provisional nature of their "mooner ways." They didn't pretend to know everything from the start. They just compiled routines and insisted everyone do things the same way. But the first couple of times people had new ideas about how to do things, the chiefs were dismissive. "It's more important to work together than to be perfect," they said. "We'll talk about that later," they said, "after we've finish the food storage." Or "after we finish the water system." They kept finishing projects and never did start talking about new ways of doing things.

To be fair, it wasn't like they lacked for novelty or had settled into a rut. Anything new on Earth or on one of the habs inevitably made its way to the moon. All they had to do was add it to their habrick price list, and a few months later there it was, floating slowly down their tether. They had to figure out new "mooner ways" every time something new came to them.

And even though their Declaration and its addendums were comprehensive, it certainly wasn't encyclopedic. Nobody had ever tried to build a lunar society before. They got into new areas, unexplained territories, all the time. The

341

people who wanted to hold off on talking about fundamental changes actually had a good point, Maringka thought. Between the new innovations from Earth and from the habs and the new situations that arose daily, there was plenty of change for them to deal with. You couldn't rebuild your ship beneath you every day if you wanted to get anywhere.

Maringka sat up and took a drink from her watbot. How, she wondered, could you tell the difference between mopping floors, which lent itself to ritual stability, and raising chickens, where trying new things could lead to real improvements? How could they find the right balance between keeping things the same forever and constantly changing them? She felt like they'd found their balance up here for a moment, but only because of all the new stuff constantly dropping down their tether at their command.

That's what threw the 4C so far off kilter today, Maringka thought. Their young leaders were confronted by somebody else's new innovation and a crisis they couldn't control—a crisis developing just 384,000 kilometers above them, close enough that anyone with a decent telescope could see exactly what was happening. She shouldn't be surprised people were freaking out.

In retrospect, they'd had plenty of warning. Over the past eight or nine months, they'd seen a wave of rocket launches from Sohae, in North Korea. The North Koreans, a country so impoverished that nobody there had ever even

342

tried to buy habricks, were launching a rocket almost every other week. But they weren't launching any rockets to L_1, where everyone else was going. Instead, the North Koreans sent the first five or six of their rockets to a relatively low and unstable orbit, just a little bit higher than the old International Space Station, which had finally been decommissioned just last year and was expected to plummet to Earth in a couple of months. That was puzzling, but hardly concerning. Their next rocket, however, and the ones that followed it, went where nobody had gone before—to L_5, about a fifth of an orbit behind the Moon. At L_5, like L_1, the gravitational pulls of the Earth, the Sun, and the Moon all more or less balanced out, so once the North Korean rockets got to L_5 they could stay there fairly easily for a relatively long time.

Before the firstmooners built the tether, in fact, L_5, not L_1, had been the presumed location of the first space colonies. Sudomo told Maringka once that there'd actually been something on Earth called the "L_5 Society," but it had never amounted to much of anything. If you didn't build a lunar tether, Sudomo told her, it probably made more sense to colonize L_5 or its mirror image L_4 because remaining in free fall around those points required less energy than maintaining position at L_1 did without the tether and its counterweight.

Today the first part of the North Koreans' plan

343

became clear. They'd launched a manned ship to the same low orbit where their first set of rockets was slowly falling out of the sky. Their astronauts had already performed one spacewalk and maneuvered one of their rockets into an almost identical orbit as their ship. People were livid. They feared and distrusted the North Koreans and knew that, whatever they were doing, they weren't doing it for the mooners' benefit. That's what terrified them.

The mooners had grown complacent, Maringka thought. The constant stream of luxuries and valuables tumbling down their tether every day for the last two years had them thinking they'd be on top of the world forever. She'd seen that in the 4C meeting today. Teon, the brash young man whose influence on the council seemed to grow by the week, insisted that the North Koreans would corrupt them all. "An existential threat," he'd called them, as if hundreds of North Korean space troopers were going to take over L_1 and drop down the tether to invade Touchdown. All that would do, Maringka thought, was force them to cut the tether and screw everyone. But she kept her mouth shut.

Maringka's position as an honorary adviser made her one of the twenty or thirty mooners with omninet access for official purposes. During the meeting, they'd netted North Korea long enough for her to learn that it had, so far, stubbornly resisted joining the United Peoples and Nations, that it had engaged in wide scale reforestation efforts for

344

over a decade but was one of the few nations still burning coal to generate electricity and discharging waste directly into the ocean, that increased flooding from climate storms had caused massive famines in seven of the past ten years, and that because it was more than 30 degrees north of the equator and diplomatically isolated, North Korea had received little climate change relief. She'd seen enough to know that this miserable little country was no real threat to them.

But to many mooners, North Korea was strange and different, she thought, just like she and the rest of the mooners must seem strange and different to the North Koreans. They didn't even mop floors or raise chickens the same way. To some leaders, strangeness and difference are precious gifts that can be carefully stoked into flames of fear. Fear can forge empires.

And so at the meeting today, the 4C embraced their fears and convinced itself that this North Korean ship and its crew of five or six posed an existential threat. Because they were scared, Maringka thought, they could only speak in the language of fear. Maybe they'd subconsciously accepted that since they'd taken over the *piece de resistance* of Earth's most powerful organizations and were trading the habricks that represented people's only shot at escaping Earth for anything they wanted, they'd never be loved. It was Spartan fear, not just the growth of Athenian power,

345

which made that long ago war inevitable, Maringka remembered. North Korea was hardly Athens, but were they Sparta? She was pretty sure Sparta won that war, but she also remembered that it didn't actually work out so well for the Spartans, who were themselves conquered soon afterwards.

Nobody was going to conquer the moon any time soon, she thought, curling back up in her artfibe and resting her head on her pillow. Certainly one ship with five or six North Koreans wasn't any real threat. But it was different, and the 4C didn't know what the North Koreans were doing. That scared them and their fear made them determined to share their fear with their enemies—the North Koreans, the habsters, the United Peoples and Nations, basically the rest of humanity. And so, at the urging of Teon and his supporters, they'd started down the path to building what Teon called "the ultimate weapon in our fight for survival." They planned on drilling 24 small, 100-centimeter-wide tunnels through the center of the Moon at regular intervals. Then, they'd pack those tunnels with high explosives and build a lot of motors. That was it. "Then all of humanity will be subject to us and will do all that we wish!" Teon had assured them. He'd really said that, Maringka thought with disbelief, in a council meeting, on the moon.

Teon's theory was that, by setting off their explosives in a carefully controlled sequence, they could surgically split

346

the Moon, which weighed about 73 and a half septillion kilograms, into 48 neat little chunks, each weighing only about one and half septillion kilograms. Then, he said, they'd use the motors to steer their little chunks of the moon wherever they wanted. They'd have to move the moonlets in pairs, Teon explained, so they could spin them around each other and compensate for the lower gravity. In fact, spinning chunks of the moon around each other would actually create a higher gravity, almost .74 g according to Teon, which meant less time on centrifuges and longer lives for all of them. Planning around their tunnels meant all of their infrastructure would be positioned to not only survive the transition but would wind up in more strategic positions. "It would be challenging," Teon said, "but in the end our lives will be so much better after we blow up the moon."

In addition to improving their own lives, Teon promised that blowing up the moon would have appalling consequences for the rest of humanity. It had been hard for Maringka, who'd never forgotten that she was the daughter of a proud fishing family on a small Pacific island, to listen to his description of what breaking the moon in 48 pieces and moving them around in their orbit would do to the ocean's tides. Earthquakes would become stronger and more common, Teon promised, and volcanos would spring to life around the globe.

And while the Earthers faced water, fire, wind and

347

shaking earth, the habsters would have it even worse. Their tiny ineffectual engines were built on the assumption that L_1, the platform, and the counterweight would be there forever to provide the friendliest possible conditions for maintaining a stable orbit. Disconnecting the tether, Teon assured them, would be a mercy. If it stayed attached, the counterweight and the one and a half septillion kilogram chunk of the moon it was attached to would start rotating around the platform, knocking habs around violently. The habs themselves, he guaranteed, could not maintain orbit and would fly off harmlessly into space or plummet to Earth in flames.

This was the only way for the few thousand of them on the moon to protect themselves from the habsters, the North Koreans, and the rest of the Earthers, Teon insisted: to have the power to destroy them all. "The power to destroy," he told them, "is absolute control." Once they showed the rest of humanity they had such power, Maringka thought, the 4C would demand that their so-called enemies submit to their control. The rest of humanity would undoubtedly resist, just like the mooners had risen up against their Earther employers.

Staring up at the plain white ceiling of her quarters Maringka couldn't believe it had come to this. They'd given their leaders and the 4C so much control over the Moon and the mooners that their egos and ids would never again be satisfied by anything less than total control of all humanity.

They saw threats everywhere. Even if they blew up the Moon and slew their enemies, Maringka thought, they wouldn't be satisfied. They'd still be obsessed with the idea that somebody, somewhere, somehow threatened them. And they'd be right, she realized, because that threat to their mooner ways could be something as small as mopping a kitchen floor in a different order or exercising chickens in higher gravity. Needing to control everything made them vulnerable to anything—any little change that found some small success threatened to expose the weakness of their whole mooner way.

Chapter Eighteen

Grok

L_1 Platform

November 5, 2022

Standing in the middle of the platform, looking out over the assembled habsters waiting with various degrees of skepticism to hear him speak, all Grok could think was that the sky above the port really was the color of television tuned to a dead channel. It was the glow of the moon reflecting off the invisible exhaust trails the habs left behind as they slowly orbited the platform, he told himself. Just reflections of a reflection. Nothing to worry about. Just another speech. All he could do now was share his truth. It was up to these people to decide what, if anything, to do with his ideas. He owed them only honesty.

"Good day," Grok began, hearing his words echo through the open comtacks. "My name is Grok Martin. I'm not a habster. I'm not one of you. I'm a stranger, a guest here. Some of you invited me to your convention to share my thoughts on how people can best live together up here because for the last fifteen years I've been one of the people operating the Escuela Neuvos Talentos, the School for New Talents, on the South Pacific coast of Nicaragua, near the village of El Ostional." Pausing to look out over the crowd, Grok felt people tuning in. He had their attention and he couldn't help thinking for a moment about Julio's father, his friend Jose.

Jose was one of the first Nicaraguans to reach out to Grok and his compadres and, eventually, the first to enroll his child in their school. Julio, who was fifteen now, played the guitar beautifully and looked like a model. But about five years ago, when Julio was ten, Jose and his wife Catalina had left him in Grok's care and emigrated to Sacramento so that they could help take care of Catalina's mother and work at Catalina's cousins' restaurant. Soon after they arrived, Catalina became pregnant with their second child. There was some problem with their visa paperwork, and they were scared to take Catalina to a doctor even as she began having more and more trouble with her pregnancy. Their visa problems persisted, and four months later Catalina miscarried. She bled to death in her mother's bathtub before Jose could convince her to go to the hospital, even if it meant being deported. Jose had to come home alone and tell Julio.

If he succeeded here today, Grok told himself, tragedies like that wouldn't happen in space. Of course people would die, but they'd live or die *together*, in solidarity, as equals, with the same choices open to all of them. It was one thing to choose not to go to a hospital, or not to have a hospital to go to, Grok thought. It was quite another thing entirely to watch helplessly as other mothers and their children went into a hospital, knowing your wife and your child could not receive the same treatment.

"The new talents we try to learn at our school," Grok continued, "are talents for living in a closed environment. So, to start, I have to explain briefly what I mean by a closed environment and what makes it different from an open environment—even if you perhaps think that should be somewhat obvious, considering where we are." He heard a single brief chuckle, then silence. These people had accomplished the impossible, he reminded himself. They weren't to be taken lightly. They were serious.

The glowing static sky above him continued to be a distraction. There was something hypnotic about it, he thought, continuing to run through familiar explanations. "The first thing I want to say about a closed environment is that it's not really closed. In an absolute sense, there's only one possible closed environment: the entire universe *sub specie aeterni*, everything viewed across eternity. We're not here to talk about that, or about the questions of cosmology and theology it implicates, as fascinating as those might be." It was surprising, Grok thought, that there weren't any overtly religious habs yet. He would have expected somebody to obtain a bunch of habricks and build a space monastery by now. In theory, he'd convinced himself, his framework had plenty of space for monasteries but no room for fanatics.

"A closed environment, a closed society, as I use those terms, is just one where additional resources are not freely available. An open society, on the other hand, is one where additional resources are freely available." Grok felt, more than heard, mutters of agreement rumbling around the open comtacks. "As I look up at your habs now, of course, I can see that they are subject to many external influences: they feel the gravity of the Sun, the Earth, the Moon, each other; and to a much lesser extent, millions of other bodies. Sunlight shines on them and is reflected. Radiation sweeps through or bounces off. So to an extent those resources are freely available. But your habs are also enclosed, limited, and finite in a way which a parcel of land, even an island, on Earth, or even on the moon, is not." Grok heard more murmurs. He couldn't actually see any habs, but he'd made his point. Habsters knew what a closed society was.

Shifting to a more academic gear, Grok found himself thinking about his friend Hannah, who was writing her dissertation in philosophy at the University of North Texas in Denton, just north of Fort Worth. She supported herself and her daughter Martha by teaching introductory classes as an adjunct instructor at Midwestern State in Wichita Falls, Tarleton State in Stephenville, and sometimes at Angelo State in San Angelo. Hannah averaged about 800 miles a week and twelve or fifteen hours on the road, depending on traffic. She had a part-time job driving between her part-time jobs. Such was the state of the academy today, Grok thought. It was a good reminder not to get too academic.

"When I started thinking about the best way for people to live in closed societies, I did not start from scratch. I started with a framework, a collection of working hypotheses. The first of those is an idea sometimes attributed to Gandhi ("a nation's greatness is measured by how it treats its weakest members"), or to Jesus in Matthew 25:45 ("whatever you did not do for one of the least of these, you did not do for me"), but perhaps most clearly stated by his Holiness, Pope John Paul II ("a society will be judged on the basis of how it treats is weakest members"). The proper measuring stick for society, under this framework, is how it treats its most disadvantaged, least well-off person. The best society, the society a rational person would choose, is the best society in which to be the least well-off person. That is not a new idea, and I borrow it without shame. It has a distinguished pedigree. But I will say, and here I do advance my own views, that this framework, this hypothesis that different societies should be evaluated from the point of view of the least advantaged person, is infinitely more applicable to closed societies than in open societies."

He'd met Hannah, Grok remembered, at a conference in Houston where she'd been a reader on a panel discussion of Howard Gall's failed submersible project. There'd been four or five papers presented. The papers criticized just about every aspect of the tragedy, but what Grok remembered the most was Hannah's comment. There's no such thing as failed experiments, she said, just failed scholars who can't figure out how to learn from them. Just so, Grok thought, and there's no such thing as failed people, just societies that haven't found places for them yet.

"You probably know the truth of that better than I," he continued, "having actually lived up here with each other. To start with, closed societies are infinitely more vulnerable than open societies. On Earth, when somebody makes a bad choice, they generally hurt themselves the worst, and they can always leave, just move on somewhere else. On a hab, on the other hand, one bad choice can easily kill everyone and nobody can just get up and leave. You know that. That's why you instinctively look out for each other up here a lot more than you did back on Earth. Failures, whether social or individual, have exponentially greater consequences in closed societies. In addition, closed societies demand greater efficiency. That applies both to people and to resources. On Earth, somebody who makes bad choices can survive on the margins of society, just getting by, for a long time, continuing to make more and more bad choices. On Earth, sadly, you can waste a lot of resources, and a lot of people, for a long time. On a hab, on the other hand, you can't afford to marginalize people or waste anything at all."

Nobody on Earth ever thought of marginalized people as costs, Grok knew. They didn't have to. Their margins weren't that tight. They had the luxury of thinking of them as failures. He paused again, thinking about Harvey, a friendly old Sioux Indian he'd only met once, at the Sitting Bull memorial in Cannon Ball, North Dakota. Harvey had been a point guard, and he told Grok about the year his high school team went to the state tournament with such pride in his voice that Grok never forgot his story. Harvey and his teammates stuck together their whole lives out there on the plains in a forgotten town with 86% unemployment and even greater poverty. Harvey and his teammates and their community weren't failures, Grok thought. They were victims of a failed system that let them live and die drunk, unproductive lives. They struggled to share their wisdom, pride, and togetherness with future generations. That could never happen on a hab, Grok assured himself. Margins up here were way too tight to waste talented teammates like Harvey on welfare checks and cheap beer. They had to find places for everyone or start shoving each other out the airlocks. Grok hoped it never came to that.

"For these reasons—less waste, higher efficiency, greater vulnerability—I hope you will try to evaluate your future alternatives from the perspective of the least advantaged among you. You, however 'you' define yourselves, cannot build lives in space as disconnected individuals. You cannot succeed up here at the expense of others. You can only survive as a team. And any team is only as strong as its weakest link."

Grok hated sports. Probably because his mom obsessed so much about that football game where she met his dad. But even through the distorted lens of his hatred, Grok couldn't deny that he'd seen sports teams make people better. Not just better players. Better people.

"Look around at the ten people closest to you right now," Grok continued. He stopped and saw people glancing around but not really engaging. "No," he insisted, "I mean *really look*. Really take a second to appraise ten different people. It doesn't make a bit of difference whether you've known them since you were babies or you've never seen them before in your life. Just really look at them and try to imagine what kind of people they are." After another moment of silence, people started moving around carefully and Grok could hear comtacks opening and closing.

He gave them a few minutes. "Now," he barked, "ask yourselves this question: is there any single set of laws; any one constitution; any particular morality, that would make one particular hab the best possible place for all ten of those people to live?" Grok knew it sounded like a trick question and felt their confusion. "That is the second thing I'd like you to consider," he continued. "That there is no single society that is best for everyone. That's the second principle

I'm here to share: one size does not fit all.

"Of course, that's not my idea either," Grok added. "I'm stealing that from a Harvard philosophy professor who once famously wrote 'utopia will consist of utopias.' Habtopia will consist of habtopias. Everyone will have the same choices available, but not everyone will have to make the same choices.

"The next principle I'm here to talk about comes from an even more famous philosopher, Immanuel Kant, and from most of Earth's great religious traditions. Almost all human religions, in one way or another, promote some version of what people call the Golden Rule. Jesus said, 'In everything, do to others as you would have them do to you; for this is the law and the prophets.' Muhammad, peace upon him, said, 'Not one of you truly believes until you wish for others what you wish for yourself.' Hillel, the great Jewish teacher, said, 'That which is hateful unto you do not do to your neighbor. This is the whole of the Torah. The rest is commentary.' Confucius said, 'The basis of all good conduct is loving kindness … do not do to others what you do not want done to yourself.' 'Treat not others in ways you would yourself find hurtful' is how the Buddhist Udanavarga puts it. In the Hindu Mahabharata, we learn, 'This is the sum of duty; do not do to others what would cause pain if done to you.' The Native American teacher Black Elk believed, 'All things are our relatives; what we do to everything is what we

358

do to ourselves.' And the Quaker George Fox calls us to 'walk cheerfully over the world, answering that of God in everyone.' All those holy teachers shared this lesson that moral rules must apply equally to everyone.

"Kant's version of this Golden Rule is called the Categorical Imperative. It can be stated in different ways: 'Act as you would want all other people to act towards all other people,' 'Act only according to maxims all other rational people should follow as a universal law,' and so on. Many, of course, would object to my putting the Golden Rule and the Categorical Imperative in the same category and painting in such broad strokes. There's obviously a lot to talk about here, with different philosophical traditions arising from different orientations to the world and arriving at different ways to formulate this concept.

"But the people who invited me made it clear this wasn't an academic conference. So I'm going to skip right to my bottom line, such as it is, by way of one final short detour. If I have anything new to offer to humanity's long and distinguished conversation about these ethical imperatives, it is that I don't like to use words like 'rights,' 'duties,' and 'justice.' Instead, I like to talk about choices. You can't see rights, or duties, or justice, but you watch people make choices every day.

"This principle—that we should talk about ethics and morality in the language of choice—has perhaps an equally distinguished philosophical heritage. Over the last 150 years or so, philosophers and physicists have gradually realized Heraclitus was right: everything is flow and nothing does last forever. But again, our project today is to see what, if any, useful principles I have to offer you, not to tell stories about how I came to them. So the third principle I'd like to offer you is that people aren't things that have rights; they're events who make choices."

Grok paused. He was used to people tuning him out at this point, but they seemed interested, or at least respectful. "I'm not going to make any long-winded argument about that," Grok continued, "I'm just going to ask you to consider it. I'm going to ask you to consider whether it's more useful, whether it will keep you alive up here longer, to base your rules on the choices you see each other make rather than on things you've never seen with your own eyes, like 'rights,' 'duties,' and 'justice.'"

He still had their attention, Grok thought, but at the cost of skipping lightly across some very deep intellectual terrain in a horribly cavalier fashion. It seemed disrespectful. He shook his head and smiled, thinking of Father Romero, the kindly old priest at the Iglesia Catolica between El Ostional and Rivas, who'd been his friend since the first days of the Escuela. They tried to dine together on Tuesdays. Many times Grok tried to explain his thoughts to Father Romero, only to get lost and tie himself up in subtle complexities and ungrounded intuitions. "Why do you think God cares about rigorous proofs?" Father Romero would ask him. "God only cares about whether we are becoming better people; whether we are building a more loving world. He does not care about truth. He only cares about redeeming people and saving souls!" Grok hoped the habsters shared that mindset.

"So," Grok concluded, "the fourth and final principle I'd like you to consider is what I call the Golden Imperative: Don't make choices for other people." He paused, knowing from experience how anticlimactic that seemed after his long windup. "That imperative has two sides to it. The most direct, and probably easier to grasp, is not doing things to people against their will. Rape is a prime example of that. Rape is wrong because it's making somebody do something they didn't choose to do. It's immoral to decide whom other people have sex with. Most people agree with that pretty intuitively.

"Historically, of course, rape was something of a problem for moral systems based on so-called rights because for a long time women were thought not to have any rights. Yet, of course, we see women make choices all the time. That is one reason I like to talk about choices, which we can see people make, and not rights, which are only intellectual fictions. It's a lot easier to explain why rape is wrong in the language of choice than it is in the language of rights.

"The other side of the Golden Imperative, however, is perhaps less intuitive. Do not do things that depend on other people not being able to do them. Being a king is wrong, on this view, because it's a choice that is not, by definition, available to others. It's making people not do something they might choose to do if they could. Being king necessarily involves taking everyone else's choice of whether or not to be king away from them. Being the king, by definition, means nobody else can choose to be the king.

"That side of the Golden Imperative," Grok continued, "is perhaps more challenging and, for us, less intuitive. But if choice is the fundamental moral trait our ethical imperatives seek to protect and serve, then making people not do things, just as much as making them do things, is unethical. It's taking choices away from people. That has quite a few implications for life in a closed society. First, it means that every ethical organization is open to everyone; that nobody can justly prosper by excluding others."

Ironically, Grok thought, most of these people built their habs just exactly because they thought they could prosper by excluding the rest of humanity. But the rest of humanity weren't playing by these rules and so, for the moment, didn't count.

"So these are the four principles, the four ideas, I've come here to share with you," Grok concluded: "'you,' however you define yourself, are only as strong as 'your' weakest link; one size does not fit all; people are events who make choices, not things that have rights; and don't make choices for other people." They were still paying attention, he thought. That's all he could ask for. The rest was up to them. "Those ideas are what we learn at our school. That's the framework, the set of hypotheses, which we use to try to live together in a sustainable and ethical manner.

"By now you're probably asking yourself about the practical implications of these abstract ideas. For example, by combining the first, third, and fourth principles, we get 'the best society for me to be the least well-off person is one in which every organization is open to me, should I choose to make the same choices those in that organization are making.' That, it seems to me, is accurate. If I'm most concerned about the least well-off person, or if I think I might wind up being the least well-off, then I want to maximize the opportunities for that person. The most ethical society is the one which gives its least well-off member the most opportunities for improvement by ensuring that every organization is open to him or her, subject only to his or her willingness to make the same choices those in any particular organization are making.

"But let's stop for a second and put that into some context. Some of the things you all have to do, on all of your habs, in one way or another, are produce water and air, grow food, and process and recycle bodily waste." He saw nods of agreement. "There are different ways to do these things, which is one of the reasons I think different habs with different people should run by different rules. That's where the second principle applies: one size does not fit all.

"But as far as I know, none of your habs do any of those things in an exclusionary way. None of you make water, or process waste, for just some of the people on your hab. You all do it all together." Grok saw people nodding. "Can you imagine," he asked them, "a hab with two or three different water production systems, each run by and for a subset of the habsters on that hab? That would be insane. It would be totally inefficient.

"In the early stages of hab life, when just keeping yourselves alive and your habs in orbit is miraculous and consumes most all of your time and energy, it may seem obvious that a hab should only have one hydrosystem which serves everyone. But I believe you are going to get better at living up here. I believe there will come a time when keeping people alive on orbiting habs is commonplace, not miraculous. As a result, you will begin to have free time and take on new responsibilities. You will have new options and make new choices and form new organizations. As life in space becomes more complicated than mere survival, it may no longer seem obvious that everyone should all do things together. So I want to talk a little more about a couple of ramifications of this principle that your choices, your organizations, your ways of providing food and processing waste, should be open to everyone who chooses to make them.

"First, it means the end of classes, castes, and clans. In a society that does not permit its members to make choices for each other, there can be no proletariat class, no class of citizens who have nothing to sell but their labor. In a society that does not permit its members to make choices for each other, there can be no caste of citizens who are limited from birth to certain choices. In a society that does not permit its members to make choices for each other, there can be no royal birthright or clan of nobles. This does not necessarily mean the end of wage labor—if freely chosen— but it means that the worker can always, if he or she chooses, decide to become a part of the enterprise, to make the same choices as those entrepreneurs are making. It is possible," Grok speculated, "that somebody will choose to just sell his or her labor, but it will be impossible for them not to have any other choices available.

"Second, it means there won't be any rock stars in a closed society." Grok had only been at L_1 for a few hours, and hadn't gotten to meet many of the habsters yet. He knew most of them were young and he worried about dating himself but decided to risk it. "I call this the Courtney Love corollary," he proceeded, hearing a few chuckles of understanding. "If somebody wants to be in their favorite band, like Nirvana," he explained, "then that band, that organization, has to help make them part of it; has to help those people make the same choices they're making." The first hundred or so times he'd tried to explain this, he'd used Yoko and the Beatles. Now even Kurt and Courtney were outdated.

"You can't be a rock star," Grok concluded, "when all your fans can join together in your band. That isn't to say there won't be places for music, for art, in closed societies, but in a much more participatory role, with far, far, fewer boundaries between performers and spectators." Grok was confident that Kurt—and John before him—would have wholeheartedly supported that idea. Farewell to all royalty, musical or otherwise.

"Other than that, there's not a lot I can say about what choices will work in closed societies, in your habs, because I don't know. Nobody knows. Nobody's ever done it and you're the ones up here figuring it out, making it work. I'm suggesting a framework. I'm saying that, for something to really work up here, for people to live well in habs for a long time, it has to work for everyone. You're going to have to succeed through inclusion, together, not by excluding or marginalizing people or building on the backs of others. Habs are too vulnerable. There's just no room for those inefficiencies up here." Not just inefficiencies, Grok thought, but externalities. Externalities were the real costs of exclusion. Costs that, over time, made societies less and less 'open.' People in closed societies couldn't rely on externalities and so had to do things together right from the start. "So," Grok summarized, "those are the four principles I'm here to encourage you to think about: 'you' are only as strong as 'your' weakest link; one size does not fit all; people are events who make choices; and don't make choices for other people. Those are the principles we've learned at our Escuela.

"Finally, I'd like to share two things we've learned as we've tried to learn, teach, and live together by those principles." As always, when Grok starting thinking about innovation he thought about Basil and Sybil. They'd come together from Leeds with their two children to El Ostional a long time ago, when the Escuela was not even two years old. They'd been innovators all right. They'd installed waterwheels and generated electricity and built three story chicken coops that stayed cleaner and drier and produced more eggs. They'd died together, Grok remembered, crushed under a log in the river, after just a year or so. Grok would never forget their faces, after they'd finally dragged them out from under that log. They were smiling, as if death was just another new adventure for them. These people, Grok thought, had that same endless optimism.

"The first thing we've learned," Grok said, "is not to be more attached to choices than to people." Crackles and

367

mumbles rolled around the open comtacks and he saw confusion on the faces of the habsters around him. "Choices are tools, people are ends. This is sometimes most apparent in the transition from old to new ways of doing things," he explained. "When you've done something in a certain way—made a certain set of choices—for some time, and experienced some measure of success, it's tempting and even natural to become attached to those choices. They're familiar, comfortable, even reassuring. So when somebody else comes along and says she has a new way of doing things, there's a natural inertial resistance; a loyalty to the past."

Grok smiled, remembering the outrage at Basil's electrical network, which supplemented hydropower with power generated by humans on stationary bike generators. If you wanted power, you had to get on a bike and charge the batteries. But some people, for whatever reason, couldn't ride the bike, or didn't have time, and so on. And so they started negotiating with others to charge their batteries in exchange for food, or perhaps Spanish lessons, or whatever. After a few months, they'd invented a new currency to facilitate their trades. That really pissed some people off. They'd gotten used to living without money and were passionately against its reintroduction. "When people introduce new ideas," Grok said, "the community needs to be sensitive to this, and everyone else needs to check their

368

priorities and remember that people are more important than the choices they make."

Once his 'powerpesos' had stirred everyone up, Grok remembered fondly, Basil insisted on grouping about it. He listened to everyone speak, to everything they said about money, about each other, about the past and about the future. And then, in his simple Yorkish fashion, he brought them all back together. "All we have, all we are, is our process," Basil had reminded them. "This is where our process led. These are the choices we've made. We have to trust the process, trust our choices. If we don't, we need to start over or give up." The funny thing was, Grok recalled, a few years after that nobody ever used 'powerpesos' again.

"The second thing is that children need to be exposed to different choices. We've found that people who grow up knowing only a single set of choices, a single way of life, have a harder time appreciating and creating different ways of life than people who experience different ways of life during childhood. Just as, I believe, your habtopia will consist of habtopias—that there is no single perfect way to live in space—I also believe, and our experience shows, that habsters who experience different ways of life during childhood will grow up with more respect for other people's choices and become more capable of making new, innovative choices themselves. Based on our experience, I would suggest that you institute some kind of rotation policy,

369

where every habster child spends six months or so every other year or so living on a new hab. Because if your children, your descendants, are going to get better and better at living in space, in closed environments, they're going to have to be as innovative as possible. I would also suggest that you have some kind of similar rotation policy for everyone, so that nobody is ever stuck on any one hab. And I would suggest that you have some sort of policy for 'retiring' habs that run on choices nobody wants to make any more.

"But now I'm crossing the line," Grok apologized. "Those are questions for you, the habsters who are actually living up here, to debate. As your guest, I can only share these four principles we've learned. Even if you adopt them, or some version of them, it must be you—according to those very principles!—who decide how to implement them. My opinions are, by definition, irrelevant."

Epilogue

Rally

Milikapiti

May 4, 2029

Like a jellyfish flung by the mighty ocean waves to a special beach, Rally felt as though the abyss of space had thrown her down here for a reason. She just didn't know what it was. She'd been in Milikapiti for two days now. She'd danced; she'd sung; she'd swum in the ocean. But she still hadn't opened the plastiff box with 'Forever' carved in the ends from her dad's asteroid; she still hadn't visited her grandmother's grave; and she still hadn't told anyone who she was. She was waiting to share those things with her mother, whose plane had just landed.

She first came here almost twenty years ago, when she was still just a little girl who loved animals. G'Sille was so proud, showing her and Grok all the places she loved as a child, and even the ones that still hurt her a little bit. On that trip she and her family had stayed at the house of one of G'Sille's childhood friends, Kim, whose family never left Milikapiti. Rally had walked by the house a couple of times. It looked the same, but she hadn't seen anyone home. This time she was staying in one of the shelter rooms at the Milikapiti Women's Centre.

Until a few years ago, she could have stayed at the

fishing lodge, but it had been inundated by a storm. It was completely gone now. People salvaged anything of value and the rising waters took the rest. Hardly anyone came to Milikapiti for the fishing any more. Snake Bay was flat and shallow. There was only one relatively deep trench that ran from just southeast of Don Point to just northeast of Point Strath where the sea floor dropped as much as twelve or fifteen meters below the surface. But the rest of the bay was almost all less than five meters deep and warmed quickly under the hot sun. As the waters warmed and rose, the fish migrated, or died, while the people fought stubbornly against the climate storms.

More than two dozen storms had ripped across the island since Stanley convinced her to go look for her father in the asteroid belt five years ago. People here had fared better than most of the South Pacific and had only faced more than one storm in a week two times. Doubles, people called those, and there'd even been a few triples in the Philippines. Those were the real killers. One storm left people exposed and the next finished them off. It was like catching fish by exploding a reef and sweeping up the helpless bodies.

Rally had never been fishing. According to her father, her mother's family had been legendary fisherfolk for generations, but G'Sille never talked much about them. Rally knew that G'Sille's father, Rally's grandfather, died

372

when G'Sille was still just a very young girl. The Australian authorities took G'Sille from her mother after that and sent her to the Retta Dixon Home in Darwin—infamous for its horrific history of abuse of indigenous children. G'Sille never talked to Rally about her time there.

Retta Dixon was finally shut down in 1982, when G'Sille was thirteen. Luckily, she was taken in by foster parents who believed in education and sent her to school. Most of the other orphans from the home were put to work at menial tasks and spent the rest of their lives doing manual labor in Darwin. G'Sille not only graduated from high school, she secured a scholarship and a stipend through the Kulbardi Aboriginal Centre to study nursing at Murdoch University outside Freemantle. Rally remembered seeing her mom's scholarship notice in a scrapbook at the Escuela when she was twelve or thirteen. It was the only memento of her mom's childhood she'd ever seen.

G'Sille graduated with honors and spent several years doing volunteer and charity work in Laos, Zambia, and Guatemala. In all those places, she'd told Rally once, clean water was a constant struggle. And it was a struggle in Milikapiti now. The rising waters flooded the sewage ponds and contaminated almost half the water system. In just the last year or so, Rally learned, they'd had to replace the water main that ran alongside the burial ground park north of the city, the water main on the east side of the community church in the center of town, and the main furthest south closest to the sewage ponds. Rally had never had to deal with a contaminated hydrosystem herself, but it sent shivers through her heart. It was every Spacer's second worst nightmare, almost as bad as fire. At least here, she thought, people could build fires on the beach and boil their water. But it was still terrifying.

Rally's parents met three years before she was born, in 1996. Her father had told the story dozens of times. He was younger than G'Sille, barely two years out of college, and had managed to secure a position in the topographic division of the U.S. Geological Survey mapping hydroflow for the National Streamflow Information Program. Rally liked to imagine Grok sitting at his terminal painting oceans blue like Peter O'Toole in that old Lawrence of Arabia movie.

And like Lawrence, his cartography career was short-lived. But instead of the desert, Grok got sent to the jungle to assist a regional hydrologist with his IT for a slide show presentation at a water resources assessment and management conference in San Jose, Costa Rica. Grok was just 22 and had never traveled abroad before. G'Sille was older, more sophisticated, and had lived abroad for most of her life. Yet somehow, as her dad told it every time, the very first night he was there he walked alone in the dark to the cheesiest, least authentic café in San Jose—Rick's Café

374

Americain at the Hotel Dunn Inn—and walked out next to the light of his life.

They'd stayed together for 27 years, right up until the morning Grok left for Stanley's asteroid. Rally could still seem him there, lying on his crazy synthwood bed in the middle of the asteroid with Howard's hand clasped tightly in his. It was the only image of him alone, without G'Sille, that had ever really stuck in Rally's mind. They'd always been together for her. Now, watching her mother walk surely and confidently down the ramp off the small turboprop, Rally realized for the first time that she was 60 years old and had been living without Grok for almost six years now, never knowing for sure he was dead until the first reports from the *Farluk* reached her last year.

G'Sille was smiling, Rally saw, and she held her head high. The runway at Milikapiti faced southwest, so as G'Sille exited on the port side of the cabin down the ramp she could look out over the entire town and across Snake Bay to the Timor Sea as the sun set over the hills on the spine of Yermainer. It was a magnificent view. Rally wondered what it meant to her mom. No place is ever beautiful enough to make people forget all the bad things that happened to them there.

Usually there were only a few passengers arriving at Milikapiti. Today, however, it seemed like most of the town was waiting on the side of the runway with Rally. When the cabin door swung open people began singing and cheering with great gusto. As soon as G'Sille was about to step onto the runway, Rally saw a girl of twelve or thirteen spring out of the cabin and hold a football over her head triumphantly, spurring the crowd to even greater cheers. Soon exuberant young Tiwis in football jerseys were spilling out of the plane onto the runway, people were rushing to embrace them, and everyone was singing, dancing, and hugging each other.

Rally stayed focused on G'Sille. Moving cheerfully through the crowd, sharing hugs with a few and smiling at all, G'Sille slowly made her way across the runway until she stood next to her only child. Rally felt her tears begin as she threw herself into her mother's arms. She hadn't cried, not since before that day the year before last when she found her father's body in the middle of the asteroid. Now, in her mother's arms, all her tears came pouring out. G'Sille said nothing, just held her and rocked slowly back and forth in a rhythm that felt like the ocean.

"I'm so sorry," Rally finally managed to say haltingly. "I don't…." "Shh," her mother assured her. "I'm here with you. It's fine. Let it out." They held each other tightly and Rally cried for a few more minutes. She noticed that some of the people who'd been singing and dancing were now standing and looking nervously at her and G'Sille and she stopped crying and pulled herself together enough to straighten up, keeping tight hold of her mother's hands.

As they began to move, one of the older women who'd been watching them stepped hesitantly forward with a look of concern and asked G'Sille something in Tiwi. Rally saw her mother hesitate a bit, then she replied in the same language and the old woman's face lit up with the biggest smile Rally had ever seen. Rally felt the old woman's heart reaching out through her smile to lift Rally out of her grief. The old woman chattered reassuringly at G'Sille and patted her arm several times in a comforting way.

Rally could see the old woman looking back at them periodically as they followed the jubilant crowd down the road past the market garden towards the library and into town. "What did you tell her?" she finally asked her mother, seeing the smile that remained on G'Sille's face. "She asked what was making my daughter cry," G'Sille replied, "and she wanted to know how she could help us. I told her your father is buried in a cold, distant, lonely place and we've come here for his *pukamani yiloti*, his final memorial ceremony. I told her you were sad because we did not have songs or *pukamani* poles of our own for him or *pamajini* armbands to wear." G'Sille smiled again. "I bet your dad never could have imagined how many songs and poles she's going to bring our family for his *pukaman yiloti*."

"But Mom," she said hesitantly, "Dad wasn't from … wasn't a … didn't believe …"

"I know," G'Sille interrupted. "And a lot of the time

377

I don't know if I'm a Tiwi; if I'm from here; or if I believe anything at all. But I never got to be part of your grandmother's death, never got the chance to grow up into this world and experience these things. And besides, do you want to be the one who tells her we're not going to have a *pukamani yiloti* for your father?"

No, Rally didn't want to do that. Her dad would have approved, she thought. He'd always been fascinated by indigenous peoples, felt a bond with them. In a way, her father had dedicated his life to the idea that no authentic appropriation could ever be inappropriate or disrespectful— that everyone should be able to make the same choices as everyone else, no matter where they'd been born, what color their skin was, or what they'd done before. He would have been just as excited to help that old Tiwi woman plan her *bat mitzvah*.

After they got to town and secured a room for G'Sille at the Women's Centre, they walked over to Milikapiti's only commercial food service, the Sports & Social Club, where the triumphant young footballers and their families and friends were celebrating, along with seemingly everyone else in town. They quickly learned that the team had defeated teams from Darwin and Alice Springs in an annual tournament, the young Tiwis winning the event for the first time in several years. They got to meet some of the youngsters, who did not appear to be at all curious about

378

why the two women who looked so much like them did not live with them or have any family in Milikapiti. They didn't talk about Grok, or the past, or the future. They just enjoyed the moment together with the villagers.

After they'd eaten, as the sun was starting to set over Snake Bay, Rally and her mother left the Club and walked down to the beach together in silence. "He left us something," Rally suddenly blurted. "On that asteroid?" her mother replied. "Yes. He left us something on the asteroid in a plastiff box with '*YILOTI*' carved in the ends. It's one of the only Tiwi words I remember, because of that song you used to sing me: '*Nyirra juwuriyi yiloti*, my friend forever.'"

G'Sille smiled. "*Ngiya mantanga yiloti*," she sang back to her daughter as they sat down together on a beach log. "My dear friend forever. *Nyirra juwuriyi yiloti* is a different line from that same song: 'she's gone forever.'" G'Sille looked straight into Rally's eyes. "I can't believe you remembered that. I used to sing that song for my mother, wondering whether or not she was still alive, whether she'd ever get to meet you." "I wish I had gotten to meet her," Rally replied, feeling again the sorrow from her mother's childhood trauma. "You're meeting her in the song," G'Sille said softly. "That's what she would have said. She always said songs connect us together, even with people we've never met. She sang so beautifully."

"Dad used to sing that song too," Rally said,

remembering a time on the bluff south of Playa El Ostional
with Grok howling along with the monkeys, "but he wasn't a
very good singer." "No," G'Sille laughed, "he certainly
wasn't." "Maybe I learned it wrong from him," Rally
wondered. "You recognized it carved into a plastiff box in
the middle of that asteroid," G'Sille solemnly replied. "Just
like he wanted you to. So I'd say you learned it just fine.
What did he leave in it?" "I don't know," Rally replied.
"I've been waiting to open it with you."

"No, you should open it alone. Or maybe you should
wait and open it with your own child someday." G'Sille said.
"Don't you want to know what's in it?" "He didn't leave it
for me," G'Sille said quietly. "He knew I never wanted him
to go to that asteroid. There was nothing for me there. He
knew when he left that you'd chosen that spaceship group.
He knew your group would succeed. He must have known
that if anything happened to him, his father would reach out
to you and your group. Stanley always wants the best and
never takes no for an answer. Grok knew that if Stanley sent
anyone after him it would be you. So I'd say that whatever's
in there was meant for you: not me; not Stanley; not anyone
else."

Rally was taken aback. She'd assumed the carved
"*YILOTI*" on the box was as much a coincidence as anything,
even if it had seemed like a message to her the moment she
saw it. She'd assumed that whatever was inside the box was

for public consumption, for prosperity, some kind of essay or manifesto, not something private for her alone. She should have trusted her first instinct like her mother always said. Her mother was always so perceptive. Rally had no doubt that she was right and Grok had left the box for her. But Rally felt really bad for reminding G'Sille that Grok went to the asteroid without her.

"Yestrey's going to have a baby," she said, suddenly wanting to change the subject. "That's wonderful!" G'Sille replied, a smile lighting her face. "Which hab is she on now?" "She's back on the *Habalone*," Rally replied. "She and her partner spent a full rotation on the platform shuttle group. That let them visit every hab, to see where they felt most comfortable, but in the end they decided to go right back where they started." "Was she already pregnant?" G'Sille asked. "Of course not," Rally said. "She told me all about it. They grouped with everyone on the *Habalone* and Yestrey and Pieter, he's the partner, told them they wanted to rotate back to the *Habalone* and have a baby. Everyone was happy for them, and excited for them to come back, and excited about having a baby on the *Habalone*. So then they grouped the math, and everyone agreed they could make enough vitsups to add a baby, and so they all decided together for Yestrey to be a mom. She said she thinks there are others who want to do the same, and that they'll have enough vitsups and energy for four or five new people really soon."

"So Yestrey's baby's mates already chose her before she's even been born," G'Sille mused. "Well of course," Rally said. "Yestrey and Pieter couldn't just go having babies by themselves!" "Of course not," G'Sille smiled. "But that was always such a big concern in our project, the tension between family and mates, and how people were going to work out being together in those different ways. You used to worry about that so much, remember?" "I did? I don't remember that. Spacers have to all move forward together. There's no surplus to waste on tension! So all their mates on the *Habalone* are excited about Yestrey and Pieter becoming a bigger family; excited about the *Habalone* growing organically."

Rally looked out over the gentle waves of Snake Bay as she said that, thinking that people here might not be so enthusiastic to hear about the *Habalone* having a baby instead of rescuing an Earther. But nobody here seemed the least bit concerned about any of that. When she'd landed at Xichang, in China, she'd seen the desperate crowds surrounding the launch port, and the crew warned her not to go outside. On the bullet train down the Xi Jiang river valley to Guangzhou she'd seen the resentful, angry stares. In the Sidney airport and again at Darwin, there'd been more stares and more resentment in the faces of those who could tell where she was from. Here in Milikapiti though, nobody seemed jealous, or even the least bit curious.

"People here don't look at Spacers like other Earthers do," Rally mused. "Why do you think that is?" "How do other Earthers look at you?" her mother replied. "How do they know who you are?" "Some can tell," Rally told her. "And some of them look angry, like we've taken something from them." "Well," G'Sille smiled. "I highly doubt anyone here has any fear of you taking anything from them! But look," she pointed back down the beach, "here comes our benefactor. We can ask her!"

Rally followed G'Sille's gesture and saw that it was indeed the old woman from the airport walking slowly towards them with a friendly wave. Rally could already feel her beautiful smile lifting her spirits. "Hello!" the old woman called, surprising Rally. "She speaks English!" "Of course she does," G'Sille replied. "But at the airport," Rally started. "At the airport," G'Sille said, "I imagine she wanted to find out more about us. Are you scared of her? Do you think she's going to take something from you?" Rally looked again at the woman's kindly smile and back at her mother's grinning face and laughed at herself a little bit.

"Of course not," she said, taking her mother's hand as they moved forward to meet their new friend. "Good, good," the old woman said as they came together and exchanged handshakes. "It is good for family to be together," she told them as if it were the most obvious thing in the world. "It is," G'Sille agreed, "and I hope we are not keeping you from your family." "No, no," she replied with a deep laugh, "sometimes family has to spread apart to come back together."

"Whose family?" Rally asked. "Who are you?" "My name is Leonie Pamantari," the woman replied. "I have lived in Milikapiti my whole life, through good times and bad. I have seen many people go away from Milikapiti and watched a few come back home." "Leonie Pamantari," G'Sille said softly. "I remember you! I did not recognize you ..." "It is no matter," Leonie assured her. "I am very old and you were very young then! And we had pictures of you. They did not let you take pictures of us."

"Rally," G'Sille said, "this is Leonie Pamantari. She had a sister ..." "An older sister!" Leonie interjected. "An older sister," G'Sille continued. "whose name was Carla. Carla Pamantari. Carla married a handsome man named Norm Kerimerini. Carla and Norm I do remember: they were my grandparents; the parents of your grandfather Austin Kerimerini." "Your father?" Rally exclaimed. She'd learned more about her mother's family in the last five minutes than she had in her whole life.

"Yes, my father," G'Sille said. "Austin Kerimerini. I haven't heard his name in 50 years." "We have not forgotten him!" Leonie assured her. "And we have not forgotten you either!" She smiled again. "We do not forget things very well. That's what we do: we sing, we dance, and we remember things."

"I don't remember him very well," G'Sille admitted. "He died when I was just five or six, very soon after my sister was born." "Sister?" Rally thought. This kept getting crazier and crazier. Her mom had never said anything about having a sister. "Yes," Leonie replied, "your sister Maringka. She came back home to visit last year you know?" Now it was G'Sille's turn to look shocked. "I haven't seen her, seen Maringka, since she was adopted all those years ago, right before I started Uni. She was just 11. Adopted in Darwin by Chinese diplomats, of all people, and I went off and never saw her again. Does she live in China? Do you know how to reach her?"

Leonie's smile disappeared. "I'm not sure anything but our songs can reach her now. She was only here for two days. Her body was very frail, like she'd been under a great weight for a long time. She came back home from the moon you know! But I don't know if she had the strength to make it back there." *From the moon* Rally thought. She had a long lost mooner aunt! Rally hoped she was still alive, that she'd somehow get to meet her someday. "I couldn't take care of her," G'Sille said. "I was supposed to take care of her in Darwin and I just couldn't. It was just too much."

"Maringka would not agree," Leonie assured her. "Her body was frail, but her spirit was strong!" "She was

385

such a shy girl," G'Sille remembered. "Just four years old when they took us to that place." "She grew up to be a strong woman," Leonie assured them. "She did not like telling her stories, but I heard enough to know that she stood for the truths of the many against the fears of the few. She lived a good life, and she never stopped loving you."

Leonie's smile returned as she turned to look at Rally. "She regretted having never had children," the old woman said about Rally's aunt she'd never met, "and it would have made her happy to see you come here with your mother to honor your father and your family." "I would be happy to see her," Rally replied, trying to imagine the stories Leonie heard. She'd never really talked to a mooner, never imagined being related to one before.

"I had an uncle," G'Sille began. "Peter Kerimerini!" Leonie exclaimed. "The famous writer!" "That's right," G'Sille remembered. "He used to tell us such stories!" "He passed on," Leonie told them sadly, "but his daughter Bindi, my niece, still lives in Wurrumiyanga and she and her husband Adi have four beautiful children." Her cousins? Aunts and Uncles? Rally was having trouble keeping up with all of her mother's new relatives.

"How did you know it was me?" G'Sille asked. "I never imagined anyone but my mother would remember me. And, as you probably know, her family . . ." G'Sille's voice trailed off as she looked down at the sand. Rally looked at

386

her and then looked quizzically at Leonie. "Her family did not approve of your father," Leonie said, talking to G'Sille but looking at Rally. "And then when he died saving those children and became a hero they were shamed by their disapproval. Unfortunately, they took their shame out on his widow, especially after her children were taken away. But we should not be sad today because other people made bad choices decades ago!"

"How could I not know it was you?" Leonie continued. "Anyone can see your Tiwi blood. Anyone who lives here can tell you don't live here, and haven't lived here for a long time. Anyone whose family had people taken by the whites remembers them. And," she laughed again, "like I said—we have pictures! I didn't recognize you earlier, at the airstrip, but I went home and looked at pictures and remembered how proud Maringka had been of her sister who earned a university scholarship and looked after her in Darwin all those years. And so now I came back to see if you look like your picture, and you do! So I cheated!" Leonie laughed again, the most infectious laugh Rally ever heard.

"I feel so sad, so stupid." G'Sille said sadly, "There were so many of you here, all these years, and I never reached out, never thought that anyone but mother would remember me. Even when I brought Rally and her father here, years ago, I never asked about anyone but mother, never reached out to Uncle Peter, or Bindi, or anyone." "Yet here you are with your daughter and both of you have visited amazing places and done wonderful things," Yeonie countered. "We shouldn't be sad today because we made bad choices years ago!" G'Sille smiled and nodded her head. "What's important is not that we were forced apart," Leonie told them, "but that we're together here and now. Nothing ever ends!"